PAPA'S DAY

To my two Muses, KT and Tori

JUSTIN KASE

Copyright Notice

Chapter One

Sometimes you can't tell a story from the beginning because it doesn't really start to make sense until you're halfway through it. This is one of those. So I guess I'll start in Cobb's Station, New Jersey. Cobb's Station is a gated bedroom community tucked away in an old apple orchard just off the interstate. It consists of a couple of hundred nearly identical ranch style homes, huddled together behind an eight-foot high brick wall. I had come there on a mission early that Saturday morning, but at the moment I was wavering on the sidewalk in front of one of the houses. I removed my glasses, polished them on a coat sleeve, started to replace them, and then, on a sudden impulse, slipped them into my shirt pocket. I tried to remember what I intended to say and wondered for the eleventh time why I was putting myself through what was sure to be an unpleasant experience. This reluctance to proceed with my self-assigned task was complicated by a vague, but insistent message from my bladder. I was tempted to walk back to my car and drive to the nearest public restroom, but after a few more minutes of curbside vacillation, I convinced myself the pressure I was feeling was merely another sign of nerves, and with one final, longing glance towards my parked car, I squared my shoulders, strode quickly up to the door, and rang the bell.

A couple of minutes crept by without a response. I was just turning to leave when I heard a key rattle in the deadbolt. I waited patiently for further developments, but the door stubbornly remained closed.

"Hello?" I finally ventured. "Mr. Bolero? My name is–"

"What do you want?" asked a voice from behind the door.

"My name is Walt Callisto and I–"

"Is this about an outboard motor?"

"I'm sorry, what did you say?"

"Boat motor. Is this about a boat motor?"

I was confused. I had memorized a short introduction that I felt would quickly outline the reason for my visit, but I had practiced it in front of a mirror which had courteously refrained from interjecting questions about boat motors.

"No! Uh – No, sir, I'm not here about a boat motor." Flustered, I decided it might be better to skip my prepared remarks and get right to the point. "I – I think you might be my father."

At this point, the door suddenly swung open. The man who opened it seemed younger than I had expected and, in the harsh sunlight, I could detect no trace of a certain bony protrusion that I had expected to see at the corners of his eyes. We both had dark hair and brown eyes but after that our body types diverged rather radically. I've always favored a sort of slender, athletic appearance where Mr. Bolero clearly subscribed to a more muscular, big-chested persuasion. In a word he was robust, and I was a 40 Regular who was beginning to have doubts about the efficacy of using a casino computer program for genealogical purposes.

A polite cough made me realize that I had been standing there staring at the man without saying anything for several seconds. I gathered my thoughts and began again.

"Mr. Bolero –"

Before I could finish the sentence, he stuck out a bronzed hand adorned by several large rings and flashed a dazzling smile. The arm extended toward me was thick, well-muscled, and sported a large gold Rolex nestled in a dense growth of black hair. "Charles Bolero. Everyone calls me Charlie!"

Taken aback, I proffered a slimmer, un-bejeweled hand that suddenly seemed embarrassingly pale and hairless. "Uh, my name is Walt, Walt Callisto–"

Charlie grabbed my hand and pumped it enthusiastically. One of the big rings he was wearing pinched my palm with every downward stroke.

"Good to meet you," he boomed and laid his free hand on my shoulder. "I gather you think we're related in some way?"

"Y-yeah," I stammered. "I believe you're my. . . that you might be my biological father."

Charlie laughed. He had one of those loud, musical laughs that show a lot of teeth. "Don't tell me you're going door to door hunting for your papa!"

He released my hand but continued to grip my shoulder. I glanced down and saw that the ring that had been pinching me was a big gold college ring. I had to squint, but I could make out the letters 'SPU' spelled out in dark green gemstones. This discovery temporarily boosted my confidence.

"I'm not going door to door," I objected stiffly. "I've done a lot of research, and I believe a sperm donation you made to a fertility clinic in 1984 was used to impregnate my mother."

"Oh, I see," Charlie smiled and gave my shoulder another little squeeze. "So you're the product of a test tube romance! Well, I'm happy for you, but you need to do some more research. I never made a deposit at a sperm bank – in 1984 or any other year."

"Are you certain?" I asked, feeling my voice and confidence beginning to falter.

Charlie grinned and placed his other hand, the one wearing the big college ring, on my other shoulder.

"Dead certain! And speaking confidentially," he gave me a lecherous wink, "back in those days I was a little too busy making sperm deposits in coeds to make any in banks!"

Then he squeezed both my shoulders, threw back his head, and laughed heartily. I blushed in spite of myself. When I had rung the doorbell, armed with the results of a year's research, I had been nearly certain Charlie Bolero was my anonymous sperm donor. But now in the face of his embarrassingly convincing denial, I was no longer sure of my facts. Suddenly, I wanted to be anyplace other than where I was at that particular moment. Adding to this feeling was a renewed and urgent call from Mother Nature. This time there was no mistaking the sensation as just nerves. I definitely had to go.

"I'm sorry to have bothered you–" My voice sounded hoarse, and my eyes were beginning to sting. I was angry with myself. I had resolved not to become emotional.

"Don't think a thing about it. I just hope you can turn up your real papa. I can imagine how you feel. If I were in your shoes, I'd be trying to do the same thing."

Charlie took his hands off my shoulders and leaned forward a little. "But, just out of curiosity, where are you getting your information? I thought those sperm banks kept their records strictly confidential."

I wanted the conversation to end so I could go back to my car, drive to the nearest gas station, and ask for the restroom key. I didn't want to explain about the casino's computer program or how Charlie's college photo had ended up in its database, so I said the first thing that came into my head. "All that changed recently. They passed a new state law."

"Really?" Charlie stuck his hands in his pockets and leaned against his door. "Huh! I hadn't heard about that. So, when you requested information about your sperm donor, my name came up?"

"Not exactly. They gave me another man's name, but when I traced it, I ran into a dead end."

Charlie tilted his head to one side and tapped his chin with a manicured finger. "Well, then, how did you come up with my name?"

"It's a little complicated, and now that I'm here, it doesn't make a whole lot of sense anymore. Look, I'm – I'm sorry I bothered you, but I really need to go now. I – I have a, another appointment." I took a step backward.

"Sure! I understand. These things happen," Charlie said, "but if you happen to be in the area, feel free to drop by. I wouldn't mind hearing how my name ties into all of this."

I nodded, turned, and carefully walked away. Even though it was still broad daylight, I felt as though I was walking through a fog. I had parked my black Cadillac Esplanade halfway down the block, and when I reached it, I turned and looked back toward Charlie's house. I blinked, took my glasses out of my pocket, put them on, and took another look. The porch was empty, the door was closed, but I thought I had seen a flicker of movement in one of Charlie's windows.

I found a restroom in a convenience store on the edge of Cobb's Station just in the nick of time. When I had driven down earlier that morning, there had been a thick mist wafting through the grass and obscuring the trees along the winding, two-lane blacktop leading from the interstate to Cobb's Station. That mist and the depressing miasma that had settled into my mind at Charlie's house had blown away by the time I regained the interstate. Now that the twin pressures of confrontation and nature's urgent call had been relieved, it seemed clear to me that Charlie's reaction had been just a little too nonchalant for a man who had been blindsided by a stranger claiming to be his son. And those questions about boat motors, through a closed door. What had that been all about? Charlie sure seemed like a man with something to hide.

"Damn it!" I muttered and struck the steering wheel with my fist. "He was trying to con me."

Because of the college ring I had seen on Charlie's finger, I knew, at the least, that I had found the same Charlie Bolero who had attended Southern Pennsylvania University during the time my mother had been artificially inseminated. Other than that, I had nothing to show for the two-hour drive from my hometown in Jupiter, New York. I had planned to ask Charlie about his medical history, but that was only a pretext to elicit the answers I really craved, answers to questions that had haunted me since I had first learned that I was a sperm-donor baby.

Chapter Two

I had lied to Charlie about one thing. There was no new law in New York State allowing children conceived from donated sperm to learn their biological father's identity. Like in most states, sperm and egg donation in New York is largely unregulated, and nearly all fertility clinics routinely guarantee the privacy of both the donors and recipients of sperm and eggs. I lied because I had surreptitiously obtained the records of my mother's sperm donor from a sympathetic clerk.

The name on those records was Carl Wilson, Jr., and Wilson had listed Box 893 at a Pack & Mail store in Burn's Creek, Pennsylvania, as his address. That mailbox turned out to have been rented by another man named Chris Fulton. The manager of the Pack & Mail had told me that most of the store's mailboxes were rented by college students from Southern Pennsylvania University in nearby Canton, so I had searched the SPU alumni website for both names, and found neither. I had also tried locating the two men on a couple of DIY 'people finder' websites and had even spent a few hundred dollars on a professional locator service. All of these efforts were fruitless. Neither Carl Wilson nor Chris Fulton had been a student at SPU during the 1980s, and there was no record of either man living in Burn's Creek or in the Canton, Pennsylvania, regional area during that period. I had run out of ideas, money, and the will to continue the search for my birth father. Then I met Jason Singletary.

Jason was a lanky, self-professed computer geek who had hired on at the Ace Car Rental agency in my hometown shortly after I got the job managing it. Jupiter was a small town and, over the years, I had noticed this gangly kid striding around town with a laptop hanging off one shoulder and haunting the only coffee shop in Jupiter that offered a free Wi-Fi connection to the Internet. But Jason was younger and home-schooled, so we had never actually met.

After we began working together, I discovered that, like myself, my new assistant had never known his own father. Jason's mother wouldn't talk about it, but Jason had learned from an older cousin that his father had run off with a country music singer.

Confident of his sympathy, I told Jason of my own unsuccessful search for my biological father. After listening to my story, Jason speculated that both Carl Wilson and Chris Fulton were aliases for a SPU student. He suggested that my biological father had sold his sperm to defray his college expenses, and assumed multiple identities to sidestep rules limiting sperm donations to one clinic. Jason knew about these rules because he had a friend who worked at a fertility clinic. She told him that most fertility clinics had access to the Fertility Clinic Association's confidential database, which, among other things, was used to determine whether a potential sperm donor had ever donated at another clinic.

Jason didn't think I should give up my search for my biological father, so he offered to help me. He then proceeded to amaze me by persuading his friend at the sperm bank to let him have ten minutes alone at her workstation. Jason cross-referenced the Pack & Mail address with records in the Fertility Clinic Association's database and printed a report. It turned out that 63 donors had used Box 893 as their address. Most of the donations were made over a four-year period, during months that coincided with the fall and spring semesters at SPU. Jason pointed out that all the first names began with the letter C, and that nearly half of these aliases used Charles or one of its diminutives as a first name. Inspired by this observation, Jason and I went back to the SPU online yearbooks and made a list of all the male students with first names like Charlie, Charles, Charley, Chas or Chuck who had attended SPU between the years 1982 and 1986. We ended up with six hundred and eighty-one suspects. The task seemed hopeless at that point, and we stopped working on the project for several months, until one day when Jason came running into Ace Car Rental waving a casino brochure in the air.

"Biometrics!" shouted Jason. "Facial Feature Analysis! Walt, we've got to go to Atlantic City! I have a friend there who will let us use this cool computer program that spots cheats and advantage players."

"How's that going to help us?"

"We can use this program to compare the geometry of your face to all those Charlies who attended SPU."

"How?"

"Yearbooks."

"But what if I've taken after my mother?"

Jason said it didn't matter which side of the family I favored. Then he explained that biometrics didn't measure superficial physical characteristics like hair and skin color, but analyzed the geometry and texture of facial features, like bone structure. He also thought the trip to Atlantic City might be a good opportunity to try out his blackjack system. So Jason spent the next three days downloading photos from the SPU online yearbook and practicing blackjack on his computer. That weekend we drove up to Atlantic City, and after losing three hundred dollars playing blackjack, Jason contacted his friend in casino security.

I had never seen the inside of a casino monitoring room before. It reminded me of the bridge on the spaceship Enterprise. Bert, the captain of all these 'eyes in the sky,' was a gigantic bearded black man. Jason introduced me as his 'partner in crime' and handed over a DVD labeled "SPU CHARLIES."

Bert sat me in a chair next to his console, asked me to remove my glasses, and took my portrait with a digital camera. A few minutes later, my face popped up on one of the monitors. Bert's huge black hand manipulated the mouse, bringing up a menu that slid down in front of my electronic portrait. He made a selection from the menu, and pressed a couple of keys.

"Now the program is analyzing the size, shape, angle, depth and placement of your eye sockets, along with the distance between them," Bert said. "This feature is as unique as a man's fingerprints, and almost impossible to disguise. Our software measures seventy different landmarks on the human face. Now it's drawing a mask made of vertices. Pay special attention to the vectors around the eye sockets, nose, and lips. The geometric relationship between these areas creates a mathematical model of your face."

Bert turned to me and grinned. "Now you're in our database. The next time you walk into our casino, you'll pop up on our 'Perp Alert' screen, and the guys in this room will watch you like a hawk!"

I managed an anemic chuckle. "I promise to leave my counterfeit slot tokens at home."

Bert brought up another window on the monitor, displaying several stamp-sized faces. "Our recognition software is not infallible, and it'll occasionally initiate a 'Perp Alert' on somebody who just happens to have a strong enough resemblance to another face in our database. If it happens too often, we increase the threshold in the tunable parameters for that particular Perp. Like I was telling your friend Jason here the other day, during the last five years we've run this program, we noticed something interesting about our false alarms – the people tripping them were often closely related to the Perps!"

Bert did some rapid typing, and a block of photos appeared on his monitor. "All of these six snapshots triggered a 'Perp Alert' for a notorious card counter. We call him Sticky because he's always eating peppermints while he's playing 21. These first three pictures are Sticky in various disguises. Our recognition program spotted him even when he was wearing that beard and those thick black-framed glasses. These next two guys triggered Sticky's 'Perp Alert' too, and in each case they walked right up to a high stakes 21 table and started playing. When we brought this one in for a chat, we discovered he was Sticky's brother, and this one here turned out to be his first cousin. After that, we increased the threshold on selected landmarks of Sticky's facial mask. His two relatives are free to play here anytime they want, because it turns out that just looking like Sticky doesn't mean you can count cards like him. When we consulted our software designer about this problem, he told us some of the physical characteristics his recognition program measures, like eye socket depth and orbital separation, are dominant male traits that are often passed on to males of the next generation. But – and this is a big but – see this last picture here? Total stranger. He doesn't even play 21. He just happened to have the right stuff to reach the threshold and trip the alarm. So this little experiment might narrow the field for you, but it's not foolproof."

I assured Bert that since everything Jason and I had done so far was mostly supposition anyway, I would take any results his computer program produced with a generous portion of salt.

Bert loaded Jason's disk and brought the first page of photos up on his screen. "Whoa! Pretty low resolution!"

Jason had used Photoshop to cut photos out of the yearbook pages on the SPU alumni website. Bert enlarged one of the photos until we were looking at a screen full of smudgy dots.

"Well," Bert said, "it's not much worse than the images we get from our security cameras, so it should still work."

I was a lot less confident than Bert. The photos looked extremely grainy to me. Bert did something with his mouse that caused small, flashing frames to appear around the photos on his screen. Then he brought up a window where he entered information into several fields.

"I just instructed the program to search through all the photographs on this disk for a match to Walt's orbital configuration," announced Bert.

"What?" I asked, concern rising in my voice. "You're only looking at their eyes? How strong an indication could that be?"

"I've set the threshold to ninety-nine percent on all of the parameters, so any results we get on this run ought to be pretty conclusive. The orbital configuration includes about twenty of the principal landmarks of facial recognition, including the depth of the sockets and the width of the nose. And like I said before, the orbital ridge and its associated cavities are a dominant male trait, so that's the feature most likely to be passed down to a son."

I watched as a succession of twenty-year-old yearbook photos flashed by on the screen. Little frames of interlocking triangles were forming around their eyes, and numbers flashed under their faces as the students paraded past on Bert's screen.

"Nope," Bert announced as the last of the images flickered off of his monitor. "No match. I'm going to lower the threshold on some of the landmarks and run it again."

Bert noticed the concerned look on my face. "Don't worry; I'm only making tiny adjustments to some of the tunable parameters. I'm still keeping the bar set higher than we do for the 'Perp Alert,' and besides, you're going to check out any hits we get anyway, right?"

I nodded numbly, and watched as the parade of Charlies began to flash by again. Maybe my biological father wasn't among them. After all, just because this serial sperm donor used that name more frequently than the other names didn't mean that his real name was– The loud, simulated ring of a fire bell interrupted my thoughts.

"Bingo!" Bert announced, and we all leaned forward to stare at the screen. Staring back at us with a mocking smile were the handsome tanned features of Charlie Bolero, BA, class of 1986, majors in Business and Science, and memberships in several professional fraternities. I studied Charlie's grinning face, trying and failing to see some slight resemblance to my own.

"He doesn't even look like me!" I complained.

Instead of saying anything, Bert selected Charlie's picture and copied it into the window that held my mug shot. He made both portraits the same size and placed them (father and son?) side-by-side. Then he placed a rectangular outline over the eyes of each man, and replaced the image outside that outline with a solid black background so all that was left showing were the eyes, from the eyebrows down to the tip of the nose. My picture was sharp and clear, while Charlie's portrait was grainy and slightly blurred. My skin was pale next to Charlie's bronzed hue, and my eyes were squinting, while Charlie's eyes shone like polished marbles. Despite these differences, the effect was stunning. The brow, the bridge of the nose, the shape of the sockets, and the placement of the eyes were identical. The most startling similarity was the lower bony rim near the outside corners of the eyes. I had always noticed a little bulge there where the bone of the socket merged into my temple. I thought I could see a slight shadow cast by bulges like mine on Charlie's face.

"Is this the only match? If you ran it again, would we get other candidates?" I asked.

"It was the only match on this run. If I lowered some of the thresholds and ran it again, we might get a few more choices, but the lower the threshold the less accurate the match. Besides, according to Jason, this group of photos is only a small subset of a much larger number of possible subjects. If we ran your mug shot against all those other students, we would probably get lots of matches. Not that I could spare the time just now for a search of that scope."

"You know," Bert said, patting me on the shoulder, "this little parlor trick is a just a phenomenon we noticed since we began using this facial recognition software. When Jason told me about the search for your father, I told him about what our program could do. I thought it might help. Who knows whether it really stands up to scientific scrutiny or not? But, hey, if this guy does actually turn out to be your father, I'd sure like to know about it." With that, Bert patted me on the shoulder again, wished us a good day and returned to his surveillance.

Jason started searching the web as soon as we got back from Atlantic City. The SPU Alumni site did not have a current address for Charlie Bolero, and he didn't show up under any of the 'people search' websites. For a while, it looked like we had hit another dead end, and then, just for the hell of it, Jason decided to check the car rental agency's database to see if someone named Charlie Bolero had ever rented a car from an Ace Car Rental location. A quick search in Ace's network turned up a customer with the name of Charles Bolero, and the shocking thing for me was that this man lived only a couple of hours away in Cobb's Station, New Jersey. I wasn't confident we had found the right Charlie, but Jason insisted on my driving up the very next Saturday. He even offered to go along.

I wasn't sure if a face-to-face confrontation with this Bolero guy was the most prudent approach, but I was positive I didn't want an audience. So I declined Jason's offer to accompany me and suggested that a phone call or a letter might be better than suddenly showing up on Charlie's doorstep. Jason wasn't having any of it. He said he didn't want to give Charlie the chance of refusing a visit from me. In the end, I relented, and early that Saturday morning, I drove to Cobb's Station and my frustrating meeting with Charlie Bolero.

Chapter Three

After I left Charlie's house, I drove back to Jupiter, New York, pulled into Ace Car Rental, and parked in the back where Jody and Pitch, two teenagers who were supposed to be detailing rental returns, were goofing off. I tossed my keys to Jody, who snatched them from the air without looking up from the magazine she was reading. I walked into the agency through the back door to find Jason playing GO on one of Ace's computers. Jason loved the game and played it online with fellow enthusiasts around the world. I vaguely understood GO was a strategy game where players attempted to wall off their opposition with little coin-shaped markers. Jason had told me the game of GO was ancient and took years to master, which in my opinion were two good reasons for avoiding the game entirely.

Jason looked up as I came into the room. "Hey, Walt! What's the news? Is Charlie your pop or not?" Instead of answering, I collapsed into a chair and looked down at my hands. Jason stared at me. "You mean he denied it? I can't believe he had the nerve to deny it! Did you tell him about our evidence?"

"We don't have any 'evidence,' Jason. All we have is a bunch of phony names and a theory." I pulled my glasses off and tossed them onto my desk.

"So was this guy even the right Charlie Bolero? The one from the yearbook?"

"Yeah. I saw his school ring."

"And he claimed he hadn't made all those deposits in all those sperm banks using all those fake names?" Jason asked, keying in a new move in his online game of GO.

"He said he'd never made a donation under any name."

Jason looked up from his game with raised eyebrows. "Did he really?"

"Yeah," I said glumly, picking up my glasses and polishing them on a shirtsleeve.

"Well, well," Jason mused and then suddenly chuckled. "You know what?"

"What?

"When I was in the Fertility Association's database, I only searched for names that used that rented mailbox in Burn's Creek."

I shoved my glasses back on and studied Jason. "Yeah, so?"

"Charlie said he'd never donated sperm before, right?"

"Why?" I asked, starting to get excited. "Do you think he might have sold sperm under his own name?"

"That's exactly what I think. I bet the first time Charlie made a donation he did it under his own name at a fertility clinic close to his college. If there's a clinic in Canton, he sold his sperm there. He probably made the maximum number of donations at that first clinic, and then when he went to another clinic to start a new round, they told him – the answer, please, Mr. Callisto?"

"That he could donate sperm at only one clinic!"

"Exactly. But does that discourage your biological pop? Nope! He just manufactures a new identity and begins his career as father to the masses."

"Jason, you're a genius! Now we just need a record of Charlie's first donation. Do you think you can get your friend to help us out again?"

"Way ahead of you," Jason said, returning to his keyboard. "I'm sending her an email as we speak."

After that, Saturday afternoon car rental customers kept Jason and me too busy to continue our discussion. Ace Car Rental had just advertised a new promotion in the local newspaper and on its website. The promotion, called 'The Saturday Night Special,' advertised Ace's new luxury cars at unusually low rates for customers who came in after 4 PM on Saturday and returned their rental cars by Sunday noon.

At one point during the afternoon rush, we started to run low on clean cars, so I went out back to crack the whip. I found Pitch and Jody embroiled in an argument over whose turn it was to drive the cars through the car wash and who had to vacuum out interiors and dry the cars. I was trying to impose an equitable solution on their disagreement when I saw a little red Mini Cooper pull into the lot.

A tall wood fence surrounded the rear area of Ace Car Rental, but the Mini Cooper had parked just in front of the open gate, giving me a clear view of the little car. Even though the agency's car wash stood about twenty yards from the gate, the vision of the Mini's driver transfixed me. The late afternoon sun streaming in through the Mini Cooper's windshield bathed the driver's face in an ethereal glow. It was the most beautiful face I had ever seen. I was amazed a girl like this could exist in a town the size of Jupiter without my knowledge.

I threw a towel at Jody with a terse "Pitch washes, and you dry, Jody," and before Jody could protest my arbitrary decision, I headed towards the Mini Cooper to see if I could possibly assist this angelic apparition. I was nearly to the gate when the passenger door of the Mini Cooper opened, and a bronzed- skinned man, still engaged in a conversation with its driver, climbed out of the little car. I froze in mid-stride. I felt a surge of panic, and my legs, seemingly of their own volition, propelled me behind the fence and out of sight of the Mini Cooper. I looked back towards the car wash to see Jody staring at me. I was desperately afraid the porter would attract attention, and tried to wave her off, hoping she would take the hint and go back to work. But Jody just stood there, goggling, her arms hanging down by her sides and her clean drying towel soaking up a dark black liquid from the pavement. It seemed like ages passed before, despite a variety of frantic 'go away' gestures on my part, Jody began moving toward me. I couldn't decide whether she was the dumbest teenager we had ever employed, or was simply being obstinate because I had made her dry the cars. I decided to risk a quick look around the fence. When I discovered the Mini was gone and the coast was clear, I scuttled over to the store's back entrance and ducked inside.

I crept down the hallway and carefully peered into the customer area. There stood Charlie Bolero, calmly proffering his identification and insurance cards to Jason. From what I could see in that one quick glance, Charlie was perfectly sanguine, smiling and chatting with Jason like an old pal. I leaned back against the wall in the little hallway and tried to calm down.

I couldn't think clearly; little tendrils of the fog that had shrouded my mind earlier in the day had begun drifting back into my consciousness. I wondered what Charlie was doing at Ace. I knew there wasn't a car rental agency in Cobb's Station – that little community in New Jersey was mostly houses; but I thought there must be one a lot closer than Jupiter.

I found my thoughts drifting back to the girl who had driven Charlie to the agency. I could still see her sitting behind the wheel of the Mini Cooper, suffused by the light of the setting sun. The afterimage of her face made it difficult for me to concentrate on the mystery of Charlie's visit to Ace Car Rental. 'Who was she?' I wondered.

I crept closer to the corner of the hallway and tried to listen to the conversation between Jason and Charlie, but all I could hear was the impatient murmuring of other customers. I peeked around the corner again just in time to see Jason and Charlie step out into the front lot. I rushed into the office and around the counter, ignoring the questions customers were posing as I swept by them. I ran up to the window and watched as Jason and Charlie performed a ding patrol around a brand new Lincoln Town Car. Charlie pointed out some invisible blemish on the driver's door, and Jason noted it on the contract. Then Jason handed Charlie his copy of the contract and held the driver's door open for him.

I turned and tore back around the counter, vaguely aware of customers shouting in frustration behind me. I ran down the little hall and out the back entrance, where Jody was polishing the back window of my black Cadillac Escalade. I ran to the Escalade and jumped into the driver's seat. As I drove out of the lot, I could see Jody in my mirror, still holding her dirty towel. Goggling.

Chapter Four

I caught up with the Lincoln as it entered the northbound ramp of the interstate.

"Where the hell is he going?" I exclaimed, and then wondered if I shouldn't be asking myself the same question. I didn't really know why I was following Charlie, but nothing seemed to make a lot of sense lately. In fact, the last year of my life seemed like one big blur.

My current state of confusion had begun on my twenty-first birthday. My parents had treated me to a weekend in Atlantic City, where I had participated in the traditional rites of passage for a freshly emancipated male – drinking and gambling. The next morning I had awakened in my hotel room suffering from a big hangover. While searching my luggage for Alka-Seltzer, I came across an envelope addressed to me in my mother's handwriting, carefully folded inside a pair of my boxer shorts. I opened it with a grin, expecting to find a stash of emergency cash placed there in case I blew all my money at the casino. Instead, I found a hand-written letter relating the story of a young couple who had endured years of heartache and disappointment in their unsuccessful attempts to conceive. My parents had eventually settled on sperm donation as the only viable solution for their infertility. My mother apologized for waiting so long to tell me about the circumstances of my conception. She knew I had a good heart and, now that I had reached adulthood, the maturity to realize my true father was the man who allowed his wife to be impregnated by another man's sperm in order to have a son.

I finished the letter, then in a state of shock made worse by a bad hangover, called my mother and asked for the name of the fertility clinic she had used. My mom had wept for five minutes before she had been able to answer my question.

At the time, I was in my last year of business college. When I returned to school, I contacted my mother's fertility clinic only to learn that I needed prior written authorization from the sperm donor to access my mother's records. I wasted a couple of months writing various state agencies in an attempt to circumvent the clinic's policy before discovering that, unlike adoption agencies, fertility clinics in New York state are largely unregulated.

When I received no relief from the state authorities, I decided to make a personal visit to the clinic. The receptionist working there that day was a temp who seemed sympathetic to my situation. She hadn't been working at the clinic long, but she had heard that some donors signed wavers allowing the offspring of their recipients to contact them after their twenty-first birthday. This news was the first ray of hope I had experienced in two months, and I held my breath while she looked up my mother's records on her computer. After paging through several screens, she looked sadly up at me and said that my donor had not signed the waver. Then the receptionist asked me if I would like to fill out a release just in case my donor decided to contact me. I didn't believe there was much chance of that happening, but the temp seemed to think it would be worthwhile, so I reluctantly agreed. She asked me to wait while she went to find a release form. As she left the room, she gave me a brief, though clearly significant, wink. I had seen enough movies to know what that gesture meant. I struggled with my conscience for about two seconds and then, feeling incredibly guilty, reached over the counter, turned the temp's computer monitor toward me, and quickly scribbled down the name and address of my mother's sperm donor.

The information I stole that day had led to the dead end at the Pack & Mail and several weeks of futile detective work. During this period I began skipping classes and blowing off tests. I found I couldn't concentrate on my future until I had settled the question of my past. I ended up dropping out of college and taking a job as sales manager of the Ace Car Rental location in my hometown.

I had made great progress during my time at Ace Car Rental, but now that I had run out of an office full of customers in order to follow Charlie Bolero, I wondered if I would still have a job when I got back to the office.

The ringing of my cell phone interrupted my thoughts. I fished it out of my pocket and thumbed the speakerphone button.

"Hello, Jason."

"Walt! Where the hell are you!" blared Jason out of the cell phone's speaker. "Didn't you see all those people waiting for their damn Lincolns?"

"I'm following Charlie."

"Why are you following Charlie? And why did you tear out of here like a crazy man? You upset the customers, Walt. I had to lie to settle them down."

I grinned. Good old Jason. "What did you tell them?"

"I told them one of the cars had just left the lot without a spare in the trunk. When you found out, you ran to the front of the building to see if you could catch the customer, but he had already left, so you jumped in a car and drove off to intercept him."

"They bought that?"

"Yeah. In fact, everyone was really impressed at how seriously you take the safety of your customers. I told them Ace Car Rental would never think of letting our customers brave the interstate without a spare in the trunk."

"No one asked why I didn't just call him on his cell phone and ask him to drive back to the lot?"

"So you're a little impulsive. It's the thought that counts. Now tell me what you're doing."

"Following Charlie," I said, checking to make sure the white Lincoln was still up ahead. "Don't you think it's just a little strange he showed up here on the same day I visited him in Cobb's Station?"

"Coincidences are always strange, Walt; that's why they call them coincidences. Look, Charlie was very talkative. He told me he caught a ride with a friend who was coming to Jupiter for a visit with an old school chum. He just came along to keep her company and go to a business dinner. When they got to town, he discovered the dinner had been canceled, so rather than stay in a motel with nothing to do, he decided to rent a car and drive back home."

"But he's headed south, away from Cobb's–"

"So he's going on a little side trip. It doesn't matter. Wherever he going, he's meeting his friend back here tomorrow morning."

A thrill ran through me. The girl in the Mini Cooper would be returning to Ace Car Rental! The thrill faded when I remembered Charlie would be there as well. I wasn't ready to face Charlie again. I wondered how I could get a few minutes alone with the Mini Cooper girl. Maybe she would arrive before Charlie, or maybe I could talk to her while Charlie was inside the office checking in–

"Jason! You have to do me a favor!" I exclaimed.

"Hey, why don't you do me one first and come back to the lot? We've got customers roaming around trying to select their own rentals, Jody and Pitch aren't doing their job, and we're out of coffee. It's a zoo here, Walt."

"Okay, okay, I'm getting off at the next exit, but when I get back, I'm going to ask you to do me a big favor!"

"That's what I'm here for, Walt. See you when you get back."

I pulled off at the next ramp and drove across the overpass toward the southbound lanes. As I rode above the freeway on the big concrete overpass, I could just make out the white Lincoln as it disappeared in the distance.

I went back to work, and it was well after nine in the evening when I finally pulled into the Ganymede Terrace Apartments. There had been a lot of customers taking advantage of Ace's 'Saturday Night Special,' and afterwards Jason and I had spent a few minutes doing paperwork and a couple of hours discussing Charlie and the girl in the Mini Cooper.

The noise of my key turning in the lock of my apartment door elicited the plaintive mews of an angry cat. "Poor Io!" I exclaimed. "I'm so sorry! Let's go fix your supper right now!"

Io raced ahead of me and bounded up onto the counter to supervise while I prepared her meal. I set a Target shopping bag I was carrying on the kitchen table, opened a can of cat food, and mixed some dry kibble into it. Satisfied with my preparation, Io hopped down and waited by her water bowl. I set the food down, gave Io a little pat as she attacked her supper, and then walked into the living room to check my messages. A luminous sky-blue '2' flashed on the small LCD display of my answering machine.

My mother thought all answering machines could only record messages that were less than thirty seconds duration, so she tried to cram everything into one long and breathless run-on sentence:

"Hello Walt I'm sorry I missed you because I wanted to invite you to Sunday dinner although I'll understand perfectly if you can't come since I know you have more important things to do than share a meal with your family even though you live only ten minutes away and haven't visited or even called home in the last two weeks much less bothered to even drop us a postcard but I also wanted to let you know that I'm making your favorite rosemary steak with a delicious potato casserole so I'll save a place for you in case you come and if you do please bring some ice cream for the cherry bunt cake because we want to have a little impromptu birthday celebration for you and honey, you know I love you Bye!"

Just listening to one of my mother's messages left me gasping for breath. The second message was just ten seconds of background noise with an abrupt click as someone on the other end of the line hung up. When I listened to the message again, I thought I could hear someone's breathing accompanied by road noise and the muted sound of a car engine. While I was listening to this silent message, Io rubbed against my leg and mewed loudly. I stooped down, rubbed her head, and scratched her ears. She leaned into my hand and arched her back so I could scratch that too. After a couple of minutes of familial bonding, I stood up and walked back into my kitchen to get the Target shopping bag. Io trailed the bag and me as we walked back to the living room. I pulled a BB pistol and a tube of pellets out of the bag. I ripped open the blister pack, removed the toy gun, and stuffed the cardboard and plastic packaging back into the Target shopping bag.

Then I set the bag on the floor by my front door and walked across the room to my recliner. I sat down, loaded the air pistol's magazine, and worked its pneumatic pump a few times. Using both hands, I took careful aim and shot a pellet into the concentric red rings of the Target bag's logo. I smiled, set the BB pistol on the end table beside me, picked up a well-worn anthology of eighteenth-century British poets, and leaned back in my recliner. I spent the remainder of the evening, Io purring in my lap, reading poetry and dreaming about a girl in a sunlit Mini Cooper.

Chapter Five

Sunday morning brought a fleet of luxury vehicles cruising back into Ace Car Rental. I had just checked in a tired, sallow-faced youth with the suspenders of his rented tuxedo pants hanging limply at his sides when I felt a tap on my shoulder. I turned to see Jason nodding towards a white Lincoln Town Car just pulling into the lot. I referred my next customer to Jason's station and strode down the hallway toward the back entrance. I found my way temporally obstructed by a generously-proportioned woman brightly attired in what looked like a floral print pup tent. After stepping aside to allow her ample form room to squeeze out of the restroom and past me, I sprinted through the rear exit and made for the gate opposite the carwash. I saw Jody squatting at the rear of the carwash gloomily vacuuming out the back seat of a midnight blue Lincoln Town Car. Pitch was just driving a mud-caked Cadillac Escalade into the rear service area as I reached the gate. The kid in the rented tux had reluctantly paid a cleaning fee for what I suspected was an amorous misadventure in the muddy Escalade. 'Excellent,' I thought. Both of my young porters were occupied with their duties; now to see what kind of shot Charlie had left for me. I peeked around the gatepost, and quickly withdrew again. I had seen the red Mini Cooper parked in my line of fire, its fabric top down, its golden-haired owner listening to the radio and enjoying the morning breeze.

The Mini had apparently pulled in next to Charlie's Lincoln while I was negotiating the hallway. Its presence had turned a casual shot from the hip into an Olympic medal attempt. I couldn't risk shooting over the Mini Cooper, because in addition to endangering its beautiful driver, I would certainly be seen making the shot, so I decided to shoot around the Mini. I drew my BB pistol from my pocket and dropped onto one knee with my left arm resting on my upright knee. In this position, I could see the fat rear end of the white Lincoln extending past the bumper of the little Mini. I steadied my pistol across the wrist of my left arm, held my breath, and squeezed off a shot. I was rewarded by a dull ping as the pellet ricocheted off the metal skin of the Town Car's rear fender. The head of the girl in the Mini Cooper jerked around in the direction of the noise, her hair lofted into the air by the sudden motion. As I ducked back behind the fence, I was left with the vision of a graceful neck briefly visible under its swirling curtain of gold hair.

I straightened up and dusted myself off, then turned to see Jody, her mouth gaping and her eyes distended beyond a mere goggle and well into the bulging realm of the truly popeyed. I took her by the wrist and guided her back to her station.

"Well, Jody," I said, handing her a towel, "I think I discouraged the little rascal! If you see any of his friends scampering around back here, just let me know, and I'll deal with them."

"Deal with what, sir?" asked Jody, holding her drying towel up in front of her like a shield.

"Why, the field rats, Jody. I expect you've seen them nesting in the supply closet and running about under the cars. If they think they're being hunted, they'll move on to another territory. That's why I pop them with this whenever I see them," I said, brandishing the BB pistol. "Understand?"

"Uh, yeah," Jody said, nodding doubtfully. "Mr. Callisto?"

"Yes, Jody?"

"Isn't it my turn to drive the cars through the wash?" she asked, pulling on one of her pigtails and trailing the end of her towel back and forth on the dirty pavement.

The tone of her voice sounded innocent, but I wondered if I had just become a victim of a teenage blackmailer. "Sure, tell Pitch I said so."

Jody scampered off to give Pitch the bad news, and, slipping the BB pistol back into my pocket, I walked back to peer around the gate. I got there just in time to see Jason performing a ding patrol with Charlie. When they came to the left rear fender, Jason knelt down and rubbed the little dimple the BB had left in the Lincoln's smooth white finish.

"Uh-oh," Jason said, "it looks like you picked up a little gravel here."

Charlie bent over and looked at the ding. "How about that?" he remarked. "You know, I never heard a thing!"

"I did!" Both men looked around to face the girl in the Mini. "I heard a little pop just a minute ago, like something hitting the side of a car."

I had already ducked back behind the fence when the girl had started speaking, but I could picture Charlie looking around for the source of the missile. I marveled at this girl's ability to distinguish the direction and character of such a small noise over the sound of her car's stereo.

"Huh!" exclaimed Jason. "Well, whenever it happened, you're totally covered by your rental insurance. No big deal, just a little paper work."

Charlie laughed. "Well, no harm, no foul, hey Leda?"

I was smiling on the other side of the fence. Now I knew her name. I couldn't wait to say it aloud. Leda.

"Whatever you think," Leda said to Charlie. "Are we ready to go now?"

"I believe I have to finish up inside, and then we can head back. Right, Jason?" Jason apparently nodded, because Charlie continued, "I'll just be a couple of minutes."

I counted to ten before strolling out from behind the fence and over to the Mini Cooper. Leda was leaning back in the seat with her eyes closed and her hand propped on the steering wheel, enjoying the music of her alfresco concert. Before I could speak, Leda's eyes flew open and focused on my face. She had astonishing amber eyes of the kind that the poets describe as gold, and the unkind, as yellow. The poet in me began praising the flecks of gold suspended in Leda's twin pools of amber light—

"May I help you?"

I panicked. Leda had stolen my line, and I was at a loss for words. Now she was smiling. It was the most beautiful smile I had ever seen, but before my mind could compose a verse about how wonderful Leda's teeth looked between her lips, she brought me back to earth with another question.

"Do you talk? Or do you just like staring at girls?"

"Yeah! I mean no, or rather – I can talk, when the sun is not blinding me to the world of sound." I flushed, astonished and embarrassed by my own words.

"How pretty," laughed Leda, "Are you a poet?"

"No, I'm the manager of this Ace Car Rental location. I was about to ask you if I could be of assistance when you, uh, asked me first."

"Oh, I see," she said, indicating the waiting customers visible through Ace's windows, "you came out here to make sure that any potential clients loitering in your parking lot were being served?"

"The press of commerce must yield to the slightest desire of beauty," I answered, amazed and mortified to hear another line of verse coming out of my mouth.

"So you are a poet after all, and I'm sort of your muse du jour, huh?"

I stifled an ode to her golden eyes, and tried to regain control. "I'm sorry," I said smiling weakly. "I guess I'm just a little nervous."

Leda laughed. "Most guys just crack jokes when they're nervous. I like your approach better. I like those thick, black glasses you're wearing, too."

"You do?"

"Yeah. They look good on you. Makes you look confident, and honest, just the thing for a poet. Where did you come from anyway? I just opened my eyes and there you were!"

"I – I saw you pull into the lot a couple of minutes ago, and I ducked out the back to–to meet you," I stammered, feeling anything but confident or honest. "I came from the back service area over there," I said, pointing to the gate.

"Hmm," murmured Leda speculatively, looking at the gate. "I was here for about five minutes before you showed up. Were you watching me from behind the fence?"

"I was held up by one of our porters," I answered truthfully. "She wanted a different job assignment."

"Oh, I see. You had to stop to help another girl,"

"Jody. She's a sixteen-year-old tomboy in pigtails."

"I understand," sighed Leda in mock resignation. "Poets are often drawn to these freckle-faced Lolitas; it's tragic, really."

"I thought you were the Lolita," I said, "sans freckles and pigtails, of course."

"I'm covered with freckles," Leda giggled, "and I'm ancient. I bet I'm older than you, poetry boy."

"I never speculate on the age of beautiful young ladies, but I'll be twenty-two this coming Tuesday," I said.

"Oh! And how are you going to celebrate your birthday, poetry boy?"

"I was hoping you would celebrate it with me," I said.

"I never celebrate birthdays with poets unless I know their names, Mister–?"

She left the question hanging, waiting for me to fill in the blank. I hesitated. It had suddenly occurred to me that if I gave her my real name, she might mention it to Charlie. Then Charlie would tell Leda about me showing up on his doorstep earlier that morning. Then both Charlie and Leda would think, perhaps with some reason, that I was some kind of nut. I heard myself giving her my mother's maiden name.

"Galilei," I answered, and then reflexively covered my breast pocket with my hand. Luckily for me, my Ace Car Rental Badge had fallen victim to my preoccupation with the morning's activity, and still rested in my desk drawer.

"But my friends call me Walt," I finished lamely.

"Galilei!" exclaimed Leda. "Like that restaurant in Juno?"

If not for the danger of providing further evidence of a diminished mental capacity, I would have slapped my forehead. I had forgotten about my Uncle Vincenzo's restaurant. It was just off the Juno exit a few miles south of Cobb's Station – and something of a local tourist attraction.

"Yes," I answered cautiously.

"My mom and I love that place! Our ranch is off the next exit. Are you related to the owner?"

"He's my uncle." 'On my mother's side,' I thought to myself.

"Your uncle's restaurant would be a wonderful place to celebrate your birthday! I could meet you there!"

"Well, it's kind of a noisy–" I dithered, ecstatic that she had just agreed to go on a date with me, but desperately trying to come up with a legitimate reason to deflect her suggestion of the venue. I could see how a family restaurant would seem like a really safe place for a girl to have a date with a man she had met in a parking lot, but if I took Leda there, I was sure to be unmasked. On the other hand, if I tried to talk her into going somewhere else, she might decide not to go at all. I decided I would just have to be prepared to confess all on Tuesday night. "But I would be honored to introduce you to Uncle Vinny and his family. Of course, in order to introduce you, I'd have to know your name . . . "

"Leda – and that's all you're getting until Tuesday. Hey, it's a longer drive for you than me. Would seven be too early?"

"Seven's good. I can get Jason to cover for me," I replied, a little dizzied by the pace of events.

"Good, it's a date!" Leda grinned. "Now scoot before Charlie comes back. I don't want him knowing my business!"

I was floored. I had been wondering how I was going to beat a quick retreat when Jason buzzed my pager, but Leda had solved the problem by shooing me away, and she wasn't even going to tell Charlie about me. I had needlessly lied to Leda about my last name.

"Okay. Well, great! I'm, uh, really looking forward to –"

My plan had worked perfectly up to this point, but now instead of simply saying I'd see her on Tuesday and walking away, I was about to blow the whole thing with some nervous babbling. Then an amazing thing happened. Leda suddenly grabbed my shirt and pulled my head down to her level. I had to grab the side of the Mini Cooper's door to keep from falling into the car.

"Walt," she said, just inches from my face, "I'll be there. Now you really have to go." Then she gave me a brief, warm, intoxicating kiss and shoved me away. "Now scoot!"

I scooted.

Chapter Six

After stopping by a store to get ice cream, and by my apartment to change clothes and check on Io, I drove a few miles out of Jupiter and turned onto a narrow, potholed farm road. I was now in what my familial father (as opposed to the biological one) called cole country, cole being certain leafy green vegetables such as broccoli, cabbage, cauliflower, kale, radish, and others. Chiefly cabbage. New York grows more cabbages than any other state.

I drove past two miles of fields before the handsome green cabbages gave way to the homely discolored leaves of rutabagas. Rutabaga is also a cole crop and the vegetable that my parents grow on our farm. I turned onto the little dirt road that led through the rutabaga fields to my parents' farmhouse. I saw my father, Elmo, doing some work on a rutabaga harvester in the tractor barn. As I drove into a large graveled area that serves both as parking lot and front yard, Dad waved and then turned back to his maintenance chores. I parked and crunched through the gravel to the kitchen door, which, as in most cole country homes, was the front door.

My mom, Beatrice (everyone calls her Bee), was cutting some rutabagas into a pot. She looked up and smiled when I walked through the door.

"Don't worry, son, these aren't for the potato casserole. Your father wanted some mashed rutabagas and carrots with his dinner, but you don't have to have any."

I hated rutabagas. Over the years, Mom had mashed rutabagas with carrots, peas, onions, potatoes, cheese, and any other defenseless food items she had in the kitchen. She also made a variety of 'special' rutabaga dishes like rutabaga casserole, puffs, Parmesan, soup, and 'chicken surprise' where the surprise was rutabaga. I had eaten rutabaga boiled, roasted, fried, barbequed, broiled, fricasseed, and cooked on a stick. I didn't want any more rutabagas.

"None for me, thanks," I said, giving her a hug.

My mom grabbed my neck with her free hand and started gently weeping. "Oh, Walt, happy birthday! I hope this year goes better for you, son. I really do."

"Aw, Mom, please don't start again. Everything's going great."

She let me go, returned to cutting rutabagas, and started again. "I know, son. Everything's great. You quit college with just a year to go, you take a dead-end job renting cars that are impractical to own, you live all alone in a tiny apartment, and you haven't brought a girl to meet your mother in over a year." She fished in her apron pocket, found a crumpled tissue, and dabbed her nose. "Oh, everything's just great."

I sat down at the kitchen table, and considered cheering my mom up by telling her about Leda. Then I remembered that the restaurant where I was meeting Leda belonged to my mom's brother, whom I had passed off as my *father's* brother because I was using my mom's maiden name as my last name. I decided it would be imprudent to disclose the existence of this new girl friend to my mother at this juncture.

"I might have found my biological father," I said.

Instead of answering, Mom got up and walked to the sink with her pot of rutabagas.

"I drove up to Cobb's Station yesterday to see him."

She filled the pot with cold water and brought it over to the stove.

"He was about my height and had the same color eyes, but his skin is either naturally darker or he owns a tanning lamp."

She set the rutabagas on a gas burner and turned the knob until bright blue tongues of flame appeared under the pot.

"And he claims he's never donated sperm before."

"Well, then, why don't you leave the poor man alone and just give up this obsession of yours?" she asked. "It's ruining your life, not to mention the lives of your family."

"Mom, the man's lying. And besides obtaining an accurate medical history of both my parents, I'd kind of like to know who my siblings are, naturally conceived and otherwise, so I don't end up marrying one of them."

"Well, for my sake, I hope you're talking about marrying one of your sisters, and not one of your brothers." She gathered some spices and a small mortar and pestle from a cabinet next to the stove and carried these items over to the kitchen table. "It's silly to even worry about it, Walt. You know the odds of marrying one of your donor's other children are astronomical."

"Not in this case, Mom. My biological father made over six hundred sperm donations under sixty-three different names."

"I don't believe it!" she said, sliding into a chair opposite me. "Six hundred? How's that possible? How could someone get away with such a thing? When did you find this out? How did you find this out?"

I told my mother, in as much detail as I could, how I had tracked down Charlie Bolero.

"You know, dear, all this is fascinating," she said thoughtfully, and measured some dried rosemary leaves into her mortar. "And I think all your detective work has been brilliant, but if you really wanted to nail this man, it would help if you had an eye witness."

She began grinding the rosemary, and looked up at me with a little smile. I could hear the crunch of the rosemary stems as the pestle pulverized them. "I saw him."

Now I thought I knew how Jody felt when she was goggling at me, because I could feel my own eyes bulging from their parent sockets. "But the fertility clinics never let their clients even see pictures of the donors," I objected.

"No, they didn't show me a picture. They had to protect the privacy of the donor. They only gave me his background and physical description, along with a list of health certifications, IQ scores, grade averages and so forth. Most of which, from what you tell me now, were probably fake."

"Well, then, how did you see him?" I asked.

"I insisted; in fact, I threw a fit on the day of my insemination. I wanted to make sure my baby would grow up looking like the rest of our family, and I didn't trust anyone else's judgment. I was hysterical, I screamed, cried, and just as I was getting ready to call the whole thing off, one of the nurses told me my donor was actually at the fertility clinic. Back then, a lot of clinics only performed what was known as fresh insemination, where the sperm was taken directly from the donor and immediately implanted. The nurse said if I would just behave, she'd let me take a quick look at the donor. She took me down the hall and briefly opened a door. She made some excuse to the man inside about a wrong room assignment. I saw his face for only a moment, but I was satisfied with his appearance, so I went through with the insemination."

"Wow! So if I showed you Charlie's yearbook picture, you might recognize it?"

"If you only showed me his picture, I don't think either of us could trust the results. After all, it has been over twenty-two years – well, I guess twenty-two years and nine months to be precise," she laughed. "In order to have any confidence in my recollection, I think you should mix this man's photo with some others."

I thought that was an excellent idea. I said I would pick out about a dozen of Charlie's fellow classmates and make a little deck of cards. I was excited about my mom's unexpected contribution. I knew she didn't approve of or understand my desire to establish the identity of my biological father, and I appreciated the help she was giving now. I was about to tell her so when my father struggled through the door carrying a large burlap bag.

"Hey, Walt!" He grinned, set the bag on the table, and pulled the sides down to expose the largest, most unattractive, rutabaga I had ever seen. "I found another renegade! This one weighs over thirty-eight pounds!"

My father grew two crops of rutabagas a year. Occasionally, both the harvesting machine and the plow would miss a few of the homely vegetables and these renegades, as my father called them, would continue to grow until he happened across them in the field. Every time he found one of these monsters, he called the local paper, and the Jupiter Satellite cheerfully published a picture of my dad and his flesh-eating rutabaga. He had half a dozen newspaper clippings of these happy discoveries on the wall of his office in the tractor barn.

"Great, Dad! That ought to make a world-record rutabaga casserole," I joked.

"No, son, it's too old and tough for a casserole. This big fellow is slated for chips!"

I had forgotten about rutabaga chips. Despite my abhorrence of everything else rutabaga, I did like the chips. Fried to a crisp and heavily salted, rutabaga chips tasted much like their potato chip cousins, only chewier.

Once my father was in the house, all conversations about my search for my biological father were banned. Mom had kept my genealogical endeavors secret from Dad, and I was grateful for this deception.

Mom shooed Dad and me off to wait for dinner in the 'sitting room,' whose walls and every otherwise unoccupied surface displayed the images and momentos of Callisto family history. These included sheaves of correspondence from catalog, telephone and utility companies stacked in chronological order among untidy piles of books, magazines and newspapers. We retreated into this working farm's version of an urban living room and pretended to watch television while engaging in the abbreviated conversation of a father and son already familiar with each other's views. In between questions about the state of each other's occupations, updates on mutual acquaintances, and comments on local and foreign affairs, I found myself sneaking glances at my father's strong, careworn features in the flickering light of an unseen television program and wondering why I would ever want to give another man an excuse to call himself my father.

Chapter Seven

I arrived at Ace Car Rental on Monday morning in too good a mood to pay any attention to the antics of my two porters, so when I noticed Pitch and Jody by the carwash embroiled in yet another one of their incessant arguments, I started to just wave at them and walk into the office. But when Jody saw me, she started hollering and gesturing for me to come look at something. I really wanted to go inside and tell Jason what my mom had revealed to me, but the range of possible catastrophes resulting from the application of Pitch's and Jody's judgment compelled me to take the safer course and begin walking towards the carwash. Halfway there, I realized I was looking at the same white Lincoln Town Car that Charlie Bolero had turned in yesterday morning. I didn't think their argument could possibly have anything to do with the tiny ding I had made in the Lincoln with my BB pistol. The young porters never noticed the dings they made, much less any that customers caused. Yet, Jody's continued gestures in the direction of the Town Car made it increasingly clear as I approached the carwash that her disagreement with Pitch had something to do with the state of the white Lincoln.

"Okay, calm down," I said, upon arriving at the Lincoln's side. "Just start from the beginning – no, no, one at a time, please. Jody, you go first."

"Somebody stole the tires off this car," Jody said defiantly, and glared at Pitch.

I looked at the tires on the Lincoln. They looked okay to me. I knelt down and read the size and manufacturer information on the tire. "These look like the original manufacturer's executive edition tires to me, Jody, the same ones that are on all the other Town Cars in the lot. What's wrong with them?"

"That's what I told her, Mr. Callisto," Pitch said.

"And I told you the original tires had been swapped for some older ones of the same kind!" retorted Jody.

"Well, I'm sure that makes a lot of sense to you, but–"

I interrupted Pitch's comeback with an impatient wave of my hand. "Jody, why do you think the tires have been switched?"

"They're too smooth. All the other new cars make a sound like Velcro being pulled apart when I drive them into the car wash. This one hardly made any sound at all. When I came out of the car wash, I looked at the tires real careful, and I noticed all those crinkly little lines between the treads are almost gone. They're mostly still there on our other new cars."

I examined the tires again and then walked across the lot to look at the tires on another new Lincoln. Then I checked its odometer and walked back to the white Lincoln to compare mileage. The two readings were within about five hundred miles of each other – not enough to account for the difference in tire wear.

"Pitch, finish drying this car and move it to a slot in front of the store. Jody, I think you're right about this. Thanks for bringing it to my attention. Let me know if you notice anything else."

When I walked into the office area, I found Jason breakfasting on coffee and crullers. Jason saluted with his coffee and waved at the box of assorted pastries by the coffee maker. "Good morning, poetry boy," grinned Jason. "Have a donut."

Blushing, I grinned and poured myself some coffee. "I knew I shouldn't have told you about that. Your kind doesn't understand the language of true romance."

"You owe me every juicy detail, you ingrate. I put my butt on the line for your little balcony scene yesterday. Customers tend to blow their gaskets when you make them fill out accident forms and then start 'having difficulty' with their credit cards. Why didn't you signal me when you finished hitting on her?"

"I'm sorry, I think I just wandered around singing until I felt my pager go off. But I appreciate you risking your skinny butt. I know you don't have any to spare."

"My pleasure, poetry boy. How was supper at your mom and pop's? Did you bring me some leftovers?"

"I can't believe I haven't told you yet! My mom told me the most amazing story last night. I was just coming in here to tell you about it when Jody detoured me to show me something odd about that white Lincoln. I don't know which thing to tell you about first."

"Jody's always noticing odd things," Jason said. "Tell me what your mom said."

I told Jason about my mother being allowed to sneak a look at her sperm donor, and her idea of trying to select the face she had glimpsed twenty-odd years ago from a group of yearbook portraits. Jason liked my card deck idea and said he would print a lineup of similar faces from the 'SPU CHARLIES' disk along with Charlie Bolero's picture, on cardstock down at the local Kinko's.

Then I told Jason about Jody's discovery. Jason said he had heard of customers exchanging tires on rental cars, but no one had been caught doing it at the Jupiter location. He fished around in his desk, pulled out a ruler, and followed me outside to the white Lincoln Town Car. Stooping down, he measured the depth of the tread in different spots on the tire and then walked over to a black Lincoln parked nearby and measured its tire treads in the same manner. Jason said the tires on the black Lincoln were only about 3/32nd deeper than the tires on the white Lincoln. He pointed out that other factors beside mileage would affect tread wear including tire pressure, temperature, driving speed, and cargo weight. The white Lincoln might have just had some harder miles put on its tires. Then Jason decided to open the hood of the white Lincoln. After looking at various components in the engine compartment, he did the same with the black Lincoln. Then he opened the doors of both cars and looked around inside the driver and passenger compartments. After about five minutes of poking around, Jason shut the hoods and waved for me to follow him back into the office area.

"I think Jody's on to something," Jason said, plopping down in his chair. "The tires were definitely switched, the battery warranty expires a year earlier than the one in other car, and when I looked in the engine compartment, I saw some shiny spots that shouldn't be there."

"So, do you think Charlie did this?"

"I don't know." Jason picked up a telephone directory and began leafing through the business pages. "We got the new Lincolns three months ago. It could have happened anytime since then. I thought I'd email a few Ace Car Rental locations and some of our friendly competitors later on to see if they've noticed any parts exchanges lately. Who knows, this might end up giving you a little leverage over Charlie."

Pitch and Jody worked only half a day on Mondays. With businessmen from out of town picking up their four-day rentals, Mondays were hectic in the morning but slow in the afternoons. I decided to catch up on some paperwork while Jason went down to Kinko's to print the student photos of Charlie and some of his fellow classmates on card stock.

I was sorting through Sunday's contracts when I came across Charlie Bolero's contract with the insurance claim attached. I didn't want to commit insurance fraud, so I removed the form and tossed it into the trash. Then I flipped over the first page and looked at the copies of Charlie's driver's license and insurance card. I noticed that Charlie had different addresses on his rental agreement, driver's license, and insurance card. Having multiple home and business addresses wasn't all that unusual, and I wasn't sure what I intended to do with the information, but I jotted down the addresses and put them in my wallet anyway.

I finished sorting and filing the contracts and had started running a report on the prior week's activity when the phone rang.

"Ace Car Rental, may I help you?" I asked. There was no answer, so I tried again. "Hello, is someone there?" Again, there was no answer, and I was about to hang up when I heard a low, raspy voice say my name.

"Walt?"

I stiffened. The voice sounded strange and threatening. The effect was like a stage whisper heard from the tenth row of a theater.

"Yeah?" I ventured.

"Don't you remember me? You insisted on meeting me."

"Look," I said, "why don't you just stop playing games, and tell me what you want?"

There was a burst of giggling from the other end of the line, and then a warm female voice crooned, "But, Walt, I thought you liked playing games."

"Leda?"

"Yeah, silly, who did you think it was? Don't answer! I don't want to know. I hope I didn't scare you."

"No," I lied, wiping my brow, "but you've got a pretty wicked whisper there. How did you learn to do that?"

"Drama classes. That was my 'Pazuzu the Demon' voice from 'The Exorcist.' I called to check up on you. I wanted to make sure you actually worked at the car rental place."

"Why? You don't think I just hang around car rental agencies picking up cute girls, do you?"

"I was thinking more along the lines of a mad writer who lures beautiful women to his loft and tortures them with his poetry."

"Aw, I thought you liked my little tributes in verse," I teased.

"I did. They were sweet, but the thing I liked best was what you didn't mention."

"What was that?" I asked.

"My eyes. The first thing most guys say to me is 'You have gold eyes!' like no one else had ever noticed them before. I know I have gold eyes because just about everybody I've ever met points them out to me. You were the first guy to ever notice me before my eyes."

I sent a quick prayer of thanks up to my guardian angel. The first things I had seen yesterday were Leda's striking amber eyes. The only reason I hadn't said anything about them was because I had managed to stifle that last line of verse.

"You have gold eyes? I didn't notice. I guess I was too busy looking at your boobs." I heard another burst of giggling from Leda's end of the line.

"Watch it, poetry boy," laughed Leda, " you're on thin ice."

But it sounded to me like I was on solid ground. We traded quips a while longer and then discussed Tuesday's assignation at my uncle's restaurant in Juno. I was tempted to tell Leda my real last name then and there, but decided that the reasons for my deception were too complex to tackle over the phone.

A few minutes after I finished my conversation with Leda, Jason walked into the office and spread out a small deck of cards on my desk. Each card had a black and white portrait of a college student printed on it. "What do you think?"

I was impressed with the amount of detail Jason had achieved in the images. The original portraits had been cut from a scanned yearbook page he had downloaded from the SPU alumni web site. He had enlarged the tiny pictures to fit on two-by-three-inch cards.

"You must have enhanced these in Photoshop," I said. "They look great!"

"Nah, Photoshop can't do this. I dropped by my house and ran them through a new program that uses an advanced AI filter specifically tuned for facial reconstruction. That's what took me so long."

"Artificial intelligence? But how do you know the images are faithful to the originals? They might just be fun house distortions."

"Here, look at this one of Charlie Bolero. You can tell it really captured him. This program was written by a retired spook. It's the best image enhancement software for faces in the civilian market."

I had to admit the picture of Charlie Bolero looked like a young version of the man I had seen in Cobb's Station. The other pictures Jason had chosen from the 'SPU CHARLIES' disk were close enough in general appearance to be his cousins. My mom was going to have a challenge on her hands picking Charlie out from the rest of the deck. That is, if it really was Charlie my mom had glimpsed all those years ago.

Jason left me thumbing through the picture cards while he went back to his own desk to check his email.

"Well, crap!" exploded Jason. "I guess we won't be finding out if Charlie donated sperm in his own name anytime soon."

"Why not?"

"Because my friend doesn't work at the fertility clinic anymore."

Chapter Eight

I had timed my arrival at the Callisto rutabaga farm that evening to coincide with my dad's nightly office work. Each evening after dinner, my father spent a couple of hours in the tractor barn working in his office. I suspected that, besides conducting farm business, he used his office respites as an opportunity to do a little uninterrupted reading, surf the web, or just snooze. Now I was watching my mom, as she looked at the decades old images of SPU students spread out on her kitchen table.

"They're all so much alike," she murmured.

"I know, Mom," I said. "We tried to assemble a group of similar looking faces to make sure our chief suspect didn't stand out."

"Well, you certainly succeeded in doing that," she said, gathering the picture cards into a deck so she could shuffle through them one at a time, "because none of them jump out."

I watched as my mom went through the little deck of cards. She looked at each face in turn, and then flicked them to the back of the deck like a card player sorting suits in a game of trumps. After going through the deck a couple of times, she began dealing the cards into two stacks. I tried to avoid looking at the faces on the cards as they were assigned to each stack, because I didn't want to influence my mother's decision. She picked up the smaller of the two piles and spread them out on the table. I risked a quick glance and saw she had chosen three cards out of the deck of twelve. I was thrilled to see that one of the three was Charlie Bolero. My mom didn't notice my reaction because she was busy studying the three faces.

"The nose on this one isn't quite as I remember," she said, reducing her selection of cards to two. Then after a little more thought she held the two cards up for me to see.

"Both of these faces look a lot like the person I saw twenty-two years ago. This picture is the closest of the two," she said, wiggling the picture in her right hand. The card in her right hand was Charlie Bolero.

I didn't know whether to feel disappointed or excited as I drove back to Jupiter. Although my mother thought Charlie Bolero looked like the man she had seen in the fertility clinic all those years ago, picking two people out of a lineup when you're only looking for one does not inspire a lot of confidence in the identification.

I pulled into a Kickapoo drive-in and ordered coffee, burger and fries from the mini-skirted waitress who skated up to my Escalade. While I was waiting for my meal, I took out my wallet and retrieved the addresses I had copied off Charlie's rental agreement. Then I punched the address listed on his driver's license into the Escalade's GPS navigation system. The screen showed the destination to be on an intercoastal canal only about a one and a half hours' distance from Jupiter. This seemed strange to me. My dad had taken me fishing out of a marina on that canal, and I didn't remember seeing any houses in the area. The waitress rolled back up with my order and asked me to partially lower my window so she could attach the tray to it. I gave her a big tip, promised not to drive away with the tray, and started eating my Kickapoo burger with relish, the appreciative variety, not the pickled condiment. By the time I had finished my meal I had come to a decision. I was going on a late-night expedition.

Even with the help of the turn-by-turn directions provided by the Escalade's GPS navigation system, I still had difficulty weaving my way through the maze of roads and cul-de-sacs servicing the marinas and warehouses on the intercoastal canal. When the navigation unit finally announced that I had arrived at my destination, I found myself in a small gravel parking lot facing a nondescript metal warehouse. The street address painted over a metal and glass door was barely visible in the dim light emitted by the door's papered-over window. I got out of my car and walked up to the door. As I approached, a motion sensor mounted on the side of the building caused the halogen floodlight to flare on. Using my hands to shield my eyes from the bright white light, I peered through a small slit where the brown paper affixed to the inside of the glass did not quite meet the side of the window frame. Only one dim light bulb lit the interior of the building, but I could make out what appeared to be a large boat motor, a forklift, various crates, and boxes. I could also see two boat slips, one empty and the other holding a large commercial-looking vessel floating quietly in the dark water, its access to the canal closed off by a large roll-up metal door.

The security light on the wall above my head suddenly flickered off. With the glare of the security light gone, I could see more details inside the warehouse. I noticed the forklift had an odd-looking cradle of heavy fabric straps attached to its forks. I could also see what looked like cowlings, lower casings, a propeller and other items that had obviously been removed from the outboard engine, lined neatly along a workbench next to the metal stand to which the boat motor was attached. I was trying to read the labels on some of the boxes when I heard the deep growl of a boat motor coming up the canal. I thought this was probably a sports fisherman returning to a marina I had seen farther up the canal, but as I waited for the boat to pass by, the large metal door in front of the empty boat slip started rolling up into the ceiling. I briefly thought of making a dash for my car, but I knew this would trip the motion sensor on the security light. If this was Charlie pulling into his warehouse boat slip, I didn't want him to see the security light go on. Since I hadn't seen a car parked in front of the warehouse when I drove up, I assumed Charlie would leave the same way he came. I decided all I had to do was wait quietly by the door until Charlie left again.

A sleek fiberglass power boat backed slowly into the warehouse, the bright yellow boat fenders hanging from the sides of the slip bobbing up and down in the froth of the prop wash. I could see Charlie, facing sideways, sitting with one knee on the pilot's chair so he could watch the progress of the boat's stern and bow, expertly guiding the big powerboat into its berth. I was impressed with the calm competence of Charlie's seamanship. My dad had let me dock his fishing boat several times, and I was never able to effect the perfect combination of power and steering required to ease a large boat like this gently into its slip.

Charlie hopped out of the powerboat and made her fast to the slip's cleats. Then, pulling a remote out of his shirt pocket, he lowered the slip's big metal door. Charlie walked out of my view, and suddenly the warehouse was flooded with bright, white light. I flinched away, my dark-adjusted eyes flaring with the orange afterimage of the sudden illumination. When I looked back into the warehouse, I saw Charlie driving the forklift over to the stern of the big powerboat. Charlie lowered the cradle of fabric straps around the boat's motor, and after strapping the big motor in and loosening its clamps, lifted the motor off of its transom with the forklift. I could see the back of the forklift rise as its forks took the weight of the big outboard. Charlie slowly drove the boat motor, swaying gently in its cradle of fabric straps, over to an empty metal stand next to the stripped-down motor. After carefully lowering the motor onto the stand and clamping it securely in place, Charlie released the straps and backed the forklift out of the way. I watched with fascination as Charlie proceeded to remove the cowlings, lower casing, and other external parts from the big motor. When he had finished stripping the boat motor, Charlie began reinstalling the parts that he had just removed from the powerboat's motor onto the other motor's chassis. When he was finished, Charlie carefully removed the prop from the powerboat motor and installed it on the other motor. I felt a stabbing pain in my back and realized I had been hunched over watching this strange procedure without moving for nearly an hour. I carefully straightened up, fearful of triggering the motion sensor of the security light. I hoped Charlie was not planning to begin some kind of repair work on the newly stripped motor. I was tired and wanted to go home. I looked back into the warehouse to see Charlie strapping the replacement boat motor into the forklift's fabric cradle, then I watched as the motor was carefully driven back to the powerboat and lowered into place. After securing the replacement motor to the boat's transom and reconnecting the fuel and control cables, Charlie disappeared from view again and the bright warehouse lights were extinguished. I waited for the motor of the slip's roll-up door to hum into life, but instead I heard approaching footsteps. In a panic, I dove for the cover of a metal trash dumpster just as Charlie was opening the door. The security light flared on and I saw Charlie, his arms full of collapsed cardboard boxes, pushing through the door. I squirmed further behind the dumpster and held my breath as Charlie's footsteps approached. Then I heard the lid of the large metal trash container slamming open and the sound of cardboard boxes being thrown inside. The lid of the dumpster slammed shut, and I endured a long silent pause before the sound of footsteps finally resumed. I was beginning to relax when I suddenly realized Charlie was heading in the direction of my car! I risked a peek around the corner of the dumpster and saw Charlie peering into the Escalade's front passenger window and then testing the surface of the hood with the palm of his hand. At this point I had been at the warehouse for the better part of two hours, and I felt sure the Escalade's engine was cold. Charlie looked around the lot, rubbing the back of his neck, and then walked to the edge of his drive to peer into his neighbor's compound. When I had driven by that building, I had noticed its parking lot was crowded with a couple of boats and an old truck. After a couple of moments, Charlie walked back to the Escalade, took a small rectangle of paper from his pocket, and scribbled something on it with his pen. Then he slipped the small note under the windshield wiper and returned to his warehouse. I remained sweating behind the dumpster until I heard the roar of the big powerboat begin to fade away as Charlie Bolero cruised back down the inter-coastal canal.

Chapter Nine

"You look like someone ran you down, scraped you up, and buried you," Jason said, when I drug into work the next morning.

"Then I look a lot better than I feel." I poured a cup of coffee, walked over to the window, and stood looking out with my back to the room.

"Well?" Jason finally asked.

Without turning around, I held up two fingers.

"She picked two guys out of the deck? Was one of them Charlie?"

"Yeah," I said, walking back to my desk and sitting down.

"Then it looks to me like we've got the right Charlie. It doesn't matter that your mom picked a second guy. The point is Charlie looks like the guy your mom saw in the clinic, and the facial recognition software thinks you resemble him. He's your sperm donor, Walt. You just have to decide how far you want to push it."

"It's not that simple, Jason. He denies donating sperm, I can't get medical records or anything else without either his cooperation or proof of parentage, which I can't get without a DNA test, and I have to get Charlie to consent to it if I want the results to be legally valid. In other words, I need Mr. Bolero's cooperation, and now I think I have a way to get it." I laced the fingers of both hands together behind my head, and with elbows outstretched, leaned back in my chair with a grin on my face.

"You found something on Charlie, didn't you?"

"I feel I should warn you at this juncture that just the act of listening to this story could make you a party to an unlawful negotiation, that is, unless you happen to be a lawyer," I said.

"Blackmail?" grinned Jason. "Bring it on."

"I think I saw Charlie swapping out some boat motor parts last night." I proceeded to tell Jason about the strange events I had witnessed the night before.

"Wow, that's an amazing and scary story, Walt," Jason said, when I had finished. "He could've caught you, knocked you over the head, and dumped your body in the canal. I guess there's no doubt about who swapped the tires on that Lincoln now. So, do you have a theory about what he's doing with those boat motors?"

"Yeah, but let me hear yours, first. I know you've got one."

"Well, if it works like the car scam, it's obvious he's buying used outboard motors with a lot of hours on their meters, but in fair mechanical condition. He's careful about the motor he buys, because he doesn't want it to break down right away. He specializes in one or two popular models used in the rental and excursion business. He locates a rental with the same model motor, but with a lot fewer hours, and then he motors over to his warehouse, transfers all the exterior components to the pre-stripped chassis of the other outboard, including the control panel with its hour meter, and then takes the tricked-up high-hour engine back to the boat rental place. The boat rental agent probably won't notice the switch, because the motor looks the same on the outside with all the decals, identifying numbers, scratches, dents and paint scrapes that it left with, and the hour meter only shows the increase in time that would be expected for the period of the rental. When the switched motor finally runs into a problem, the mechanic repairing it will likely blame the accelerated wear on poor maintenance, hard use, or just outright abuse – and if the switch is discovered, the rental agent has the same problem we have with the white Lincoln: establishing when the switch took place."

"Bravo!" I applauded. "Now, how does he sell his stolen boat motors?"

"Probably through some kind of used marine equipment outlet."

"Like a company that sold remanufactured engines?" I handed Jason a business card. "Charlie left me this on my windshield last night."

"I noticed your vehicle parked here last night," read Jason. "Please call me at the number on the reverse." Jason flipped the card over and read the other side. "Sea Tech Limited, Remanufactured Marine Engines, Ottawa, Canada, Charles Bolero, Account Representative, 315-555-8763."

"The thing that bothers me," I said, "is why Charlie would go to so much trouble to sell stolen boat motors when he could probably make just as much money selling legitimate outboards without the risk of being put in prison. It's like that white Lincoln. Why would someone in Charlie's position bother to swap tires that are only a little more worn than the tires he's replacing?"

Jason studied my face for a moment. "Why do any of us do what we do, Walt? You're confusing motivation with motive. Charlie might think he's stealing parts from rental cars to save money, but he's really doing it so he can feel superior to everyone else."

"You mean he's doing it for kicks."

"Yeah. On the other hand, I think Charlie's stealing boat motors for the money. He could buy a good used marine outboard with high hours for around three thousand, and sell a remanufactured boat motor with full warranties for at least ten grand. If you subtract the costs of the old motor, the boat rental, and miscellaneous overhead, Charlie would net at least five grand from each transaction. Greedy crooks get caught, so I bet he only sells one every couple of weeks, but that would still bring in a hundred and twenty grand a year for only a couple of days' work a month. I call that a pretty sweet little racket."

"Well, what do you think about me confronting Charlie with his scams as a way to force him to cooperate?"

"It might work, but you'd have to be careful how you played it.'

"Yeah. He might just decide to close up shop and challenge me to prove he did anything wrong. There must be thousands of boat rental agencies up and down the coast; I don't know where he gets his boat motors from, or who he sells the stolen ones to, for that matter. If I scared him, he could just get rid of his last 'remanufactured engine,' and pretend Sea Tech went bankrupt."

"Yeah, or he could just give you a one-way boat ride," grinned Jason, "which brings up the subject of the note. Don't you think it sounds a little threatening?"

"No, Charlie thinks the car belonged to someone from a neighboring warehouse with a crowded parking area. I saw him walk to the edge of the drive and look into their parking lot."

"Are you sure? What were you driving last night?"

"That black Escalade. Why?"

"What were you driving Saturday morning when you visited Charlie in Cobb's Station?"

It was a little after five in the afternoon when I pulled into Ganymede Terrace apartments. I had meant to get away sooner, but a discussion with Jason and a last minute spate of business had delayed my departure. Jason had received several replies from other agencies to my inquiry about parts swapping on rental vehicles. Apparently, these thefts occurred on a regular basis in larger markets, with tire swapping the most prevalent and easiest to detect. Most of these rogue customers substituted extremely worn tires and occasionally returned rentals with different brands and sizes of tires on the same car. Some of the rental agents who returned Jason's email reported finding worn vinyl bucket seats substituted for leather captain chairs, Kmart car radios in place of Bose stereo systems, and in one instance an entire high performance Cadillac North Star V8 engine replaced by a grease-caked, valve-clanking motor well on its second trip around the odometer. As Jason had pointed out, moderation is the key to a successful criminal enterprise, a virtue he found sadly lacking in most of these rogue customers, but seemingly abundant in the character of Charlie Bolero, because none of the cars in which thefts were discovered had been rented by him.

With Io's calico tail flashing in my wake, I proceeded directly to my living room to call my Uncle Vinny. Galilei's Famous Italian Restaurant had been a fixture on the outskirts of Juno for nearly twenty years. Galilei's owed its renown as much to its décor as to its homey Sicilian dishes. The interior of the restaurant was plastered over with tributes to famous and not so famous Italian scientists, explorers, artists, and musicians. Each dining area was dedicated to a different branch of Italian endeavor, with grandiose names such as 'Explorers' Pavilion,' 'The Hall of Scientists,' and 'Gallery of the Arts.' It was like dining in a tourist museum.

"Uncle Vinny? It's me, Walt."

"Walt! How's Bee and Elmo?"

"Mom and Dad are both fine, Uncle Vinny. Look, Uncle Vinny, I'm meeting a wonderful girl for dinner tonight at your place, and I'd like you to do me a small favor."

"Hey! A beautiful girl! Wonderful news! Hey, Lois! Walt is bringing his girl to meet us!" I couldn't make out my aunt's answer over the clatter of dishes and other kitchen noises, but it sounded enthusiastic. "Don't you worry about a thing, Walt. For you, anything. If it's money, don't even ask. Your money is no good here–"

"No, thanks, Uncle Vinny; it's not money. It's–a little embarrassing. You see, this girl was with a friend of her mother's, and for reasons that are too complicated to go into right now, I didn't want this friend to know I was talking to her–so I introduced myself as Walt Galilei, so he wouldn't recognize my name if she mentioned meeting me."

"So she thinks I'm your father?"

"No, you're still my Uncle Vinny, except now you're on my father's side. I'll straighten it all out as soon as I get there. The problem is I'm running late. I'd be really grateful if you could just put her in the Explorers' Pavilion and keep anyone from accidentally spilling the beans until I get there."

"Okay, Walt, I'll be your Punchinello, just for the night, and when you arrive and reveal my brother Benny is really my sister Beatrice, I'll come in and claim my applause. Now, who is this lovely signorina I have to deceive?"

"I only know her by her first name, Leda. She'll be there by seven."

"Leda? With the beautiful gold eyes?"

"Yeah, how did you know–"

"Lois! Our Walt is dating the beautiful Leda Lobrelei! They're coming here tonight! Thaw some shrimp!" I could hear my aunt's squeal in the background. "Lois is very excited. Leda's a wonderful girl; I'd tell a thousand lies if I were in your place. Leda and her beautiful mother Himalia Lobrelei come in here all the time. They're nice people."

I guess I shouldn't have been too surprised that my uncle knew Leda; Uncle Vinny made a point of visiting with his customers, and Leda had mentioned that she and her mother loved Galilei's. "Thanks, Uncle Vinny! You always come through for me–"

"I can't deny you, Walt; you're my sister's only son. Now, get going. You mustn't let the beautiful Leda wait too long! I'm so proud!"

My uncle was singing an Italian love ballad when I hung up. "Lobrelei!" I said aloud, "Leda Lobrelei!" I thought her name was as beautiful as her eyes. I had put down the phone and was about to go take my shower when I noticed the message light flashing a pale blue "2" on my answer machine. The first message began with the muffled sounds of a car engine accompanied by the distant roar of tires on concrete pavement. That call ended abruptly about three seconds into the message. The second message had the same background noise for the first few seconds, and I was about to push the erase button on my answering machine when a warm, friendly voice began speaking.

"Hello, Walt? I hope this is the Walt Callisto who came to my house on Saturday morning. If not, then please ignore this message. You know, Walt, after you left Saturday morning, I couldn't shake the feeling you were still a little confused. I think we should have another, less hurried, discussion so we can clear up any lingering doubts you might have. I'll be out this evening until at least ten, but you can call any time after that."

I stood in stunned silence while Charlie left his phone number and best wishes. After searching and finding pen and paper, I replayed the message and wrote down Charlie's cell and home telephone numbers. Charlie was right about my state of confusion, but now it was mixed with a measure of relief. I had been dreading a second confrontation with this man who, in my opinion, was a glad-handed sneak thief, but now that I had an invitation, I felt more confident about obtaining Charlie's cooperation, especially after I had revealed what I knew about Sea Tech. I took my shower, donned chinos, loafers, a white shirt, and a heather sports jacket, fed Io, and left my apartment singing an Italian love song.

Chapter Ten

Leda's little red Mini Cooper was parked near the front entrance of Galilei's Famous Italian when I pulled up in the Escalade. I jumped out and hurried to the entrance fearing that, despite the arrangements with my uncle, the false beard of my mother's maiden name was being torn away before I had a chance to explain.

"Buon sera, figlio della mia sorella!" exclaimed Vinny, rushing forward to embrace me as I entered the restaurant. I knew my uncle was trying to say 'Good evening, nephew' in Italian, and not getting it quite right. When Vincenzo Galilei was in his restaurant, he had the habit of speaking loudly in poor Italian, and using exaggerated gestures like a comic Italian chef in a TV commercial. This was a little embarrassing for me, although I had to admit that Galilei's customers seemed to enjoy my uncle's antics.

"Good evening, Uncle Vinny. I see Leda's here. Is everything okay?"

"Don't worry, Walt. I've taken care of everything," Vinny said in a conspiratorial tone. "She just arrived. I set a table for her in the Hall of Scientists, and I've told Tony not to go in until you arrive. By the way, Leda told me today is your birthday!"

I had a frightening vision of the entire restaurant staff singing Buon Compleanno around one of my uncle's blazing Pans de Spagna Italiano, a special brandied flaming sponge cake.

"Actually, Uncle Vinny," I said, "I've already celebrated my birthday with Mom and Pop. Leda and I are just having a quiet little dinner."

"She's a beautiful girl, Walt. Tell her I'm making Alfredo del Gambero Galilei in her honor."

I promised to pass on my Uncle Vinny's compliments and set off toward the Hall of Scientists, taking a short cut through the Explorers' Pavilion, which served as both the main dining hall and a quarry-tiled thoroughfare to the smaller dining rooms. The Explorers' Pavilion's walls were covered with spotlighted paintings of famous navigators and adventurers such as Giovanni da Verrazzano, Amerigo Vespucci, Giovanni Caboto, and Marco Polo. There was a huge baroque fountain featuring Christoforo Columbo at the far end of the room, flanked by short hallways on either side. These led to the kitchen and rear dining rooms.

I took the right-hand hallway to the Hall of Scientists, where I found Leda standing among the room's empty dining tables. She was reading a plaque under one of the photographs on the wall, her hair and eyes gleaming in the soft glow cast by the squat amber glasses that my uncle used for table candles. I stood in the doorway for a moment, watching her lips move, as she traced the lines of text in the dimly lit room. She finished reading, looked up, and smiled at me.

"Hey! I didn't know there were so many famous Italian scientists! See this stony-faced guy in this portrait? He's Guglielmo Marconi. He invented radio. Listen to what it says about him: 'In 1900, he took out his famous patent No. 7777 for tuned telegraphy.' Isn't that weird? Patent number 7777 filed right at the turn of the century? It sounds made up, huh?"

"Look at this one," she said, moving to an old black-and-white group photo. "See, this is a picture of the Manhattan Project team. See that little man on the end? That's Enrico Fermi. He built the world's first nuclear reactor - under a football stadium during World War II!"

"Yeah, I know. He also has an element named after him."

"Which one?"

"Fermium."

"I think you're making that up."

"No, really, it's element 100 on the periodic table. Fermi has a unit of measurement named after him, too."

"Yeah?" she smiled, "and what would that be?"

"The Fermi."

Leda placed one hand on her hip and waggled the fingers of her other hand in a come hither motion. When I obeyed her summons, she grabbed my jacket lapels and drew me within a couple of inches of her face.

"You're full of crap," she said smiling.

"No, really," I gulped, staring into Leda's gold eyes, "it's an atomic measure of energy down at the electron level."

I imagined there were probably trillions of Fermi roiling in the amber maelstroms of Leda's eyes. I could imagine all those countless crackling electrons leaping from their perilous nuclear orbits and incinerating hapless suitors she caught lying to her. I decided the sooner I could square myself with Leda the safer I would be, so I took Leda by the hand and led her over to the corner table that my uncle had set up with place settings, wine glasses and a carafe of Galilei's house Chianti.

"Leda," I said, pulling out her chair for her, "there's something about my last name I need to tell you about."

"Oh, I already know." Leda said, plopping down and scooting her chair under the table.

"You do?" I asked, amazed. "Who told you? My uncle?"

"No, I just read about it on a little plaque under Galileo's portrait."

"Oh! That. No, that isn't–"

"Sit down. I want to tell you something kind of weird."

I sat down. I wanted to interrupt her and explain about my search for my biological father and how it had led to Charlie and why I had to give Leda my mother's maiden name, but Leda's will was too strong. She wanted me to sit and listen, so I sat and listened.

"Ok, now don't take this the wrong way. I don't want you to think I'm one of those fatal-attraction chicks or anything like that, so don't go getting creeped out, but in a weird way, our meeting each other may have been written in the stars. You wouldn't be able to tell by looking at my mom now, but when she was young, she was a whacked-out New Age mystic type. She wore weird costumes and magic charms to school and went to a lot of spooky séances and Black Sabbath concerts. When I was born, she named me after one of Jupiter's moons, because she thought it had some kind of cosmological significance. All of Jupiter's moons are named after Greek gods or their women – 'Leda' for the one Zeus seduced while he was disguised as a big swan. Now, here's the weird part: Galileo was the first astronomer to discover Jupiter's moons – you're related to Galileo, and I'm named after a Jovian moon! Get it? We were destined to meet each another!"

"Wow," I said, and limited my remarks to that monosyllable. Sooner or later, Leda would have to know my last name was not Galilei, but now that she thought there was some mystical connection between her first name and my borrowed last name, I was afraid to broach the subject.

"You're not freaked out, are you?" asked Leda.

"No," I said quickly, "I love mythology. I named my cat Io. She was another one of Zeus's lovers, and one of the moons Galileo discovered."

"Io? Really? You didn't just make that up to humor me, did you?"

"No, it's on her name tag. You can check it out if you want to."

"Wow, just think, Walt," Leda said, leaning forward, and touching my hand, "you're eating dinner with one moon and going home to another. Maybe I should go home with you to check out Io's name tag."

I blushed and felt a surge of warmth suffuse my body. I was desperately trying to think of a clever reply when my cousin Tony entered the room with the antipasto tray.

"Hey, Walt! Happy Birthday! Pop had me make you this nice antipasto. We got some anchovies on little pieces of crusty pasta dura, some fresh bocconcini and ripe tomatoes with a drizzle of oil and a little basil, some beautiful figs wrapped in prosciutto, some olives and some of that pickled baby corn you like," Tony said, placing the tray between us. "Hi, Leda!"

I looked up at Tony in terror. I had momentarily forgotten that Leda and her mother frequented my uncle's restaurant. I wondered how well Tony knew them. I remembered my Uncle Vinny knew their names, but he often knew the names of customers who only came through town once or twice a year. I was afraid Tony might blurt out my real last name, but Leda eased my fears by cutting Tony off before he could get started. "Hey, Tony, your cousin and I are just getting to know each other, so don't go blabbing things you think you know about me."

"I'm the soul of discretion," protested Tony, grinning and holding his hands out in supplication. "I would never reveal the confidences of a beautiful woman."

"Shut up, you nut! I've never confided in you. Your cousin here," she said turning to me, "thinks he knows all about me because he chats up my mom and me when we eat here."

I noticed Tony casting a nervous glance in my direction. My cousin was about five years older than me and married to a fiery Italian beauty whose jealousy was legendary in the family.

"Well, then, I have some catching up to do. How do you feel about shrimp?" I asked, raising a warning eyebrow at Tony when Leda wasn't looking.

"I love shrimp," Leda answered.

"Well, you're in luck tonight," Tony said, taking his cue. "Just for you, my pop is making his famous Alfredo del Gambero Galilei. He butterflies and grills large, succulent gulf shrimp and serves them over a bed of homemade spinach linguini covered with the best Alfredo sauce in New Jersey. He makes his Alfredo sauce using only butter, Parmesan, and wine. No cream. My pop says the butter and cheese makes its own cream. We have customers who come all the way from Atlantic City just to taste our Alfredo."

"It sounds yummy. Please tell Vinny what a sweetheart he is for making it for us," Leda said.

Tony went back to the kitchen, and I breathed a sigh of relief. I decided I would wait until after the meal to reveal my real last name to Leda. I poured Leda and myself some Chianti, and we both sampled the antipasto.

"I love these little cheese balls. What did Tony call them?" asked Leda.

"Bocconcini."

"Is that Italian for little balls?"

"No, it's a type of freshly made mozzarella."

"What's Italian for little balls?"

"I don't really speak Italian."

"You don't? I thought you would've picked some up from your father. Doesn't your father speak Italian?"

"Not very much. We're fifth generation Italian-Americans. The last people to speak fluent Italian in my family were my great grandparents."

"But your Uncle Vinny speaks Italian."

"If you could speak Italian, you'd realize my Uncle Vinny can't. He bought one of those 'Speak Italian in 30 Days' DVDs when he opened this restaurant and learned just enough to be dangerous. His Italian-speaking customers try to help him become more fluent when they visit, but they don't try very hard because they know it's just a part of his act, like this Italian museum all around us. How about your family? Do your mom and pop speak Italian?"

"Do I look Italian?"

"No, but – I mean, your last name sounds Italian."

"Who told you my last name?"

"My Uncle Vinny."

"Yeah, well, we're not Italian. At least Mom and I aren't. Louis Lobrelei was mother's second husband. Now, he was Italian. I remember going to a family reunion in Chicago just a few months before he died. I was about seven years old. There must have been a hundred people there, aunts, uncles, sisters and brothers, lots of old folks and about a million little kids who treated me like their real cousin. A lot of those people spoke Italian, and they could really cook Italian too. Everyone was very demonstrative, you know. They laughed and argued a lot, and they cried and hugged each other a lot. We haven't been back since his funeral. I guess I miss being a part of that family."

I was impressed with this story. I thought it revealed all I really needed to know about Leda. I found her desire to be part of a big family attractive. In fact, Leda was beginning to feel like part of my family already. I realized now I had felt some kind of familial connection the first time I saw her glowing face through the sun-splashed windshield of the Mini Cooper.

Without mentioning their last name, I told Leda about Mom, Dad, and the rutabaga farm. I told her about growing up in an extended Italian family and how nearly everything she had described about her stepfather's family applied to mine, especially the arguing part. My family had plenty of loud, embarrassing arguments when we got together – just not in Italian.

Leda told me about how her mother, Himalia, had sold their house and gone on the road shortly after her husband's death. At first she had taken Leda with her to various points of interest in the US and Canada. Then after a couple of years of traveling around, Himalia, concerned about her daughter's education, decided to put Leda in a Catholic boarding school in West Virginia. Himalia then expanded her expeditions to the four corners of the world, coming back to West Virginia during school breaks to take Leda with her to some of her favorite travel destinations. Leda went on from boarding school to attend a women's college in Florida. When she graduated, Himalia took her on a trip to Paris, and then surprised Leda by announcing she had bought a horse ranch in New Jersey.

The casual way in which she related the tale of her mother's travels, her own private education and Himalia's recent real estate acquisition, made me suspect Leda took her mother's obvious wealth for granted and would be surprised to find anyone intimated by it. Cole country farmland was expensive, so my family wasn't exactly poor, but I had gone to public high school in Jupiter, attended a state university and my only trip out of the states had been a brief jaunt to Canada when my family had visited Niagara Falls, so even though she didn't act like it, I suspected Leda might be out of my social sphere.

By this point, the remains of the antipasto had been removed and replaced with large colorful platters of steaming green pasta, smothered in my uncle's famous Alfredo sauce and topped with enormous grilled shrimp. Through glasses blurred by steam, I watched Leda snatch a butterflied shrimp from the verdant linguini turf and bite through one of its delicate pink wings.

"Hmm, yummy!" She grinned, licking Alfredo sauce from her fingers.

I smiled and took my glasses off to wipe them. I thought this was the perfect moment to reveal my true identity.

"Leda, remember the other day when I met you outside Ace Car Rental?" Leda nodded and took another bite of shrimp, her gold eyes flashing in the candlelight. "Well, there is something I'd like to explain about my name—"

"Hush!" Leda said.

"I beg your pardon?" I asked, taken aback.

"Shut up for a second! I think I hear my mother!"

Chapter Eleven

"Leda!" Himalia hallooed from some remote part of Galilei's Famous Italian Restaurant.

"Crap," moaned Leda, "she's hunting us down."

"Where are you, dear? Shout, so I can find you," Himalia called.

"I'm sorry," Leda said, burying her face in her hands. "It wouldn't occur to my mom to simply ask the waiter where we were."

"Oh, uh, that's all right," I said, trying to be diplomatic, "your mom's shouts will just blend in with Uncle Vinny's."

"So you don't mind?"

"No, of course not." I did mind of course, but I wasn't stupid enough to admit it. "I'm looking forward to meeting your mom."

"Okay. Just remember, you asked for it." Leda grinned and then stood up and hollered, "We're back here, Mom! In the Hall of Scientists."

There was a clatter of high heels rapidly approaching, and then Himalia stepped into the room. I realized my mouth was hanging open. I snapped it shut and tried to stop staring at Leda's mom, but it was like trying to not look at a traffic accident.

Himalia had big, red hair, with glitter in it. Red, not copper, or burnt orange, but red like a stoplight. And she was dressed to kill. I had to admit she had an excellent figure, because I could see most of it. She was wearing tight black Capri pants that stopped about six inches short of her shapely ankles, which were adorned by the bright red straps of her high heels. The first few buttons of her long sleeved iridescent green midriff blouse were unfastened, and her ample chest was still heaving from her little run. Like her daughter, Himalia also had striking eyes, but of an unusually clear hazel color, much like the agates I used to covet when I played marbles back in the second grade. Trembling a little from some nameless trepidation, I stood up to meet Leda's mother.

Himalia gave us a dazzling smile and hurried over to throw her arms loosely around her daughter's neck, spreading her hands like little wings to protect her long ruby nails. Looking at me over Leda's shoulder, Himalia gave me a bright little smile, and I could have sworn I saw one of her gleaming hazel eyes wink at me.

"I saw your cute little red car out front when we pulled up, and I said to Charlie, there's Leda, I just have to run in and say hi while you park the car!" Himalia burbled.

"Of course you did. Mom, meet Walt Galilei. Walt, this is my mother. She's not always this sparkly, and that's not her normal hair color."

"Isn't it marvelous?" Himalia asked patting her glittered hair. "It's a special hairspray that they just got in at Lydia's. Believe it or not, the color and the glitter are all in the same can, and they just sprayed it on!"

I found myself unable to speak. I was petrified by the prospect that the Charlie Himalia had just mentioned might be the same Charlie I knew.

"Walt! Compliment my mom's hair!" Leda demanded.

"Oh, excuse me," I apologized, suddenly regaining the power of speech, "I was confused. For a moment there, I thought I was meeting Leda's sister. I'm delighted to meet you, Mrs. Lobrelei, and your hair is absolutely stunning."

Himalia took my extended hand, wrapped the warm fingers of her other hand around my wrist, and drew my hand up toward her breast, her long red nails gently pricking my skin.

"Why, Leda, I do believe you've found a true gentleman." Then, turning back to me, she said, "Please call me Himalia, Walt."

Her nails dug into my skin a little more as she gave my hand a squeeze. I was worried that the hand Himalia was holding might inadvertently brush against her breast, so I brought my other hand up and placed it on top of the hand sandwich Himalia had made for herself.

"Sure...um, ah, Himalia," I stammered, as I tried to gently extricate my hands from Himalia's grasp.

"And he's shy, too. Isn't that sweet?" Himalia said, pulling my hands against her breast.

It was at this moment that I became aware of Charlie Bolero standing in the doorway. He wasn't smiling, but I didn't think he was frowning either. If anything, Charlie appeared to be mildly perplexed.

"Well, hello, everyone. I hope I'm not interrupting anything," Charlie said.

"Oh, get in here, Charlie, and stop being silly," Himalia gushed. "I want you to meet Leda's new boy friend."

This was it, I thought. I was about to be exposed as a liar. Charlie entered the room and stood by Himalia. She released me and put her hand on Charlie's shoulder.

"Walt, this is my friend Charlie Bolero. Charlie, I'd like you to meet Walt Galilei."

I winced at the introduction and was barely able to watch Charlie's reaction. But to my surprise, Charlie merely smiled pleasantly and extended his hand. After staring at Charlie's hand for a moment, I, in something of a daze, offered mine. Charlie took it and clasped my arm with his other hand in a move reminiscent of Himalia's handshake.

"Happy to meet you," Charlie said warmly. "What was your last name again?"

I stared at him in disbelief. I was certain Charlie was playing with me, and I wasn't going to give Charlie the pleasure of seeing me squirm. I decided to preempt Charlie by telling Leda my real name right in front of Charlie and her mother. Then I intended to warn Himalia about the criminal activities I had witnessed at Charlie's marina warehouse on Monday night.

"I'm actually quite proud of my name–" I began. I felt a little odd trying to denounce a man while he was holding my hand, and I was wondering how to disengage his grip when Charlie suddenly interrupted me.

"Galilei!" exclaimed Charlie, pumping my hand. "I remember now, like the name of this restaurant. Well, then, you must be related to Vinny! I'm delighted to meet you, Walt. Vinny's a wonderful guy, and I'm sure you share all of his best traits."

"Vinny's his uncle," said Leda. "He made us this marvelous Shrimp Alfredo dish."

"Which is probably getting cold," said Charlie, releasing my hand. "Please don't allow us to ruin your meal. Himalia, why don't we get a table in another room, and let these young people finish dinner?"

"But, Charlie, can't we dine with them?" asked Himalia. "I want to get to know Walt."

"No, dear. They wouldn't want us to watch them eat while we waited for our dinner. We can all go out together some other night," Charlie said, putting his hand around Himalia's waist to gently urge her out of the room.

"That's Charlie for you," smiled Himalia, patting Charlie's shoulder, "our little Miss Manners. It was delightful meeting you, Walt, and I'm really looking forward to seeing you again. Oh! I have an idea! Walt, do you ride?"

"Ride?" I asked weakly.

"Horses, darling," breathed Himalia. "We have the cutest little ranch only a few miles from here. You could come over some afternoon, and we could all have a lovely trot through the pastures."

"Oh. Uh, sure. That sounds fun," I said, a little uncertainly.

"Wonderful! Leda, I'm depending on you to make all the arrangements."

"Okay, Mom. Enjoy your dinner."

Himalia hugged her daughter, gave me a smile, a little wave, and clacked out of the room on her red high heels. I couldn't be positive, because Charlie was smiling and waving at the time, but I thought I saw a fleeting glint of warning flash from Charlie's eyes as he turned to follow Himalia.

"Congratulations on surviving Hurricane Himalia," Leda said, plopping back into her chair. "Let's eat and get out of here before she decides to come back."

I collapsed into my own chair, unsure of how to proceed. Events seemed to have spun out of control with the arrival of Himalia and Charlie. Now I had to explain my deception to both Leda and her mother. I knew I needed to clear matters up before they became any more complicated, so I resolved once again to confess everything to Leda the moment we finished dinner.

While we ate our meal, Leda told me about her mom's horse ranch. Elara Downs was a thoroughbred broodmare farm about twenty miles north of Juno. For years, Elara had enjoyed a nationwide reputation as a top breeder of champion racehorses and broodmare sires. Although Elara still owned some top tier broodmares, the facility's reputation had suffered in recent years due to a series of unfortunate events. The previous owner, Emily Taurus, a widow in her sixties, told Himalia that operations at the ranch had deteriorated badly after the death of her husband.

Himalia had kept all the old staff on and even retained Emily as the farm manager, so the day-to-day operation of the ranch remained virtually unchanged. Now, however, Elara had the capital needed to pay expenses and repair its image. Emily was immensely grateful to Himalia for saving the ranch. To show her appreciation, she insisted on giving Himalia the antique furniture and rugs that decorated Elara's antebellum style mansion. The day they took possession of the ranch, Emily had introduced Charlie Bolero to Himalia and Leda as both a friend and client. Leda had disliked him at first sight.

"It was his smile," said Leda, "like his mouth was smiling, but his eyes weren't. They didn't match, you know? But, as you can see, my mom liked him. He's just her type. She loves agreeable people, whether they're faking it or not."

I knew this was my cue. "I'm glad you don't like Charlie, Leda, because now I can tell you why I don't like him either. This may surprise you, but despite that little act he put on when you introduced us, I knew Charlie before tonight."

"You dinged Charlie's rental!" gasped Leda, pointing at me like she was picking me out of a lineup. "You did, didn't you? I thought I heard a little ping sound while I was waiting for him in my mini!"

I was amazed. "How did you know?"

"Girls are intuitive, Walt. Besides, I saw you ducking back behind the fence."

"I'm sorry," I said, blushing and lowering my head. "It was a stupid thing to do, but I needed to talk to you without Charlie finding out. I saw you, just for a moment, dropping him off the day before and, well, I just had to meet you, and I had this unresolved issue with Charlie that– "

At this point, I looked up to see how well Leda was reacting to my confession, but I found she wasn't even looking at me. Instead, she appeared to be looking over my shoulder at someone behind me. I stopped speaking and turned to see my Uncle Vinny standing in the doorway. My uncle looked a little apprehensive.

"Salve, Walt; salve, Leda. I just wanted to check and make sure you had everything you needed," Vinny said, giving me a meaningful glance that I didn't quite understand.

"Vinny, your shrimp and pasta was just exquisite!" Leda exclaimed. "What did you call it again?"

"Alfredo del Gambero Galilei," said Uncle Vinny.

"Well, it was the best meal I've had here yet," Leda said.

"Thank you so much–"

"And the pasta! What did you call that green pasta?" Leda asked, turning toward me.

I noticed Vinny was nodding his head sideways like he had a crick in his neck and silently mouthing some kind of message.

"Oh, uh, spinach linguini," I answered.

"Yeah. The linguini was scrumptious. Was it homemade?" she asked, turning back towards Vinny.

When Leda wasn't looking, I shrugged my shoulders to indicate I didn't understand Vinny's message, but my uncle just kept nodding towards the front of the restaurant.

"Yes, we make all of our own pasta. Oh, by the way, Walt, you'll never guess who your cousin Tony sat in the Explorers' Pavilion while I was busy in the kitchen."

"I can't guess, Uncle Vinny. Who?" I wondered what my uncle was trying to say.

"Your mom and pop."

Reeling in shock, I watched helplessly as an eerie blue light slowly dawned behind my Uncle Vinny. With growing dismay, I realized what this blue glow meant. I could smell the aroma of burned sugar and brandy, and I could make out the voices of my parents among the chorus approaching the Hall of Scientists. I felt betrayed by my idiot cousin and let down by my Uncle Vinny, my Punchinello, who was now sheepishly standing aside to let Tony bring in a flaming Pan de Spagna Italiano. My Aunt Lois followed with a tray of gelato slices made up of pistachio, vanilla, and strawberry flavored stripes, like little

Italian flags, while my mom and dad, along with several Galilei waiters and waitresses, crowded in behind her singing the birthday song:

Buon Compleanno a Te,
Buon Compleanno a Te,
Buon Compleanno cara Walt!
Buon Compleanno a Te!

Like a nightmare in a Fellini film, the members of the birthday procession gathered around me singing the same silly verse over and over. Bizarrely, I heard someone singing counterpoint in a shrill, enthusiastic, soprano. The discordant sounds didn't appear to be coming from anyone directly in front of me so I looked over at Leda, but she wasn't singing. She was staring at someone on the far edge of the group near the door. I followed her gaze and was horrified to see Himalia's big red bouffant hairdo, glittering in the glow of the burning sponge cake and bouncing to the beat as she belted out the lyrics of the birthday song.

When they finished singing the final chorus, my Aunt Lois gave me a kiss and wished me a happy birthday.

"I'm sorry we can't stay and have cake and ice cream with you, but somebody has to work around here." Then my aunt led the waiters and waitresses back to their stations. My Uncle Vinny gave me an apologetic shrug and followed his wife back to the safety of his kitchen. Everyone else assembled around our table.

"Here you go, cousin; you can do the honors." I realized Tony was holding a cake knife out to me. "When I discovered your parents didn't even know you were here, I leapt into action and arranged this little sorpresa per il tuo compleanno!"

I stared at Tony and wondered vaguely if the cake knife, which was an abbreviated spatula with a cutting edge, could be used as a deadly weapon. Unable to think of another, socially acceptable course of action, I stood up and reluctantly accepted the knife from my cousin. I cut a wedge of cake with flickering fingers of blue flame dancing on top, placed it on a slab of gelato, and handed it to my mother.

She took the plate, gave me a one-armed hug, and whispered into my ear: "Smile, dear, it's not that bad." Then she turned and addressed the rest of the party. "Walt is a little surprised to see us – you see, we just celebrated his birthday Sunday night, and here we are again." Everyone laughed appreciatively, and Leda reached over and gave my hand a squeeze.

"Don't worry, Walt," Mom said. "Your father and I just decided to pop in on Vinny and Lois. We're not stalking you!"

This produced more laughter, and I felt my eyes tear up. I wondered if my mom would still want to hug me when she discovered my deception. I loaded another slab of ice cream with flaming cake and handed it to my father. When I looked up, I saw Himalia was next in line.

"I guess I'm crashing your party," Himalia grinned, reaching for the plate of burning cake I was holding. "I sort of joined your birthday procession on the way back from the lady's room." She turned to my parents. "Hi, I'm Himalia, Leda's mother."

"Mother! Wait until you're introduced," Leda complained. "I haven't gotten to meet them yet."

Himalia moved closer to her daughter, forcing me to reach over the blazing Pan de Spagna Italiano in order to hand a plate of cake and ice cream to her. 'Good,' I thought, I would introduce them and avoid using last names. But before I could speak, Himalia reached down with her other hand, the one that wasn't reaching blindly for the plate, and patted her daughter on the head.

"Oh, don't mind Leda," Himalia said. "She's just miffed because, like you, I popped in on her unexpectedly."

"Then allow me to make the introductions," Tony said brightly.

I would have shot my cousin a venomous look, but I was busy trying to put the plate in Himalia's blindly groping hand. She was looking at her daughter instead of at the plate, and she kept missing it. I was concerned she might accidentally put her hand into the flaming birthday cake, so I grabbed her wrist with my other hand and guided her hand to the plate. Himalia turned around and smiled at me, clasping my free hand in hers. "Thank you, dear. Happy birthday."

"Uncle Elmo, Aunt Bee, I'd like you to meet two of our most attractive customers, Leda and Himalia Lobrelei! Mrs. Lobrelei, Leda," Tony said grandly, "I'd like to introduce you to Walt's parents, Mr. and Mrs. Callisto!"

Himalia's smile suddenly vanished behind a frown of confusion. She swiveled her head to look quizzically at Tony, then at my parents, and then back at me. My face was burning brighter than the flaming confection we were both holding.

"But, Walt, dear," Himalia said, "didn't you say your last name was Galilei?"

"Mom! Let go of his hand!" Leda said.

"Hush, Leda, I'm trying to determine this young man's real last name," Himalia said. "Well, Walt, which is it? Galilei or Callisto?"

"Mother!" Leda shouted. "Let go of his hand! His sleeve is on fire!"

I looked down at my arm and was astonished to see thick yellow flames curling around the sleeve of my heather sports jacket. Himalia shrieked, threw herself on me, and started trying to pull my sports jacket off. Rushing to help me, Tony knocked over the table holding the flaming Pan de Spagna Italiano. Himalia and I tripped over the table and fell on the cake. Leda, thinking fast, grabbed the carafe of Chianti and poured it over my sleeve, her mother, and the smoldering remains of the cake.

After Himalia and I had been disentangled and helped up from the floor, a cursory inspection revealed the most grievous injuries sustained by either party to be a singed jacket, purple wine stains on Himalia's Versace blouse, and a broken heel on one of her red shoes. Himalia seemed to have lost all interest in ascertaining my real last name. She insisted that Leda immediately take her home, and sent Tony to inform Charlie of her decision. Her gold eyes looking larger than ever, Leda gave me a little shrug as she helped her mother hobble out of the room.

As soon as she was satisfied her son hadn't been burned by flaming sponge cake, my mom started questioning me about Himalia's confusion over my last name.

"Walt, that lady? Himalia, was it? Why did she think your name was Galilei?"

I moistened a napkin in my water glass and used it to wipe the red mud of cake and wine from my glasses while I thought about my answer. I considered telling my mother that Himalia had just gotten my uncle's name mixed up with my own, but I knew that would only make matters worse. Besides, I didn't like lying to my parents. On the other hand, I didn't want to say too much in front of my father. He didn't know I was trying to trace my biological father and explaining why I was using my uncle's last name would involve explaining who Charlie was and why I had contacted him in the first place. I put my glasses back on and looked at my mother. Her face had gone pale, and she seemed to be looking at something behind me. I turned to see Charlie Bolero standing in the entrance of the Hall of Scientists.

"Hi. I heard about the fire, and I thought I would check on you."

Chapter Twelve

Much later that same night, if Jupiter and Mars hadn't already sunk beneath the horizon, they would have seen me sweating bullets inside the darkened interior of my parked Cadillac Escalade, just down the street from Charlie's house in Cobb's Station, New Jersey. I was trying to talk myself into getting out of the car, marching up to the door, and hammering on it until Charlie answered. After the embarrassing events at my uncle's restaurant, I was more determined than ever to prove that Charlie was my biological father.

After appearing in the door of the Hall of Scientists asking after my welfare, Charlie had introduced himself to my parents. I was watching Charlie's face at the time and couldn't detect the slightest change in expression when my dad responded by introducing himself and my mom as Bee and Elmo Callisto. I still couldn't understand why Charlie hadn't shown any surprise when I had been introduced as Walt Galilei or betrayed even the slightest twitch when later my parents introduced themselves as Mr. and Mrs. Callisto. Elmo and Charlie chatted briefly about the dangers of flaming sponge cakes and how fortunate I was to escape the accident without serious injury. During this conversation, I noticed my mother sneaking little glances at Charlie and quickly looking away when Charlie returned her gaze. Eventually, Charlie excused himself by saying he had to get back to his house to do a little paperwork.

Seemingly dismissing her concern over my multiple surnames, my mom suddenly announced that the dinner she and Dad had ordered before being summoned to my impromptu birthday party had probably already been served, and they needed to return to their table before it got cold. My father patted me on the back and ushered Mom back to their table. As she left the room, she gave me a worried look. This bothered me more than anything else that had happened that night. I don't like making my mother worry.

I removed my glasses, mopped the perspiration from my forehead with my sleeve, and slipped my glasses into my shirt pocket. Then I got out of the Escalade and walked up to the front door. Except for the yellow porch light that flared into life when I approached, the house seemed quiet, dark, and vacant. I tentatively knocked on the front door, producing a dull tapping sound that I doubted could be heard in the back of the house. I waited a few minutes, listening for signs of life stirring within the house, and then tried ringing the doorbell. The bell was either broken or the house was extremely soundproof because I could hear nothing. Several tedious minutes crawled by without any response. I began to wonder if Charlie was even home.

After waiting a while longer, I stepped off the low brick platform that served as a front porch and walked across the front yard to the driveway. Tall wooden gates blocked access to the back of the house, but by pulling myself up on the top rail of one of them and craning my neck, I was able to see into the backyard. All the windows I could see in the house were dark. I had decided Charlie was not home and was lowering myself back to the pavement, when I noticed a faint neon glow seeping from under the rubber gasket of the closed garage door. The garage itself was steeped in dark shadows, but I was able to make out a large three-car garage with a mother-in-law apartment perched above it.

I hauled myself up, threw a leg over the top of the gate, and then hung there, teetering between indulging my desire to climb on over and obeying the voice of reason that was urging me to go back to my Escalade and give Charlie a call. After all, Charlie left his telephone number on my answering machine, not an open-ended invitation to drop by unannounced late at night and climb into his backyard. But that's exactly what I decided to do. I didn't want to give Charlie any notice. I wanted to just appear, suddenly, like an avenging angel, demanding truth from a deceitful sire who was refusing to recognize his progeny.

I swung my other leg over and dropped to the pavement, suddenly realizing, as the jolt of impact passed through my frame, that there could be a vicious dog charging toward me at that very moment. Cursing myself for a fool, I braced myself for a ravenous attack by the kind of slavering hellhound I imagined a man like Charlie might keep in his backyard. But, after several uneventful moments had passed, I decided it was probably safe to make my way over to the garage.

Not wanting to bang on one of the large metal garage doors, I looked around for a people-sized entry door. I didn't see one in the front, so I followed a sidewalk around a tall hedge to the side of the garage. There, under an exterior staircase leading to the mother-in-law apartment, I found a three-panel wood door with a small diamond-shaped window set into its upper panel. With my knuckles poised to rap on the door, I found myself hesitating on a threshold once again. I agonized over the advisability of surprising Charlie in the middle of whatever he was doing in his garage. Surely, I thought, Charlie's offer of a meeting had demonstrated his good intentions, and bursting into his garage with accusations of outboard motor fraud might just shatter that goodwill.

I was preparing to leave when I caught sight of Charlie through the door's little diamond-shaped window. He was lugging a large metal tank over to a brightly illuminated workbench. At first, I thought it might be a propane tank, but it seemed a little too large and the wrong shape. As I watched, Charlie put this container onto a chair next to the bench and began donning a long pair of cotton gloves. He took some care to pull the elastic wrists of each glove up over the sleeves of the heavy wool shirt he was wearing, before he put on a pair of safety goggles. When he removed the lid of the big tank, its thick metal brim instantly turned white with frost. Even though I felt a little uncomfortable spying on Charlie for the second night in a row, I was not going to leave now.

Charlie set the tank's lid to one side on the workbench and picked up what appeared to be an oversized, steel coffee thermos. I noticed the rim of this container also frosted up when its lid was removed. Charlie carefully placed the thermos back on the workbench so that it was adjacent to the metal tank. Because the tank was elevated by the chair it sat on, the lids of both vessels were on a level with each other. He reached a gloved hand into the interior of the steel tank and slowly drew up a metal cylinder so that it was just barely visible in the neck of the tank. He inserted a finger of his other hand into the cylinder and carefully drew out a flat metal rod until a small translucent tube attached to the bottom of the rod emerged from the cylinder. The tube appeared to contain a number of thin white sticks that looked remarkably like tiny soda straws to me. Rapidly, but with the measured deliberation of a man handling high explosives, Charlie carefully transferred the metal rod with its tube of straws into the interior of the oversized thermos. After completing this operation, Charlie replaced the tank's lid, tightened the thermos cap, straightened up, and with an obvious air of relief, wiped perspiration from his forehead with the sleeve of his heavy wool shirt. Then he pulled off his gloves, removed his goggles, stripped off his shirt, and placed them on the bench. I ducked to one side as Charlie picked up the tank and started lugging it back to where he had gotten it. As he passed by the door, I glimpsed something strange that drew me back to the window for a closer look. What I had seen, as it had passed through the door's small diamond of glass, was an odd mottled pattern on the right side of Charlie's bronzed back. Peering through the little window, I could see that Charlie's back was disfigured by several markedly lighter squares of skin, much like a checkerboard, proceeding out of the waistband of his Dockers and gradually fading into a dense black growth of hair as they approached the region of his right shoulder.

I pulled back from the door and even though it was a cool evening, I discovered that, like Charlie, I also needed to wipe perspiration from my brow. I wondered if those peculiar squares were some kind of bizarre tattoo, or the result of some old injury, or perhaps the refurbished sites of donor tissue excised to repair a bad burn on some other portion of his anatomy. Whatever their origin, I decided I had seen enough.

I didn't know what I had just witnessed, but I was entirely certain that I didn't want to confront Charlie at that particular moment, so I made my way, as quietly as I could, back around the hedge and down the driveway to the gate. There was a latch on this side of the gate, so instead of climbing over again, I carefully opened the gate, stepped through and then closed it as quietly as I could. It squeaked a little but I was confident the noise wouldn't carry into the garage.

As I walked down the street toward my Escalade, I marveled at what a mysterious character Charlie had turned out to be. The stolen tires, the strange scene at the marina warehouse, and Charlie's failure to show any surprise at finding me masquerading under a false name had already confirmed my unfavorable first impression, but this mad scientist act in the garage had just put the icing on the cake. It all made me rather hope Charlie would turn out not to be my father after all.

"Walt?"

I froze in mid-stride. My first instinct was to run for my car, but pride made me put my foot down and turn around. Even from a half block away, I could see Charlie standing in the open gate shining a flashlight in my direction.

Chapter Thirteen

"Is that you, Walt?" Charlie asked again.

"Yes." I wanted to sound confident and defiant, but my answer came out thin and raspy. I cleared my throat and cupped a hand to my mouth. "Yeah, it's me, Mr. Bolero. Sorry. I hope I didn't disturb you."

"Not at all, I was just working in the garage. Come on back. We'll go inside and have a little talk."

I noticed Charlie didn't have to shout to be heard. Like an actor in an amphitheatre, his voice simply carried the distance with its warm, conversational manner still intact.

"I thought you weren't home. Uh, does your doorbell ring in the garage?" I asked as I came abreast of Charlie. I was glad Charlie wasn't shining his flashlight at my face, because I knew that I was blushing.

"No," Charlie replied with a faint note of amusement in his voice, "but I think you might have inadvertently rattled my gate. It has a driveway alarm that sounds in the garage when it's opened, and you might have moved it enough to trigger it."

"Yeah. I'm sorry. I did try the gate," I lied, feeling my face flushing even more. "I thought I'd try knocking on your kitchen door, but the gate was latched."

"Well, I'm glad you tried the gate, because I really wanted to see you. Come on inside." He shut the gate and led the way to the front door. As we neared the porch, the motion-sensitive fixture by the door clicked on and bathed us in amber light. I noticed Charlie had pulled on a white polo shirt and was carrying a large yellow flashlight in his right hand. Charlie tucked a second article that he had been holding in his left hand under the crook of his right arm in order to retrieve his door key from his pocket. I was startled to recognize this object as the oversized steel thermos into which Charlie had transferred the tube of frozen straws.

Charlie opened the door and turned the lights on. As we went through the house, I caught glimpses of comfortable, well-appointed rooms. I had expected a house cluttered with the paraphernalia of extralegal activities, like heavy wooden crates and stacks of expensive merchandise, but nothing of the kind was in evidence. In fact, I thought wryly, Charlie's home looked much more orderly than my own apartment.

Charlie ushered me down a photo-lined hallway and into a dimly illuminated, wood-paneled library situated near the back of the house. The dark oak floor-to-ceiling shelves that consumed most of the wall space were populated entirely by hardback books, and one corner of the room was dominated by a massive partners' style oak desk accompanied by two empire-era leather wingback chairs of the sort I had previously seen only in old Sherlock Holmes movies. All the hardbound books lined up on their dark oak shelves, the tall leather chairs, massive desk, heavy brass lamps, and other decorations in the room exuded an almost spiritual masculine quality that I found a bit oppressive.

Charlie set the flashlight and the thermos down on his desk and switched on an oil-rubbed brass banker's lamp equipped with a cigar-shaped, acid-green glass shade. He clapped his hands together, rubbed them briskly, and then waved toward the cushioned depths of one of the red leather wingback chairs.

"Please, Walt, have a seat. Can I get you anything? How about a soda? Or would you care for a beer? I think I have a couple of Heinekens in the fridge."

I didn't answer immediately because I felt a little nonplussed by Charlie's solicitude. I had imagined the atmosphere of this meeting to be of a more contentious, confrontational nature, and Charlie's apparent concern for my comfort was throwing me a little off-track. I gingerly lowered myself into the seat of the big wingback chair. The cushion felt softer than I had imagined and the oily fragrance of the leather reminded me vaguely of little league baseball. I was feeling a little too comfortable leaning back into the tufted depths of the chair, so I made myself sit on the edge of my seat and lean forward to face my adversary, who was still awaiting my drink order.

"Or perhaps this late hour calls for coffee?" Charlie inquired. "You seem a little tired and distracted."

"I'm fine, thanks," I said tersely.

"Well, in that case, let's discuss your problem and see if we can find a mutually satisfactory solution."

He sat down in the other chair and leaned back into the shadow cast by its wings. His features disappeared into the gloom, but I could still see his eyes, and when he spoke, his teeth seemed to float in the dark, like the Cheshire cat's smile in Alice in Wonderland.

"The other day, you told me my name wasn't listed as your sperm donor when you obtained your records and yet, somehow or other, you still traced the donation to me. At the time, you didn't want to go into details on just how I came into the picture, and you left saying you had made a mistake. When you drove away Saturday afternoon, I thought you still had some doubts. And judging from the events of the last couple of days, I'd say I was right. Now, it would help me to help you if you could tell me how your detective work led to my door."

His elbows resting on the arms of his chair, Charlie steepled his hands and waited in the leather recesses of his lair for my response. Events weren't proceeding exactly the way I had imagined they would. I had expected this meeting to start with my renewed assertion of Charlie's parentage, followed by Charlie's continued denial of culpability, forcing me to threaten him with exposure of the outboard motor scam, which would hopefully result in Charlie's capitulation and an agreement to have a parental DNA test performed.

"Okay, I guess I owe you that much."

I described in detail how Jason and I had reached our conclusions but I was careful not to reveal how or where we had obtained confidential records from the fertility association or the true nature and location of the facial recognition system at the Atlantic City casino.

"Ok, let's see where we are," Charlie said when I finished my account. "First, you traced your sperm donor to a rented mailbox that turned out to be rented by someone else. Then you connected that mailbox by some undisclosed method to sixty-three other donors, all of whom made sperm donations and listed this same rented mailbox as their address. Correct so far?"

"Yes."

"Then you reached the obvious conclusion that those sixty-three donors were all the same person, who for some reason felt compelled to hide his true identity."

"Yeah, because fertility clinics don't want donors who have already made donations at another clinic."

"Well, whatever his reason, I think your deductions are perfectly sound up to this point. It's when you jump to the conclusion he was a student at SPU because it's one town over from this Pack & Mail store, that your investigation starts to look shaky."

"But you're forgetting about the average age for donors and the four year span of the donations."

"I said shaky, not improbable. It's a reasonable conclusion, but any number of other possibilities comes to mind. For instance, this man might have been a gypsy of some sort, say an undocumented immigrant who made his living by conducting a variety of petty scams. I encountered a number of shady characters in and around Canton when I was at SPU. I think they prefer college towns because they can blend in with the students."

"Maybe, but don't you think it's a little unlikely this guy would've hung around for exactly four years, which just happens to be how long it takes to get a bachelor's degree?"

"Apparently, he didn't hang around. He was traveling up and down the eastern seaboard donating sperm – remember? Canton may have just been his home base. But, let's assume, as you did, that he was a student at SPU and even go so far as to accept your next leap of logic that identified this student as a man named Charles or Charlie because all the first names started with the letter "C," and a lot of them were diminutives of that name. Then your next logical step would have been to compound a list of students with that name, which you did, then examine the circumstances of each student on that list to determine if he would be a likely candidate, which you did not do. Instead, you brought their photographs to some programmer working at an airport, a mall, or some large facility where security is important, and you had him analyze the photographs using facial recognition software in an unprecedented and unproven manner. Then when you sought confirmation of the results from your mother, based on a two-decade-old glimpse of her sperm donor, by mixing my photo with only eleven others, you felt vindicated by my photo turning up in a selection that comprised twenty-five percent of the sample. Does that about cover it?"

"Well, I don't think it was–"

"She initially selected three photos, that's twenty-five percent of twelve. If you had shown her all six hundred-odd photos, and she had selected a hundred-fifty of them, you wouldn't have felt so confident about the results, would you? If all your other assumptions about the donor being a student at SPU, his being named Charlie, and the validity of using facial recognition software to pick your papa from hundreds of twenty-year-old photographs turned out to be valid, you would still be left with a two out of three chance you were barking up the wrong tree. Which you were, of course, seeing that I never donated sperm in the first place. But that's beside the point, because I believe we can resolve all your doubts about me very easily, and set you back on the path to finding the real donor if you still want to. But first I'd like to ask you a couple of questions."

I sat looking at my hands folded on the desk before me. I had struck that pose to project a sense of relaxed confidence in front of Charlie; now my hands looked as if they were folded in supplication. I quickly withdrew them to the arms of my chair and looked my host in the eye. Charlie's face was visible now that he had leaned forward into the glow of the banker's lamp, and his dark brown eyes seemed at once sympathetic and stern. I guessed he was about to bring up the events at the restaurant that night or maybe even my presence at the marine warehouse the night before. Whatever it was, I resolved to be forthright in my answers. I wasn't ashamed of my actions, and I was determined not to hide from this man.

"Okay. Shoot."

"First, how did you meet Leda?"

"May I ask why you think that's any of your business?" I was astonished by my own frosty words. I could feel the heat rising into my face, and realized my fingers were digging into the soft leather of the chair arm. I took a deep breath and relaxed my grip on the chair. "I mean, if you think I hunted Leda down in order to get at you, then you're mistaken. Our meeting each other was a coincidence."

"Well, life is a string of coincidences, Walt, but, just to ease my concerns, I'd appreciate it if you could tell me about this one."

I had an odd feeling of déjà vu. This was the second time in a less than a week that I had heard an expression about coincidences, and it seemed strange to hear it coming from Charlie. I considered my answer. I had resolved to tell Charlie the truth despite the consequences, but I was afraid of what the answer might do to my chances with Leda. That is, if she hadn't already dismissed me as a lunatic after everything that had happened that night. After considering the mess I had made at the restaurant, I decided that telling Charlie the truth couldn't make matters any worse than they already were.

"I met her at the Ace Car Rental location I manage in Jupiter," I said.

Charlie's expression suddenly went blank. His appearance reminded me of one of those movie androids whose silicon brain suddenly overloads under the stress of some unexpected event. Just as I began to wonder if an explosion was imminent, Charlie suddenly broke into a grin and snapped the fingers of his left hand with the gesture ending in a finger pistol shaped from a cocked thumb and a tanned index finger pointing at my chest.

"You work at the place I rented the Lincoln from on Saturday! You must have met Leda when she dropped me off."

"She drove off before I could talk to her Saturday. I actually met her when she came to meet you on Sunday."

"What a remarkable coincidence – I receive an unexpected visit from you Saturday morning, and I unknowingly returned the favor that same afternoon. Well, this certainly explains a lot of things." This last observation was addressed half to himself and half to me. I wondered what puzzle I had just supplied the missing pieces to. Had Charlie just realized I dinged the rented Lincoln with a pellet gun, or that I got the address to Charlie's warehouse from his driver's license?

"This explains a little mystery I've been wondering about," Charlie said, leaning back in his chair and pitching a new steeple with his fingers.

I waited apprehensively for accusations of insurance fraud, theft of private information provided in a business transaction, and criminal trespass, fully prepared to respond with my own recriminations of auto parts theft, boat motor fraud, and allusions to the suspicious activity in his garage. But instead of exploding in a torrent of allegations, Charlie erupted in a toothy chuckle that danced in the dark of the chair's big wings.

"I think I know the reason for your strange behavior at the restaurant this evening, but I'd like to hear it from you," Charlie said as he leaned out of the gloom again to study my face.

"Oh, you mean my alias," I said, as a wave of relief washed over me. "Yeah, well, when I met Leda Sunday morning, I really wanted to get to know her. But I was afraid of giving Leda my real last name because you would've jumped to the wrong conclusions if she happened to mention our date in front of you. And I couldn't just come out and tell her I had seen her with a man I suspected of being my biological father."

"No," mused Charlie, "I don't think that would've worked out too well. I think I probably would have felt an obligation to inform her about your inquiry. And believe it or not, I actually sympathize with you and the dilemma you found yourself in. But why in the world did you choose the name of a popular restaurant? Wasn't that likely to lead to complications?"

"Because it's my mother's maiden name and the first name that popped into my head. I didn't think about my uncle's restaurant until Leda mentioned it, and then one thing led to another, until I found myself playing the fool at the most embarrassing birthday party of my whole life."

"Cheer up, Walt! Fate makes fools of us all. If you escape its kind attentions with only a small wound to your dignity, you should count yourself among the fortunate few."

"Look, coming here has been a mistake. It's my night for mistakes. Sorry I bothered you." I stood up and turned to leave.

"Wait, Walt. You can't leave until you get what you came for."

I stared uncomprehendingly at my antagonist. "What did I come for?"

"Answers, Walt, answers. You're plagued by questions. Let me help you answer some of them."

I turned back and saw Charlie leaning forward into the light and peering up at me from the depths of his big leather wingchair. The green light illuminated a web of fine lines etching the smooth brown skin around his worried-looking eyes. I was puzzled by this show of concern. Charlie had won, hadn't he? I was running away, just like I had Saturday morning. Why should he care?

"Sit down, Walt. I think I can help you."

I sat back down, this time leaning back into the chair and letting the soft cushions envelop me. I hadn't realized just how tense I had been. The smooth leather felt good against my tired muscles. Charlie was smiling approvingly at me. I wondered what he wanted.

"Walt, if you were convinced I was really your papa, why didn't you ask me to take a DNA test?"

"Because I didn't think you would," I said dully. "Why, are you volunteering to take one now?"

"As long as you're willing to pay for it, I don't see why I should object, Walt."

"Oh." I found this unexpected victory a little disconcerting. I searched around in my tired brain for the appropriate response. "Okay, then. I guess I need to find a clinic near you that you can meet me at and–"

"It's a lot easier to do than that, Walt. Just go on the web and 'Google' the words 'parental DNA test'."

"A mail order DNA test?" I asked suspiciously. "How accurate could that be?"

"Extremely accurate. They use the same labs the clinics do. Check it out."

"Okay, thanks. I'll look into it and get back to you," I said, trying to sound more grateful than I felt. I was wondering how Charlie knew about things like the availability of DNA tests and why he was so willing to take one. I knew I should feel jubilant over Charlie's agreeing to take a DNA screen, but considering the things I had discovered about him in the last twenty-four hours, I couldn't help feeling skeptical about his true intentions.

"Good. Now that's settled, I insist on making you some coffee. It's a long drive back to Jupiter, and you must be exhausted."

I watched him get up, and suddenly had an inspiration. "Thanks, I could use some coffee, but you don't have to make a fresh pot. I'll just have some out of your coffee thermos." And without saying another word, I reached for the handle of the metal thermos Charlie had placed on the desk.

Charlie placed a hand on my wrist to stop me from unscrewing the lid. "I'm afraid that thermos doesn't contain coffee."

I gazed innocently at my host's face. "Oh, I'm sorry. What do you have in it?"

"Actually, it contains horse semen."

Chapter Fourteen

I felt the cool air of Charlie's library playing over my tongue and realized my mouth was hanging open.

"Hor-hor-horse semen?" I stammered.

Charlie smiled at my bewilderment and gently removed the metal thermos from my grasp. "That's right, frozen horse semen, or thoroughbred equine sperm, or as I like to call it, frozen gold. This thermos is full of liquid nitrogen, and you have to be careful when you uncork it. That's why I stopped you. I'm taking it out to Himalia's broodmare farm early tomorrow morning. Oh, that reminds me; I need to be sure to bring Thunder Tom's papers with me."

I watched as he opened a drawer on the partner's desk and removed several cardboard file folders. He sorted through these until he found the one he wanted and placed it in a leather briefcase that he pulled from under his desk.

"I'll just go put this next to my bed so I won't forget it in the morning, and then I'll make you that coffee. Make yourself comfortable. I won't be long. I'll tell you about my two-year-olds when I get back." Charlie said this over his shoulder as he left the room carrying the briefcase in one hand and the thermos in the other.

I attempted to voice my acknowledgement of Charlie's comments, but my motor responses were still suffering from cognitive backup. His two-year-olds? I guessed he meant some horses that he owned or had a share of. I didn't know just how common it was to keep horse sperm in a garage, but I believed that was what was in that thermos, and since Charlie didn't appear to care if I knew about it or not, it was probably perfectly legitimate. I shook my head. It appeared the only arrow I had left in my quiver was what I had witnessed at the marine warehouse the night before, and now that Charlie had volunteered to take the DNA test, there seemed no reason to bring it up.

I stared down at my hands. They were pale and slim, with long, tapered fingers that my mother called 'artistic.' Charlie had large, tanned, well-proportioned hands, with straight, broad-tipped fingers. I thought Charlie's best argument of the night should have been the simple observation that he didn't look like me. Before DNA and blood tests, and without firsthand knowledge, appearance was the only way people had of gauging kinship. Based on appearance alone, I didn't think any reasonable person would ever conclude that Charlie and I were related. I formed a steeple with my hands like Charlie had and stared disconsolately at the pale curving roof of my fingers. I realized that I had reached a dead end. Charlie wasn't my biological father.

I stifled a yawn. If Charlie didn't make it back with that coffee soon, I was afraid I might fall asleep in my chair. I got up, stretched, and looked around. I noticed Charlie had left some of his file folders piled on the desk. The tab of one was sticking out of the stack with some of the bold black lettering visible. I stretched again, pulled my glasses out of my pocket, and polished them with my shirttail. Then, feeling the faintest tinge of embarrassment, I slipped my glasses on and looked across the desk at the pile of folders. I could make out the word 'Sea' on one of the tabs, but the rest of the label was obscured by the folder on top of it. My face burning, I leaned across the desk and pulled the folder out a little so I could read the rest of the tab. It read 'Sea Tech / stripping and assembly.' Abandoning all sense of propriety, I jerked the folder out of the pile and opened it.

The folder contained several slim technical manuals that had been printed on laser paper and stapled together. The title page of the first manual read:

PREPARING, PACKING, AND SHIPPING ENGINE CORES

Sea Tech Limited

Remanufactured Marine Engines and Transmissions
Ottawa, Canada – www.seatechlimited.com © 2005

Inside was a series of black and white photos illustrating the removal of the cowling, casing, control panel, prop and other exterior components from a large, marine outboard engine. It had detailed step-by-step instructions describing the proper sequence of dismantling the casing, along with numerous close-up shots showing the location and method of removal of various wires and linkages, with illustrations of various tools and exactly where and how they were used.

I flipped through the manual and saw more instructions and photos on the mounting of the stripped 'core' into a special shipping crate, and the installation of a series of metal straps and foam blocks to prepare it for transport. The next manual detailed how to prepare a customer's rebuilt core for delivery. It had a similar array of photos and instructions detailing the installation of all the components that were removed in the first technical manual.

I was looking at a third manual dealing with mounting a completed engine on a boat's transom and connecting the wiring and steering mechanisms when I heard a cough behind me. I jerked guiltily and turned to face Charlie. He was standing in the doorway holding a tray loaded with a pot of coffee, cups, and sandwiches. He had a strange expression on his face that I couldn't read.

"Would you allow customers at your car rental agency to go through your business files?" Charlie asked coldly.

My face fell, and it took all my courage to look Charlie in the eye. I had just discovered in the last five minutes that I had completely misjudged Charlie Bolero, and now I was afraid Charlie was about to judge me and find me lacking. I stood there, still holding the file folder in my hand, searching for some explanation or apology that would erase the last five days of unjustified hatred towards a person I now realized must be a unusually patient and generous man.

"Mr. Bolero, I – I'm so sorry. I don't know what to say. These last few days have been so confusing. I want you to know I really appreciate everything that you've–"

"Oh, forget it," Charlie said airily, brushing by to place his burden on the desk. He then took the file folder from my hands, walked around to his side of the desk, gathered up the rest of the files, and replaced them in the drawer they had come from. "I suppose you were only curious about what I do around here. I'm pretty sure you've never heard of anyone keeping thoroughbred horse semen in his house before, and I bet you'd like to know just how I'm able to afford even one race horse, much less two. Sit down; have some coffee. Try one of these sandwiches."

I was mystified. Charlie's outrage had come and gone so quickly, I wasn't sure if it was ever there. But I was grateful for my host's leniency, and I did have a lot of questions about racehorses and boat motors, so I sat down, accepted a mug of coffee, and took one of the sandwiches.

I spent another hour in Charlie's library discovering, among other things, that the generation before me had found a bachelor's degree just as useless as my own had. After trying a series of different careers without success, Charlie finally settled into the food and beverage industry. After several years of climbing the corporate ladder at Ogden Federated Foods, he found himself overseeing the concessions at a number of thoroughbred racetracks. During this period, Bolero had become acquainted with some of the top owners, trainers, and handicappers in the country. After watching the fortunes of these sportsmen rise and fall with the seasons, he decided that, besides the tracks and concessions, the only people in the business who ever made big money were a handful of lucky horse owners, and their key to success seemed to be winning the genetic lottery.

At this point in his story, Charlie's features had softened, and his eyes glistened as he recounted just how much money those lucky few were making. He told me he knew he had reached a dead end at Ogden, because Ivy League MBAs occupied all the upper rungs of their corporate structure – and he only had a BA in business from a state university. So, when he heard one of the owners he knew was forming a syndicate to purchase a foal sired by the son of a Triple Crown winner, he begged to be allowed in. Small investors like Charlie were not normally allowed into syndicates of that size, but his acquaintance, an extraordinarily successful stockbroker named Daniel Brookshire, made an exception. He had received some timely information about the food service industry from Charlie, and this was his way of returning the favor. Their horse won its maiden race and went on to become one of the top ten two-year-olds of the season. The syndicate gave Charlie his share of the profits and then bought him out. He was too grateful for being allowed a share of the horse in the first place to object to being barred from future earnings, so he just thanked his friend for his help and applied his winnings to a thirty-percent stake of a promising gelding named Thunder Tom. This horse was sired from a son of the same Triple Crown winner that had sired the first foal he had invested in. But Thunder Tom broke down in his third race and had to be destroyed.

Charlie was devastated. Not only had he lost his investment, the syndicate was also deeply in the red. The other members of the syndicate were law partners, and they scheduled the debt settlement meeting at their office. At the meeting, he was pleased to find that his share of the debt was somewhat less than he had expected, because Thunder Tom's frozen sperm was being sold to a harness horse breeder. Charlie had been a little surprised to hear a gelding could have sperm. Then he learned the syndicate had collected it prior to Thunder Tom's castration. He then asked why they couldn't get a better price for the sperm, thus reducing his share of the debt even further. They said it was a good offer because even with Thunder Tom's impressive lineage, he was still an unproven sire who had broken down in his third race. That's when Charlie asked if he could buy the sperm himself. His partners were amused, but agreeable, so Charlie got a loan on the equity in his house and paid off the syndicate. Now he was the proud owner of a can of frozen sperm, but without the necessary funds to produce a foal with it.

When he began asking other owners, trainers and hangers-on at the tracks to invest in his frozen assets, he got some odd reactions. Most of his acquaintances simply demurred without comment, but when a trainer actually laughed in his face, he realized there must be something he was expected to know about artificial insemination that he didn't, so he approached the man who had let him into his first syndicate, Daniel Brookshire. His friend sat him down, and gently told him the facts of thoroughbred horseracing. Mr. Brookshire told him about the Jockey Club, which is the breed registry for all thoroughbred horses foaled in the US, Canada, and Puerto Rico. It was founded in 1894 by a group of racehorse owners and breeders determined to bring some much-needed order to a chaotic sport. Charlie knew some of this, but what he didn't know was that out of the twenty-odd horse registries in the US, which included everything from quarter horse to harness racing, the only registry that would not register foals conceived through artificial insemination was the American Jockey Club. Now Charlie knew why his partners had seemed so amused when he had offered to buy Thunder Tom's sperm. Mr. Brookshire told Charlie that his only options were to sell Thunder Tom's sperm to breeders of standard-bred horses, export any foals produced by his sperm to Lysithea – a country he had never heard of – or simply keep Thunder Tom's sperm in cold storage and wait for things to change. Mr. Brookshire also confided to Charlie that he and many other owners and breeders were lobbying the Jockey Club to lift their ban. Charlie decided to wait it out.

As the months passed, he found himself strapped by the added expenses of loan payments and cold storage fees for Thunder Tom's unrealized progeny. He looked into the latter expense and discovered he could maintain the frozen sperm himself by paying for the container it was in, moving it to his house, and simply topping off the liquid nitrogen protecting its contents every couple of weeks.

Even after turning his garage into a cryogenic storage facility, Charlie still found himself sinking ever deeper into the mire. Finally, out of desperation, he decided to look into the possibility of bringing his horse's sperm, or a foal produced from it, to the foreign country his friend had indicated would register Thunder Tom's offspring. After some research, he confirmed the Lysithean Breeders Club would register the artificially-conceived offspring of sires listed in the American Jockey Club to race in their country, but just how one went about doing this seemed to be a mystery. Finally, he hit on the strategy of tracing the origins of Daring Get-Away, a recent American-bred champion on the Lysithean racing circuit. It turned out Daring Get-Away was foaled at Elara Downs, a prestigious broodmare farm only a few miles from his home. He drove down to Elara Downs the next day. The owner, a recently widowed woman in her sixties, was sympathetic towards Charlie's predicament and put him in touch with Prince Hassan Bin Alman, a horse owner in Lysithea who had sponsored the successful American horse. Prince Hassan Bin Alman responded to a long letter from Charlie by first pointing out that live cover and not artificial insemination had been employed in the breeding of Daring Get-Away. Nevertheless, he was perfectly willing to sponsor Thunder Tom's foal with the Lysithean Breeders Club, in addition to handling all the other aspects of training and racing the horse, provided Charlie could meet all expenses. He took the trouble of including a summary of costs associated with Daring Get-Away's career in Lysithea, and added the compensation for his services over and above his expenses would be a fifty-percent share in any purses won.

Elara Downs, up to that point, had not used artificial insemination, but was interested in trying it if Charlie wanted to pay for the experiment. So all Charlie had to do was come up with a small fortune, and with a little luck, he could turn Thunder Tom's sperm from a cold liability into a hot asset.

So, armed with the results of his research, he expanded his search for investors to the Internet. His search failed to produce any legitimate investors, but one of the respondents to his emails, after declining to invest in one of Thunder

Tom's foals, suggested he might be able to raise the capital he needed by selling remanufactured marine outboard engines. Normally he was skeptical of any offer of employment received over the web, but since he had obtained this contact from a list of potential investors with triple-A credit ratings, he decided to look into it. He was glad he did, because it turned out that the same people who patronize racetracks also owned huge motorboats. Within a year he was earning more money selling Sea Tech outboard engines part time than he did from his job, so he quit his job. He told me the profit margin on these remanufactured boat engines was enormous. Sea Tech had found a way to use NAFTA to avoid taxes on Japanese-made engines by importing 'used' motors without their cowlings and casings as 'engine cores' to Ottawa, where they were supposedly rebuilt, then re-exported to the states as a Canadian product remanufactured from American-supplied engine parts. In reality, the engines were remanufactured at the same plant in Japan where they had originally been made. Sea Tech was careful never to say this in any of their literature or even to their sales representatives, but Charlie had found checklists and inspection tags written in Kanji tucked into the shipping crates of rebuilt engines. Charlie's customers, both private individuals and excursion outfits, used their boats a lot, and he was kept busy swapping their exterior components onto rebuilt engines. Occasionally, a cowling, prop or control panel would need to be replaced as well, so he started keeping a stock of these items in his warehouse.

Within a year of leaving his job, he had saved enough money to match Thunder Tom's sperm with a couple of medium-priced broodmares at Elara Downs. Those pairings had resulted in two remarkable foals that had both gone on to win several races in Lysithea.

Charlie told me he had recently reached the point where he could afford to stop selling Sea Tech motors and spend all his time on breeding racehorses. When I asked Charlie if he was going to sell his boat motor business, he said that Sea Tech Limited didn't allow the transfer of a franchise to a second party, and in any case, he wouldn't feel comfortable putting someone else into a business that he now believed to be skirting the edge of the law.

I was impressed with Charlie's integrity. I wondered how I could have so completely misjudged the man. I reflected sadly on how, now that it seemed evident Charlie was not my biological father, I had come to admire him as a truly gifted and resourceful man of unusually high character.

It was past midnight when Charlie finally walked me to my car and shook my hand. He told me that he frequently visited Himalia's farm and hoped to see me there soon. I agreed with this sentiment, but secretly doubted that Leda or her mother would still want me to visit their ranch after the restaurant debacle.

Charlie then reminded me to check into the parental DNA tests on the web, and I promised to do so while privately wondering why I should waste the money. I got in my Escalade and drove back toward Jupiter. As I made my way down Charlie's street, I glanced in my rearview mirror, and in its reflection, I could see Charlie standing by his driveway, watching me.

Chapter Fifteen

Jason had agreed to open Ace Car Rental Wednesday morning in order to let me sleep in after my big date, so it was well after ten when I drove into the middle of an improvised hockey rink that Pitch and Jody had erected in the carwash. Pitch quickly moved the trashcan 'hockey net' out of the Escalade's path while Jody put up brooms that had been used to swat a rubber ball 'puck' up and down the narrow building that housed the automatic car washing equipment. I threw my keys over my shoulder as I strode towards the office and heard them jingle as Jody snatched them out of the air.

When I walked into the office, Jason looked up from his never-ending game of correspondent GO and gave me an appraising stare.

"You look cheerful," he said.

"You know, Jason, I feel cheerful," I said, surveying the black sludge in the coffee pot. "Hey! You let the coffee run out."

"It's nearly noon. Forget coffee. Tell me how your big date went."

"We always make fresh coffee for the noon rush," I complained.

Jason sighed, logged off his game, and got up to make coffee. "The noon rush on Wednesday consists of about six customers. Now stop stalling, and give me the details."

I sat down at my desk and watched Jason rinse out the pot. I thought through the events at the restaurant and tried to decide the best way to describe what had happened. It seemed like there were too many people involved for it to be called a 'date.'

"Well?" prompted Jason. "You don't need to wait until I'm finished, you know. I can make coffee and listen too."

"It was a farce."

"A farce?"

"Yeah, you know, a grossly exaggerated play or movie full of clever word play and embarrassing situations."

"So if everything went wrong, why are you in such a good mood?"

"I didn't say I was in a good mood. I said I was cheerful. There's a difference. One is about how you feel about what's already happened; the other's about your outlook."

"You can't feel lousy and cheerful at the same time, Walt."

"Maybe you can't, but I can have one lousy night and still be cheerful about the future."

"I don't want to hear about your future. I want to hear what happened last night. If I wanted to discuss philosophy, I'd call my mother."

So I put my hands behind my head, leaned back in my chair, and ran through the events at my uncle's restaurant. I touched on my aborted attempts to reveal my actual last name, the unexpected arrival of Himalia and Charlie followed by the unexpected arrival of my parents, the surprise birthday party and the humiliating exposure of my false identity. When I finished describing rolling around on the floor with Himalia and the flaming sponge cake, I sat up and discovered Jason leaning up against the file cabinet still holding the pot of water. "Hey!" I objected, " I thought you said you could make coffee and listen, too."

"That sounds more like a horror show than a farce," Jason said, coming back to life and pouring the water into the coffee maker's reservoir. "So Bolero was there too! Wow. And he didn't rat you out?"

"No. When Leda introduced me as Walt Galilei instead of Callisto, he didn't bat an eye."

"He didn't? Huh. Oh! I bet he played along because he didn't want Leda's mother to know about his little hobby back at college!"

"That's what I thought at the time, but I found out a lot about Charlie last night, and now I think he played along because he was being considerate."

"That guy?" Jason stopped making coffee again and turned to stare at me. "Come on, Walt, snap out of it. A guy like Bolero doesn't do anything out of consideration for someone's feelings."

"Well, Jason," I said, gently taking a pre-measured bag of ground coffee out of his hand, "we might've been all wrong about Charlie."

"What do you mean?"

"I went to see him last night after that disaster at Uncle Vinny's, and he suggested taking a parental DNA test before I even brought it up."

I thought Jason's reaction looked a lot like Jody's did when she was surprised. After a moment of goggling at me, Jason shut his mouth and gestured at the pre-measured coffee packet.

"Are you going to make coffee or not?"

I finished making the coffee, and, between customers, told Jason about the trip to Cobb's Station. Jason showed a keen interest in Charlie's frozen racehorse sperm and was fascinated by the markings I had seen on Charlie's back. But even after hearing about the Sea Tech technical manuals and Charlie's story of how he had gotten into the remanufactured boat motor business, Jason was still skeptical. I mentioned the invitation Charlie had left on my answering machine, and he repeated his theory that Charlie had recognized my Escalade in his warehouse parking lot the night before. He suggested Charlie could have prepared the Sea-Tech manuals in advance and left them on the desk for me to find. I dismissed his suspicions as too convoluted, and told Jason about how the folder of technical manuals was almost buried under the other folders on the desk. Jason then speculated that Charlie had done something to draw my attention to the folder, at which point I declared that any speculation about Charlie's possible involvement in criminal enterprises wasn't relevant anymore now that he had volunteered to take a DNA test. Jason cautiously agreed with this conclusion, as long as precautions were taken to ensure that Charlie didn't pull a fast one, like substituting another genetic sample in place of his own.

Jason had heard about the parental DNA tests that were available on the Internet. He thought that as long as we were working with a reputable lab, the results were probably as accurate as those obtained through a clinic. His only concern was that Charlie might try to swap out the cotton swabs when I wasn't looking. He told me he would research the available DNA kits on the web and devise a sampling protocol that would prevent Charlie from cheating. I wasn't eager to go through with the tests anymore, but I reluctantly accepted my friend's offer, because I wanted Jason to be convinced that we had fingered the wrong man.

As I thought about this, I realized Charlie had expressed the same concerns; he wanted me to have proof that he wasn't my biological father. To me, this was another affirmation of Charlie's good intentions.

Later in the afternoon, during a lull in business, I decided to phone Leda and try to explain why I had given her my uncle's last name. I still didn't have her phone number, but I remembered that her mom's ranch was called Elara Downs. I grabbed a cold drink out of the refrigerator, walked out into the back parking lot, and wandered over to a quiet corner for a little privacy. I called information on my cell phone and was pleasantly surprised when they were able to connect me to the main business number at the ranch. I took a sip of my coke and waited for Leda to answer the phone.

"Good morning!" sang a sultry voice. "You've reached Elara Downs, home of the most beautiful broodmares in New Jersey. May I help you?"

When I recognized the voice, I aspirated some of my Coca-Cola. I tried to cough an intelligible response into the phone, but only succeeded in spraying coke all over it.

"Hello?" Himalia repeated. "If you're a sexual deviant, you'll need to breath a lot louder. I'm not getting anything on this end."

"Mrs. Lobrelei!" I managed to croak, "please don't hang up. It's me, Walt Callisto, and I –" I would have gone on to apologize to Himalia for my actions the night before, but she interrupted me.

"Walt! How nice to hear from you! Leda was just frantic with worry that you would be put off by our silly little accident last night. But I knew you would understand because you obviously come from quality people. I'm sorry I had to leave before I was able to chat with your charming parents. I do hope to see them again soon. But just listen to me chatting away when you probably want to talk to Leda. Hang on just a scoch, and I'll get her."

She left me hanging in a fluffy cloud of surprise and amazement. After the previous evening's events, I had expected Leda's mother to be a little cool toward me, and her positive attitude puzzled me. Before I could speculate further on Himalia's puzzling lack of reserve, however, Leda picked up the phone.

"Walt! What did you say to my mother?"

"Err, nothing. She didn't give me a chance."

"Good! Did you clear up your name change with your parents?"

"Well, no, I was about to, but Charlie Bolero dropped by before I had a chance, and the subject didn't come up again before I left."

"Well, at least he's good for something," said Leda. "Look, I covered for you with Mom by telling her that I was confused. I told her I got your last name mixed up with the name of the restaurant, and you didn't notice because you're shy and got all flustered meeting her last night. She liked that explanation. It appeals to her vanity. So you got the story straight?"

I wasn't sure what to say so I just mumbled an affirmative, "Uh huh."

"Great, now, Mr. Callisto, why don't you come out and visit me at my mom's horse ranch this evening? You can meet some of the ranch hands, and maybe even get to watch some artificial sex."

"Um, artificial sex?" I asked, feeling my temperature rise.

"Yeah, if everything's just right, the vet might try to inseminate Frisco Gal this evening. She's the top broodmare at Elara Downs. You might find it interesting. It's very high tech and controversial. Our broodmare manager has his nose up in the air about it. They were going to do it this morning, but the vet wasn't sure if the old girl was ready to ovulate or something, so they postponed it until tonight. Come on over. You'll have fun."

I was mystified by how easily matters had been smoothed over, but I was grateful to have another opportunity see Leda, so I got directions to Elara Downs and promised to be there by seven.

A few hours later, I was cruising up the interstate listening to the symphonic strains of Queen. I liked the upbeat energy of their music. Since Elara Downs was a little closer to Jupiter than Juno, I could leave around five-thirty and still get to the ranch by seven. Ace closed at five on Wednesdays, but since I had to swing by Ganymede Terrace so I could change and spend a little time with Io, Jason still had to close up for me.

Lack of sleep and all the long road trips had made me nearly worthless at work over the past few days, and I was grateful for Jason's patience and support. I knew my friend was still suspicious of Charlie, but Jason hadn't been present last night and gotten to know Charlie like I had. Just before I left Ace Car Rental, Jason told me that he had located a DNA test kit from a big lab used by hospitals and clinics. This kit was a little more expensive than some of the others, but it collected two samples from each person instead of only one. Jason especially liked the color-coded shafts on the sampling swabs. He said that would help ensure Charlie didn't try to switch them out with one he had hidden on his person. I was certain Charlie wouldn't try anything of the kind, but I was happy to bear the additional expense if it would help ensure the validity of the test. I already knew what the outcome would be, and I wanted Jason to accept the results when they didn't end up meeting his expectations.

I turned up the volume on Bohemian Rhapsody until I could feel the bass vibrate the hairs on the back of my neck. It was a beautiful evening with the setting sun providing a symphony of color to complement the music playing in the black Escalade. Although the lyrics were sad, I like this song and when the chorus started singing, I joined in on the refrain:

Thunderbolt and lightning very very frightening me
Gallileo, gallileo, gallileo, gallileo,
Gallileo figaro magnifico – magnifico oh oh ohoooooo!

Singing in a loud falsetto and rapping out the beat of the music on my steering wheel, I was feeling better than I had in a long time. I felt as though I had spent the last year living in a dark fantasy in which the man who had casually sold the seeds of his creation played the part of Beelzebub. Now I decided it was time to abandon fantasy and concentrate on the future. 'After all,' I thought, misquoting Samuel Johnson to myself, 'it matters not how you begin life, but how you live it.'

I was rocking to 'We are the Champions' when I left the interstate. I was impressed to discover that Elara Downs was actually printed in big white letters on the highway exit sign. I followed the ramp down to a spacious blacktop road lined on both sides by miles of white, cross-hatch fences enclosing endless rolling pastures of green grass. Leda had said their ranch was the fifth gate on the right, and I carefully counted ranch gates to ensure I didn't pass it, but I need not have bothered. The huge whitewashed brick columns with their massive wrought iron gates would have been impossible to miss. Elara Downs was spelled out in large gilded letters that arched over the gates from and to the out-flung hooves of two gigantic iron horses rearing high atop the majestic brick columns. I pulled up to the intercom and pushed the call button.

"Ye_?, Wh_ '_ th_re?" crackled the speaker.

"It's Walt Callisto." The sound quality was dismal. I felt like I was ordering a meal at a drive-thru.

"Walt_r ki_s a toad? Wh_t d__ y_u say?

I couldn't understand the speaker, but I thought I recognized the voice.

"Mrs. Lobrelei, it's me, Walt. Remember? We fell on the cake—"

"Th_t d_mn sp__ge c_ke! Of c__rse, __me on __ W__ter D__r!"

The big gates slowly creaked apart, and I drove my Escalade under the iron horses and down the curving drive. The driveway was a lot like the road leading to it – a spacious blacktop lane lined on both sides by immaculate white fence rails. I was just wondering how long this driveway could possibly be when the fence finally gave way to a majestic colonnade of spreading oak trees and a rambling antebellum style mansion. The driveway culminated in a circle around an impressive equestrian fountain with offshoots leading variously to a portico, a large garage, and a gate to the rest of the ranch. As I pulled up to the front of the house, Leda came roaring up in a Kelly green, gas-powered golf cart.

"Hop in. You're just in time."

"Is it okay to leave my car here?"

"Just leave the keys in it. One of the hands will move it for you."

I jumped in next to Leda, and she took off towards the gate that I had noticed earlier. Just as I thought we were going to ram into it, it slid out of the way and let the cart through.

We passed several buildings and a row of paddocks before Leda skidded to a stop in front of a handsome brick building that looked more like an upscale community center than a barn. It had large sliding doors in the center of the building and a small parking area with an ordinary entry door to one side. The sign above the door identified the building as Breeding Barn 1. Leda leaned over, grabbed me by the neck, gave me a one-armed squeeze, and kissed me so hard it left my lips tingling.

"Come on," she said, "let's go in and watch Frisco Gal get laid."

Chapter Sixteen

In the fading golden glow that often marks the gauzy border between night and day, I watched Leda as she hopped out of the golf cart and trotted over to the door. The almost liquid quality of this amber twilight imbued her skin and hair with that radiant texture one normally sees only in Renaissance paintings. For the first time in my life, if only for a moment, I felt totally free of angst. All of my thoughts, my very being, were concentrated into this one crystalline moment of beauty and clarity.

"Walt!"

The crystal shattered into a million fragments, and I realized Leda was standing in the open door waiting for me to follow her. Feeling a little disoriented, I slid off the golf cart's bench and tottered after Leda into the Breeding Barn.

The door let into a handsome knotty pine reception area decorated with contemporary furniture and images of champion racehorses. No one was behind the reception desk, and Leda led me through another door and down a wide hallway with a beautiful vaulted pine roof. About halfway down the hall, I realized the white-walled rooms we were passing were actually horse stalls – beautiful stalls with translucent panels of some kind of plastic in the sliding doors that fronted the hall. Through the translucent panels, I could see the silhouettes of thoroughbreds patiently standing in their stalls.

In the middle of the building, we came to a junction that led to a large room with a lofty cathedral ceiling, white walls, and a white floor. A freestanding double stall with waist-high walls stood in the center of the room. Its white tubing and movable plastic panels gave it a clinical appearance. Several people were standing next to a long stainless steel bench laden with an assortment of equipment. They were watching a slender white-haired gentleman rub a metal paddle across the belly of a nervous-looking mare housed in one side of the twin stalls. Leda grabbed my hand and pulled me toward the group.

"We're just in time," she whispered. "That's the vet, Dr. Norton. He's performing an ultrasound now to check the condition of Gal's ovaries. That red-faced man standing next to him is Dean, our broodmare manager, and the older lady standing on the other side watching the monitor is Emily Taurus. She used to own this place, but now she's our farm manager. Of course, you recognize Charlie standing over there with the goofy look on his face. Mom is back at the house, and you'll probably meet some of the other hands at dinner."

Charlie was leaning up against the stall cradling the big steel thermos I had seen at his house the night before. He looked a little pensive, like an actor about to go on stage.

Dr. Norton straightened up, put the paddle back in its cradle, and replayed the sonogram he had just made. He conferred quietly with Dean, the broodmare manager, and pointed out something on the monitor. Then he looked up and noticed Leda and me watching them.

"Leda, I see you've retrieved your young man. Excellent. I'm happy he was able to get by that pestilential speaker system at your gate. You may want to show him the rest of the facility while I palpitate Frisco Gal here, as it may offend your tender sensibilities."

Charlie, stirred from his thoughts by the vet's remarks, smiled and waved, but remained where he was.

"No, that's okay, Doc," retorted Leda. "I'll just hold Walt's hand."

"Why, is he squeamish?" Dr. Norton asked with a little smile. "Better hold his nose while you're at it. The odor is worse than the sight."

He turned back to his cart and donned a pair of rubber gloves that went all the way up to his elbows. He picked up a large tube of ointment, squirted a generous amount into the palm of one of his gloved hands, and lubricated the surface of one glove up to his forearm. Holding his arms up, he gave Dean a nod and walked around to the rear of the horse. Stroking her flank and speaking softly to her, Dean pulled Frisco Gal's tail up and held it out of the way for the vet.

Dr. Norton slowly inserted his fingers into the mare's rectum, and like a man putting his arm into a heavy winter coat, gradually inserted hand, wrist, and forearm into Frisco Gal's rear. Dean kept stroking the mare while speaking to her in a low voice, and, except for snorting a little and shifting her feet, she seemed to barely notice this intrusion into her nethermost regions.

With a look of concentration, Dr. Norton kept his arm inside the mare for about six seconds, and then slowly withdrew it into the open air. As he did, an intense wave of fetid odor swept across the room and knocked out my sense of smell.

Smiling, Dr. Norton stripped off his gloves and disposed of them. "Okay, Charlie, we're ready for the sire."

Charlie snapped out of his reverie and treated the room to a wide grin. "Excellent! If Frisco Gal is ready to receive him, Thunder Tom is ready to stand to her."

"Then where is he?" asked Dr. Norton

"I beg your pardon?"

"Your tank, man," Dr. Norton said impatiently. "Did you leave it in your car? If so, you best go get it. We need to strike while the iron is hot."

Charlie held up his thermos and started to reply, but Emily Taurus raised a hand to indicate that he should remain silent.

"I'm sorry, Edwin, I meant to tell you about Charlie's precautions. You were not in attendance at Thunder Tom's last two inseminations. You remember the little fire we had a couple of years ago."

"Of course, I do, Emily," Dr. Norton said. "It nearly ruined you."

"Yes, and the destruction of Running Fool's sperm made Charlie aware of how dangerous it is to have a stallion's entire production in one location."

Dr. Norton's gaze darted to the big thermos hanging by its strap from Charlie's hand. "You mean to tell me your sperm bank transferred some of the sire's sperm into that small vessel?"

"Actually," Charlie said, calmly walking around the stall, "I maintain Thunder Tom's sperm myself."

"Why would you do something so blasted stupid when certified storage facilities are so cheap and readily available?"

"Edwin, please, Charlie is a good customer," interjected Emily.

"Your customer, Emily. My liability."

"You have no liability, Edwin. You make us sign a waver, remember?"

"Yeah, that's true," he smiled, "but you know I'm only trying to protect you and your mare here."

"I'm afraid none of these mares belong to me anymore, Edwin," she said gently, "but I'm still responsible for them, and I wouldn't do anything to compromise their well-being. Charlie's extremely knowledgeable in the handling of frozen sperm. He's demonstrated his expertise at two inseminations prior to this one, both of which resulted in successful pregnancies."

"That's impressive," mused Dr. Norton, "One hundred percent, first cycle fertility. In that case, as long as all the proper documents are in order, we'll proceed."

"I have them all right here, Edwin, and I assure you they're in apple pie order," Emily said, holding up a clipboard.

"Okay, then," Dr. Norton, said clapping his hands together, "due to the unusual circumstances, I'm going to take an additional precaution. Dean, would you please step into the lab and fetch a microscope and a specimen slide."

For the first time since I had known Charlie, I detected a faint look of apprehension in his demeanor. As Dean hurried off to get the additional equipment, Charlie approached Dr. Norton and spoke to him in a lowered voice.

"Because," Dr. Norton responded in a normal voice, "I want to establish that your horse's semen demonstrates progressive motility and has an acceptable level of "lyced" sperm. Improper thawing or freezing can cause sperm to rupture, and excessive levels of damaged sperm can add dramatically to the risk of uterine inflammation."

Charlie nodded enthusiastically, as if he was agreeing with the vet, but he appeared a little upset to me. "Yes! You're right; I've read about that. I was only a little concerned about the amount of time it would take to examine the sperm in the microscope, but you're definitely doing the right thing, and I appreciate your looking after my interests. Since I've made things more difficult for you, I was wondering if I could help out in some way, perhaps–"

"Yes, you can hold that blasted coffee thermos of yours while we retrieve the sperm. I don't want to be responsible if it falls over and empties its contents all over damnation. Dean!" He shouted in the direction the broodmare manager had gone. "Bring back another pair of goggles and gloves!"

"No need, Doctor," Charlie said, pulling the two items from his coat pocket. "I've brought my own."

"So I see," Dr. Norton said, sounding more than a little annoyed. "Then for your benefit and the edification of our two young guests, let me outline the procedure we're going to follow."

Leda and I moved closer to the steel bench, and Dr. Norton pulled a sheaf of papers out of his back pocket and referred to them.

"Emily has provided me with the thawing recommendations for the straw size and extender formula used in Thunder Tom's sperm. I have prepared this equipment in accordance with those instructions. Now to begin with, Charlie, how are the straws situated in that coffee thermos of yours?"

"Actually, Doctor, it's not a coffee thermos," Charlie said stiffly. "This is a certified single canister Dewar, and the straws are situated just as they are in a full-sized tank. They're in a goblet attached to the lower portion of a cane, and the cane is isolated inside a canister."

"Oh, I see," Dr. Norton said, looking somewhat mollified. "Well, as you know, we only have three seconds to transfer the straws, to avoid damage to the sperm. While Charlie holds his thermos, I'll raise the goblet high enough in the vessel to transfer five straws into the warm water bath where they'll remain for exactly forty-five seconds. I will then dry the straws on this sterile cotton pad, open them and pool the contents into this incubator. As I begin this task, I'll place a tiny sample from the first straw I decant onto a slide. While Dean quickly prepares the specimen for examination, I'll complete the pooling and take a quick look into the microscope. If all is well, I'll remove the AI gun from its warming holster and draw the sperm into its chamber. While I'm doing this, Dean will swab Frisco Gal's perineal area with Betadine and hold her tail out of the way. I will then insert the nozzle of the AI gun and complete the insemination. During this procedure, I don't want to hear anyone, other than myself, make the slightest sound. Is that understood?"

Like children who want their teacher to know how cooperative they are being, the other four adults in the room all nodded their heads in response to Dr. Norton's question. Dean walked back into the room carrying the microscope and a small box of slides and solution.

"Excellent," Dr. Norton smiled. "I hope the stage on that thing is equipped with a slide warmer."

"It sure is, Doc," Dean replied, plugging the microscope into a power strip and placing it on one end of the steel bench. "We use it to check motility in sperm from live stallions."

"As opposed to the frozen ones no doubt," Dr. Norton said with a chuckle. "Our broodmare manager here doesn't approve of artificial insemination. Dean, when I decant the first straw, I'll deposit a sample onto a slide. I want you to quickly prepare the specimen in the same manner you use on fresh sperm and place it in the microscope."

"Will do, Doc."

"Fine. Then Charlie, if you and your thermos will position yourselves at this end of the work area, we'll begin."

Charlie moved next to Dr. Norton, put down the thermos, and donned his safety glasses and gloves. Dean put on latex gloves and safety glasses, sterilized a slide, and placed it on the stage of the microscope to warm. Dr. Norton pulled on his gloves and a pair of plastic goggles.

"Ok, Charlie, you may open your vessel. Good. Now, can you raise the canister? Good. Now can you slowly draw the cane up until the rim of the goblet just clears the edge of the frost line? That's it, slow and easy, a little more–there. Now just hold what you got."

Dr. Norton reached into the mouth of the canister with a long pair of tweezers, rapidly removing five straws in succession, placing each one into a device sitting next to the thermos, and pushing a button on its built-in timer after the last straw was immersed. Charlie, having lowered the canister into the thermos and replaced its cap, remained at the bench, nervously watching the procedure. I wondered why Charlie appeared to be so anxious. It seemed to me that Dr. Norton knew exactly what he was doing and had matters well in hand.

"I have positioned these straws in this warm water bath from left to right where they'll remain for 45 seconds," Dr. Norton continued. "The water is being maintained at a hundred twenty-two degrees. When the bell chimes, I'll remove them in the order in which they were submerged. Dean, when I remove the first straw and begin drying it on this pad, I want you to present me with the warmed slide."

Dean nodded, and they all watched the timer on the warm water bath tick down. I found myself wondering if a similar procedure was followed with human sperm, and mentally winced as a disturbing image of my mother bent over in a stall flashed into my imagination. The bell's chime brought a welcome end to this vision as I watched Dr. Norton remove a straw from its warm water bath, dry it thoroughly, and tap its end on the sterile tray containing the cotton pad. He removed a pair of scissors from a transparent box sitting on the table and snipped off the top of the straw. He placed a fingertip on the cut end and held the straw over a tube cradled inside the incubator the scissors had come from. Then he cut the bottom end off the straw, took the warmed slide from Dean and positioning it under the straw, allowed a tiny drop of fluid to drop onto the slide by quickly removing and replacing his fingertip on the top of the straw. He handed the slide to Dean, allowed the rest of the semen to flow into the tube, and set the expended straw aside on the sterile tray. He rapidly decanted the other straws into the tube, then turned to the microscope and briefly examined the slide Dean had just prepared.

"Excellent motility, plenty of very strong swimmers, and a minimum of debris," Dr. Norton announced as he looked up from the microscope. "If Thunder Tom's foal runs like these spermatozoa, you'll be a rich man, Charlie."

Charlie smiled faintly, but he still looked tense to me. Dr. Norton nodded at Dean, and while he was removing the AI gun from its warming holster and drawing the pooled sperm into its nozzle, Dean was swabbing antiseptic solution on what Dr. Norton had referred to as Frisco Gal's perineal area. He held her tail again and spoke in a soothing voice while Dr. Norton gently eased the long tube of the AI Gun into the depths of her reproductive organs. With a short push of the plunger, Frisco's intimate date with the ghost of Thunder Tom was over before she was even aware they were having sex.

There was a metallic clatter, and everyone looked around to see Charlie chasing the expended straws as they skittered across the white concrete floor.

"Sorry," he apologized as he stooped to pick up the straws. "I knocked the tray on the floor."

"Well, make sure you retrieve all of those straws, Mr. Bolero," Dr. Norton ordered crossly. "I need them for my documentation."

One of the straws ended up at my feet. I bent to pick it up, but before I could look at it, Charlie pulled it from my fingers.

"He wants these for his part of the paperwork," Charlie explained with a weak smile. "These straws have a lot of information written on them. Here, I think I have a magnifying glass on my keychain." He thrust his free hand into his right jacket pocket and immediately pulled it out again. "Wrong pocket," he said and then thrust his other hand into his left jacket pocket. "Yeah, here it is." His hand came out clutching a keychain along with the expended straws he had retrieved from the floor. Charlie held a straw up with the magnifying glass in front of the tiny black letters written on it. I just had time to make out the words: 'Thunder Tom' and "Pender Lab" followed by a date and some other names and numbers, when the exasperated voice of Dr. Norton cut Charlie's 'show and tell' session short.

"If you two are finished lollygagging, I'd like my straws back, please."

Charlie hurried over to the bench and handed the straws to Dr. Norton who took them and handed them to Emily. "Would you read the label on one of these to me, Emily, while I write it out?"

"Certainly, Edwin."

"You know, Charlie," Dr. Norton said, as he sat on a stool and fanned some forms out on the bench, "technically speaking, I'm supposed to record the information on these straws prior to insemination."

"But no one does, Doctor Norton," Charlie said. "Exposing the straws to the air for more than three seconds could kill the sperm."

"Very true, Charlie, and there is precious little time during the thawing and decanting phase, too. That's why I depend on the judgment of farm managers like Emily here, to make sure all the 'T's are crossed and the 'I's are dotted. Only her intervention on your behalf kept me from canceling this insemination. I suggest you invest in another full-sized tank if you want to avoid trouble in the future." Dr. Norton said this with a smile, but his eyes looked serious.

Charlie hesitated a moment as if he were about to raise an objection to the doctor's suggestion, and then offered him his hand. "Thank you, Doctor, I'm going to do just that, and I want to thank you for the excellent job you did tonight. I feel confident Frisco Gal will produce a outstanding foal."

Dr. Norton shook hands with Charlie, turned to Emily, and after a brief exchange, began jotting down information as she read it from one of Thunder Tom's straws. Charlie picked up his thermos and walked over to where Leda and I were standing.

"Well, Walt, I hope you enjoyed the insemination. I know I'm excited. I think we all witnessed history in the making tonight. This match between Frisco Gal and Thunder Tom is going to produce the next Lysithean World Cup winner." He grinned and patted my shoulder. "You wait and see, three years from now, you'll be watching my horse enter the winner's circle, and you'll turn to your friends and say, 'I was there the night that horse was conceived.'"

I was relieved that the nervous tension Charlie had displayed earlier was gone. "I hope you're right, Charlie, because by then, I'll probably be needing a loan." We both laughed, but I noticed Leda looked annoyed.

"Himalia has invited us all to dinner. Are you coming?" Charlie asked.

"I'm going to show Walt around the breeding barn," Leda answered tartly. "You can tell Mom we'll be in after that."

When Charlie had left the room, Leda turned around and stared at me, her extraordinary gold eyes flashing ominously.

"What?" I asked.

"Just when did you get so chummy with Charlie?" she demanded.

Chapter Seventeen

When I was nine years old, I heard the idiom 'she was looking daggers at him' in an old black-and-white detective movie. My friends and I thought the expression was hilarious, and it enjoyed a brief revival among the fourth-grade students at my parochial school. Now, as I suffered under Leda's excruciating glare, that phrase came swimming back from all those rained-out recesses and started doing backstrokes in my stream of consciousness.

"Boy, you really don't like the guy, do you?" I asked, trying but failing to sound amused.

"He's a prick," Leda said loudly, "and I thought you didn't like him, either."

I looked back to where Dr. Norton and Emily were doing their paperwork. They didn't seem to have heard Leda's outburst, but the broodmare manager, who was leading Frisco Gal in their direction, was wearing a satisfied smirk on his red face.

"You're right," I told her quickly in a hushed voice. "I did hate him, but I changed my mind. Could we go somewhere else to talk about this?"

By way of answer, Leda grabbed my arm and pulled me towards the broodmare manager and his charge.

"Hey, Dean, do you mind if Walt and I tag along?" Leda fell in behind the mare and pulled me with her. "I want Walt to hear some of your stories before we have dinner with Mother and Charlie."

Dean stopped walking and turned around to look back at me. We were standing in the passageway just outside the breeding room. "Are you a friend of Charlie's?"

"I just met him about five days ago, but he seems like a nice guy," I said.

Talking over his shoulder, Dean began walking again. "Yeah, he always seems like a nice guy. I thought he was a nice guy when he showed up here a couple of years ago. He was real friendly. He talked to all the hands, said he wanted to know all about breeding racehorses. Got close to Emily. She still thinks the world of him. Says he helped her cope after Frank's death. Her husband, Frank, built this place, made it famous. Charlie talked Emily into trying AI, that's artificial insemination, said he wanted to breed racehorses for the Lysithean circuit, only it turns out he didn't have the money to do it. Well, a year or so went by with him constantly popping in, nosing around, and putting us off with delays and promises. Then one day Charlie brought in a big client for Emily. He was a friend Charlie knew from the track. I guess you know Charlie worked in the business."

I said I knew about Charlie's job with Ogden, and Dean stuck his free hand into the air with the index finger pointing up. Viewed from the rear, it looked like a dance move, but I knew Dean was just emphasizing an important point in the story.

"Right. Charlie's friend was a big shot in thoroughbred racing. They met at one of the tracks where Ogden had the concessions. This guy, I think his name was Brookshire, was a major investor in a syndicate that owned Running Fool, the famous Triple Crown winner. Running Fool's stud fees were sky-high when they acquired him, but he got injured and couldn't perform live cover anymore. So they collected his sperm and froze it, and besides selling it for use with standard breed horses, that's all they could do with it because the Jockey Club prohibits artificial insemination with either fresh or frozen sperm. Charlie heard about their problem and recommended Elara Downs as the best jumping-off place for the Lysithean turf – which was true, because besides having produced Daring Get-Away for Prince Hassan, we also had the most sought after 'Blue Hen' mare in the country."

Saying this, Dean came to a stop in front of one of the stalls and stood stroking Frisco Gal's neck. Small fluorescent fixtures illuminated the passageway over each stall door. The light from this one was vibrating slightly, and it seemed to me to be pulsing in sync with the anger in Dean's eyes. "All of us, including me, were excited and grateful for the business. I didn't know much about AI or frozen sperm back then, but I knew it could mean big bucks for the farm."

Dean opened the stall door, led Frisco Gal in, and removed her harness. While I waited outside with Leda in awkward silence, Dean spent several minutes inside the stall, talking softly to the mare while he brushed her neck and shoulders.

"Why were you guys so quiet out here?" he asked, when he finally emerged. "You could've talked to each other while I was grooming the Gal, you know."

"That's okay, Dean," Leda grinned. "We thought Gal deserved a little post coital cuddling without a bunch of yammering going on outside her stall."

"Yeah, right," Dean replied, and I could tell by the way he said it that Leda's attempt at humor hadn't registered with him.

"Well, anyway," Dean said, "like I was saying, we were all excited about pairing a Triple Crown winner with Frisco Gal. Our Lysithean acquaintance, Prince Hassan, found us a vet who had experience with AI and knew how to fill out the Lysithean Jockey Club's registration forms. Well, the vet came and checked out Gal, and a couple of weeks later Running Fool's sperm arrives by special courier, not just a few straws like Charlie brought tonight, but the stallion's entire production in a full-sized tank. Then the vet arrived, checked out Gal, and just like this morning, said she wasn't quite ready to drop her eggs. So, Emily, the vet and Charlie all decided to make a day of it – touring the ranch and then returning to the breeding barn for another try after dinner."

"Why was Charlie here?' I asked.

"He said he just wanted to observe on behalf of his big shot friend. I wanted to bring the cryogenic tank back up to the house, but Emily said it would be safer to leave it in the barn than to move it to the house and then back to the barn a few hours later, so I locked it in the tack room. Emily invited me up to the house for dinner, and we were eating dessert when the alarms went off. The first thing you do in a barn fire is get your horses out. After that, you worry about trying to extinguish the flames. By the time we had finished moving our stock out, the fire department had arrived and put out the fire. It turns out it was confined to the tack room. Our tack room had a one-hour firewall, but the knotty pine ceiling provided a lot of fuel for the flames. The fire chief said the temperature in the tack room reached well over a thousand degrees."

"But wouldn't the sperm have been protected by the liquid nitrogen?" I asked.

"They said the nitrogen gas helped put out the fire," he said, shaking his head like he still couldn't believe it. "It all boiled out when the tank's safety valve blew."

"How did the fire start?"

"We never found out. Since I was the one who locked it up, they asked me a lot of questions about what we kept in the tack room. Besides the usual bridles, saddles, and brushes, there was damn little flammable material in that room. I had a cot and a hot plate in there for the times we'd stay all night caring for a sick horse, and I kept a few chemicals in a metal cabinet. I guess some of them might have been flammable, but there was nothing to set them off. The only other electrical things in the room beside the hot plate were the lights – and that led the chief to speculate the ballast overheated and caught the ceiling on fire. But he couldn't make an official determination because the heat damage was too extensive."

"Charlie did it," Leda said.

I turned to look at Leda, leaning up against the stall's sliding door with her arms crossed. Now the light from the vibrating fluorescent fixture above the stall was pulsing in her eyes, too. Not wishing to instigate another baleful glare from Leda, I was at pains to cast my next question in neutral terms.

"Oh, uh, how did you find out?"

"Too many coincidences," Dean answered. "Right after the fire, Emily called her contact at the syndicate that owned the horse to report the accident, and they told her it was the second worse news they had received that day."

"Running Fool died," Leda said. "They said it was a severe colic attack. They performed emergency surgery, but he didn't make it."

"Then, a few days later, the syndicate calls Emily to inform her their insurance won't pay off," Dean continued, "because custody of the sperm had been transferred to Elara Downs. And when Emily contacted her insurance company, she discovered she wasn't covered, because storing frozen sperm in a locked tack room wasn't considered due diligence, whatever that means. So, after a lot of wrangling and compromises, Elara Downs ended up losing several hundred grand on its first AI job. Brookshire claimed this was only a fraction of his losses, and the stink he made about the incident nearly destroyed our reputation."

"That's terrible. But what made you think Charlie was involved? I mean, why would he want to hurt the farm?"

"Money," said Leda. "A month after the fire, Charlie suddenly had enough money to pay for two foals at once."

"Too many coincidences," Dean said again, as we began walking back to the breeding room. "We think the Running Fool syndicate cooked the whole scheme up with Charlie when they discovered their recently acquired Triple Crown winner couldn't perform live cover anymore. They never wanted to raise horses for the Lysithean circuit. They just wanted to recoup their investment, so they got Charlie to engineer the fire and then arranged a little accident for Running Fool. You know, colic is uncommon in older horses, and when it does occur, it's rarely fatal. I think the insurance snafu was as much a surprise to them as it was to Emily."

When we got back to the breeding room, Dr. Norton and Emily were just finishing up. I noticed Dr. Norton putting a plastic bag containing the expended frozen sperm straws into his briefcase along with his copies of the paperwork. I thought that was a little curious. I had assumed the used straws would simply have been discarded.

As Dean started sweeping out the standing stall, Dr. Norton picked up his valise and escorted Emily towards the door.

"Leda, don't forget about dinner," Emily said as she approached us. "Your mom has gone to a lot of trouble, and we shouldn't be late."

"We'll be right behind you, Emily. I just want to show Walt a couple of things. Walt, this is Emily Taurus, Elara Downs's farm manager." Emily smiled and said she was pleased to meet me. "And this is Doc Norton, our cantankerous old horse doctor."

"Don't mind her, Walt. She's just miffed because I wouldn't delay the insemination until your arrival." Dr. Norton laughed and shook my hand. His grip felt more like a farmer's than a doctor's. "But I'm glad you managed to get here before we got too far along. Everything turned out for the best, as most things usually do."

Dr. Norton advised us not to dilly-dally, or he would eat our dessert. After they left, Leda and I helped Dean pack all the equipment onto a cart and move it and the folding table back to a long narrow room full of white counter tops and unfamiliar equipment.

"While Dean's putting things up in here, I want you to look at the tack room. It's just through here." She guided me through a short hall that led back to the main passageway. The tack room had a large steel double door that opened into the passageway just opposite the hall leading to the breeding room.

"It's usually locked when Dean's not here," she said as she pulled one of the big doors open. "As you can see, it's been rebuilt, but Dean says it's set up just like it was before the fire."

The tack room was much larger than I had imagined, with a lot of harness work hanging from one wall and a large rack full of saddles, saddle pads, blankets, sheets, rope and other assorted gear. There were a small bunk bed and some heavy steel shelving neatly stocked with boxes of supplies, supplements, and bottles of various preparations. It was all very spacious and free of clutter, which was what I guessed Leda wanted me to see. I had to agree with Leda that it didn't look like the kind of room that would suddenly go up in flames, but I also noticed that the knotty pine ceiling had been replaced with one of corrugated steel.

"Dean figured Charlie could've left a cell phone hidden among some cleaning rags in the metal cabinet where they used to store those chemicals." Leda indicated the assortment of bottles and boxes on the shelves. "He says all you'd have to do is wire a model rocket igniter to the ringer circuit on the cell phone and give the phone a call when you wanted to set it off."

'Yeah,' I thought, 'or a pile of oily cleaning rags could've spontaneously combusted just like they're always warning people about in public service announcements.'

Dean wasn't in sight when we got back to the lab. He wasn't in the breeding room, either, and all the lights had been turned off except for one fluorescent fixture over the stall. Leda gave me a mischievous look, grabbed my hand, and pulled me into the middle of the room, giggling, prancing, and pirouetting at the end of my arm.

"Alone at last!" she declaimed, and holding my hand above her head, she spun herself into my chest, hooking a warm leg around the back of my thigh while wrapping her free arm around my neck. Although I had spent the last few days dreaming of just such a moment, I was made oddly uncomfortable by the reality of the event. I wondered if Leda's capering playfulness was putting me off. I had never really felt comfortable letting my hair down. I had attended keg parties in college, but I had never joined in the moronic jocularity of my inebriated fraternity brothers. Even Jason, himself classified as a computer geek by most people, thought I was something of a cold fish. He often remarked that I was 'fun challenged' and needed a lost weekend of mindless debauchery to loosen me up.

I surfaced from my thoughts to find I was moving. Leda was still holding my left hand in the air, and she was dancing me backwards toward the standing stall. I draped my arm around her waist and tried to take the lead, but like a persistent tugboat gently pressing a reluctant steamer into its dock, she kept her course true and steady. We finally heaved up against the rails of the stall and Leda, grinning mischievously, reached up, removed my glasses, and shoved them into my pocket.

"You know, this stall is usually used for actual sex between a stallion and a mare. It's called live cover, and it's a lot more exciting than watching a vet poke a mare with a big plunger. Would you like to come over sometime and see some real horse sex, Walt?"

Reeling in the heady flood of warmth and fragrance emanating from Leda's body, I found myself unable to speak, but with some effort managed a nod.

"You would?" Leda asked, her gold eyes growing to enormous proportions as she moved in for a kiss. "Would you like a little preview?" I nodded again. After a couple of minutes of heavy breathing we came up for air and sagged against the standing stall. As we recovered, Leda put her head on my shoulder and looked down at our intertwined hands. Suddenly she released me and stooped down.

"Look," she said. "There's something sticking out down here. Hey, I found you a souvenir!" She stood up and slipped something into my jacket pocket.

"What is it?" I asked.

"One of those straws Thunder Tom's sperm came in. It must have rolled under the stall's floor. A couple of years from now, you can sip champagne through it when Charlie's horse wins the Lysithean World Cup."

"Yuck!" I said, and tried to tickle her ribs. Leda squealed with laughter and fell to the floor, pulling me with her. We were still giggling like five-year-olds when Charlie walked into the room and flipped on the main lights.

"Oh, I'm sorry," said Charlie, sounding a little surprised. "I didn't mean to disturb you." He stood nervously glancing around at the floor and the edges of the room while Leda and I regained our feet. I supposed that he was trying to avert his eyes without being too obvious about it. After we had stood up and adjusted our clothing, Charlie curtailed his inspection of the room and turned to us with an apologetic smile. "Himalia was worried about you and sent me to ask if you would like your dinner brought out to the barn."

Chapter Eighteen

Dinner at Elara Downs was a gala affair. The formal dining table in Himalia's antebellum mansion seated twenty and was adorned by three massive brass candelabras. Only one of these at the far end of the table was ablaze where Himalia, perilously close to self-immolation, hovered in a gossamer cloud of pink chiffon over a small group of candle-lit diners. When Leda and I followed Charlie into the dining room, Himalia hurried over, clucking her disapproval.

She told her daughter it was rude to keep their guests waiting, gave me an alluring smile, and took my hand. "Walt, I'm so happy you could attend. I want you to know you'll be perfectly safe tonight." She placed a hand by her mouth as if she were about to murmur a confidential aside, but her next words came out in a stage whisper easily loud enough to be heard by all of her guests and anyone working in the kitchen. "I made sure there would be no flaming desserts tonight."

I couldn't find a part of Himalia's body I could look at without blushing. Her scarlet, sharkskin hip-huggers and abbreviated red chiffon v-necked halter top trimmed in billows of diaphanous pink fabric feathers exposed even more of her bare midriff than her outfit of the night before, as well as an embarrassing expanse of milk-white cleavage, where twin gold and ruby pedants were hanging like ripe, errant grapes.

"They're not real, you know," Himalia murmured, bringing my attention back to her face.

"They're not?" I squeaked.

"No, they were grown in a lab."

"Uh, a leb, a lad, a lab?"

"Yes, rubies this large would be worth a king's ransom if they were genuine."

"Oh!" I exclaimed, relief oozing from every pore. "Yeah, I can see that."

"Poor Walt, you look like you've been rode hard and put away wet." She felt my forehead with a ruby-taloned hand. "Your face is flushed, and your hands are clammier than an undertaker's. Come sit with me where I can see to it that you get something in your stomach."

Still holding my hand, Himalia led me to one end of the long mahogany table and sat me in the first seat, with Leda at my side. Charlie sat down opposite me, next to Emily Taurus. Dr. Norton was on Emily's other side, and Dean was opposite him, seated next to Leda. Himalia, satisfied by having achieved the classic boy, girl, boy, girl, seating arrangement, stood at the head of the table and tapped her glass repeatedly with a fork.

"Everybody hush up. Mrs. Taurus has something to say. Emily, would you please do the honors?" Himalia sat down, and Emily stood up and addressed the rest of the table.

"In keeping with a long-standing tradition here at Elara Downs, we like to have a little toast when one of our mares receives the gift of life from a customer's stallion. In this case, the stallion is the greatly underestimated Thunder Tom, who despite breaking down in his first season has, by a miracle of modern science, managed to sire the two most promising American colts on the Lysithean circuit. We're extremely excited to have the opportunity to work with this stallion again, and we have great hopes for the foal resulting from mating him with our most valued broodmare, Frisco Gal."

During this speech, a short, slim man, dressed in a green silk jersey and dark pants, was pouring wine for each diner. I thought he moved a lot like Io, and he had sharp cat-like features, too, covered by skin resembling a tanned leather roadmap.

"Walt," Emily said, "the man serving your wine is Derek Fontaine, our Director of Operations. He and his wife prepared our dinner tonight. Derek was one of the nation's leading jockeys back in the 70s and 80s. His intimate knowledge of the racehorse industry helped make Elara Downs into one of the leading broodmare farms on the east coast. Derek, would you ask the others to step in for the toast?"

Derek left the room briefly and returned with two middle-aged women. They were introduced to me as Betty Greenberger, the farm's accountant, and Yvonne Fontaine, who was Derek's wife and the stud manager. We each took a glass of wine, and waited for Emily to make the toast.

"To a standing foal," she said and drained her glass. Everyone else in the room repeated the toast and drained their glasses. Though I felt a little foolish not knowing the meaning of the toast, I followed suit and drained my glass.

Derek, Yvonne, and Betty brought in their creation, and served it to the other guests. It turned out to be a southern style dinner of smothered steak, purple hull peas, turnip greens, and cornbread. Derek and his wife sat next to Leda, and Betty, who had initially sat next to them, picked up her plate and moved around the table to Dr. Norton's side in response to some vigorous signals from Himalia's fork. I had never had this kind of food before, and was oblivious to the dinner conversation that sprang up around me, until a remark from Dr. Norton directed towards Charlie pulled me back from the soulful delights of cornbread and turnip juice.

"Charlie, I'm truly impressed by Thunder Tom's unprecedented success as a super corporeal sire," Dr. Norton declared as he cut his steak into small, uniform pieces.

Charlie, who had been engaged in a conversation between Himalia and Emily, leaned forward slightly so he could see Dr. Norton.

"I'm sorry, Doctor, I didn't quite catch that. Super corporeal?"

"Not of this world, Charlie. Thunder Tom's performance, as a sire from beyond the grave, has been nothing short of remarkable."

Charlie grinned and spread one large tanned hand heavenward. "What can I say, Doctor? I've been truly blessed."

"Indeed. Tell me, Charlie, how old was Thunder Tom when he was gelded?"

"I believe that happened right before he became a two-year-old." Charlie said, his grin fading into an uncertain smile. "I'm not sure because I joined the syndicate when he was already racing as a gelding."

"I see," Dr. Norton said, chewing thoughtfully. "That means the sperm was collected from a horse between thirteen and twenty-four months of age. I must say, Charlie, when I saw the density and vitality of Thunder Tom's spermatozoa in the microscope this evening, I would have guessed it had come from a somewhat older stallion."

"Excuse me, Doctor," I interjected. "Wouldn't Thunder Tom have to have been at least twenty-four months old if the sperm was collected when he was two?"

Dr. Norton looked up from his plate like a man disturbed from a game of chess. "Well, normally you would be correct, Walt, but for the purposes of horseracing, all thoroughbreds universally turn two on the first January of their second year."

"Why do they do that?"

"Because two-year-olds race as a class, Walt. The schedule would be chaotic if new two-year-olds were being introduced pell-mell throughout the season."

"Oh. So Thunder Tom could've still been a juvenile when they uh, collected his sperm."

"Well, horses mature faster than you might think, Walt. Preteen might be a more accurate description for a horse entering its second year. Nonetheless, stallions usually don't develop high sperm counts until their third year. Charlie should count himself doubly fortunate because two back to back, first cycle pregnancies from the frozen sperm of a sire that young is unusual in itself. But to produce two standing foals that go on to be champions of the Lysithean turf is the stuff of legend."

"Standing foal – I know I'm showing my ignorance, but what exactly does that mean?"

"Breeding thoroughbreds is an uncertain enterprise, Walt. What with this outbreak of Mare Reproductive Loss Syndrome and other problems, not all pregnancies go full term, and not all foals are able to get to their feet after birth."

"Oh." I realized the other conversations at the table had subsided, leaving me in the center of attention. I decided to shift the conversation away from what seemed to be a sensitive subject. "You know, your mention of Charlie's horses in Lysithea reminded me of something I've been curious about. Why does the breeder's association in this country have a rule against artificial insemination?"

Dr. Norton smiled, and everybody else at the table groaned. Apparently, I had jumped from the frying pan into the fire. Emily patted Dr. Norton's hand and smiled at me.

"I'm afraid you've just pushed Edwin's button, dear. We've heard from him at length on this particular subject, and we're all just a little battle weary." She glanced over at Dean, whose face looked a little redder than usual.

"Now, Emily, we mustn't stifle Walt's natural curiosity simply because the rest of us have had our fill. He just wants to know why the Jockey Club is flailing against the winds of change."

"You know it's not just the Jockey Club, Doc."

"I beg your pardon, Dean. You're perfectly correct. An international fleet of breeder's associations and studbooks man the AI blockade that tiny Lysithea manages to evade."

"Why do they let Lysithea register AI thoroughbreds? Couldn't the Jockey Club forbid owners and breeders from dealing with Lysithea?"

"An astute observation, Walt. They could, but commerce won't be denied. Any admiral foolish enough to interfere with smuggler's sloops will wake to the smell of burning canvas. Lysithea is the pressure valve for breeders and owners who weren't born wealthy and feel oppressed by the racing world's aristocracy. Besides, Lysithea's market share in the thoroughbred racing industry is negligible."

"But their purses are among the richest in the world," Charlie said.

"True, Charlie, and I know you find that gratifying. But the big money isn't in purses. Even the richest prizes in horse racing pale in comparison to those oversize cardboard checks handed out at golf tournaments. No, the big money in racing changes hands at the auction house, like the one in Kentucky a couple of years back where 130 yearlings were sold over three days for eighty million dollars."

"'Market share. Big money. There you go again, Doc," Dean complained. "Terms like that are corrupting thoroughbred racing. Horse racing is not an industry; it's a sport. It's about testing the breed. Walt, did you know that all modern thoroughbred horses trace their origins back to just three founding stallions?"

"Uh, no."

"The Byerley Turk, Darley Arabian, and Godolphin Arabian. The first studbook was started in England in 1751, which was over forty years before compulsory recording of births and deaths of humans in that country. Horse breeders have spent nearly three centuries patiently increasing the lines and quality of thoroughbreds, and now some people want to throw all that away in the name of progress. No offense meant, Mr. Bolero."

"None taken, Dean, none taken. And if you remember from our past discussions, I share your views to a large extent. We simply disagree on how to address the problem."

Dr. Norton looked over his glasses in Charlie's direction, and smiled unpleasantly. He cleared his throat as if about to comment, but Dean spoke first.

"Now, Walt, before Doc dazzles you with the 'inevitability of technological evolution,' I wonder if you could tell me what would have happened if artificial insemination had been available back in the sixteenth century when there were only three sires available."

"Well, uh, how many mares were there?"

"Plenty. They were spread across several countries, but that wouldn't have presented a problem if they had AI. Charlie brought his dead stallion's sperm here in a small thermos bottle. If they had that kind of technology, they wouldn't have needed to transport stallions or mares hundreds of miles over difficult country hoping to arrive at their destination just when the intended mares came into season. They could've collected the sperm any old time and shipped it off to half of Europe whenever anyone needed it."

"In that case, wouldn't everything have happened just the same as it has already, only faster?" Himalia asked describing circles of rapid progress in the air with her fork.

"Not exactly. But I'd like to hear Walt's opinion."

I felt Leda give my leg an encouraging squeeze. I hesitated, trying to find the right approach to the question. I wondered why Dean wanted my opinion. I obviously didn't know anything about horse breeding.

"Well," I said uncertainly, "whenever we have a special on our full-sized luxury cars, everyone wants to rent the big Lincolns. I guess if we had an unlimited supply of Town Cars, that's all we would rent during our 'Saturday Night Special' promotion."

"See, Doc? Walt spotted the problem right away. If the Turk had been the Seattle Slew of the day, all modern thoroughbreds would have descended from the Byerley Turk. There would have been a lot less diversity, and the viability of the species would have been diminished."

"Ah. See what happens when you come out with your big guns too soon, Dean? You leave your flanks exposed. Seattle Slew sired over a thousand foals after his unprecedented career. I don't think Artificial Insemination would have improved much on that achievement, but AI would have saved owners the expense and danger of shipping their mares to Three Chimneys farm."

"With AI, there would've been ten thousand foals, Doc. Every horse on the circuit would be Slew's direct descendent. Hundreds of paternal lines would've been pushed aside in favor of the only undefeated Triple Crown winner in history, and three centuries of breeding would've been lost."

"Unwarranted hyperbole, Dean. Far from destroying diversity, AI would actually preserve and enhance the equine gene pool by democratically extending the reproductive range of all stallions regardless of their performance. Furthermore, the myth that a champion sire necessarily begets champions would soon be debunked in an AI environment. There would be fads, to be sure, but when the majority of the camp followers came up short at the finish line, they would dip back into the frozen gene pool for a different champion, and your precious diversity would thus be preserved."

"What about dam diversity?" Yvonne asked. Derek poured himself another glass of wine, and used the bottle to conceal an apologetic grimace from his wife's view.

"What about it?" Dr. Norton asked, in a slightly puzzled manner.

"She's concerned about the impact AI would have on the maternal lines, Edwin," Emily prompted from his side.

"Yeah!" Himalia seconded from the head of the table. "Let's hear the female perspective on this frozen sperm business. It takes two to Tango, you know. Tell him about it, Yvonne."

Though she stood six inches over her husband, Yvonne was a slim blond-haired lady in her early forties who was obviously unused to attention, for a rosy hue had risen around her neck and shoulders. She adjusted the straps on her gown, squared those suddenly pink shoulders, and addressed Dr. Norton.

"As you know, Dr. Norton, even with live cover, stallions pass along their genetic material at a rate of about ten to one to any given mare. With artificial insemination, that ratio could easily widen to a hundred to one. In other words, where you have say, a dozen foals from an average broodmare today as compared to a hundred foals from an average sire, in a future with AI, sires might have a thousand foals to the dam's dozen."

"Well, while I hesitate to appear chauvinistic, I fail to see how that would negatively impact genetic diversity. The cruel facts are that the majority of the characteristics thoroughbred breeders select for happen to reside in the male line."

"Edwin!" admonished Emily, "that's simply not true. If the mare is so unimportant, why is so much of the sales catalogue at auctions devoted to the dam's line, and why is Charlie paying a rather large premium to mate Thunder Tom to Frisco Gal?"

"The answer to both questions is the prominence of the sires listed in the dam's pedigree. I'm not saying that I agree with all the policies and superstitions prevalent among the owners and breeders in our industry, and as I've already indicated, I don't find the pedigree and conformation of a foal to be extraordinarily predictive of its performance, but if you're going to trace a horse's or a human's ancestors past two generations, you have to stick to either the male or female line, or that horse or human will end up being related to every individual in the entire species. In the equine and human world, we quite sensibly trace ancestry through the male line because of the male's greater potential for distributing his genetic material. And in both species, the male characteristics of superior size, strength, and stamina are what the various sporting events test for."

"Well, that's certainly what I go for – a big, strong hunk!" Yvonne quipped, causing her undersized husband to deliver an elbow to her ribs. "Ouch! But as you see, I settled for brains and stamina."

"I'm a breeder, Doc," Dean said, "and I disagree with you about the importance of the dam in selective breeding. Horses might get their strength and stamina from their sires, but they get their heart, or rather their spirit, from their dam. In a live covering, you can feel it in the room as the stallion stands to the mare and joins his spirit with hers. That's what's missing in test tube reproduction, the heat, the passion, and the blood. More than DNA is exchanged in a live encounter, and that's a fact."

"That's a load of romantic folderol, Dean. You're not some superstitious aristocrat who believes in this spirit of the blood nonsense. You were educated at Texas A&M, for Pete's sake."

"I'm not so sure, Doctor." Everyone turned to face Charlie, who had adopted Himalia's silverware baton technique, but with a knife held up in place of a fork. "There's more to heaven and earth than meets the eye. I believe that something–what was that term you used, oh yes, super corporeal. I believe that a super corporeal essence is exchanged between a man and a woman, or in this case a stallion and a mare, when they make love. Evidently, Thunder Tom's progeny have been able to win races without this ineffable ingredient of passion, but I've often wondered what effect its absence might have on the development of a human child."

Dr. Norton dismissed this comment with a contemptuous wave, but Himalia and Emily continued discussing the concept with Charlie for the rest of the meal, while the others talked about a range of topics from the car rental business to an ex-Jockey's perspective on handicapping.

After dinner, Leda and I sat outside on her back porch, cuddling and talking for hours. I thought Leda was probably bursting with curiosity about just what my connection with Charlie Bolero was, and I had come prepared to tell Leda the whole story, but after she and Dean had made it clear just how much they despised Charlie, I was somewhat hesitant about broaching the subject. I decided that unless she asked me about it, I would put off telling her about my quest and how it had led to Charlie until after I got the results back from the DNA test. At least that way, I would have proof that the man Leda hated most in the entire world was not my father.

Chapter Nineteen

Thursdays at Ace Car Rental were spent getting ready for Friday. Pitch and Jody were busy servicing the car wash when I pulled into the lot, and Jason was alphabetizing the week's contracts when I walked into the office.

"Are you saddle sore this morning?" Jason asked, without looking up from his sorting.

"We didn't go horse riding."

"Well, how was your date?"

"Do you remember the time we went to the top of the Empire State Building?" I asked, helping myself to a cup of coffee.

"Yeah," Jason said, grinning. "You were shaking so bad I thought we'd have to tranquilize you to get you down." He picked up a stack of folders and carried them over to the filing cabinets.

I followed, describing, with the hand that didn't have a cup of hot coffee in it, the awe-inspiring panorama of New York City as viewed from a hundred and two stories above the ground.

"It was beautiful and terrifying at the same time." I put my coffee down on the top of one of the filing cabinets in order to demonstrate the full majesty of the spectacle with both hands. "Leda's like that. She comes at me like a Bengal Tiger, and I just stand there, petrified by this amazingly beautiful creature that's about to rip my head off."

"Hmm, it sounds like you might be feeling a little ambivalent."

"A little?"

"It's probably just stage fright. After all, you haven't been on a date in over a year."

"No. It's not just that. Sure, I'm a little rusty, but if it was just that sort of–you know, recreational dating thing I used to do in college, I don't think I'd have any problems. But this is different, Jason. This is serious." I hit the top of the filing cabinet for emphasis, and upset my coffee cup, spilling its contents down the side of the cabinet. Jason quickly closed the file drawer to prevent the hot liquid from ruining his paperwork.

"Oh, crap!" Jason said, staring at me.

"Yeah," I agreed, trying to mop up some of the coffee with some blank notation forms I had grabbed off the top of the cabinet.

"No, I mean, you have some kind of crap on your coat sleeve."

"Where? Did I get some coffee on it?"

"No, it's some kind of nasty looking brown stuff. Take off your jacket."

I took off my coat and examined it. I found a moist brown stain on the elbow of my right sleeve. I grinned at Jason.

"Yeah, it's crap all right, horse crap. I was wearing this jacket last night because I ruined my heather sports coat at the restaurant the other night."

"How did you get horse manure on your jacket? Did you and Leda do a little rolling in the hay?"

I blushed. I didn't want to confirm Jason's surmise.

"No, I must have brushed against a horse stall or something. Look, I have another jacket at the cleaners. I'm going to go get it, and give them this one." I quickly left the office before Jason could ask any more embarrassing questions.

My drycleaner happened to be one of Ace Car Rental's neighbors. All I had to do to pick up or drop off my laundry was walk around the wood fence dividing the two businesses. The little Korean woman who usually served me had apparently seen me coming and had my dry cleaning hanging on the hook next to the cash register when I walked in.

"Hi, Mr. Callisto. Good morning to you. Look." I looked and saw she was pointing to a little paper envelope pinned to one of the clear plastic bags protecting my dry cleaning. "We find something in pocket!"

I thanked her and handed her my soiled jacket. While she was writing a receipt, I tore open the little brown envelope that had been attached to my laundry. It contained a ballpoint pen and a receipt from a Mexican restaurant. I remembered spilling a glass of iced tea on myself the last time Jason and I had lunched there. I was hard on jackets.

When I returned to Ace, I found Jason back at his desk sorting through more paperwork.

"If you didn't go horse riding yesterday, what were you doing in the barn?" Jason asked, looking up at me over a sheaf of rental contracts.

I knew my friend wouldn't be happy until he had the full story, so I rolled my chair over to his desk and began telling Jason about the artificial insemination of Frisco Gal. Jason wasn't surprised by Dr. Norton's negative reaction to Charlie's single cylinder Dewar, and when I recounted Dean's story about the tack room fire, the destruction of Running Fool's sperm, and Dean's suspicions about those events, he stopped alphabetizing contracts and made me tell him about the insemination process in greater detail. When I mentioned seeing Dr. Norton collect Thunder Tom's expended straws, a familiar light sprang into Jason's eyes. I knew that look meant poor old Charlie was about to be found the perpetrator of yet another elaborate scheme. I sighed and propped my feet on his desk so I could be more comfortable while Jason reconstructed the dastardly crime. I hoped the DNA test Jason had ordered yesterday would arrive soon, because until there was incontrovertible proof that Charlie was not my father, I felt Jason would continue to focus all his energy into exposing Charlie's evil machinations.

"I bet you think Dr. Norton shares the broodmare manager's suspicions about Charlie, don't you?" I asked, smiling over the top of my coffee mug.

"I think Dr. Norton has an entirely different set of suspicions."

"Oh?" I questioned, a little surprised by this deduction. "How do you figure that?"

"From a couple of things Dr. Norton said, and the fact he's holding onto those used straws, even though he's already recorded the data on them. I think I know what Charlie's up to, but first I want to know if Dr. Norton said anything else about Charlie's frozen sperm or the way he transported it to the farm."

I thought about this question while I sipped my coffee. At first I couldn't remember anything I hadn't already told Jason, but then I recollected Dr. Norton's remark to Charlie about how unusual it was to find healthy sperm from a stallion as young as Thunder Tom. I told Jason about this and how it had led me to ask about just when a racehorse turns two.

Jason laughed. "I think you might have upset a little trap Dr. Norton was setting for Charlie. I think Dr. Norton suspects the sperm Charlie brought to Elara Downs last night wasn't Thunder Tom's."

"Oh, so you think Dr. Norton is going to have the residue in those straws tested to see if the DNA matches Thunder Tom's?"

"No, I think he'll have it tested and compared to the DNA profile of Running Fool."

I stared at Jason for a few moments without saying anything. I respected my friend's analytical abilities, but in this case, I thought Jason's train of deduction had gone seriously off the tracks.

"So you think Running Fool's frozen sperm wasn't destroyed in the tack room fire?"

"I think what they recovered from the charred remains of that tank was Thunder Tom's sperm inserted into counterfeit straws with Running Fool's information printed on them."

"You should write detective stories. How could Charlie substitute a perfect replica of Running Fool's, tank complete with all its contents and markings? And how could he be certain no one would run a DNA screen on the sperm?"

"Anyone investigating the fire might have examined the sperm under a microscope to see if they had survived, but no one would've thought to test the DNA to see if the contents of those straws actually were Running Fool's sperm. If the Jockey Club ever changes its mind about AI, a Triple Crown Winner's straws would be worth tens of thousands of dollars each, but it wouldn't have occurred to anyone that a small-time huckster would want to substitute his horse's worthless sperm for Running Fool's in order to breed AI foals that he could only race in Lysithea. I'm sure the purses he's winning there seem like a lot of money to Charlie, but they're chicken feed compared to the titanic sums that change hands at auctions for thoroughbreds. In other words, Charlie was operating under the radar, like someone counterfeiting one-dollar bills. I don't think anyone would've ever suspected him of anything, if Dr. Norton hadn't come along.

"After you told me about that nitrogen tank full of frozen sperm Charlie kept in his garage, I did a little research on the net. All of the various kinds of tanks, canisters, canes, goblets, and straws used in the storing of frozen sperm are readily available from a number of suppliers. Charlie would have needed to know the precise type and number of straws used in Running Fool's tank, the exact information and style of printing on those straws, and any identifying information on the canisters and the tank in order to pull off the switch. But his friendship with Emily Taurus and his position as the middle man between Elara Downs and the Running Fool syndicate would have provided him with the necessary access."

"That's a fascinating theory, Jason, but I'm afraid that's all it is. And it's full of holes, too. Dr. Norton might be suspicious of Charlie, but he may simply suspect him of substituting sperm from a non-registered horse in place of Thunder Tom's. Charlie worked in the racing industry, remember? If he wanted to do something crooked, he could've gotten high quality sperm under the table a lot easier than setting fire to a tack room, counterfeiting a whole tank full of frozen sperm straws, and then trying to pass his famous stolen horse sperm off as Thunder Tom's. By the way, how did he manage that part? It's not like he could change the labels on the straws, because you can't expose them to room temperature for more than three seconds without damaging them, you know."

"Give me a break, Walt, I haven't had time to work out all the details yet, but the reason Charlie would take all those risks is pretty obvious. He had access to Running Fool's sperm, and any frozen sperm he could have gotten under the table wouldn't have been a Triple Crown Winner's. Charlie had a once-in-a-lifetime opportunity and he grabbed it."

"Well, it all sounds pretty far-fetched to me. I think you're going overboard because you want to justify picking him out as the serial sperm donor. You'll probably change your mind when we do that DNA test."

Jason laughed and told me we would find out whether the DNA test changed his mind about Charlie soon enough. He had ordered the kit sent in an overnight envelope.

I hadn't talked to my mom since the disastrous night at my Uncle Vinny's restaurant. I knew she was waiting for me to explain Himalia's confusion over my name, so when lunch rolled around I walked outside to give her a call. Pitch and Jody had finished restocking the consumables in the car wash and had just begun performing safety checks on the few cars that were still left in the back lot. I walked around to the front lot and called Mom on my cell phone.

When I heard my mother's voice, I knew I couldn't tell her that Leda had simply gotten my last name mixed up with my uncle's. Since I was a small boy, my policy when dealing with my mother had always been the truth or nothing. Sometimes that had meant some creative obfuscation and stonewalling, but I had never lied to her.

"Hi, Mom."

"Walt, I'm glad you called. I was a little worried about you."

"Everything's fine, Mom. I'm sorry about that misunderstanding at Uncle Vinny's. It was entirely my fault. I gave Leda your maiden name because I didn't want Charlie to find out I was seeing his friend's daughter." I paused for a moment to see if she wanted to comment at this point. When she didn't say anything, I proceeded to bring her up to date. "In case you're wondering, Leda straightened everything out with her mother, and I went to their thoroughbred horse farm last night. You should have seen it, Mom, it was fantastic–"

"What about that man?"

I noticed Pitch and Jody coming through the gate to continue their safety checks on the cars parked in the front lot, so I decided to walk back to the rear lot.

"I'm sorry, Mom, I didn't catch that. What man?"

"The man who introduced himself to us at the restaurant."

"Oh! That was Charlie, Mom, the guy I was just talking about." I walked toward the carwash to check on Pitch and Jody's work. "He's the same Charlie I told you about Sunday night, the one Jason and I thought might be my biological father, only it turns out we were completely wrong about him."

"I–, well this sounds silly, but I thought I recognized him."

I dropped my cell phone. It skittered into the car wash like a puck in Jody and Pitch's broomstick hockey game. I went in after it, and slipped on the wet pavement. I crawled over to the phone and put it to my ear.

"Mom, are you still there?"

"Yes. What happened?"

"I dropped the phone. You say you recognized him. You mean, from that old student photograph you saw Monday night, right?"

"No. I mean, yes, from the photograph you showed me, but also from twenty years ago when I saw him sitting in the waiting room at the fertility clinic."

"But, Mom," I complained, struggling back up from the carwash floor, and trying to brush off my pants, "the guy must be fifty years old, and you only saw him for a couple of seconds twenty-two years ago."

"I'm sure he's not quite that old, dear, and I'm not entirely certain he's the same man. It was just so unexpected, meeting him there like that. I thought I recognized him, and thought you might want to know since you're, you know, investigating him."

I wandered back out of the carwash, holding the phone in one hand and gesturing with the other. "Well, thanks, Mom," I said, waving my hand in the air, "but I was wrong about Charlie. I had a long talk with him the other night, and even though he has never even donated sperm before, and couldn't possibly be my father, he's still insisting on taking a DNA test to ease any lingering doubts I might have. He's a really nice guy, Mom."

"Oh, well, that's good, dear."

"Yes. Jason checked into it and found out these tests are nearly ninety-nine percent accurate in matching a parent's DNA to their child, and one hundred percent accurate in eliminating them. So when Charlie gets a negative result, it will mean you probably just recognized him from that stupid photo line up I put you through Monday."

"Oh," my mom said quietly, "then I guess you'll have to retrace your steps and try another line of inquiry."

"I don't know, Mom. I'm starting to wonder why I ever wanted to locate my biological father in the first place. It won't change anything if I find him. I mean I'll still be the same person, and Dad will still be my real father."

"That's sweet, Walt." She sniffed a little and then bravely continued, "I always knew you felt that way about your dad. But I want you to be completely satisfied before you abandon your search, because the worse thing in the world is regret, son, and I don't want you feeling later in life that you missed your chance to know who all your relatives are."

I told Mom I would carefully consider all my options before giving up the search for my biological father, and then, after making and answering inquiries and affirmations on an assortment of other familial concerns and sentiments, I told my mother I loved her and hung up. When I had folded up my cell phone, stowed it in my shirt pocket and looked around, I realized that I had wandered back out the gate and into the front lot. A Federal Express truck stood idling next to the building, and I could just make out Jason's wiry top half, framed by one of Ace's plate glass windows, signing for a batch of overnight packages.

Jason waved an overnight envelope at me when I walked into the office. I was surprised to learn the ordinary looking FedEx envelope contained the parental DNA test Jason had ordered. I had expected it to be packed in a box or at least an envelope with a little more bulk than the one Jason showed me, but apparently all the kit contained, besides some paperwork and a return label, was four color-coded swabs in sterile plastic tubes, and a couple of pairs of disposable plastic gloves. All together, for a test instilled with so much life-changing potential for its users, the outward aspect of the DNA kit seemed strangely underwhelming to me.

Jason insisted that I immediately call Charlie to set up a meeting for administering the DNA test. I felt embarrassed doing it, but I called the number Charlie had given me anyway, because I wanted to satisfy Jason and put what I considered to be a humiliating episode behind me. Charlie answered on the first ring, and before I could finish apologizing for bothering him again so soon, invited me to join him at Ananke Race Park that evening to watch one of his horses in Lysithea run on a closed circuit broadcast at the race track's simulcast betting facility. Jason, who was listening on an extension, was urging me with frantic hand gestures and urgent whispers to accept this invitation, and then surprise Charlie by showing up with Jason and the DNA test in tow. I ignored Jason's suggestion because I believed I owed Charlie the courtesy of choosing the time and place of what could be an embarrassing procedure. When I told Charlie about the arrival of the test and my friend's desire to administer it, Jason threw his hand up and shook his head in disgust. Then Charlie surprised us both by graciously adding Jason to his invitation and suggesting that we could take the DNA test at the racetrack.

Chapter Twenty

Ananke Race Park looked curiously out of place to me. It had been built on a secluded portion of the Manhattan bypass, and provided with its own exit and entrance ramps. I felt that with its vast expanse of parking lots and giant glass buildings, passenger jets should be taking off and landing, or hordes of weary shoppers should be bundling out with their purchases. But Ananke Race Park just crouched by the turnpike like an oversized shopping mall built too far from the city to attract shoppers.

The huge brightly-lit complex with its acres of empty asphalt parking lots appeared practically deserted when Jason and I drove up to the entrance. We purchased a parking ticket from a bored attendant, and made our way to a low, brick annex where a relatively meager scattering of cars sheltered in the lee of the huge, darkened stadium. Jason recalled driving by the track when the thoroughbreds were racing and seeing the enormous parking lot full to overflowing. During the off season, a few hundred diehard enthusiasts would drive out to the track each day to place two-dollar bets, gather around television monitors running simulcast races at other tracks, and boast to each other about how they were going to clean up when the thoroughbreds returned to Ananke.

Ananke Race Park's simulcast betting parlor subscribed to the institutional school of décor. That elusive DMV mystique had been captured by the clever use of drab commercial carpeting, white acoustical tile ceilings, and cafeteria-style furnishings. The people and general atmosphere of the place reminded me of League night at the Red Spot Lanes, Jupiter's bowling alley. The air was thick with tobacco smoke; the ugly carpet was littered with discarded tickets, programs and cigarette butts; and the almost exclusively male crowd seemed unusually grim and preoccupied. Jason and I wended our way through a maze of brown Formica-topped tables, tip sheet clutching pensioners, bleary eyed, wheel-betting construction workers, and laptop-lugging amateur handicappers, until we were hailed by our host for the evening.

"Walt! Over here!"

We made our way to a table where Charlie and another man were sitting. Charlie stood up as we approached, and placed a friendly hand on my shoulder.

"Chic, this is my good friend, Walt, and I believe this young rascal's name is Jason." Chic, a slim man wearing a narrow-brimmed checkered hat, smiled and nodded at each of us in turn, flashing a mouthful of gold dental work in the process. "Jason, here, is very thorough when it comes to filling out insurance paperwork," Charlie said, smiling ruefully.

I blushed. Charlie seemed to be hinting that he knew about the little scam we had used to delay him Sunday morning while I was talking to Leda. If so, Charlie's jibe didn't seem to disturb Jason. I simply smiled and returned Chic's nod.

"You kids go ahead and sit down," Chic said, getting up. "I've got to get back to work."

"Oh, you work here at the track?" I asked.

"Yeah," Chic said, winking at Charlie. "I work at the track. I'm responsible for unredeemed tickets." He laughed, told Charlie he would see him later, and wandered off with his head down and his hands in his pockets.

"So," I said, taking a seat opposite Charlie, "they keep track of unredeemed tickets, huh?"

Charlie laughed. "Chic means he picks up winning tickets off the floor and cashes them in. He's a stoop. Take a seat, Jason. We still have twenty minutes before my race starts."

Jason, who had remained standing, frowned and held up the overnight envelope the DNA paternity test had come in. "I thought we might want to go somewhere less public to take this test," he explained.

"We don't have to go anywhere. Nobody here is going to pay any attention to us sticking cotton swabs in our mouths. Take a load off."

Jason sat down and began fumbling with the envelope. Fascinated by the underbelly of the racing world, I looked around to see if I could spot Chic searching for tickets.

"A stoop?" I asked. "You mean Chic actually makes a living finding winning tickets that people accidentally throw away? How often does that happen? I mean, it doesn't sound like you could make much of a living off the occasional two-dollar winner someone missed."

"You'd be surprised how many winning tickets get thrown on the floor," Charlie said. "During live racing season, the management of this track thinks there's enough un-cashed tickets on the floor to justify five guys constantly pushing electric sweeping machines around in the main stadium. Chic has to work fast to keep ahead of them. If you watch him, you'll see him walking along scanning the floor, turning tickets over with his toe, and if you see him stoop, it means he's found a winner. He has an amazing memory. He keeps all the numbers of all the winning horses, win, place, and show, for each race in his head – and not just for one day, but for an entire season. He once found a three-week-old Trifecta ticket worth $3800 under a trashcan. He usually just works the big events. This is the first time I've ever seen him or any stoop at a simulcast facility. That's what we were talking about when you came up just now. He thinks this place might be an overlooked hunting ground. He says even though there's a lot fewer bettors here than there are in the grandstands, the fact that several races from different tracks are being bet simultaneously means more potential for mistakes."

"Has he found anything?" I asked.

"Nah. He's been here since noon, and he's only found a couple of two-dollar show tickets. But he says he's enjoying the challenge of keeping up with the race cards from four different tracks."

"This is the reason I thought we might want to do this in private," Jason interjected, holding up a package of disposable rubber gloves. "You're supposed to wear these when you swab your cheeks."

Charlie took the gloves and examined them. "Rubber gloves?" he laughed. "You've got to be kidding."

"This lab happens to be very meticulous," Jason said, a little defensively. "They use special foam- tipped buccal swabs to collect the cheek cells, instead of ordinary cotton ones. They have each participant collect two separate samples, and they want you to rinse your mouth out if you've eaten in the last thirty minutes."

"I guess they want to make sure there's no contamination from any animal tissue you might have had for lunch," I said, trying to support my friend.

"Yeah, I could see how that would be a problem if the person being tested were a cannibal," Charlie grinned. "Okay, let's go to the men's room."

Charlie handed the gloves back to Jason and then we got up and made our way through the table area and across the teller lobby to the restrooms. There were a couple of men in the restroom when we arrived, but Charlie assured Jason he didn't mind, so Charlie and I rinsed our mouths, dried our hands, and donned the rubber gloves. The swabs were individually packaged in plastic cases and sealed in sterile envelopes. Jason carefully tore the top off one of these and let Charlie extract the red plastic tube. The tube had a cap on one end that doubled as a handle for the swab, and Charlie used this to draw the buccal swab from its sheath. Following Jason's instructions, Charlie rubbed the tip of the swab back and forth six times inside his right cheek. Jason said this scrubbing motion assured that a sufficient concentration of epithelial cells from Charlie's cheek would rub off onto the swab's foam pad. Charlie inserted the swab back into its plastic case and dropped it in a zip-lock bag that Jason held open for him. Then he repeated the process for his left cheek. My buccal swabs had blue handles, but otherwise the procedure was identical. In fewer than five minutes, we were finished, and Jason had both sets of color-coded samples back in the overnight envelope.

"What the heck are you guys doing?"

We turned to see Chic standing behind us looking totally mystified.

"Oh, hey, Chic," Charlie said. "Jason here is involved in a little epidemiological study, and he's collecting samples of the kinds of flora and fauna that ends up in people's mouths at public venues like this one."

"No kidding?" Chic said, obviously impressed.

"Yeah. He's a volunteer collector for a nationwide project run by the CDC. It's part of the whole terrorism preparedness thing," Charlie said, winking at me.

I didn't think Chic needed to know anything about our business, but I was a little troubled by the ease with which Charlie had fabricated and recounted this cover story to his acquaintance.

As we made our way back to our table, my bladder complained that I had failed to do the one thing the facility we had just left had actually been designed for, so I excused myself from Charlie's and Jason's company and headed back to the men's room.

After nature's call had been answered, I found myself washing my hands next to Chic the stoop. Chic treated me to a mouth full of gold teeth and wagged his head from side to side in a display of good-natured resignation. I didn't know exactly how to respond to this gesture, so I simply smiled and nodded.

"That Charlie's some piece of work, huh?" Chic said, proceeding to meticulously dry his hands with a series of paper towels.

"Well," I replied uncertainly, "he's an unusually thoughtful man."

"Yeah, that's Charlie for you, always thinking," Chic said, pulling a sheaf of brown paper from the dispenser and only briefly patting his hands before tossing the wad of paper onto the top of an overflowing trashcan.

"No, I meant he's considerate."

"Oh, yeah," Chic said, yanking yet another paper towel from its dispenser. "That, too, very considerate, like you said, unusually considerate." He spent a couple of moments dabbing at the little webs of skin between his fingers, then he discarded the paper towel, tipped his checkered hat to me, and ambled out of the restroom.

I suspected Chic was trying to make some kind of cynical implication, but I didn't give his remarks any more credence than I had Jason's or Leda's suspicions. In my eyes, Charlie was a man of his word; he had volunteered to take the DNA paternity test and had followed through on the offer. Besides, I thought, what kind of person would make ambiguous statements to someone he just met about the man who had introduced them? I shrugged my shoulders and turned my attention to drying my hands with one of the restroom's hot air blowers.

Charlie's horse finished in third place. That was still in the money though, so Charlie was in a good mood when Jason and I left him that evening. On the drive back to Jupiter, I recounted my encounter with Chic in the restroom. I had anticipated that Jason would pounce on this incident as fresh proof of Charlie's true nature, but Jason was uncharacteristically restrained in his comments. I chalked Jason's reticence up to the overnight envelope cradled in his lap. I believed Jason had finally realized we had picked the wrong man.

When I returned to my apartment, I found two mad females waiting for me. After I had fed and smoothed Io's ruffled fur and feelings, I discovered several angry messages from Leda on my answering machine. Leda wanted to know where I was and why I wasn't answering my cell phone or voice mail. I slapped my pocket and groaned when my hand failed to encounter my cell phone. The last-minute decision to meet Charlie at the racetrack had caused me to leave my cell phone lying on my desk at the office. I had also neglected to call Leda and let her know I was going to be out of town. I fought down a sudden sense of panic. I told myself there was no reason to be alarmed. After all, I had known Leda for less than a week. She certainly wouldn't expect me to keep her informed of all my movements. Would she? Then, right in the middle of this comforting bit of wishful thinking, my phone started ringing.

"Hello?"

"You better not complain about how late it is, you fink!"

"Leda!"

"Where the hell have you been, Walt?"

My glands suddenly sent mixed messages of terror and pleasure surging through my body. On the one hand, I was terrified by Leda's anger, while on the other, I felt extremely flattered.

"I'm… I'm so sorry for not calling you, Leda. Something unexpected came up, and I left the office in such a hurry that I neglected to call you. And I forgot my cell phone."

"Oh," Leda said. "I hope nothing bad happened."

"No, no, I just had to go out of town to meet somebody."

"Who was she?" Leda asked suspiciously.

"Not another girl. Charlie, I met Charlie Bolero at a racetrack."

"What!" Leda exploded. "You went behind my back to see that creep? After everything I told you about him? And that's why you didn't call me?"

"No, no, no. You've got it all wrong. Remember, I told you that I knew him before I met you. I had some business with him, that's all."

"Yeah, I remember. At first you acted like you didn't like him anymore than I did, then you started joking around with him at the farm Wednesday night like he was an old pal or something. I had to go out of my way to clue you in about what a total jerk he is. I thought you got the message, too. Now I find out you've been sneaking around with him again tonight–"

"Come on, Leda, I wouldn't have told you about meeting him at the racetrack if I were trying to hide it –"

"Are you working some kind of con job with him against my mother? Is that it? Is it your job to distract me while he screws my mother out of Elara Downs?"

"Leda, stop it!" I shouted. "I'm sorry. I didn't mean to yell at you, but you're jumping to all the wrong conclusions. I wanted to tell you about my situation the other night at my Uncle Vinny's, but I kept getting interrupted. Then I was all set to tell you at your ranch last night, but you and Dean seemed so upset about Charlie, I decided I'd better wait until I had more answers before trying to explain my relationship with him. Well, tonight I pretty much finished my business with Charlie, so now I'm ready to tell you all about it."

"Well, go ahead. I'm listening."

I told Leda the whole sordid tale from the very beginning, starting with finding my mother's letter hidden in my boxer shorts at my hotel in Atlantic City and progressing chronologically through all the twists and turns of my quest to its most recent dead end in the men's room of Ananke Race Park that evening. I was careful to omit Jason's suspicions about the Lincoln Town Car Charlie had rented, the two occasions on which I had spied on Charlie, and Jason's theories about the criminal nature of Charlie's business activities.

Leda couldn't resist interrupting a number of times, especially when I was trying to explain how my and Jason's trail of deductions had led to Charlie Bolero, but she was a sympathetic and attentive audience.

When I finished describing the administration of the Parental DNA test in the racetrack restroom, I paused to allow Leda to make a comment, but all I heard was some muffled, snuffling sounds. Feeling puzzled and helpless, I was eventually able to calm Leda down by awkwardly mumbling reassuring phrases into the phone like "there, there," and "everything is all right." I always felt stupid saying things like that to people when they were upset, but I could never think of anything else to say.

When Leda stopped crying, she explained that she had suspected me of allying myself with Charlie Bolero against her and her mother, but after learning about my confrontation with Charlie at Cobb's Station on the previous Saturday, she could see why I had introduced myself to her as Walt Galilei instead of Walt Callisto. Then, slightly embarrassed, she confessed to being a little disappointed at learning the true motivation behind my strange behavior, because she had secretly hoped that I was actually a detective who was only playing the part of a confused and bumbling car rental agent in order to shadow Charlie Bolero without raising his suspicions.

I was a little hurt by the confused and bumbling remark, but grateful that she believed my story. I kept the first feeling to myself and thanked her for trusting me. She laughed and admitted she didn't believe anyone would make up a story like mine. After that, to lighten the mood, she called me 'poetry boy' and told me how ridiculously sweet I had looked rolling around on the floor with Himalia in the steaming remains of my birthday cake. This was followed by an embarrassing exchange of sweet nothings whispered into telephone receivers, and an assortment of small talk.

The talk suddenly got a lot bigger when Leda remarked that since it was apparent Charlie was not my father, I wouldn't be too upset when she exposed the man for the scoundrel that he was. I cautioned Leda against any rash action and tried to dispel what I considered her unwarranted and mistaken suspicions by recounting the saga of Thunder Tom as I had heard it from Charlie on Tuesday night. I quickly curtailed this recitation, however, when Leda began to grow angry again.

With cold sweat beading my brow, I opted for the better part of valor and tacitly agreed to Leda's forcefully stated observation that although Charlie seemed like a gentleman and a scholar to me, he could still be capable of committing a vile and vicious fraud against Emily Taurus at Elara Downs. In other words, even though I was favorably impressed by Charlie and only wanted the best for him, I liked Leda a lot better, and decided to shut my trap.

The conversation shifted to our next date, and after discussing several possible venues, Leda suddenly remembered she had promised me an opportunity to witness a live stallion standing to one of Elara Downs's brood mares. A live cover was scheduled for 6:30 Friday evening. I had felt a little queasy just watching the artificial insemination of Frisco Gal, so I wasn't tremendously excited about watching a huge, massively aroused stallion climb up onto the back of some hapless mare. But since going to Elara Downs would afford me another opportunity of cuddling with Leda on her back porch, I agreed to meet her at Breeding Barn 1 to watch, as Leda put it, some real horse sex.

Chapter Twenty-One

I couldn't remember anything about my workday when I found myself at the end of it. On Fridays, out-of-town business customers, usually late for their flights, brought their rental cars back en masse, as if purposefully coordinating their last minute returns in order to create maximum congestion at the rental counter. This weekly pandemonium was compounded by the fact that Ace Car Rental didn't operate an airport shuttle. This meant customers had to cram themselves into an assortment of taxis and limousines that ferried passengers to and from Jupiter's single terminal airport.

This constant stream of customers, rental cars, cabs, and limos, along with the usual mind-numbing paperwork, tended to move Fridays at Ace Car Rental along at a rapid pace. My lack of sleep and preoccupation with Leda made this particular Friday whiz by like nobody's business, and before I knew it, my shoulder was being tapped by Jason's fingers.

"Hey, Walt, you better get going if you want to get to Leda's by six-thirty."

Startled, I glanced at my watch and gulped. It was after five. If I hurried, I might just manage to be fashionably late for the 'live cover' event Leda wanted me to see at Elara Downs. I jumped up from my desk and strode toward the back door.

"Thanks, Jason, you're a real pal! Don't stay open too late. If all the returns aren't in by six, leave a note on the door and go home."

The note I had referred to instructed customers who arrived after closing to drop their keys through the mail slot and park their rental cars in Ace's front lot with their paperwork locked inside. Customers who took advantage of this late return policy had a half-day rent added to their bill. Jason, looking concerned, accompanied me out to the Escalade, nagging as he went.

"Are you sure you're not too tired to drive?"

"You sound like my mother, Jason."

"Just trying to be safe, Walt. I hit the sack as soon as I got back last night and I still felt a little woozy this morning. You stayed up all night talking to Leda."

"Stop worrying, Mom. I used to get by with a lot less sleep in college. Just close up on time, and don't forget and come in by mistake tomorrow."

Every third weekend, a manager from another Ace Car Rental relieved Jason and me for the Saturday and Sunday shifts. Lately it was a disgruntled middle-aged man from Buffalo named Marty who complained bitterly about the long hours he had to work, comparing his job unfavorably to that of a liquor store clerk. I didn't understand Marty's attitude. As far as I knew, Ace did not require their employees to work beyond forty hours a week. But since our compensation was based on the number of rentals each location produced, Jason and I worked as many hours as we could. We were both enthusiastic about our jobs, and our efforts had been rewarded by increasingly fatter paychecks. I felt a little nervous about entrusting the store to Marty. I usually dropped by on Saturdays to check up on him, and on Sunday mornings to help check in the weekend rentals.

As I drove away from the rental lot, I caught a glimpse of Jason walking back into the office. I felt a pang of guilt for leaving my friend to close up all by himself. I knew Jason had been working more than his share of hours in the last few days, and I resolved to make it up to him.

I arrived at Elara Downs at a quarter to seven. Fearing I was late for the live cover session, I left the black Escalade cooling in front of Elara Downs' sprawling antebellum mansion and ran all the way to Breeding Barn 1. I stumbled into the breeding room, panting harder than the big, sweating stallion Dean was leading into the room. Leda and Emily were standing a little to one side of the standing stall watching Dr. Norton wrap a glossy brown mare's tail with white cloth tape. They all looked up as I stumbled into the room.

"Ah, Mr. Callisto, your timing remains as faultless as ever. You've arrived mere moments before the commencement of nature's most sacred ritual. Now, if you could just move over there by Emily and Leda, we'll get this little romance started."

Leda grabbed my arm as I approached, and pulled me next to her.

"We have to stand way over here because live cover is a lot more dangerous than artificial insemination," Leda said, giving my arm a little squeeze. "It's more fun to watch, too!"

I wasn't so sure about it being fun to watch. After witnessing Frisco Gal's artificial insemination, I had formed the opinion that the procreation activities of animals and humans were better conducted in private. The sex life of rutabagas affords surprisingly little exposure to the mechanics of reproduction, and growing up on a rutabaga farm had failed to imbue me with the unflappable reserve commonly acquired by agrarians who raise livestock. On the other hand, I was prepared to endure an equine orgy of Byzantine dimensions if it meant I could spend time with Leda, so I responded to her remark by nodding and smiling as if I were eager to watch a couple of racehorses making whoopee.

We watched in silence as Dr. Norton finished preparing the mare for her suitor's attentions. He swabbed her perineal area and adjusted a leather strap on her right front leg so that her hoof was held several inches off the floor of the stall. Dean led the stallion up to the left side of the mare and allowed him to smell, taste, and lightly nuzzle her. The mare responded to this attention by emitting nervous sounding whinnies, and shimmied about in her stall. I thought Dean looked a little worried, but he must have felt the mare was ready because he led the stallion into a position directly behind her, while Dr. Norton took hold of her bandaged tail and held it out of the way. One especially prominent feature of this rustic tableau made it readily apparent to everyone watching that the stallion was excited, enthusiastic, and ready to commence operations.

I shut my eyes the moment the stallion's rather impressive profile swung into view. At first, I told myself I was simply resting my eyes, but after hearing, smelling, and feeling the heat of those first moments of 'real horse sex,' I knew they were closed for the duration. My ears, however, were wide open, and what I heard sounded terrifyingly physical, like a fat man getting the beating of a lifetime: a crescendo of colliding flesh, piercing whinnies and shrill neighs, accompanied by hot, pungent waves of aroma submerging my already saturated senses in a fetid surf of horsy pheromones.

"That's it!" I heard Dean announce. "Do you see how he's moving his tail now? We call that flagging. He's getting ready to dismount, and when he does, I need everyone to stand clear, because we need to move fast to avoid any parting shots from the mare."

I opened my eyes in time to see the big stallion standing down from the mare. Dean was hauling hard on the lead even before his front hooves touched the ground and pulled the stallion out of range of the mare's hindquarters just in time. Despite being hobbled, the mare still managed to get off a pretty good kick, and if it had connected, the stallion would have undoubtedly thought twice about getting fresh with her the next time around.

"You look a little peaked, Walt," I heard Emily say. "Maybe you need to step outside for some fresh air."

I turned to see Emily and Leda staring at me with concern written on their faces, or at least written on Emily's face. The concern on Leda's face was hard to read, because it was obscured by a big grin.

"Aw, he's okay, Emily," she said, slapping my shoulder as if it were the fender of a reliable old truck. "This sort of thing is old hat to Walt. He's a farm boy, you know."

An hour later, Leda was still teasing me about my reaction to the live cover session as she drove her little red Mini Cooper into the parking lot of Galilei's Famous Italian restaurant. After my last embarrassing visit, I hadn't contemplated returning to my uncle's restaurant during my lifetime, much less four days after the birthday debacle, but Leda had insisted. My cousin Tony was in the lobby when we entered the restaurant. He grinned like a lunatic when he saw us, and I was afraid Tony was about to make some humorous reference to the birthday party disaster. I tried to signal Tony to go away, but my cousin ignored me, and launched into a bad imitation of my Uncle Vinny's jolly Italian chef routine.

"Buon pomeriggio, Leda! Buon pomeriggio, Walt! Entr in, entr in, vostro ospite e vostro meraviglioso supper essere attend voi!" Tony finished by sweeping his hands up in a flourish to point towards the Hall of Scientists.

I wasn't sure what my cousin had just said, but I knew I didn't want to eat in the room where my humiliating birthday party had taken place. "Cut it out, Tony! Your Italian is worse than Uncle Vinny's. It sounded like you said our supper was going to serve us to our host or something. And by the way, we don't want to eat in the Hall of Scientists, if that's where you're pointing."

Tony looked at me reproachfully and put his hands on his hips. "Well, you don't have to eat there, but that's where your dinner companion is waiting for you."

I was nearing the end of my patience. I liked my cousin, but I thought Tony had a talent for mucking things up. "Tony," I said slowly, "Leda and I are not meeting anyone, so whoever you have waiting in the Hall of Scientists must be expecting someone else."

"No, he's right, Walt," Leda said, briefly touching my hand. "I invited a couple of friends to eat with us. I hope you don't mind."

My hopes of a romantic evening suddenly dashed, I tried to hide my disappointment as I followed Tony and Leda to the room where, only four days before, I had gotten up close and personal with Leda's mother and a flaming sponge cake. As we entered the room, a slim, middle-aged man stood up to greet us. At first, I was a little surprised that one of Leda's friends was a middle-aged man, and then, when the man's crooked smile exposed a mouth full of gold dental work, I was flabbergasted.

"You must be Ralph Chicarillo," Leda said.

"Yeah. Call me Chic."

Chic 'the stoop' stepped forward and shook my cool, limp hand. "We met at the track last night, remember?" He bent a little closer and leered at me. "I bet you didn't think you'd be seeing me again so soon, huh?"

I hadn't thought I would ever be seeing Chic again. After all, we didn't exactly run in the same circles – well, of course, now we ran in the same circles. But I couldn't begin to imagine how Leda would have even heard of someone like Chic, much less have invited him to dinner.

Leda led me over to the same table we had the last time, except now it had been changed from a two-top to a four-top by the expedient of pulling it away from the wall and adding two chairs.

Chic commandeered the chair in the corner, and extracted a pre-moistened towelette from the recesses of his costume. He tore open the wet nap's foil pouch and proceeded to carefully unfold the little square of wet paper it contained. Normally, I agreed with Himalia's preference for boy, girl, boy, girl seating, but I didn't like Leda sitting next to this particular boy, so I sat next to him instead.

"So you met Chic at the track," Leda said. "You forgot to mention that last night."

I blushed, took my glasses off, and began nervously polishing them with my napkin.

"Well, we really didn't get to know each other that well–" I began and then ground to a stop. Why in the world was I being so defensive, I asked myself. After all, I wasn't the one inviting shifty racetrack reprobates to dine with us. If anyone had any explaining to do, it was Leda. I stopped polishing my glasses and gave my girl friend an austere look. "But what's this all about anyway? What's Chic doing here? How do you know him?"

"Don't harangue the girl, Walt. I invited Chic."

The comment hadn't come from either Leda or Chic. I put my glasses back on and looked up to see Dr. Norton smiling at me from the doorway.

Chapter Twenty-Two

I don't like surprises, and I didn't understand why people kept springing them on me while I was trying to have romantic meals with Leda. So, it was with an understandable degree of resentment that I watched Dr. Norton take a seat between his co-conspirators.

"You seem a tad put out, Walt," Dr. Norton observed, "not that I blame you. I expect you were anticipating a far more intimate repast than one that included a crusty old animal doctor and a character like Chic here. I want you to know right from the start that Leda arranged this gathering entirely at my request, so I could talk to you about Charlie Bolero."

I was at once surprised and angry. I would have thought Leda could have gone for at least a day without blabbing my secrets to all and sundry. Unable to think of anything to say, I turned, with as much dignity as I could muster, to stare reproachfully at Leda. "If you're thinking Leda betrayed some confidence or other, you couldn't be more wrong," Dr. Norton said sternly. "She wouldn't tell me a blasted thing beyond confirming that you and Charlie were recently acquainted, a fact I'd already determined from your interaction with him at Frisco Gal's insemination and the dinner afterward. It was only after Chic here phoned me with news of your presence at Ananke Race Park last night that I decided to talk to you about Charlie."

Still confused, I turned my stare to bear upon Dr. Norton and his odious associate. The old veterinarian simply smiled at me, while Chic studiously applied a second wet nap to the interstices of his slender fingers.

"I don't understand. Why would Chic call you about my movements?" I demanded, as if the stoop wasn't calmly washing his hands in the chair next to me. "What's this all about? Are you spying on me or something?"

"We're not spying on you, Walt. We're spying on Charlie, and if you'll sit down, I'll be happy to explain what it's all about."

I was surprised and embarrassed to discover I was now standing with my fists clenched by my sides. With a feeling of weariness washing over me, I sank back into my chair. "Oh. Uh, sorry, I'm—I'm just a little, you know, on edge, and I—haven't had a lot of sleep lately…" I trailed off and shrugged my shoulders.

"Not at all," Dr. Norton said genially. "Your reaction is quite understandable. No man likes conspiracies sprung on him at dinner. I would have approached you at the farm, but for the danger of Emily or Leda's mother finding out."

"Oh, I see what this is about," I said. "You're helping Dean and Leda. You think Charlie engineered that tack room fire so his powerful friends could collect the insurance money."

"Well, I'm not certain I agree with all of their suppositions, but I do believe Charlie contributed to the loss of the farm Emily and her husband spent a lifetime building. Emily's an old friend of mine. When I learned the details of the fire and the financial disaster that followed, I became suspicious of the circumstances surrounding the entire incident. I decided to find out what really happened, so I persuaded Emily to retire old Doc Pritchard, and replace him with myself. For the last three months, I've been observing the staff at Elara Downs, and I've concluded none of them had anything to do with the fire."

"Why would you think that anyone set the fire?" I asked. "Didn't the fire department rule it an accident?"

"Indeed, barn fires are all too tragically common, Walt, but they seldom occur in tack rooms as well organized as the one Dean maintains. I believe Charlie may have had something to do with this one, and I've enlisted Chic, to help me keep tabs on his movements."

At this point Tony popped into the room to take drink orders. During this interlude, I gave Leda a hard look that softened somewhat when I saw a glistening of concern in her eyes. Nevertheless, when she patted my hand and attempted an encouraging smile, I still bristled with indignation. I didn't appreciate being manipulated or put on the spot. I wished Leda had simply come to me and explained the situation in private.

"I wouldn't blame you if you had your doubts about my suspicions," Dr. Norton said after Tony had left the room. "After all, you haven't known Charlie long enough to know what he's really like, and you've only just met us. Leda tells me you're skeptical of her and Dean's theory, and, to be truthful, I have my own doubts about a lot of their scenario, but some of Dean's observations happen to coincide with my own. The most notable of which is that of Charlie's suddenly acquiring enough financing only two weeks after the fire to pay for the insemination, gestational care, feeding and maintenance of not one but two foals in quick succession."

"That's probably only a coincidence," I said. " Charlie bought into a company called Sea Tech about three years ago. He said it took about a year for it to begin making real profits, and several more months to produce enough money to pay for those two foals."

"Ah, see? There's something we didn't know about," he said, glancing over at Chic, who gave a little nod in return. "That certainly would explain his financing, but there's still a mystery surrounding some of Charlie's other actions."

"Like Charlie bringing Thunder Tom's sperm in that little tank instead of a full-sized can?" I asked. Dr. Norton raised an eyebrow, but I kept talking. "Tell me, Dr. Norton, did the DNA samples you extracted from those used straws happen to match Thunder Tom's profile? I assume that they did; otherwise, we wouldn't be sitting here discussing what I know about Charlie."

I knew this statement would surprise Dr. Norton, and I wasn't disappointed by the old horse doctor's reaction. A bemused Dr. Norton sat back in his chair, scratched his chin, and studied me over the top of his spectacles for several moments before responding.

"Obviously, I wasn't being quite as discreet as I had imagined. You should be congratulated on a nice piece of reasoning, Walt. Did you work that out just now? Never mind. It doesn't matter. Yes, I had the straws tested, and yes, the DNA profile matched the one on file for Thunder Tom. I told you I had my own ideas about what happened, and since you seem able to follow my reasoning simply by observing my actions, I don't feel the need to go into my theories at this point. I just want to get to the bottom of this, for Emily's sake, even if doing so doesn't restore her farm or any of her money. During my investigations, I've spoken with several people in thoroughbred circles who knew Charlie when he represented Ogden Federated. One of them was Daniel Brookshire. I've known Daniel for several years. He's a shrewd judge of horses, highly educated, and an exceedingly charming, likeable man, but a man who plays his cards close to his vest. I was unable to extract a great deal of information from him, either positive or negative, about Charlie or his involvement in arranging Brookshire's contract with Elara Downs, though Daniel did seem to betray an overly keen interest in my inquiry. So, I hunted Chic up to see if he had heard any rumors concerning Daniel Brookshire and Charlie. Chic circulates between the racetracks on the circuit, and hears more about the affairs of the rich and powerful than you would expect. He has assisted me more than once in other inquiries that I've made on behalf of thoroughbred breeders."

This last statement puzzled me. I wondered just how often circumstances arose in the course of Dr. Norton's regular duties that required him to make inquiries, and was about to ask about the investigative side of his veterinary practice when Chic decided it was time to contribute to the conversation.

"Yeah, I try to keep my eyes and ears open, and I try to be helpful. It ain't easy working in the wager salvage business, what with track cops always hassling you and bettors giving you dirty looks. So I try to make myself useful to people who can take a little heat off me. People like Charlie. As a food and beverage manager, he could tell bartenders and hamburger flippers to give me a hard time, or not. For instance, they could holler to security about me fishing through the trash and hanging around their concessions – a lot of tickets get dropped in front of the bars and pizza stands – or they could just ignore me.

So I collect any bits of information I find lying around that might help me sweeten up managers, security guards, and the like with tips on horses and info about the owners and trainers. I find that kind of stuff scribbled on people's napkins next to their leftover fries and tossed on the floor with their cigarette butts and tickets. I cash the winning tickets, and I keep any info I find up here," Chic tapped the side of his head, "for a rainy day."

He directed a sly gold-toothed grin at me, causing me to grit my teeth in order to suppress a shudder of revulsion. I thought Chic displayed an overweening pride in an unwarranted intrusion into other people's private affairs.

"I hear things, too, like in restrooms for instance and stairways and other places where people think nobody's paying any attention. You know, it's sort of funny, but people shout things at the finish line they wouldn't dare whisper in the parking lot. And they never notice me standing there. They don't want to notice me. I'm an invisible pariah, shuffling along behind them with my head hung down, flipping tickets over with my toes, and listening to every damn word they say."

"Yeah, well, it sounds like you've got a really interesting hobby there, Chic, but Doc said you were going to tell us what you know about Charlie," Leda said.

Leda had an impatient edge to her voice that made me feel a little better about her. She might have been guilty of ambushing me with an inquisition, but at least she wasn't going to let this unpleasant ticket stooper drone on about his snooping expertise.

"I'm getting to it," Chic said, looking hurt. "My hobby, as you call it, got Charlie his first piece of a horse."

"You mean Thunder Tom? The one he's breeding to Frisco Gal?" asked Leda.

"No, that's the horse he lost all his money on. His first horse was Brookshire's Paulie Boy, and it made a ton of money. If it weren't for me, Charlie wouldn't have had a piece of it. Penny-ante food and beverage managers don't usually get a taste of a Daniel Brookshire horse."

"Charlie told me Mr. Brookshire made an exception because they were friends," I said.

Chic flashed his evil-looking dental work and shook his head. "Charlie don't have friends. He has acquaintances, and if it weren't for a certain something I happened across in the valet lot, which by the way is an area that's often overlooked by your ordinary stooper, Brookshire wouldn't have given him the time of day."

"Are you trying to imply," I asked, "that Charlie used this thing you found to blackmail Mr. Brookshire?"

"Naw, Charlie's too smart for that. He returned the item in question just as nice as you please, like it was only a lost book or a wallet, and not something that could get a man permanent barred from racing. Like you said last night, Charlie's an unusually considerate man, especially when he finds somebody in an awkward situation. He'll cover for you – act like it's nothing special, and let human nature take its course. Sooner or later, you'll find yourself in a position to help Charlie in some way or other, and he'll show up to collect his pound of flesh, so to speak."

I turned to face Chic, and addressed him in a reasonable tone of voice. "You know, this all seems just a little vague. What is this thing you turned over to Charlie, and was he really aware it was an outlawed item when he returned it? Isn't it possible he was simply returning Mr. Brookshire's property like any considerate person would?"

Chic glared at me and then mimicked the first two words of my question in a high nasal voice. "*You knooow*, you're starting to sound like Charlie, with that creepy, fake friendly voice of his."

"There's no need for name calling," Dr. Norton said. "He's simply asking for a little clarification."

"He's calling me a liar, is what he's doing, and I'm not going to tell him what the item was. He might blab it to somebody."

"That is a good point, Walt," the doctor said. "I'm sure you realize that our conversation this evening is strictly confidential."

"I'm not going to tell Charlie about it, if that's what you're afraid of," I replied.

"I know you wouldn't do that, but other people's reputations are at stake as well, and I don't think we should be too specific about certain details. Charlie knew what it was. Chic demonstrated it, and suffice it to say that the racing commission would definitely prohibit this kind of item. It was inside a small zippered pouch along with some of Mr. Brookshire's other personal effects. Chic showed the contents to Charlie and explained what the banned item was used for. Charlie offered to return the pouch to its owner on Chic's behalf, and see to it that he received credit for finding it. Chic accepted this offer because he didn't have access to the Jockey Club, and he was nervous about carrying a contraband item around with him until he was able to contact Mr. Brookshire."

"I see," I said. "Instead of reporting a possible violation of racing commission rules to the authorities, Chic asked Charlie to return the item and collect a reward for him."

Chic made a rude noise that sounded like air escaping from a rubber tire and rolled his eyes. "There he goes again, Doc."

"That's hardly fair to Chic, Walt. Racetrack management doesn't view stoops as legitimate members of the wagering community. Stoops finance their gambling by retrieving tickets that management would rather go un-redeemed, and they would love to have an excuse to kick one of them out of their facilities. Filing a serious charge against a trusted member of the thoroughbred community could result in Chic being barred from every track on the circuit."

"Worse than that," Chic said. "Brookshire would've probably just claimed I planted the spar– uh, I mean the thing on him and got me thrown in the clink."

"The important thing is that this episode exposes Charlie as the kind of man who might be capable of perpetrating fraud if he stood to profit from it," Dr. Norton said.

I wasn't sure I agreed with Dr. Norton's assessment. I felt that even if everything Chic reported was true and accurate, it still didn't prove anything about either Daniel Brookshire's or Charlie's character. As Chic had pointed out himself, the banned item could have been planted in his misplaced leather pouch by one of Brookshire's enemies and left in the valet lot in order to frame him. From my dealings with him over the last week, I had found Charlie to be an intelligent and cautious person who practiced a lot more restraint than the average man. I thought that if I were able to imagine this one innocent explanation for the presence of the illegal item in Brookshire's pouch, then so would Charlie, and he might have agreed to act as a go-between simply to keep Chic out of trouble.

Tony came scuttling in balancing a tray of drinks on one hand and one of Vinny's huge Margarita pizzas on the other. I had to help my cousin set the drinks on the table, because Tony had failed to bring another waiter to assist him. Completely oblivious to the tension in the room, Tony hung around to chat up Leda after he finished serving the pizza, which made her feel obligated to introduce her guests. When Tony discovered Chic 'worked' at the racetrack, he spent five minutes complaining about his gambling losses and pressuring the stoop for tips on upcoming races. He only left after Chic had promised to give him a call the next time he had a tip on a horse.

Afterward, I found that I felt much more relaxed about the whole situation. My gregarious cousin's inane patter had somehow lightened the mood and changed my perspective on Dr. Norton's inquiry. I still felt Leda and the crusty old veterinarian were barking up the wrong tree, but I began to answer Dr. Norton's questions a little more freely. I was not completely without discretion, however, and didn't volunteer information that wasn't asked for or that was, in my opinion, irrelevant. I didn't reveal how I had met Charlie, or how I had tracked him down in pursuit of my biological father. I didn't tell the doctor about the exchanged parts on the Lincoln, or what I saw when I spied on Charlie at his warehouse and again in his garage. I didn't share any of Jason's various theories about Charlie's misdeeds, or any of my own initial misgivings or my subsequent change of heart when Charlie turned out to be so forthcoming and generous. Most importantly, I didn't tell the doctor how much I wished that the results of the paternity test Charlie had volunteered to take, in spite of all expectations to the contrary, would turn out to be positive.

Chapter Twenty-Three

Halfway between Juno and Jupiter, I nodded off – and woke up hanging upside down from my seat belt. The shock of cold water invading my nose and mouth had awakened me. The Escalade had veered off the Freeway and rolled over in a water-filled ditch. The water wasn't deep, but in my inverted position, it completely immersed my head. The airbag had deployed and was hanging down from the steering wheel, sticking to my face like a wet shroud. At first, I struggled wildly, tearing at my straps and kicking my legs in an effort to propel my body from what I perceived to be the inky bottom of some roadside abyss. Only when my struggles briefly lifted my head out of the water, and I felt cool air coming through the wet cloth of the air bag, did I realize my true peril. I knew then that I was suspended upside down in a wrecked Cadillac Escalade, drowning in twelve inches of water.

This was an impressive feat of deduction for someone who had gotten less sleep in the past five days than some people get in a single night. Though it hurt my neck to do so, I craned my head up toward my chest so my nose and mouth were clear of the water. I was still unable to expel the water from my nasal cavity because of gravity and the wet airbag covering my face. For several terrifying seconds, my neck and shoulders aching from the effort, I clawed at the wet cloth with the one hand I could move freely. When I finally pulled the cloth from my face, I drew my first full breath of air, but some of the water in my nose was drawn into my lungs, causing me to cough and choke so violently that my head dropped back into the water. Fighting back panic, I grabbed at my own legs to haul myself back out of the water and suck in another agonizing lungful of air. This only partially succeeded because my shoulder harness was pinning one of my arms and preventing it from reaching a useful handhold. I knew I could not sustain the battle against gravity indefinitely. My only chance of avoiding the ignominious fate of drowning in a puddle was to release the buckle of the seatbelt I was hanging from. That was easier said than done, because I was holding my head out of the water with the only hand that could still reach the buckle. For what seemed like an eternity, I struggled in the darkness, straining to keep my head out of the water. I found myself regretting the year I had wasted searching for a father who didn't want me, when I already had one that did. I wondered why I had always struggled against the circumstances I found myself in, when I could have simply relaxed and enjoyed the opportunities God had given me. Then, as my strength was beginning to flag, I suddenly realized I had just given myself some good advice. I took in a deep breath, released my grip on my leg, relaxed my straining neck and let my head plunge into the cold water. Fighting the instinct to immediately pull my head from the suffocating liquid that immersed it, I reached up blindly with my one unencumbered arm into the darkness above, searched for the safety belt buckle, found it and released it. My body only fell a couple of inches, and my head settled gently into the padded ceiling of the Escalade. Even though my entire head was under water at this point, all traces of panic had left me. I felt no more alarm than a man lying upside down in a wading pool. I maneuvered my legs onto the windshield, managed to roll over, and then push myself up into a sitting position in the cold ditch water.

The first thing I heard when I had righted myself was the worried voice of an OnStar™ operator announcing that their monitoring service had detected airbag deployment, and inquiring if anyone was hurt. After I got my breath back, I was finally able to assure the operator that I seemed to be uninjured, but definitely needed the services of a tow truck. I didn't know where I was, but thanks to the vehicle's onboard GPS navigation system, the OnStar™ operator did. She told me I was thirty-five miles south of Jupiter, and a tow truck was on its way. After the operator had hung up, I realized I had forgotten to mention that my car was upside down in a ditch. I supposed that I could simply wait until the tow truck arrived, but I wasn't sure the Escalade was visible from the highway, so I started looking for a way out of the wreck. The doors were stuck in the muck, but I thought I might get out through the tailgate in the back of the vehicle. The ignition key was about even with my head, and when I removed it, the car was plunged into a deafening silence. The engine had been roaring away the whole time. I was surprised. I would have expected the motor to automatically shut off when it was turned upside down. I crawled along the ceiling of the vehicle, navigating through a clutter of unseen objects that had fallen into the water. When I reached the tailgate, I felt around for a latch up near the floor, but couldn't seem to find one. Then I remembered the latch release on my ignition key. I didn't think it would work, but I pressed it anyway. There was a loud click, and the tailgate fell open like a ramp on a naval landing craft. I grunted in surprise, clambered out, and climbed up the bank.

As I stood on the shoulder of the interstate waiting for the tow truck, I tried to recall the last minutes before the accident. I had been listening to music and thinking about Leda. She had been less than satisfied with my level of cooperation with Dr. Norton's investigation. After I had taken her back to Elara Downs, she sat in my car complaining for thirty minutes, and didn't invite me in to cuddle on the veranda afterwards. I couldn't understand why she was making such a big deal of my refusal to spy on Charlie. I had told them everything Charlie had told me about Brookshire, and I had even promised to pass on anything Charlie might say in the future that related to the tack room fire, Mr. Brookshire, or Running Fool. But I had resolutely drawn the line at carrying a recorder and attempting to elicit incriminating remarks from Charlie.

Leda had railed at me, pleaded with me, and insulted me in that order. She told me that if I really cared for her, I would be happy to carry a recorder, search through Charlie's private papers, or even deploy hidden microphones and cameras if she asked me to. She expressed her fear that her mother would fall victim to one of Charlie's schemes. She became emotional talking about how susceptible Himalia was to Charlie's attentions, and how much time she was spending with him lately. When she realized I wasn't going to change my mind, Leda accused me of being a coward and jumped out of the Escalade, slamming the door after her. Forty minutes later, I found myself upside down in a ditch, and although I had no memory of going to sleep or even feeling drowsy, I was able to remember fragments of a strange dream that I must have had while the Escalade was veering off the road.

In the dream, Leda, Chic, and Dr. Norton were chasing Charlie and me around the tables of Galilei's Famous Italian restaurant. Then I found myself running in a crowd of people through the Explorers' Pavilion. When I looked at some of the people in the crowd, I noticed they all looked just like me. Then I found myself in the Hall of Scientists where the crowd had pushed Charlie into a corner. Suddenly Leda forced her way up to the front of the crowd. Grinning wickedly, she picked up a carafe and gave Charlie an evil wink with one of her golden eyes. As Leda drew her arm back to throw, I flung my body in the way of the lethal liquid. That was when I woke to find I was drowning.

The tow truck arrived before my clothes had dried out, and the state police pulled up after the driver had already turned the Escalade back over on its wheels and was hauling it out of the ditch. I was amazed at the extent of the damage I could see as the wrecked SUV lurched up the bank into the work lights of the tow truck. Both the police officer and I stopped doing paperwork in order to look at it. The roof and windshield were caved in on the passenger's side, and the hood and fenders were crushed all the way down to the rubber of the front tires. I felt a cold shiver run down my spine. It seemed like a miracle to have escaped with my life, and I was about to say as much to the officer when I noticed a black Lincoln Town Car pull out of the slow-moving stream of rubber-neckers. After the highway patrol had arrived to add its flashing blue lights to the yellow ones on the tow truck, traffic had backed up on the freeway. The Lincoln parked on the shoulder about eighty feet down the road, and a man got out and began walking back. When he came in range of the tow truck's work lights, I recognized him.

"Good evening, Officer," Charlie said, nodding at the patrolman. "I thought that looked like your car, Walt. What in the world happened?"

"I'm afraid he fell asleep at the wheel, sir," the officer said. "Are you related to this young man?"

"No, Officer, but we're close friends. I can drive him back to his home when you're finished with him. What a wreck! Are you certain you're not injured? Where are your glasses?"

I touched my face where my glasses normally resided. They were missing. "I don't know. I guess they're still in the car."

"I'll go see if the tow truck operator can retrieve them for you," Charlie said, and went off to talk to him.

"That's a good friend you have there," the officer remarked. "Get him to take you by a hospital on the way home. You need to be checked out for internal injuries. You'll be happy to know I'm not going to give you a traffic citation, but I want you to read this and be more careful in the future."

The officer handed me a 'Driving Drowsy and Fatigue' pamphlet printed by the Governor's Traffic and Safety Committee, then went over to talk to Charlie, who was watching the tow truck driver pry open the driver's side door on the Escalade. I could see their silhouettes talking and gesturing to each other. I heard Charlie laugh, saw him nod, and shake the officer's hand. After the tow truck driver managed to get the door open, Charlie borrowed a flashlight and rummaged around inside the Escalade for a couple of minutes before emerging with my glasses and rejoining me on the shoulder of the road.

"Did you notice there aren't any rumble strips cut into the shoulder along this section of the road?" Charlie asked, handing me my glasses. "If there were, you probably would've waked up in time to avoid the accident. Hey, I was just talking to the officer, and he wants me to drop you by the ER in Jupiter just to be on the safe side."

"No, that's okay, Charlie, I can catch a ride with the tow truck driver," I said, taking the glasses and shoving them in my pocket. "Really, I don't need to go to the ER, and I don't want to take you out of your way."

"Don't worry about it. I'm going that direction anyway. I was headed up to my warehouse to do a little work. Like I said the other night, I'm getting out of the business, so I need to finish up a few things and clean out my space before I vacate the lease."

"But it's nearly midnight. Isn't it kind of late to be cleaning out your warehouse?"

Charlie laughed and slapped me on the shoulder. "I'm used to working late. I'm a night owl just like you. Now come on, I promised the patrol officer I'd take care of you."

So I found myself sitting on several layers of newspaper in Charlie's car listening to details of an automobile accident Charlie was in when he was my age. I wasn't listening very closely, because I was preoccupied by all the problems that my car accident was going to cause for me with Ace Car Rental. Ace might pull my company car privileges or perhaps even let me go over the incident. I was wondering if volunteering to pay Ace's insurance deductible on the Escalade would help alleviate matters with Ace when I realized that Charlie had segued from the story about crashing his custom Chevy van on the way to an outdoor music concert, to a story about some sexual conquest he had made there.

"I was never a fan of Black Sabbath, but their rock concerts was the place to go when you wanted to get your freak on, if you catch my drift, and this babe was a world class freak. She was wearing so much crystal jewelry she glowed in the dark, which was a good thing because it was after nine by the time my roommate and I had hitchhiked from the place we left my wrecked van. Away from the lights of the stage, you couldn't really see the faces of the girls you were hitting on, but not being able to see each other clearly kind of made things more exciting for both of us. She had a voluptuous figure, so I imagined that she looked like Ann Margaret, and I think I might have helped her imagination along by telling her I was a member of one of the bands that had opened for Black Sabbath at the concert."

"Really?" I was a fan of vintage rock music, and wondered who Charlie had impersonated. "Who opened for them?"

"Glass Bird."

"Glass Bird!" I laughed. "Don't tell me she bought that! Which member?"

"I tried to be evasive, but I think she got the idea I was Charlie Vonante."

"The drummer?"

"Yeah. Well, I had already given her my real first name – and he was the only Charlie in the band."

"You're lucky she didn't ask you to drum out a few riffs." Even though I was a little dismayed by the behavior of this younger version of Charlie, it was still a funny story, and it made my current problems seem a little less dire. "So what happened after that?"

"We ended up making love in a closed hotdog stand."

"A hotdog stand!"

"Well, it was a kosher hotdog stand."

"What difference does that make? Are you Jewish?"

"No, but she might have been."

"I'm guessing you probably didn't see her again after that."

"No, as a matter of fact our little love nest was rudely invaded by the return of the hotdog vendor. I think we scared him as much as he scared us, because he fell over backward when we both suddenly sprang up out of the darkness. I jumped over him and ran off carrying my pants in one hand and my shoes in the other. I guess the girl ran in another direction, because I didn't bump into her again."

When we arrived at the Emergency Room in Jupiter, I convinced Charlie to drop me off at the entrance and stood just inside the door until I saw him drive away. Then I called Jason to pick me up. When Jason heard about the accident, he was just as insistent as Charlie had been about my being checked out, so I reluctantly submitted to a strenuous series of questions, scans, and probes so my friend could rest easy about my health.

On the way to Ace, I told Jason about the car wreck and some of what had transpired at Elara Downs, the restaurant, and my ride home with Charlie. Jason wasn't awake enough to respond in detail to my account, but he perked up during Chic's story. He said he had a theory about what was in the leather pouch Chic had found at the race track, and he intended to check it out on the Internet when he got home. Jason also commiserated with me over the blow-up I had with Leda in front of her home after our dinner date cum ambush, but confidently predicted Leda wouldn't stay mad for very long.

It was nearly dawn by the time I drove into Ganymede Terrace's parking lot in a new white Escalade. When I opened my door, my calico cat greeted me in an uncharacteristically solicitous manner. Instead of yowling angrily or ignoring me completely as she normally did when I was late, Io rubbed her mottled flank back and forth against my ankles and allowed me to pick her up and cuddle her in my arms. I thought she must have been able to sense my recent brush with death and was trying to comfort me.

After I had finished bonding with Io and feeding her, I hurried hopefully into my living room to check the answering machine. I found a lonely, fluorescent blue zero, glowing balefully in the machine's 'number of messages received' window. Leda hadn't called.

Chapter Twenty-Four

The following afternoon, feeling like I had lost a fight with a jackhammer, I rolled carefully out of bed and tottered to my living room to make a phone call. After several rings, I finally got a recording stating that Elara Downs, the foremost broodmare facility in the northeast, was closed on Saturdays, but thoroughbred owners interested in breeding their horses with the finest bloodlines in the industry could leave their message at the beep.

Beep! "... Hello, this message is for Leda. Hi, Leda, I just wanted to let you know that I had a little accident on the way home last night and didn't get back to my apartment until four AM– So if you tried to call me, that's where I was. It looks like I lost my cell phone as well, but I'm going by the office later on and you can call me there– if you want to. I'll try to call you again from there, too. I have the rest of today and most of tomorrow off, if you want to go out somewhere. Well, I guess I'll talk to you later. Bye for now."

I hung up the phone feeling I had just left the most pathetic phone message in the history of dating. I wondered why the designers of answering machines weren't required by law to provide a way for people who left messages on their diabolical contraptions to modify or delete ill-considered messages.

I showered and dressed as best as I could, and after a mutual exchange of civilities with Io, hobbled out to my new car. I had chosen a brand new fully loaded white Escalade ESV with a sunroof. If Ace Car Rental decided to jerk my company car privileges on Monday, I wanted to spend the rest of the weekend in the best SUV on the lot.

When I pulled into Ace's back parking lot, I found Pitch and Jody chattering and gesticulating by the smashed remains of my black Escalade. I couldn't guess how it had ended up as the morning's entertainment for my teenage employees. I had asked the tow truck operator to take it to the dealership that Ace used in Jupiter to maintain their GM vehicles.

Pitch hurried back to the carwash when he saw me walking up, but Jody stayed to goggle. She seemed to be having some difficulty deciding just where to direct her look of amazement. First she stared with open mouth and bulbous eyes at me, and then she gaped with equal enthusiasm at the caved-in roof of the Escalade. I sought to focus her attention by interposing myself between the wrecked Cadillac and Jody.

"You're alive!" observed Jody.

"Yes, Jody, thanks for noticing. Do you happen to know who brought this car here?"

"*You* know," she said accusingly, "the tow truck guy."

"I meant, who sent it over. I'm trying to determine if the dealership sent it over, or if the towing company brought it over here by mistake."

"Oh. I don't know. Marty signed for it."

My heart sank. I had wanted to handle the paperwork on the accident personally, so I could put the matter in the best light possible. I had turned on my heel and started to stride toward the office when Jody called after me.

"Hey, Mr. Callisto!"

I turned, fully expecting the daffy girl to ask if I wanted the wrecked Escalade washed and detailed.

"Do you want me to look through your old car for your stuff?"

"Thanks, Jody," I said, feeling surprised and not a little guilty about my unkind thoughts. "I'd appreciate that. But please be careful not to cut yourself on anything."

I left Jody happily rummaging through the wrecked Escalade, and entered the office through the back door. When I came to the end of the hall, I was presented with a rear view of Marty's bald head cushioned on the hairy arms he had folded behind it. He had his feet propped up on my desk and, contrary to Ace's rules and local ordinances, he also had a lit cigar, smoking like a chimney, sticking out of his fat, florid face.

"Marty!" I said sharply, and immediately regretted doing so. I didn't like Marty smoking in my office, but I couldn't afford to make him angry either.

Marty took his arms from behind his head, swung his feet down, and turned around to look at me. "Oh, hi, Walt. I was kind of worried about you. Glad to see you're up and around."

"Thanks. Look, I'm sorry I snapped at you, but you know we're not allowed to smoke in the office."

"I only do it when there's not any customers around." He picked an empty pickle jar off the desk and waggled it at me. "Look, when I see a customer driving up I just drop my stogie in this little bottle and screw on the lid. Pretty clever huh?"

"Well, that would extinguish the cigar all right," I said, "but what about the odor that's still in the room?"

Marty took one more puff off his cigar, dropped it in the pickle jar, screwed on the lid, and dispersed the smoke by waving his pudgy hands around. "What odor? I don't smell anything, do you?"

I thought the room smelled like a wet baboon, but I decided it might be impolitic to say so. "Never mind, but I'd appreciate it if you left your cigar in its bottle while you're in the store."

"No problem, Walt. It's your store, and you should have things your way."

"Thanks." I paused for a moment, searching for the right words to frame my next question. Marty might not know who wrecked the Esplanade, and I didn't see any reason to inform him. "Uh, I see they dropped that wrecked car off in the back lot. I thought it was going to the dealer – do you know why it was brought back here?"

"Oh, that was my doing, Walt. Ace doesn't send wrecks to the dealer. They just collect the insurance and write them off. You should know that."

"But I thought we sent them to the dealer for an evaluation first."

"Not if there's any obvious structural damage. I had the dealer send it over here when he called about it this morning. You probably didn't know the procedure because your location hasn't had any bad wrecks since you took over."

"Yeah, well, I need to use my desk for a little while, so maybe you could take your cigar for a walk."

"Sure, sure." Marty said, heaving himself out of his chair. "Going to catch up on some paperwork, huh?"

I sat down and started tapping on the keyboard. After banging away for a few moments, I realized Marty was still waiting for an answer.

"Oh." I said, looking around like I had just noticed him standing there, "Sorry Marty, yeah, I'm doing paperwork. I'm going to look in the company's website for an accident form."

"No need for that, Walt. I already took care of it."

I blanched and stared at Marty in disbelief. "What did you do?"

"Like I said, I took care of it, filled out the paperwork, and turned it in for you."

"But you couldn't have filled it out," I shouted. "You didn't even know what happened!"

"Sure I did," Marty said calmly. "The police report was sitting in the fax machine when I came in this morning."

I slapped my forehead. I had forgotten that I had given the highway patrolman my fax number. But at the time I had thought the report would take days to be completed. Why, I asked myself, was I cursed with a hyper-efficient policeman? I slumped down in my chair and put my face in my hands.

"My location went a whole year without any of our customers having a serious accident, and then the manager of the store totals a $70,000 Cadillac."

"Hey, I didn't think about it that way," Marty said. "That's pretty funny."

I lifted my head and gave him a sour look. "Yeah, real funny," I said quietly, and then I continued with my voice getting louder and shriller with each word. "Why did you have to file the paperwork, Marty? Didn't you think I might want to do it? They could take away my company car. I might even lose my job!"

At first Marty seemed stunned by my outburst, but then he laid a solemn hand on my shoulder, and contorted his fat, red features into an absurdly lugubrious expression.

"Yeah, I'm afraid you're done for Walt," he said gravely. "You'll never work in the rental car business again." Then he started laughing so hard he had to sit down on my desk. "Nah!" Marty said after he had finally recovered his breath. "I've wrecked three cars, and they never did anything except make me start driving old, ratty, smoked up cars. The important thing is to report the accident right away, so they can file their insurance claim. I didn't know how long you might be out of the office, so I did you a favor. Take it from me; you're not losing your job or your car privileges. In fact, Ace will probably be tickled pink you're not filing a workman's comp claim. So just relax and pick out another car to drive. Just don't rub it in their faces by choosing the newest car on the lot as your replacement." He grinned at me and shuffled out the front door with his pickle bottle.

My face burned with embarrassment. Did Marty know I was driving the new Escalade? I felt foolish and relieved at the same time. Marty might not be the most enthusiastic employee in the Ace organization, but he had been working for them a long time and probably knew what he was talking about.

While Marty was out walking his cigar, I exchanged the keys of the new Cadillac Esplanade for an older, black Lincoln Town Car. Then I made another attempt to phone Leda. This time Himalia answered the phone, and she sounded even more ecstatically happy than normal.

"Hello, Himalia, this is Walt. Is Leda around?"

"Walt! It's so nice to hear your voice. No, I'm afraid Leda's not around. She drove off in her little red car. I hope she's going shopping, because she needs to find a dress for the wedding."

"Wedding?" I asked, suddenly feeling like I had been plunged headfirst into the drink again. "Leda's getting married?"

"Don't be silly, Walt. I'm the one getting married. I thought Leda might have mentioned it to you, but of course, I just found out last night. You remember Charlie Bolero? Well, he popped the question last night during our date, and then after I swooned in his arms, he drove me home and rushed off in the middle of the night to close down some business of his. He said he wanted to get rid of any unnecessary distractions before making me happy became his full-time job. Isn't that the silliest and most wonderfully romantic thing you ever heard of?"

"Er, uh, –" I thought it was silly and a little odd that Charlie hadn't mentioned his engagement to me. Had it slipped his mind, or was he leaving it up to Himalia to make the announcement in case she changed hers? "Yes, very. I'm sure you'll be very happy. Charlie's a great guy. I'll have to give him a call and congratulate him. By the way, could you give me Leda's cell phone number?"

"Oh, my dear, haven't you noticed? Leda never answers her cell phone. Oh, she carries one in her car because I make her, but she keeps it turned off. She thinks cell phones are an invasion of privacy. It drives me crazy. I can never get hold of her."

I empathized with Himalia's frustration. My parents had an "emergency phone" in their car, too. I couldn't even persuade Mom to call me on my cell phone because she thought it was too expensive. "Yeah. I have the same problem with my mom–"

"I would adore chatting with you all day, Walt," interrupted Himalia, "but I have a lot of web surfing to do. We want to have a cozy, intimate little wedding, with guests from our farm and some of our neighbors, and I need to find a string quartet or a five-piece orchestra that'll fit in your Uncle Vinny's restaurant. That's where I thought we'd book the wedding and the reception because it has that romantic Mediterranean thing going for it and, as you probably know, Charlie is of Greek extraction. I'll tell Leda you called, and if you happen to see her first, remind her she has some shopping to do."

After she rang off, I sat at my desk trying to process all the implications of the bombshell Himalia had so casually tossed in my lap. Charlie was Greek; he was going to marry Himalia; in Uncle Vinny's Restaurant; Leda didn't use cell phones; and she was out somewhere in her Mini Cooper. I knew all these new developments portended some ominous event in my near future; I just couldn't quite make out the shape of the approaching disaster.

"Hey, I'm back!"

I looked up to see Marty standing in front of me with his pickle jar.

"Look," Marty said, "you don't have to stay here all day. It's your day off. Go recreate or procreate. I have everything under control here. Just come back tomorrow and help me check in the weekenders like you usually do. I really appreciate you coming by on Sunday mornings. That's why I went out of my way to help you today."

I didn't have the heart to tell Marty that the real reason I helped him on Sundays was because I didn't want my regular customers pissed off by the indifferent service of a dissatisfied relief manager.

"Thanks, Marty, I'm always glad to help. See you tomorrow morning." I stood up and started to walk slowly out the door, already immersed in thought about Leda, Himalia, and Charlie.

"Oh, Walt, there was something I wanted to tell you."

I stopped at the door and turned to see what Marty wanted.

"Jason called me up Monday and asked if I had ever had any cars returned with a part switched or missing. I told him that I've had plenty of rentals come in with everything from tires to engines changed out. Then he asked me if I had ever rented to a guy named Charlie Bolero. When he asked me, the name didn't sound familiar, but I've been thinking about it and now I do remember a guy named Bolero that rented a Lincoln from me about a year ago. I think he said he was changing a boat motor out or something in the area, and he just needed a car for the day. I didn't see him arrive, but I know his customer picked him up the next morning because I heard them talking about how great the new engine sounded. After he left, I noticed something a little off about that Lincoln – the tires were cleaner than when they went out. I thought it was kind of odd, so I took a closer look and they did look a little more worn than before, not much, just a little. I mean, it's like they were changed, but the tires that were put back were nearly as good as the ones that were taken off. It didn't make sense to me, so I shrugged it off. He could've changed out the filters, the battery and other consumables, and I wouldn't have noticed because I didn't check them. Anyway, it might not mean anything, but you might mention it to Jason."

Chapter Twenty-Five

As I pulled away from Ace Car Rental, I saw Leda pulling in. When I honked my horn to get her attention, she made a rude gesture with her left hand and flew past me. I knew she was angry with me, but I thought this sort of behavior was just a bit over the top. I made a U-turn, drove back into the lot, and parked behind her. Leda jumped out of her car, then ran toward mine shouting and shaking her fist, but when I rolled down my window, her expression instantly changed from rage to joy.

"Oh, Walt, I'm so glad it's you. I thought you were Charlie!" she exclaimed and reached through the window to hug my neck.

"Why would you think that?"

"Because his big ugly car looks just like this one." She suddenly released me and stepped back, sparks of anger flashing in her eyes once more. "This isn't his car, is it?" Understanding suddenly dawned. Having taken Marty's advice to avoid selecting the newest car on the lot in place of the wrecked Escalade, I was driving a black Lincoln Town Car closely resembling Charlie's.

"Look around you, Leda," I said. "We rent Lincolns of every color, and we have at least a dozen black Town Cars like this one."

"Oh," Leda said. "What happened to your SUV?"

"Well, when I was driving back from Juno last night, I–"

"Oh, never mind," she said, cutting me off with an impatient wave of her hand. "Just park this ugly piece of crap and get in my car. I need to talk to you."

"But where are we going?"

"It's a surprise. Just hurry up."

I inwardly groaned. I hoped she hadn't arranged another little meeting with Dr. Norton and Chic. I also felt Leda should have displayed a little more curiosity about my missing Escalade. I was eager to talk to Leda, however, so I obediently parked the Lincoln in an empty spot next to the gate. As I climbed out of my car, Leda drove up and retracted the roof on her Mini. I stepped into the little car and we sped off. When I noticed we were taking the interstate, I raised a quizzical eyebrow at Leda.

"Oh, don't look so concerned," she said crossly. "We're not going far."

After we had driven along in silence for a couple of minutes, I decided it was up to me to get the conversation rolling, so I began to tell her about my accident again.

"You were asking about my SUV. Well, you're never going to believe what happened –"

"Look, Walt, I don't want to talk right now. Just lean back and enjoy the ride. Okay?"

I was hurt and confused. She asked me to ride with her because she said she needed to talk, but when I tried to talk to her, she bit my head off. I pressed up against the door on my side of the car, and moodily watched downtown Jupiter slide by. It was a beautiful day, very much like the previous Saturday, when I had caught my first intoxicating glimpse of Leda. Now I stole another look at her as she piloted the miniature red car through the afternoon freeway traffic. Her face was glowing, her hair was streaming in the wind, and her angry golden eyes were glowing in the sun. It didn't seem fair for Leda to look so breathtakingly beautiful while she was being so mean to me.

Leda pulled into valet parking at the Marriott, grabbed a garment bag from the back seat of the Mini Cooper, and jumped out without waiting for an attendant to take her keys. I hurried over to the valet booth, tipped the clerk, and got a receipt. Then I ran into the hotel's lobby just in time to catch sight of Leda going into an elevator. I put on a burst of speed, and just barely managed to slip through the doors before they closed.

"Here, take these. I need to fix my hair," Leda said, thrusting the garment bag at me.

Still panting from my dash through the lobby, I took hold of the plastic hooks protruding from the top of the garment bag, and gave voice to the frustration I was feeling.

"What's your hurry?"

Leda glared at me for a couple of seconds, and then suddenly burst into tears. Feeling like the worst kind of cad, I swept Leda's limp, sobbing form into my free arm. Leda pushed her damp face into my shirt, and her sobbing gradually subsided as I rocked her in my arms and repeatedly apologized for snapping at her.

The elevator door opened on the concierge floor. After taking a moment to brush her hair and repair her makeup, Leda took the garment bag from me, grabbed my hand, led me along the hallway to the door of a large suite, and rang the bell. After a couple of moments, a tall girl dressed in a pink dressing gown and wearing curlers in her hair opened the door.

"Leda!" she complained, "you didn't say you were bringing a man over."

"Surprise!" Leda said, and brushed by the girl, towing me along behind her.

The room I was pulled into contained all the amenities of a first class luxury suite: a giant plasma screen television, a full-sized kitchen, a fully stocked bar and half a dozen beautiful, half-naked women. I had dreamed of situations like this, but under the current circumstances, I was finding the reality a little awkward. I wanted to look, but I didn't want Leda to see me looking, so I chose the safer course of not looking at the girls at all. While Leda and the other girls were embroiled in an argument over whether she should have brought a man with her, I pretended to admire the flat screen television, and evinced an intense but completely synthetic interest in the décor. In desperation, I finally retreated to the bathroom to admire its sumptuous appointments.

When I came out ten minutes later, I was relieved to find the girls had covered up. There appeared to be a private conversation in progress, so I headed towards a stool at the breakfast bar. Leda apparently had other ideas, and patted an empty spot next to her on the large, semicircular leather sectional she and her friends were sitting on. As I gingerly lowered myself between Leda and a bouncy looking girl in a kimono, I was treated to a panoramic display of seven seductively clad women. Conscious of Leda's gaze, I smiled nervously and endeavored to fade into the upholstery.

This gathering was obviously some kind of reunion, and I couldn't help wondering why Leda had dragged me along. When she said she wanted to talk to me, I had expected her to drive me to some secluded spot, tearfully announce her mother's engagement, and try to browbeat me into helping her sabotage Charlie.

The sound of loud laughter interrupted my thoughts, and I suddenly realized that Leda was describing in embarrassing detail my reaction to the live cover session I had endured at Elara Downs the previous afternoon.

"He was so cute. I think he kept his eyes closed through the entire thing," Leda was saying.

"Leda!" I interjected, sounding louder than I meant to, "I was feeling ill, remember? I told you I hadn't been getting enough sleep–"

"Oh, don't be mad," said the kimono-clad girl next to me. "Leda was paying you a compliment. We all think you're just wonderful. Don't we, girls?"

All the women voiced their agreement. The girl in the pink bathrobe and curlers added to the kimono girl's remarks.

"While you were in the bathroom, we were all talking about what a gentleman you are, Walt," she said, looking at me with that steady gaze people use when they want to demonstrate how sincere they are being. "It's rare to find a man who averts his eyes when he's pulled into a room full of half-naked girls."

"Yeah," said the kimono-clad girl, "I can see why Leda likes you. You're cute and polite."

"I'm sorry, Walt. I didn't mean to embarrass you," Leda said, squeezing my leg. "We were just discussing a friend of ours who accidentally became engaged to her first cousin, and I said it was a shame she wasn't a horse. Nobody got the joke, so I had to explain how we intentionally inbreed thoroughbred horses at Elara Downs."

"Yeah," chimed in kimono girl. "Then I asked Leda if she had ever watched them actually breed the horses, and Leda started describing the live horse sex session you two watched yesterday. She wasn't making fun of you; she was just pointing out how you're a gentleman around horses, too."

This statement initiated a fresh round of laughter, and I felt my embarrassment deepening still further. "Yes, Walt," said the girl in curlers, "you obviously have a highly developed sense of decorum and we think that's really admirable."

"Well, if you think I'm so wonderful, why are you laughing?" I snapped.

The girl wearing the curlers gave me a disappointed stare, stood up, came over and squashed in between me and the bouncy girl in the kimono, causing her and the other girls to shift towards their end of the couch. She took my hand in hers and turned on her sincere gaze.

"Because it's funny, Walt," she said patiently. "It's only natural for friends to laugh at each other's foibles. Laughter is only mean-spirited when mean people are doing the laughing. You don't think we're mean people – do you, Walt?"

"No," I finally mumbled, not really certain what I thought anymore.

"Good, because when you're dating Leda, you're dating all of us." She waved one hand to indicate the other girls sitting on the couch. "We're like sisters, Walt. We all shared the same dorm at college, and we all had absentee parents who were either too busy making money or traveling around the world. So we decided to form our own little family. My name is Maia. The rest of the girls call me Mother because I'm the oldest. Leda's the youngest, and we like to think of her as our little golden child. You might know Alice." She released my hand and patted the knee of the kimono-clad girl next to her. "She lives here in Jupiter."

"Well, actually, I live in Kale with my dad," Alice said, "but I always tell everyone I live in Jupiter because no one knows where Kale is."

I knew where Kale was, but I wouldn't be likely to know Alice. Kale was an exclusive gated community on the outskirts of Jupiter with its own school, country club, and shopping center. Kale residents often visited Jupiter to shop and dine at some of the stores and restaurants, but only gardeners, air conditioning repair men, and the cream of Jupiter's society saw the inside of Kale. This didn't amount to a lot of people since Jupiter's society was principally made up of farmers, small town merchants, and factory workers who thought church picnics, PTA meetings, and basketball games comprised the highlights of the social calendar.

"So, Walt, do you think our friend should tell her fiancé that she's his cousin?" Maia asked. She had casually tossed me this hot potato after I had been introduced to the last girl on the couch, a redhead named Sara who was working on her MBA at Brown. Sara was the fourth member of Leda's group in an Ivy-league graduate program. Maia had deferred her higher education while exploring the world of high finance as an intern at a prestigious Wall Street firm, and Alice was working in her father's pharmaceutical company, leaving Leda as the only member of the group who hadn't chosen a career thus far.

I could see the expectant faces of Maia and the rest of Leda's half-dressed surrogate family peering at me from all around the semi-circular couch, waiting for me to answer Maia's question.

"I couldn't say. I mean, personally, I generally agree with the social and religious conventions prohibiting marriage between close relatives and of course there are negative biological consequences involved—"

Maia stopped me by reaching over and taking my hand again, this time clasping it between both of her hands. This constant hand-holding tendency of Maia's was beginning to wear on me. In the first place, it seemed like too intimate a gesture for an attractive girl I had just met to be making, especially in front of my girlfriend, and secondly, once my hand was ensnared in this tender trap, I was unable to think of a polite way to withdraw it.

"Walt, I wasn't asking for a sociological lecture on the incest taboo. I just wanted to know, based on your unique perspective, if you thought she should tell her fiancé or not."

It took a moment to process the implications of Maia's statement and then, once I understood that Maia was referring to my special status as the product of an anonymous sperm donor, I looked accusingly at Leda only to find her boldly returning my gaze.

Maia drew my attention back to her by squeezing the hand that she was holding captive between her own. "Of course she told us about your situation, Walt. We're her family."

My feeling of betrayal quickly evaporated as I realized I had shared many personal details about Leda with Jason. I took a breath and endeavored to answer the question again.

"Oh. Well, I guess if I found myself engaged to my first cousin, I'd have to tell her. I mean – she would have the right to know something like that, wouldn't she?"

"But, what if the, uh, wedding preparations were in a really advanced state?" asked Alice, leaning around Maia for an unobstructed view of me.

"That would just make the need to tell my fiancé about the situation more urgent," I answered, thinking Alice looked a little less bouncy than before.

"But what if things had gone too far?" Alice insisted. "What if the wedding ceremony *had* to proceed?"

I was unable to imagine why a wedding couldn't be canceled unless their friend was pregnant and opposed to abortion. But if that were the case, why was Alice being so oblique about it? The moment I asked myself this question, it struck me that the 'friend' they were discussing might be present, and Alice was trying to be delicate in order to spare her feelings.

"In that case, I'd have to think about when and how I told my fiancé about our family ties. I'd still have to tell her, but I might wait for a time and place that would minimize the trauma to her and, uh, other family members."

Alice nodded vaguely and settled back in her place with a thoughtful expression. Maia smiled at me and released my sweaty hand after giving it a final squeeze.

"That's what I was saying while you were admiring our bathroom, Walt," Maia said. "There are a few things in life that can't or shouldn't be undone, but ceremonies and paperwork can always be modified or reversed."

Leda patted my knee, beaming up at me like a proud parent. Now I discovered my curiosity had been piqued, and since my contribution to the discussion had been so well received, I felt that I could risk asking a question.

"Maia, how did your friend find out her fiancé was her cousin?"

"Well, Walt, Alice knows the story much better than I, so I'll let her tell it."

Maia and Alice briefly engaged in one of those silent exchanges of lip-contortions, head shakes, and obscure gestures women use when they don't want men in the room to know what they're saying. Then Alice turned to me with a reluctant air and recounted how their friend, who was from a wealthy family, had recently discovered that the young stockbroker she was engaged to was adopted. After learning he had been unsuccessful in tracing his birth parents, she decided to make finding them her wedding gift to her fiancé. So, utilizing financial resources a young stockbroker could only dream of accessing, she hired an exclusive firm that handled these kinds of inquiries for her class of clientele.

They had begun with the adoption agency and were able to discover the name of the young man's mother right away. She had used a go-between to give up her child to the adoption agency, and that intermediary had since passed away, but this obstacle, which had proven an impassable roadblock for her fiancé, had readily yielded to the investigative power of the inquiry agency.

Alice said her friend could have stopped with this achievement and presented her betrothed with the priceless gift of a long lost mother, but she wanted to find his birth father as well. So she authorized her inquiry agency to fly a team out to California in order to interview her fiancé's birth mom who, with a little financial incentive, had provided several possible candidates for the father.

With the help of her fiancé's hairbrush and some DNA samples surreptitiously collected from the various birth father candidates, Alice's friend finally got what she wanted. When she opened the agents' report and scanned the information, she was shocked to find that her fiancé's birth father was also one of her own uncles on her mother's side.

"Uh," I said to Alice, "you know, after hearing your friend's story, I think I might have been wrong when I suggested she should wait to tell her fiancé about her discovery."

"No, Walt," Maia interrupted, touching my arm. "Your first response was the correct one. We wanted your opinion because you know in your heart this nightmare could happen to you. And your mind is a moral mind, Walt. It values life over society's conventions, and that's a good thing."

There was something about her expression, and the way her fingers were resting lightly on my arm, almost like that small gesture of restraint adults use to silence a talkative child in a public forum, that gave me the impression that Maia considered the subject closed.

But I was worried about the consequences of my remarks, and now I was fearful about the way Alice's friend would construe my lightly-considered opinions on such a serious, life-changing topic. So, ignoring the frown that suddenly appeared on Maia's face and the tightening fingers on my arm, I sought to clarify my earlier comments.

"Alice, if you do mention my remarks to your friend, I want her to know that what I might do in similar circumstances is only idle speculation on my part. I don't really know what I would do, and I don't think anyone else can tell her the best course of action either. This is an extremely personal issue. She should follow her own heart, and not the advice of other people."

Alice stared at me for a couple of moments, then suddenly jumped up and ran from the room, followed shortly by three of the other girls who obviously wanted to comfort her.

I sat in stunned silence. Maia was glaring at me with a mixture of disgust and amazement. I was reluctant to turn and see how Leda and the one other girl who had remained were reacting to this development, and before I could steel myself to look, Maia gave voice to her disappointment.

"Walt, haven't you ever heard the expression 'leave well enough alone?' We've been talking to Alice about her situation for hours before Leda showed up with you and her problem. I only asked for your input because Alice requested it when she heard about your background. You seem like an intelligent and thoughtful young man, and I assumed you understood from the way I was asking that I wanted you to give Alice some support for a difficult decision she had already made. There was absolutely no call for you to start moralizing. Just who the hell do you think you are anyway?"

"Aw, give him a break, Maia," Leda said. "He didn't know Alice was the 'friend' we were talking about."

"A child would've known it, Leda. You shouldn't have brought him along in the first place."

"I had to bring him, Maia. We already discussed this, and I don't want to go into it again in front of Walt. Alice asked for his opinion and he gave it to her – his honest, unvarnished opinion. It's her own fault if she can't handle it."

During this exchange, I was cringing between the warring parties like a canary in a catfight, and I noticed that Sara, the only other girl still in the room, was staring down at her hands in an attempt to ignore the fight.

I was upset about Alice, hurt by what I thought was unfair criticism on Maia's part, and annoyed with Leda for putting me in this position. On that point I agreed with Maia. I didn't see why Leda had felt compelled to bring me with her to the hotel. I suddenly felt very tired. I guessed I still hadn't caught up on my sleep yet, and it was beginning to look like the sore muscles and bruises from the car wreck were about to get some competition from a throbbing headache. I took off my glasses, rested my face in my hands, and let the argument rage on around me.

Chapter Twenty-Six

"Okay, you're right," I heard Maia say to Leda. "I'm so used to you and the rest of my girls being able to read my mind that I just expect everyone to. I guess Walt here, like most members of his sex, is simply used to a more direct form of communication. Besides, this might turn out for the best. I think Alice needed a catharsis to help focus her mind, and when she recovers, I'm confident she'll choose what's best for herself and her – well, for herself. Come on, let's make up."

I felt the sudden warmth and pressure of two warm bodies press against me as the two women embraced each other over the top of my huddled form.

Well, I think we've finished with Alice's problem for the time being," Maia said. "I guess we can tackle your little predicament now."

"I don't want to do mine without the rest of the family present," Leda said.

"Too bad. They're going to be busy calming Alice down for the next twenty minutes, and we're running out of time. We're supposed to be getting ready to go out to dinner, and then some of us have early flights we need to catch in order to get back to the real world. Wake up, Walt. We need your help on this one, too."

I straightened up, put on my glasses, and looked suspiciously at Maia and Leda's smiling faces. I could tell by their expressions that I had been right. Leda had arranged another ambush, much like the one at my uncle's restaurant the day before. But this time, thanks to my conversation with Himalia, I had prior warning, and I was ready for her.

"You girls can discuss this one without me," I said.

"Don't be sore, Walt," Maia said. "I was wrong to jump down your throat, and I apologize. Come on, we really need your help."

"I'm not sore, Maia. I just don't think I can help."

"How do you know you can't help?" demanded Leda. "We haven't told you anything about my problem yet."

"I know because I talked to your mother earlier today when I was looking for you, and she told me about her engagement. I'm sorry you don't like Charlie, but I won't help you sabotage his relationship with your mother. "

Leda stared at me, her face flushing redder than I had ever seen it before. Then she suddenly drew back her left hand and punched me on the arm. The blow stung. Leda could really punch.

"You jerk!" Leda shouted, punching me again. "Why didn't you say something when you first saw me?"

"Hey! Stop that." I said, my voice rising with the frustration I was feeling. "You never gave me a chance to tell you, Leda. You just drove up in your little red car and started ordering me around. You wouldn't even listen when I tried to tell you about the wreck I was in last night."

"Wreck? You were in a wreck?" Leda cried, and punched me on the arm again. "Why didn't you call me, you jerk?"

Then Leda grabbed me by the neck and started sobbing on my shoulder.

"You have to make allowances for Leda," Maia said, smiling in a motherly way at the tender display. "She's been a little overwrought lately."

Maia looked on with approval as I sought to comfort Leda by repeating the process that had been so successful in the elevator. As Leda's sobbing subsided, I began to recount the events of the previous night. When I started describing the harrowing details of waking up with my head underwater and the ensuing struggle to escape, Sara, who had been sitting quietly on the far end of the couch, slid over next to Leda with the rapt expression of a child listening to a ghost story.

When I got to the part of my account where Charlie drove up in his black Lincoln, Leda's eyes grew stormy again.

"What the hell was he doing there?" Leda demanded. "Did you call him to help you?"

"No, Leda, my cell phone was still under water at the time. That's why I couldn't call you. Jody found it for me today when she cleaned out the wrecked Escalade, but I think it's probably ruined. Charlie just happened to be driving past on the way to his warehouse, and he recognized my car."

"I thought you said my mother told you about her engagement," snapped Leda. "Did you say that because you were afraid of telling me you heard about it from Charlie?"

"There you go jumping to conclusions again," I complained and started to tell her I had never lied to her and never would, but then remembered that I had inaugurated our relationship with a lie and had kept up the pretense for several days. "Charlie didn't happen to mention it. Maybe he didn't think it was any of my business, I don't know, but he spent most of the trip telling me stories about his college days."

"I bet he was a real scumbag when he was in college," Leda said.

"Based on the story he told me, I'd say he was a typical fraternity type."

"That's what I thought," Leda said with satisfaction.

"Well, Walt," Maia said, "I bet you're black and blue under your clothes and could do with a little rest, but unfortunately, we're on a tight schedule, and I promised we'd help Leda decide what to do about her mother's wedding."

"Why should she do anything?" I was amazed to hear myself asking and reflexively attempted to shield my sore arm from renewed attack.

"Because I don't want a creep like Charlie for a stepfather!" yelled Leda, and started to draw back her fist again, but this time her arm was stayed by a sharp command from Maia before the vengeful blow could fall.

"Stop it, Sunshine!" Maia said. Leda lowered her fist and glared at me, her eyes boiling like twin stars on the verge of going supernova. Maia regarded me with a judicious eye. "I thought you didn't want to be involved in this discussion, Walt."

"I'm sorry, Leda," I said mournfully. "I'm sorry. It was stupid of me to say anything. I'm sorry, and I apologize. This is strictly a family problem, and that's why I shouldn't be involved. In fact, I think it might be better if I just step outside while you and Maia discuss it. Don't hurry. I'll just go down and wait in the lounge."

I stood up to go, but found my exit blocked by one of Maia's shapely legs.

"Sit down, Walt."

"But, I think it's probably better if–" I wavered.

"Sit!" Maia commanded, and, much to my own surprise, I sat.

"Oh, let him go, Maia. He doesn't want to help. Go on, Walt, get the hell out. I wouldn't want you to compromise your precious ethics," Leda said bitterly.

"That will be enough from you, Sunshine," Maia snapped. "Sara, take Leda back to check on Alice. I need to have a few words with her boyfriend."

"He's not my boyfriend. I hate him!" Leda shouted, but allowed Sara to escort her from the room, leaving me shaken and apprehensive but waiting obediently on the couch.

"Now, let's sort this thing out, shall we?" Maia said, as she turned back to me. I prepared for the impending interview by shoving my hands under the cushions. This turned out to be a needless precaution, however, because Maia didn't attempt to hold my hand. In a sudden change of tactics, she simply leaned back and crossed her arms.

"Walt, just how long have you known Charlie?"

"About as long as I've known Leda–I met them both on the same day and–"

"So you've known Charlie for about a week," Maia said.

"Uh, yeah, but it seems like a lot longer–"

"A week isn't long enough to know anything about a man, Walt. Your feelings about him are just that, feelings. When you first met him, you were convinced he was your father. You told Leda you didn't like him or trust him, and then less than a day later you were seen joking with him at her mother's horse farm. Your feelings about Charlie changed not because of anything you found out about him, but because he gave you or appeared to give you his full cooperation, and you felt guilty about initially distrusting him."

"Well, that's not true, or not entirely true, anyway. He volunteered to take a parental DNA test after I had already found out I'd been wrong about him all along."

Maia let out a sigh and sadly shook her head. "Walt, you're still not confident about Charlie's innocence. I can hear it in your voice. Deep down, you still have grave reservations about him you won't admit to, because you feel guilty about prejudging him. When a confidence man wants to establish trust in a mark, he often encourages false suspicions about himself, and then plants evidence where the mark is sure to find it, proving his innocence. It's just a trick to gain your confidence. That's why they're called confidence men."

"But that's not what happened in this case."

"No, in this case, you conveniently provided Charlie with something he could easily disprove, and once he discovered your connection to Leda and Himalia, he went out of his way to disprove it. It's paid dividends, too, because now you're one of his biggest supporters. You only met Charlie a week ago, and yet you dismiss Leda's suspicions out of hand even though she, Dean and the people you had dinner with last night have known Charlie far longer than you. Doesn't that sound a little imprudent to you?"

"Yeah, I guess." I nodded wearily. "Look, I'm tired and frankly I don't see the point of arguing. It doesn't matter anyway. Leda hates me, and I'm probably never going to see her, her mother, or Charlie again, so why don't you just let me go home and get some sleep?"

"Leda doesn't hate you, Walt. She's just upset by your lack of confidence in her. You don't know her like I do. She's a marvelous judge of character, and if she says Charlie's a fiend in human shape, then he's the devil incarnate. You know, she told us you gave her a false name when you first met. She said it was obvious you were lying about something, but it was equally apparent to her that deceit didn't come easily to you, and it was this characteristic above all others that caught her interest that day.

"Despite what she said, she respects you for standing up for your principles. She just thinks you should give a little more credence to her assessment of Charlie's character. I like you, Walt, and I think I might be able to fix things up between you and Leda, if I knew a little more about your relationship with Charlie."

I took my glasses off and rubbed my eyes. "What do you want, Maia?"

"You could start by telling me about whatever this thing is that still bothers you."

Maia was right. I had been harboring doubts about Charlie since Marty told me about the rental in Buffalo. I had been thinking about Charlie's preference for Lincoln Town Cars. Not only did he own one, he also rented them. This wasn't too strange on the face of it, but it had been my experience that most customers rented a different vehicle from the one they had at home, just to try something different.

So, after asking for and receiving assurances from Maia that what I told her would go no further, I related the two incidents where apparent parts switching had been detected on Town Cars that Charlie had rented. I also pointed out how ridiculous it would be for someone with the kind of money Charlie had to risk going to jail simply to exchange one set of used tires for a slightly less used set of tires.

This didn't seem to bother Maia, because, like Jason, she thought Charlie might be doing it just to keep in practice. But she also praised me for not assuming Charlie's guilt simply on the basis of coincidence and insubstantial circumstantial evidence.

By degrees, and with some additional coaxing, along with repeated assurances that she would hold anything I told her in the strictest confidence, I told Maia the story of how Jason and I had come to select Charlie as our prime suspect and how frustrated I had been after my first confrontation with him on Charlie's front porch. I told her about watching Charlie work on the boat motors, and Jason's theory about where he got them and what he did with them. I recounted the chance meeting with Charlie at my Uncle Vinny's restaurant, and how I later watched Charlie transfer frozen horse sperm in his garage. I recounted the story Charlie had told me in his study at Cobb's Station, and how I had gotten caught looking at Charlie's papers on his desk. I emphasized how the boat motor company manuals and franchise information that I had found on Charlie's desk had changed my mind about Charlie's character, before Charlie made the offer to take the parental DNA test. I described the artificial insemination of Frisco Gal, and Jason's theory about how Charlie might have stolen Running Fool's sperm. Then I stressed the point that I had discovered perfectly logical and legitimate reasons for all of Charlie's actions, reasons which had made Jason's theories and my own suspicions seem silly in retrospect.

"Okay, Walt, I think I understand how you feel now," Maia said, after I had finished telling my story. "I don't think you can help Leda expose Charlie or sabotage his wedding. You felt free to spy on him when you thought he wasn't being honest with you. You rummaged through his papers when you thought he was a crook, but it's not in your nature to spy on him, now that you think he's an honest man. Even if Leda convinced you to cooperate, it would backfire, because your conscience would be sure to give you away. You're just the kind of person who gets caught when you try to tell a lie or deceive someone. It's a rare quality to find in a man these days and Leda's lucky to have found you. That's what I'm going to go tell her right now. Why don't you wait until she comes out? I'm certain she'll want to see you before you leave."

"Well, actually, I sort of have to wait. Leda brought me over here in her car."

"Oh. That wasn't very farsighted on Leda's part. You can't come to dinner with us. It's a family function. We need to get you a taxi. Why don't you just relax? I'll call the concierge."

She patted my leg, stood up, and went to join the other girls. I got up from the couch and wandered around the room examining the things I had only pretended to look at earlier.

I wondered if Leda would really want to see me before she went out. She had seemed hurt and angry when she left the room. For that matter, I thought, even if she did come back into the room, ready to forgive and forget, I wasn't sure if *I* wanted to continue seeing Leda if she was going to denounce me every time I wasn't in total agreement with her. It was time I grew a backbone, I told myself, and perhaps I should let her know that if we were going to continue seeing each other, she would have to moderate her attitude. "Yes, sir," I said out loud, "I'm going to lay down the law!"

"Hi, Walt."

I turned and was confronted by a shining vision in white. Leda was dressed in a simple white gown that fastened across her bare right shoulder with a gold clasp. She had tied up her hair, revealing in the process a long, graceful neck that, in some mysterious way, spoke to my primal depths. I was dimly aware that I should say something, but my heart was banging away like a kettledrum, I was having trouble breathing, and incredibly, a soft, white mist seemed to have risen around Leda. Leda smiled and began to stride like a goddess in her firmament through the translucent swirls and whorls of what looked to me like a rapidly growing fog. By the time she reached me, the billowing clouds around Leda were so dense I could just make out the golden glow of her eyes and the dim shadow of her hand as she reached up to remove my glasses.

"That's funny, your glasses are all fogged up," Leda marveled. She pulled my shirttail out and used it to polish my glasses before gently replacing them on my face. "Do you like my gown? We're all wearing them tonight. It's sort of like our official uniform."

I nodded vaguely, but I wasn't looking at her dress. My eyes were too busy tracing the magical curve of Leda's neck where it merged into her naked shoulder. Here I found my attention drawn to the little gold clasp that secured the gown's single strap. It was a cunning device of Cyrillic characters inscribed under a group of classic feminine profiles. I reached out a tentative finger to touch the proud beauties sculpted across the top of the clasp, but Leda intercepted my hand and pressed it to her warm skin.

"That's just our school pin," she murmured. "I'll let you take a closer look at it later, but now I have to go out with my friends. I'm sorry I yelled at you. I know I've been demanding an awful lot for someone you barely know, but I want you to hold on tight and try to be patient with me just a little while longer. Maia and all my friends were impressed with you, and that's important to me because they're my second family. Now, I want you to take my keys and drive my car back to your apartment, and when we're all done here, I'll have them drop me off and we can – visit," Leda said, moving my hand into warmer regions.

A thrill ran through me at the thought of Leda coming to my apartment. The sterner side of me tried to point out that this was a good opportunity to lay down the law about her imperious attitude, but that side of me was knocked down and pummeled into silence by all of my other sides. I told Leda where the Ganymede Apartments were, gave her my apartment number, and let her escort me to the suite's front door. As Leda was giving me a goodbye smooch, I became aware of observers and turned to see a very regal looking Maia, accompanied by what looked like a host of young goddesses attired in their shining white raiment. Maia's glossy black hair gushed fourth in a fountain of dark ringlets through a small gold hoop that had replaced her hair curlers, and she had traded her pink dressing gown for one made of a flowing, diaphanous material that was eye-searing white in places where it billowed, and disturbingly transparent where it clung.

All of the girls had put their hair up in various ways, and though some of their gowns draped over one shoulder, and others over both, and some were gathered, while others fell away in smooth flowing folds, all of them featured the small gold clasp.

"Whoops," Leda said patting my transfixed, and yes, goggling face, "time to go!" but before she could shove me out the door, one of the beautiful young goddesses ran up and hugged my neck. She held me tightly in her embrace for a long moment, and it wasn't until after she had released me and rejoined the others that I realized that she was Alice.

Chapter Twenty-Seven

The little red Mini Cooper looked like a giant red beetle invading the cole crops of Jupiter's farming community as it zipped along the blacktop on its way to our rutabaga farm. Only a week before, these rolling fields of broccoli, cabbage, and cauliflower, the foot soldiers of the vegetable world, wouldn't have rated a second glance from me. But on this morning, the endless ranks of squat, unpretentious plants, marching in their tens of thousands, up and down the hills and dales of my childhood countryside filled me with a deep sense of pride. I found myself pointing out and commenting on the various varieties of kale, collards, and cabbage, like a Hollywood tour guide holding forth on the homes and personal habits of movie stars.

Comfortably sprawled in the Mini's passenger seat, with her bare legs propped up on the dashboard and her golden hair, which she had knotted into two long pigtails, flailing in the wind, Leda seemed to be enduring this agricultural lecture with remarkably good humor. She even asked questions about the different colors and conformations of the plants and encouraged me to go into greater detail about the harvesting and transport of leafy produce.

During all this happy exposition, I kept stealing looks at my comely passenger, who had prepared for this bucolic expedition by donning blue jean cutoffs and a gingham blouse knotted high above her midriff like Mary Ann on Gilligan's Island. Leda radiated the kind of wholesomeness that started forest fires. It was as if the professor had created a hybrid of Ginger and Mary Ann. And I was bringing her home to meet my parents – that is, to properly meet them, in circumstances that didn't involve identity fraud, flaming sponge cake, and wrestling on the floor with my girlfriend's underdressed and oversexed mother.

Adding to my pleasure in this Sunday morning outing was the fact that Leda herself had suggested it. In fact, she had insisted on it after learning I had neglected to tell my mother about my car accident. What with one thing and another, I hadn't talked to my mom for nearly two days, and I hadn't been surprised to find another one of her breathless, run-on sentence, conscience-pricking messages waiting on my answering machine when I got home Saturday evening.

"Hi honey, I hadn't heard from you since Thursday and I was just wondering if you had gotten any results from that test or if you had begun another search for your, ah – donor and I wanted to know if this was the weekend you have off and if it is, if you would like to come out tomorrow for Sunday dinner or, if you're up early enough, meet me at Mass, because God knows how long it's been since you've been, but I'd love to see you either way so, oh . . . If you do come, could you drop by Maggio's and pick up a flat of fresh strawberries and a box of whipping cream, the heavy kind not that light stuff, because since you didn't get any the other night, I'm baking you a sponge cake!"

The mention of sponge cake had made me shiver, though I did want to have Sunday dinner with my parents. I hadn't seen them since the embarrassing events at my uncle's restaurant Tuesday evening, and a family dinner in Mom's farmhouse kitchen would go a long way toward rehabilitating my image as a sane and loving son. But I didn't return her call, because I wasn't certain what I would be doing on Sunday.

Leda's parting kiss at the door of the luxury suite had been full of promise, but her words, in my view, had been vague and open to interpretation. I had driven her red Mini Cooper to my apartment as she had suggested, but I wasn't clear on Leda's plans for the balance of the evening. The way Leda had whispered the word 'visit' at the door of the Marriott suite and the fact that she had sent me home in her car seemed to suggest a very passionate evening in store for me, but after spending a couple of frenetic hours prepping my apartment I had begun to experience doubts.

In the midst of my preparations, it had suddenly occurred to me that Leda might have been using the word 'visit' in its literal sense. Perhaps she only wanted to see where I lived, meet my cat, see what kinds of books I had, have a nice long chat and try to hash out the differences that had come between us.

Becoming increasingly agitated with each passing minute, I had asked myself what Leda would think if she walked through my door to find my overhead lights turned off and my table lamps turned to their lowest setting? This thought had caused me to rush around the apartment flipping on the overhead fixtures and turning up my table lamps to their full, 150-watt settings. Io, who had curled herself into a comfortable ball of calico fur on one end of the couch, had leapt up, squinted reproachfully at me, and stalked indignantly from the room.

With all the lights on, the tray of fruit and cheese I had laid out on the coffee table along with a bottle of Chardonnay suddenly seemed obscenely suggestive. The wine as well as the fruit tray had been Jason's suggestion. I had stopped by Ace on my way home to help Marty close up and found that Jason had dropped by for the same reason. I took the opportunity to tell him about Himalia and Charlie's engagement, Leda's sudden reappearance, and some of what had happened at the Marriott.

When Jason heard about Leda's impending visit, he had insisted that I go home. He also insisted on helping Marty close up the next day. Jason assured me that he didn't have any plans for Sunday other than watching a couple of documentaries on the science channel which he could easily TiVo to watch later. We chatted about the evening in store for me as we walked out to the parking lot, and Jason was grinning from ear to ear as I pulled away in Leda's little red car.

I grabbed the fruit tray along with the bottle of Chardonnay I had purchased to accompany it and hurried off to the kitchen to hide the evidence. I was shoving them into my refrigerator when I heard my stereo system change to a new DVD and the mellow voice of Barry White softly crooning, "You're the first, the last, my everything." I nearly tripped over my coffee table in my rush to get to the stereo.

I stabbed repeatedly at the eject button on my DVD changer until the carousel holding the recordings finally slid out of the player, then I began yanking DVDs out of the changing mechanism. The DVD changer on my stereo held a hundred DVDs and I was appalled to find I had loaded the first twenty positions with a veritable orgy of sexually suggestive titles like Je T'aime–Moi Non Plus, Try a Little Tenderness, Start Me Up, and Soul Provider.

I began shuffling through the rest of my collection for replacements. Incredibly, nearly every piece of music I owned seemed to have something to do with love or sex. After frantically thumbing through my recordings, I did find a couple of albums that appeared to be about drugs, death, and the futility of existence, but I thought that might be going too far in the other direction. Fortunately, Leda saved me from my quandary by calling up to cancel her visit.

"Hello?"

"Hi. I guess you've been wondering what happened to me."

"Oh! Hi, Leda." I tried to sound casual. "No, not really, I mean, I know you and your friends had a lot to talk over. I've just been, you know, sprucing up my apartment so you wouldn't be too shocked when you saw it."

"Well, Walt, I know I said I was coming over, but Alice and I just now got back from seeing our friends off at the airport, and I was wondering if it would be okay if I put off our visit until tomorrow. I'm kind of beat, and since this suite is already paid for, Alice and I thought we might as well spend the night."

"Oh! Sure!" I said, feeling unexpectedly relieved by the news. I didn't know why, but I was glad I didn't have to deal with the possibility of an amorous encounter with Leda in my apartment. I hoped I didn't sound too happy about her not coming over, and decided to amend my response. "I mean – if you're tired, you really shouldn't be driving. Look at what happened to me."

"Yeah, Walt, that's a good point, though I hadn't really been planning on driving home tonight."

"Oh." At these words, a warm glow suffused my body, and I wondered if she was implying that she had meant to stay the night if she had come over. Just in case this wasn't what she was saying, I decided to place another interpretation on it to demonstrate I wasn't making any assumptions about her intentions. "Uh–right. I forgot. I have your car."

"Maybe we could have lunch tomorrow if you don't have other plans."

"No. I mean I don't have any other plans. My mother wanted me to come over for lunch, but I wasn't going to go if you were in town."

"Oh, well, I guess you better have lunch with your mom then. She probably wants to make sure you weren't hurt in that wreck."

"No, that's okay, I can have dinner with you. My mom invites me to lunch every Sunday. She doesn't even know about my accident yet."

"You mean you didn't tell your mother that you almost drowned in a ditch either? You idiot! Women have instincts, Walt. We know when bad things happen. It makes things worse when you don't tell us about it. I want you to come pick me up tomorrow morning, and then we're going to drive to your mom's place and relieve that poor woman's mind."

I happily agreed to this proposition. After we finished our conversation, I set my alarm for 6 AM so I could call Mom before she left for church in the morning and let her know I was bringing a guest to Sunday dinner.

Mom appeared at the back door when Leda and I pulled into the gravel parking lot behind my parent's farmhouse. Before I could turn off the engine, Leda had jumped out of the Mini Cooper and run to meet my mother. The two embraced as if they had known one another for years. It wasn't the first time I had seen my mother hug someone she barely knew, but I was always baffled by this easy affinity women seemed to have for each other. I felt that the sensible reserve most men practiced in their relationships was more appropriate for everyday wear, and would never have considered embracing a girlfriend's father no matter how long I had known him.

I retrieved the flat of strawberries along with the box of whipping cream from the back seat, and was about to follow Leda and Mom into the house when my father hailed me. I turned to see him, dressed in his working uniform of kaki pants and red plaid woolen shirt, waving for me to join him in the barn. Somewhat apprehensive about my mother and Leda being out of earshot in the kitchen, I hesitated for a moment and then, carrying the flat of strawberries with the box of cream balanced on top, walked across the gravel yard to the tractor-barn/farm office to see what my father wanted.

When I reached the barn, I found that he had gone into his office and sat down in his big, oak swivel chair. My father waved at a metal folding chair next to the desk. I set my burden down on the desk, reversed the chair, straddled the seat, and sat with my arms akimbo across the chair's back.

I liked this office. Diesel fumes, rutabaga dust, and thirty-five years of honest sweat permeated the air. The walls were covered with fertilizer charts, notices from the agricultural extension, calendars from pesticide companies, and newspaper clippings about the giant rutabagas Dad occasionally found in his fields. To me, the office was a memorial to the man who worked in it and a tribute to the one institution that, in Thomas Jefferson's opinion, best exemplified the spirit of the American republic.

Dad's face had been burnished by the elements into a creased leather mask ill suited to the display of emotion, but on this occasion the taut muscles of a worried man showed through the weather- worn exterior.

"What's wrong, Dad?" I asked. "Aren't you feeling okay?'

"I feel fine, son. It's your mother that worries me. She's been troubled about something since we bumped into you at your uncle's restaurant the other night."

"Oh," I said, avoiding my father's eyes. I felt guilty and ashamed that I might have upset my mother and this kind and earnest man because of my search for someone whose only contribution to my existence had been a vial of genetic material sold to a fertility clinic.

"Do you know what might be bothering her?"

"Yeah, Dad."

"Is it some kind of problem with this girl you've brought with you today?"

"No! Gosh, no, Dad, it's not anything like that." At that moment, I decided I no longer cared who my biological father was. The only father I cared about now was the one in front of me, and I was determined to make him feel better. "Look, I can't tell you much about it, but Mom won't be worried after I talk to her this afternoon."

"That's all I wanted to hear, son. Your mother has cooked a pot roast for dinner. Let's go in and see this young lady of yours."

I knew that was the end of the problem as far as my father was concerned. My dad was a man who always did what he said he would do and expected me to do the same. I picked up the flat of strawberries and the box of heavy cream, and followed my father back to the house feeling curiously lighter than I had on my trip out to the barn.

At the Callisto farm, dinner was served in the same room in which it was prepared and frequently out of the same pots and pans it was cooked in, but Mom's Yankee pot roast was always beautifully arranged on a large, cobalt blue, serving platter that had been in the family as long as I could remember. Yankee pot roast is the original one-pan meal, and Mom's version included carrots, onions, and rutabagas baked in the same black iron pot as the chuck roast.

Before I thought to warn her, Leda took a bite of one of the rutabagas and made a sour face that got one of the biggest laughs I had ever seen anyone get out of my father. An embarrassed Leda apologized and explained that while she liked rutabagas, she had expected to bite into a baked potato and was surprised by the stealthy tuber that had taken its place. I tried to ease Leda's embarrassment by telling her about all the other ways my mother had prepared the homely vegetable over the years and openly declared that I had never met a rutabaga I liked. This got a rise from my mother, who thought it was her duty to support her husband's chosen field of agriculture by getting as many people to eat his produce as she possibly could.

Mom's strawberry sponge cake was a big hit with everyone. Despite the recent trauma a similar confection had recently caused me, I inhaled two helpings and gave my mother rave reviews on the dessert. These compliments helped mollify the hurt feelings that had been inflicted by my affronts to her rutabaga dishes, and she was in a good mood when I drew her aside after dinner.

Dad had offered to show Leda the giant rutabaga he had found the week before, and to take her on a personal walking tour of a working produce farm. I followed the two just far enough into the parking lot to tell Leda I was going to stay behind to talk to my mother. Leda gave me a nod of approval, and I knew she assumed I was staying to tell Mom about my car accident. Her assumption was partially correct, but after I had filled her in on the wreck, I told Mom that she didn't have to worry about Charlie Bolero anymore. I pointed out that Charlie had proven he wasn't the sperm donor by following through on his offer to take the parental DNA test. Then I used every ounce of persuasion I possessed to convince my mother that I no longer needed to know, or cared who my biological father was.

Chapter Twenty-Eight

Mondays had never really been my favorite day of the week, but this particular Monday was the worst one I could remember. My Sunday excursion with Leda had gone amazingly well up to the point where she had dropped me off at Ace to pick up my Lincoln. From there, it had gone incredibly bad. After I had exited the Mini Cooper, Leda had slid into the driver's seat, grabbed my shirt, and pulled me down for a kiss exactly as she had seven days before. After releasing me from her embrace, she regarded me with somber, amber eyes, and announced she couldn't see me anymore.

Leda's abrupt declaration had left me paralyzed with emotion. Her little red car had dwindled into the distance before I decided that I wasn't going to allow her to simply abandon me without some kind of explanation. I took out my keys and turned to get into my Lincoln only to discover that it wasn't where I left it. After a frantic and futile survey of the vehicles parked in the front lot, it suddenly occurred to me that one of the porters might have moved the Lincoln to the back lot. Jody or Pitch would have had to ask Marty or Jason for a spare key, but that wouldn't have been too unusual. Customers who took advantage of Ace's express check-in occasionally forgot to leave the keys with their contract in the drop box. I hadn't told Marty which car I had taken, and neither he nor Jason could have known I had left that Lincoln in the parking lot to go on a spontaneous ride with Leda.

I unlocked the gate and raced into the back lot to look for the Lincoln. I hadn't been exaggerating when I told Leda that Ace had several virtually identical black Town Cars, I had to try my key in three of them before I located the one I had checked out the day before. I roared out of the parking lot without stopping to lock the gate and headed for the freeway. Five minutes later, a state trooper pulled me over about seven miles outside Jupiter and informed me he had clocked the Lincoln at over 90 MPH on his radar gun. I apologized to the officer and meekly proffered my credentials, thankful that I had rolled my Esplanade in a different state than the one I was about to be issued a speeding ticket in. If the two incidents had been connected, I suspected it could have easily resulted in the instant suspension of my driver's license. As it was, a speeding ticket, coming so soon after my accident, would probably draw some very unfavorable attention from my superiors in the Ace Car Rental organization.

While the officer checked for warrants on the computer in his patrol car, I had time to contemplate Leda's unexpected departure and felt I had reacted badly by racing after her. Now that I had cooled down, I realized that Leda would probably have given her reasons for ending our relationship if she had felt able to do so. I watched morosely as the state trooper made his way back to the Lincoln. I wished I had just gone home and waited for Leda to call me instead of getting myself into this predicament. The officer pulled out his pad, scribbled something on it, and tore off a copy for me. I was relieved to discover that I had been issued a warning instead of a citation. It was the sort of warning that automatically became a citation if I failed to complete a defensive driving class in the next ten days, but I was grateful for the opportunity to avoid a speeding ticket, and I thanked the officer profusely.

That evening I tried calling Leda at Elara Downs. I got the farm's voice mail and had to leave a message asking Leda to call me. I tried again the next morning before I went to work and again after I arrived at work, each time with the same result. I guessed Himalia had everyone at the ranch so busy preparing for her 'cozy, intimate little wedding' that no one had time to answer the phone.

My Monday was made worse by a petty act of vandalism that had occurred in Ace's back lot during the night. When I arrived at work earlier that morning, I found Jody and Pitch trying to remove spray paint off the sides of half a dozen new Escalades. There were no gang symbols or stark anti-SUV propaganda sprayed on the cars, just random swirls of red and black enamel spray paint. I suspected the damage was caused by a couple of bored, nonaligned teenagers who happened across a wide-open gate and a lot full of brand new cars.

I was angry with the vandals, but I was furious with myself for leaving the gate open. After watching the two teenage porters dab at the spray paint, I searched my pocket for my cell phone, remembered it was out of commission and headed into the office to see if I could get someone from the dealership out to assess the damage.

Jason was inundated by Monday morning business customers when I walked in, so I put off my call to the Cadillac dealer to help him catch up. I didn't think about it again until nearly noon when the press of account reps and dry goods salesmen had finally dissipated.

"Crap!" I exclaimed.

"What's the matter?"

"I meant to call the dealer and see what they could do about those Escalades."

"I called them. They told us to hit the spray paint with several light applications of paint thinner and it should begin to soften and wipe off after the fourth or fifth application."

"Won't that hurt the finish?"

"No. They said Escalades are protected by an acrylic gel-coat that's not affected by paint thinner."

"Good. That makes me feel a little better. Those cars wouldn't have been vandalized if I hadn't left the gate open."

"Oh, you came by after we closed?"

"Yeah. I left the Lincoln I was using in the lot Saturday, and Leda dropped me off to pick it up yesterday afternoon."

"Only it wasn't where you left it, was it?"

"Nope, I should have known someone would move it if I left it in the front lot too long. Anyway, I found it in the back lot, and then forgot to lock the gate when I left."

"That doesn't sound like the anal retentive guy I know. What's wrong with you?"

"Leda dumped me."

"Already? You've only known her a week. How did things go at your apartment Saturday?"

"She didn't come over to the apartment Saturday night, and to tell you the truth, I was sort of relieved when she didn't. I don't think I was ready yet."

"I'm starting to think you'll never be ready."

"Thanks, Jason, that's just the kind of support I need after my heart's been torn into little pieces."

"I'm sorry, but you don't really sound all that torn up about it."

"That's because I'm running on adrenaline. I stayed up half the night worrying about her. I've tried to call her a couple of times but no one is answering the phone at her house, and for some stupid reason, she doesn't carry a cell phone."

"At the moment, you don't either. I tried to call you twice yesterday before I remembered your phone took a swim with you in that ditch. Then I rang your house and when your machine picked up, I figured you were out with Leda somewhere."

"Yeah, we were at my folks."

"Oh. What happened? Did your dad make a crack about her yellow eyes?"

"Her eyes are gold, Jason. You've only seen her outdoors. Her eyes appear to be light amber in direct sunlight, but they're actually this beautiful, metallic gold color. And my parents loved her. We had a great time. My mom treated her like a long lost daughter, and my father took her out to see his giant rutabaga. Everything was wonderful. I was on top of the world. Jason, you wouldn't believe how astonishingly beautiful Leda looked yesterday. She had her hair tied in pigtails, and she was wearing this outfit that made her look like Mary Ann on steroids. She seemed like she was really enjoying herself, too. I don't think she likes rutabagas, but who does? She didn't give a clue anything was wrong until we drove back here, and then she just kissed me, said she didn't want to see me anymore, and drove off."

"Wow! She didn't say anything else? She just drove off? Huh! Maybe she's still mad because you won't spy on Charlie."

"She didn't seem angry. After Maia talked to her, everything seemed fine. I'm sure she's still upset about Charlie marrying her mother, but Maia convinced her there was nothing I could do about it."

"I've been wanting to talk to you about that. You didn't tell me much about what happened at the Marriot Saturday, but what you did tell me didn't give me a whole lot of confidence about anything this surrogate mother of Leda's– what was her name? Maia? Maia – or any of the rest of Leda's school chums might have said to you. It sounded to me like Leda got you over there to pump information out of you."

"You need to fight this disturbing tendency of yours to think everyone has a hidden agenda," I said jokingly. "Come on! I knew they were up to something, Jason. I'm not totally naïve. Is that why you tried to call me yesterday? Did you want to warn me about Leda's college friends – to save me from their clutches before it was too late?"

"No, it was nothing. I'll tell you about it some other time when you don't have so much on your mind."

"Hey, if it's nothing, then I want to hear about it. I need something to distract my mind. Go ahead. What did you call me for? Spit it out."

"Well, I just wanted to tell you about a documentary I watched on the Discovery channel, but it would take way too long to explain. It's lunchtime. Why don't you go out and eat a nice hot lunch? I'll go grab a sandwich when you get back."

"We'll order a pizza. What was this documentary about?"

"Okay. But this concerns Charlie and the possibility that he could still be your biological father. You're already stirred up about Leda, and this might make you angry."

"What're you trying to say? Did you get the results from the test? Is Charlie my father after all?"

"No, no, calm down. No, the DNA test hasn't come back yet, and when it does, I fully expect it to be negative. Otherwise, Charlie wouldn't have volunteered to take it. See? See how excited you got just then? This is why I didn't want to go into this right now."

"Well, I'm not going to let you stop now. Tell me about the documentary."

"It was called 'I'm My Own Twin,' and it was about chimeras."

"What's a chimera?"

"Let's order the pizza first, then I'll tell you. It's kind of complicated."

I complained that Jason enjoyed complicating everything, but I gave in and ordered a pie from Ray's Pizzeria, which was just down the street from Ace. There are a lot of pizza places in New York variously called Ray's, Famous Ray's, Original Ray's, the Original Famous Ray's, and Ray Ray's, just to name a few. I didn't know if the Ray's in Jupiter was a genuine, Original Famous Ray's pizza or just a knockoff, but they made really good New York style pizzas and delivered them faster than most of the other pizzerias in town could even make them. Less than ten minutes after I hung up the phone, we were biting into that tender, crunchy, chewy crust that characterizes New York style pizza and sets it apart from all the other cheese pies that pass for pizza in the rest of the country.

"Chimeras are essentially animals or people that are two different individuals fused into one body. It's like you mixed up pieces from two jigsaw puzzles that were cut from the same die but had different pictures printed on them. The pieces would still fit together, but you would end up with a patchwork of mismatched pieces."

"Hey, I think I remember seeing a CSI episode where the rape suspect turned out to be one of these chimera guys. There was something about him having two different kinds of DNA, too, but I thought it was just a fictional device."

"Nope, it's real."

"I thought that DNA identification was fool proof, like fingerprints."

"It's still the most definitive way to identify someone. It just turns out some people have more than one set of genetic fingerprints."

"But how do you end up with two sets of DNA?"

"The most common way is transplantation. Everyone who's ever had an organ transplant carries two different cell lines in their bodies. People can also inherit an extra cell line because of a genetic disorder called mosaicism. Fraternal twins can share some of each other's DNA through blood-vessel anastomoses during fetal development. And mothers can end up with small amounts of their children's cell lines floating around in their blood for decades after giving birth. But real chimeras are created when either one fertilized egg fuses with an extra sperm, or two fertilized eggs fuse together to form one individual. Scientists used to think chimerism was confined to Siamese twins, hermaphrodites, and other obviously bifurcated individuals, but recently they've been finding chimeras with subtle or no outward signs of the condition. Have you ever seen someone with two different colored eyes?"

"Yeah," I answered, "like one brown eye and one blue one. Why? Are they chimeras?"

"Not always. That's called heterochromia. It can be caused by heredity, trauma, and illness, but it can also be one of the outward signs of chimerism – along with other irregularities like patchy hair or skin."

"Well, this is all really interesting, but I don't see what it has to do with Charlie."

"That's just because you're not thinking clearly today. You're too tired and worried about Leda to see where I'm going with this."

"Well, hurry up and get there before our afternoon customers start showing up."

"Okay, but pay attention. In this documentary I saw, they told a story about a lady who was brought to court for welfare fraud after DNA testing proved she wasn't the mother of the children she had listed on her application. The prosecutors immediately called for her two children to be taken into state custody, but the woman, who was pregnant at the time, was so vehement in her insistence the tests were in error that the judge decided to wait until she gave birth so the same tests could be run on that child. The day she delivered, blood samples were immediately drawn from both the mother and child, and new DNA tests of the blood samples proved she was not the mother of that child either. Impossible, huh? It turns out she was a chimera. They finally found a DNA match for her children when they tested cell samples extracted from her cervix." Jason paused, again, and grinned at me. "All right, Walt, get ready. This is where I make you mad."

"I still don't see it, but go ahead."

"Put down your soda first. You might throw it at me, and I don't want to get sprayed with root beer."

"Will you just get on with it!"

"This lady had no outward signs of her condition, but Charlie does."

"What! Don't tell me you think Charlie's a chimera!"

"Now aren't you glad I made you put down the root beer?"

"You have root beer on the brain, Jason. Let me get this straight, you still think Charlie's actually my father, and you think the only reason he volunteered to take that parental identification test was because he knew the DNA in his mouth wouldn't produce a positive result."

"Precisely. I knew you'd get it."

"What makes you think Charlie's a chimera?"

"Don't you remember telling me about those light and dark squares of skin on his back?"

"Yeah, so?"

"Patchy skin can be an indication of chimerism."

"It could also be an indication of skin disease, vitamin deficiency, or lying in the sun too damn long while wearing a checkered shirt!"

"Well, it might be caused by other factors, but your sunburn theory is kind of silly."

"I was being facetious, you nitwit. You know, Jason, I used to think you were smart. In fact, I thought you were brilliant. But now that I've heard your latest crackpot theory, I'm beginning to think you're just a computer geek with an overactive imagination."

"See? I knew it would make you mad."

"I'm not mad. If it weren't for you, I wouldn't have met Leda, and I wouldn't have gotten past that stupid obsession about finding my biological father. I realized yesterday that I didn't care who my sperm donor was, and I told my mother it didn't matter to me how I got here. I'm here, and I'm damned lucky to have parents who wanted me bad enough to use a stranger's sperm in order to bring me into existence. Yesterday was the first day of my life as an adult, and maybe you should think about growing up too."

That was the end of the conversation. Jason just shrugged his shoulders, finished eating his pizza, and announced he was going out to see how Pitch and Jody were doing on their paint removal project. After Jason left, I wondered if I had been too hard on him. After all, he had only been trying to help. Now that the heat of the moment had passed, I suspected I had behaved in a petty fashion toward my best friend. I resolved to apologize and thank him for all his efforts on my behalf, maybe take him out to dinner, or buy him a book on blackjack. Jason liked blackjack. Maybe I could stand Jason a trip to Atlantic City or Las Vegas. Vegas would be better; I didn't think Jason had ever been to Vegas. In my imagination, I could see Jason running his system on the high stake blackjack table at Caesar's Palace. Just as Jason was being thrown out of the casino for card counting, the phone rang.

"Hello?"

"Walt?"

"Leda?"

"No, Walt, this is Leda's mother. I need to see you."

"Himalia! Oh, God, what's wrong? Has something happened to Leda? Is she okay?"

"Leda's fine, but I need to see you. I'm in Jupiter. Is there a place we can meet? Away from your place of business?"

"Is this about Leda? Did she tell you why she doesn't want to see me anymore?"

"I can't talk about it on a cell phone. Can you meet me or not?"

"Uh, you mean like at a restaurant or something?"

"No, I don't want our conversation to be overheard. Hey! I just passed a bowling alley. Could you meet me there?"

"The Red Spot Lanes? Yeah, I guess so. Do you want to meet me there after I get off?"

"Now."

"Now?"

"Now."

I couldn't imagine what could possibly be so urgent, but I really wanted to talk to Himalia about Leda, so I agreed to meet her. After I hung up, I rang Jason's cell phone.

"Hey, Walt," Jason answered, "I'm just about finished out here. Pitch and Jody got every bit of the spray paint off those Escalades. They look great. They're running them through the car wash as we speak."

"That's great, Jason. You were smart to get on that problem so quickly this morning. You should be managing this place instead of me."

"Nah, I like being number two."

"Okay, we won't switch right this moment, but if I had to go somewhere for an hour or so, do you think you could handle the afternoon customers?"

"Sure. Is there a problem?"

"Leda's mom is meeting me at the Red Spot. I think she wants to talk to me about Leda."

"At the bowling alley? That should be interesting. Okay, I'm coming in, but there's going to be a price to pay."

"What's that?"

"You're going to have to tell me everything that happens."

"I wouldn't leave you out of the loop, Jason. You're my friend."

Chapter Twenty-Nine

The Red Spot Lanes was one of Jupiter's most prominent social venues. Everybody who was anybody dropped by the bowling alley at least once a week. I hadn't been anybody since I graduated from high school. On my drive over, I was thinking that the ever-popular Red Spot Lanes was possibly the worst place in all of Jupiter to have a private conversation. But when I walked into the bowling alley, I changed my mind. The cacophony of falling bowling pins, bouncing bowling balls and a hundred people all trying to talk over the noise was deafening. You couldn't hear what people were saying ten feet away. It was exceptionally private.

The Red Spot had twenty-four lanes, and on Monday afternoons, twenty of them were set aside for senior league play. I found Himalia waiting for me in one of the four lanes that were still available for non-league bowlers. She was bowling practice frames. I sat down in her lane's seating area, and waited for her to finish the frame. She had left the eight and ten pins standing. When I used to bowl, I usually tried knocking down adjacent pins by rolling my ball between them. Himalia picked up the spare by smoothly hooking her ball into the eight pin, causing it to shoot across the boards like a cannon shot, cleanly taking out the ten pin with its passage. I was impressed.

Himalia turned around, saw me, and strode purposefully toward the seating area. She had changed her appearance. She was wearing a simple but elegant pantsuit made of a dense toffee-colored material, and her hair was a completely natural-looking shade of red. I was amazed by this transformation. She looked like an attractive and perfectly normal middle-aged woman.

"Hello, Walt," she said, extending her hand. "Thanks for meeting me on such short notice."

I stood up and shook her hand. She seemed calm but somber, renewing my fears that some calamity had occurred.

"Please take a seat."

My heart thumping, I sat down heavily and waited for Himalia to reveal her news. Instead of sitting down next to me, Himalia leaned against the scorekeeper's desk, crossed her arms, and gazed at me like a housewife inspecting a not too fresh fish.

"Did you tell Leda that Charlie was a crook?"

"I – I – did I tell her what?" I stammered.

"Leda said you told her that Charlie stole some tires off a car you rented him. Is that true?"

I knew I hadn't told Leda about the suspected parts theft on the Lincoln, so Maia must have mentioned it to her. I was disappointed in Maia. She had promised to keep our conversation in the strictest confidence, and if she had felt a need to relate a portion of it to Leda, she should have at least tried to get the details straight.

"She probably just misunderstood me. I might have mentioned that Charlie had returned a car whose tires appeared to have been exchanged at some point, but I didn't accuse him of doing it."

"So you just left the inference hanging in the air then?"

"No, I said it wouldn't make any sense for a man like Charlie to do something like that."

"I see. Excuse me for a moment," she said, and walked over to the ball return, dried her hands, and retrieved her ball. Then she sent her ball arching down the lane into the 1-2 pocket. It was a perfect strike, and somewhere amid the fuzzy chaos of my troubled mind, I realized that Himalia was bowling left-handed.

Himalia walked back to the scorer's table and picked up a tall glass full of ice and a dark-colored beverage. She took a swallow, resumed her former position, and redeployed her fish-accessing gaze. "Did you happen to mention to Leda that Charlie stole boat motors for a living?"

I was dumbfounded by the extent of Maia's treachery. "Actually, I told one of Leda's friends about watching Charlie move the casing and control panels from one boat motor to another at his warehouse. At the time I thought it looked suspicious, but what Leda's friend obviously neglected to mention was that I subsequently discovered Charlie sold rebuilt engines."

"How did you see Charlie doing this? Did he invite you to his warehouse?"

My face suddenly felt hot, and I knew that it had probably turned the color of underdone roast beef. I wasn't sure how to answer. Himalia was Charlie's fiancé. What would he think if he learned how I had spied on him?

"You look apoplectic, Walt. Are you angry, or are you just having a stroke?"

"No, I'm sorry, I just feel a little flushed. Could I please have some of your drink?"

"Sure."

She handed me the glass, and I took a big gulp. I had been expecting diet cola. What I got was mostly rum, with a little coke in it for color. I choked and sprayed it all over myself.

"Don't you like Cuba Libres?" she asked.

"I'm sorry. I thought it was diet coke."

I handed the drink back to her, pulled out my handkerchief, and tried to blot some of the sticky liquid off my clothes.

"Well, Walt, when your daughter suddenly tells you the man you're going to marry is a crook, you need something a little stronger than diet coke."

Himalia smiled at me, tilted her head back, and drained the rest of her Cuba Libre. She set the empty glass down on the scorer's table, sat down next to me, and took charge of my handkerchief.

"Look," she said, daubing at drops of rum and coke, "I know you get flustered easily, but I need to know the truth. Leda has never liked Charlie, and I know she'd jump at the chance to break us up. When Leda told me that you were the source of her information, I was naturally a little dubious because, well, you recall that you were introduced as Walt Galilei when your name real name is Callisto–"

"Yes, but I can explain that–"

"You don't have to. Leda told me she got the names confused."

"But that's not what really happened."

"I know, dear. I knew you were hiding something the moment you set yourself on fire. But you seemed harmless enough, and I was just happy for Leda to have a boyfriend. I thought she might stop bitching about my relationship with Charlie if you were around to distract her. That's why I invited you out to the ranch, and up until this morning, everything was going just peachy keen. But this morning she told me those terrible stories about Charlie. If the things she said about him are true, I guess I'm better off without him. But if she's just trying to wreck my wedding, I'll kick her little fanny out on the street. I'm sorry. I shouldn't have said that. There must have been a Libre too much Cuba in my drink. Hey, why don't you go throw some water on your face? We'll resume questioning after you get back."

Himalia hopped up, retrieved her ball, and as I made my way to the men's room, I could hear her bowling another strike. I was grateful for the temporary reprieve, but I was surprised by her equanimity. I doubted I would be nearly as calm and patient under similar circumstances.

In the restroom, I washed my hands and face, and then moistened a paper towel and tried to remove the sticky remains of Himalia's Cuba Libre. My shirt was ruined, but I thought my jacket would probably be okay after it was dry-cleaned.

After I had done everything I could for my clothes, I stood looking at myself in the mirror. I had to decide what I was going to tell Himalia. I wanted to tell the truth, but I didn't want to create a rift between mother and daughter. I believed Maia misquoted me to Leda, but I was worried Himalia wouldn't see it that way. In addition, I really didn't want Charlie to hear about all the times I had spied on him.

As this worrisome thought passed thorough my consciousness, I felt the hair rise on the back of my neck. It had suddenly occurred to me that Charlie could already know everything. Maia might have launched a two-pronged attack. In addition to sending Leda to her mother with a misleading version of my story, she could have also sent Charlie an anonymous letter, detailing Maia's version of everything I had told her, accompanied by threats to make it all public. Jason had been right. Leda had brought me there to be interrogated, and the job had fallen to the insidiously persuasive Maia. She had adopted Leda's cause and skillfully extracted information from me that she was now exploiting to achieve her goal – breaking up Himalia and Charlie's relationship.

This thought kicked my brain into panic mode. Maia's machinations might do more than just wreck an impending marriage. It could also put my head in danger of being twisted off by Charlie, thus ruining any chance I had of getting back together with Leda. I decided that bold and decisive action was called for, and ran out of the bathroom, nearly knocking over an octogenarian bowler on the way out.

"Slow down, sonny, there's a hell of a lot more to life than bowling."

I agreed with the old coot's admonition, but I didn't have time to respond. It was nearly two o'clock in the afternoon, and I wanted to reassure Himalia about Charlie's character, take full responsibility for any slurs Leda had made against him, and drive to Cobb's Station to intercept any slander-filled letter Maia might have FedExed to Charlie's house. Even if I got there too late, I thought I still might be able to ameliorate matters by explaining my side of the story to Charlie.

I found Himalia patiently waiting for me by the scorer's table. She smiled as I came running up to the seating area.

"Well, I wasn't expecting you to sneak away, but I didn't think you'd be this eager to resume the interrogation."

"Himalia, Charlie's a good and decent man who's shown me nothing but kindness since the day I met him, and he didn't do anything wrong. The other night, Leda invited me to a little party with some of her college friends. I wanted to impress them so I'm afraid I might have said some things about Charlie that weren't true."

"So you got to talking about Charlie, and you just threw in some lies to spice it up. Is that it?"

"Yes, and I'm really sorry and ashamed."

"I imagine you are. So, tell me Walt, was the part about you being a detective a lie too?"

My mouth nearly fell open with astonishment before I remembered Leda's fantasy about me being an undercover detective. I guessed Leda had thrown that part in to boost the credibility of her allegations. I managed to disguise my sagging jaw at the last moment by nodding my head, and then looked down at my feet to show how embarrassed I was.

"You're a terrible liar, Walt."

"I know, I'm sorry. I don't know why I feel compelled to make up these ridiculous stories, but I've decided that this is the end of it. After today I'm going to get some professional help in controlling my problem." I said all this without looking up, and for a moment, I thought it had gone over in a big way.

"No, Walt, what I'm saying is you're terrible at lying."

I looked up and saw Himalia looking at me with an expression of amused pity.

"I'm guessing she didn't say I was a detective," I said.

"No, she didn't. I knew from the way you came sprinting up here that you were going to cover for my daughter."

"Listen, Himalia, Leda's innocent. She's only repeating what this friend of hers told her to say. Her name is Maia, and she's like a female Svengali. She's the one who wormed all that information about Charlie out of me, and then distorted it to suit her purpose."

"What was her purpose?"

"Huh?"

"What was Maia's purpose in getting Leda to make these allegations against Charlie?"

Checkmate. I couldn't see a way to answer the question without implicating Leda. Maia had never even met Charlie or Himalia and wouldn't have any reason to disrupt their wedding without Leda asking her to. Even if she was innocent of the methods Maia employed, Leda was guilty of instigating the plot they were used in. I sat down and put my head in my hands. I wasn't aware of Himalia taking the seat next to me until I found the top of my head being patted in a consoling manner.

"It's okay, Walt, I knew Leda wanted to wreck my wedding all along. Now, how do you know all this stuff about Charlie? Didn't you just meet him last Tuesday at Vinny's place?"

"Oh, crap." I said. My words were a little muffled because I still had my face buried in my hands. I began desperately trying to formulate a response other than 'Oh crap,' but I was distracted by Himalia's gentle pats, which, though doubtlessly well intentioned, felt like bricks bouncing off the top of my head, as my world collapsed around me.

If I had to reveal how I came to know about Charlie's activities, not only would it delay my race to Charlie's house to intercept any overnight envelopes Maia might have dispatched, it would also entail an explanation of why I had been spying on Charlie in the first place. This would then inevitably lead to the whole, sperm donor matter, and a new series of embarrassing questions.

"I didn't catch that last groan, Walt," Himalia said, mercifully suspending her head patting, "but it sounds like you're a little flustered again. Well, cheer up; I'm not going to throw Leda out on the street. I was just blowing off steam. You've assured me Charlie didn't do anything wrong, and I believe you. Everything's just Jim Dandy! Maia's evil plan has been foiled. I'm going to get married this Saturday, and Leda might even change her mind and start seeing you again."

I lifted my head and stared at Himalia with a faint gleam of hope shining in my eyes. "Do you really think so? Did she mention why she stopped seeing me?"

"No, she just marched into the office this morning and told me that you discovered Charlie had stolen parts off one of your rental cars, and suspected him of selling hot boat motors, too. She said you had made her promise not to tell anyone because you couldn't prove any of it, and you didn't want to make Charlie mad, but she didn't care anymore because you two had broken up. She didn't say why. She just said you had both agreed to stop seeing each other. Then she left the house and drove away. She probably expected me to confront Charlie and make him prove a negative. I mean – that's the problem with accusations, isn't it? No matter what Charlie said to me, I'd always have little doubts about him in the back of my mind. So I decided to drive down here to get it from the horse's mouth. I remembered you talking about your job at some car rental place, and then I found that last message you left for Leda. That's how I got your number."

I didn't know why Leda had told her mother the breakup was mutual, but the fact that she didn't give Himalia a reason for discontinuing our relationship gave me hope. If it had been anything serious, I was sure she would have mentioned it to her mother. If I could just find a way to keep the channels of communication open, I thought there was still a chance of our getting back together. Keeping the channels open meant keeping on Himalia and Charlie's good side. That would be easier to do if Charlie didn't get the idea I was trying to blackmail him. And while I couldn't be certain Maia had actually sent a blackmail letter, I couldn't take the chance she hadn't – I had to get Himalia to let me go before it was too late.

"Himalia, I know you're curious about my relationship with Charlie, but would you believe me if I simply told you that I met him a few days prior to my birthday party at my Uncle Vinny's, and because my business with Charlie was of an extremely personal nature, he covered for me by pretending we hadn't met before?"

"Yes, I would, Walt, because it has the ring of truth. It sounds just like something Charlie would do. Don't you think you could tell me a little more about it?"

"All I can tell you is that Charlie went out of his way to help me, and although I didn't find what I was looking for that day, I found a new friend. I'm glad he has a fiancé who would rather drive to another state to get at the truth, than fling a bunch of last minute accusations in his face."

Himalia grinned and gave me a big hug.

"Okay, Walt, you did a good job. There're still some unanswered questions, but you've convinced me that they're not important. I'm satisfied, and I'm heading back home. Don't worry about Leda. She'll come around when she finds out how wrong she's been about Charlie. Oh, by the way, we're having the wedding at two-thirty this Saturday at Vinny's. Leda probably won't come, but I'm sure Charlie would be glad to see you."

I walked her out to her car partly because it was the polite thing to do, but principally because I needed to see what it looked like. She was driving a cherry red Mercedes-Benz convertible. I liked her taste in luxury cars. I would be sure to duck down and pass on the blind side, if I spotted a cherry red Mercedes on my way to Cobb's Station.

Chapter Thirty

I was glad to be on the road again. There was something about going on a long, solo drive in the country that lifted my spirits and made me feel like I was in control of my life for a change. The feeling usually dissipated the moment I got out of the car, but at least I had the memory of all those uneventful miles of pavement, countryside and unseen towns I had driven through with no other interaction than the wind of my passage.

I tried to focus on the comforting feelings my long drive had engendered as I exited the Lincoln Town Car a block down the street from Charlie's house. There was more than an hour of daylight left, and though the apple trees were casting long shadows over the lawns, I was able to see the front door clearly as I drove past it. I hadn't seen an overnight envelope. This could mean Charlie had already retrieved the envelope, that it hadn't been delivered yet, or that Maia had never sent it in the first place.

But there was another possibility. Perhaps Maia had given her little packet of accusations and demands to Leda, so she could personally deliver it to Charlie's house. If she had, the envelope probably wouldn't be visible from the street. Leda would probably have just popped it through the mail slot for Charlie to find with the rest of his mail. I had prepared for this contingency by stopping at the convenience store on the edge of Cobb's Station. There, I bought the one necessary ingredient for a secret weapon that had served me well in similar situations during my grade-school days. I found the other ingredient in a trash dumpster behind the store. I assembled the device in my car, and carried it with me as I walked down the block to Charlie's house. I wavered on the sidewalk for a moment, stuck in the netherworld of indecision, and then suddenly made the plunge and walked up to the door.

I reached out a hand and rang the doorbell, ready to toss my secret weapon into the shrubbery if Charlie should come to the door. I allowed a full minute to pass before I followed up with the doorknocker. When that went unanswered, I took a quick look around and seeing no one in sight, I stooped down, pushed open the mail slot and peered in. By dent of squinting and moving my head back and forth, I was able to make out various pieces of ordinary-looking mail scattered behind the door. Then, when I put my face right against the door and looked straight down, I spotted a suspicious-looking envelope with a familiar logo on its upper left hand corner. It was an envelope from the Airport Marriot in Jupiter. I wished my friend Jason were present to witness this moment. I suspected Jason thought I wasn't able to think analytically. I was proud of the fact that I had correctly predicted Maia's actions, and had quickly formed a flexible plan of action which even allowed for the last minute acquisition of specialized tools and tactics to meet changing conditions in the field.

Holding the mail flap open with one hand, I deftly inserted the flexible metal shaft of my unauthorized mail retrieval device through the mail slot, being exceedingly careful not to allow the sides of the slot to come into contact with the adhesive matrix on the end of the shaft. After making a couple of last-minute adjustments to the geometry of the tool's metal shaft, I was able to bring the adhesive matrix into contact with the suspect envelope. With the deliberate care acquired from many tricky and perilous retrievals of everything from lost coins at the bottom of steam grates to the rescue of a neighbor's wedding band from a neighborhood storm drain, I slowly drew the letter up until I was able to pinch the corner of the envelope between the tips of two fingers and pull it back through the slot. I detached the letter from the wad of bubble gum and let the coat hanger fall onto the porch floor. I couldn't believe it! I was holding the masterstroke of Maia's diabolical plan in my hands!

"Hey! What the hell are you doing?"

I froze in the crouched position that I had assumed for fishing the blackmail envelope through the mail slot. When one is surprised with one's trousers down, one's brain often doesn't operate as efficiently as one would wish, and my brain jumped to the erroneous conclusion that my worst fears had come to pass.

"Sorry, Charlie."

"Walt, you moron, do I sound like Charlie? Turn around!"

I straightened up and turned to see Leda standing with her hands on her hips, her legs splayed, and her elbows stuck out like the wings of a fighter jet in takeoff position.

"Give me that letter!"

"Leda!" I cried, my heart overflowing with relief and pangs of unrequited love.

"Don't 'Leda' me! You just give me that damn letter, before I knock you down and take it from you."

"But, Leda, this letter could destroy people's lives. I know you don't like Charlie, but Maia has fed you a pack of lies!"

"I'm warning you, Walt. Hand it over!"

"No! You're naïve, Leda. Maia's dangerous. I bet you don't know half of what's in here."

"I should know. I helped her write it. Maia could sell bullshit to a cattle rancher, but she can't write worth a damn. Now for the last time, Walt, give me that letter!"

"Leda, I love you, but–"

I wasn't prepared for Leda's sudden rush, and she knocked me base over apex. Somehow, I managed to hold on to the letter, but Leda quickly scrabbled on top of my chest, shoved my face into the concrete, and held it there while snatching at the letter with her free hand. I prided myself on being a gentleman, and owing to my status as an only child, I had never wrestled with an older sister or any other female, other than my brief and undecided one-round bout with Himalia. Thus I was completely inexperienced in the fine art of fending off an attack by an enraged girlfriend. Leda had almost wrested the envelope from my hand by the time my shocked brain decided that the thing to do when a wild cat is sitting on your chest is to roll over. I promptly did this, and sent both of us crashing off the porch into the bushes. Having lost her hold on the letter, Leda jumped up, screaming with rage, and turned the air blue with a string of invective that would make a prison guard blush. Reeling with pain and indignation, I scrambled to my feet and made shushing gestures at her.

"Calm down, Leda! Can't we talk this over?"

"No, we can't, because you're too damn stupid. All those rutabagas your mother fed you have pickled your brain!"

"That's it. I don't have to stand here and be insulted. I'm going home." I shoved the letter into my coat pocket and started to walk away.

"Wait, Walt! I'll talk to you, but we can't do it here. Charlie's liable to come home any moment, and I don't want him to find us here."

My feelings were ruffled, but I still ached to be close to her, so I agreed to move our discussion away from Charlie's front lawn. Leda tried to straighten up the bushes, grabbed my coat hanger, and stalked down the street to my Lincoln. After we got in the car, Leda instructed me to drive around the block. When I turned into the street behind Charlie's, I recognized Leda's little red Mini Cooper parked next to an undeveloped lot. I pulled up behind the Mini and turned to face Leda.

Although her clothes were disheveled from our fight, and her hair looked like last year's Halloween fright wig, she still looked amazingly beautiful to me. I wanted to tell her how much I loved her, that I was only withholding the blackmail letter for her own good, but before I could put these thoughts into words, Leda leaned back against her door and kicked me in my midsection. The force of the blow slammed me up against my door and knocked the breath out of me. By the time I recovered, Leda was on top of me, pulling the letter out of my coat pocket. I grabbed one end of the envelope and was beginning to win the ensuing tug-of-war, when Leda, her hair flared into a wild golden mane and her bright gold eyes blazing, bared her pearly whites, and sank them into the meaty part of my arm.

"Ouch! Damn it, Leda! Are you crazy? Stop it!" Strength inspired by terror enabled me to bodily lift my assailant and fling her against the passenger door.

Leda straightened up, wiped her mouth with her sleeve, and stared down at her hand. She was holding the letter, or at least most of it. I still had a big corner of it.

"You idiot! You tore it!" she screamed, holding up the mutilated blackmail letter so I could see the damage.

I wasn't interested in the torn envelope. I was more concerned about the damage to my arm. I removed my jacket, rolled up my sleeve, and inspected the bite marks. I saw two crescents of deep indentations in my skin, but no blood. I held my arm up for Leda to see.

"You bit me!"

Leda stared at the wound she had inflicted, let her letter fall to the floor, and slid across the seat toward me with open arms.

"I'm sorry, I'm sorry. I didn't mean to bite you so hard. Does it hurt?" she wailed.

"Don't touch me!" I shouted.

Leda jerked back like a scalded child, and I was instantly sorry. I cursed myself for six kinds of a fool, and desperately racked my brain for something that would erase the harshness of my last remark, and return Leda to my arms.

"At least you didn't break the skin. For a moment there I thought I might have to get a rabies shot." I chuckled and grinned at Leda in what I hoped was a conciliatory manner.

But Leda didn't respond in quite the way I had hoped. In fact, the sudden change in her expression would have impressed any actor who had ever portrayed the mild Doctor Jekyll transforming into the hideous Mr. Hyde.

"Shut up!" she screamed, snatching up the letter and shaking it at me. "You nearly ruined everything. You don't know what's at stake. My mother's worth millions, and this creep Charlie's after her money."

"But I'm just trying to protect you from yourself," I pleaded. "No matter what you think Charlie's guilty of, you can't go around stuffing letters full of unproven allegations and threats in people's mail slots."

"You're trying to protect Charlie, not me. You always take his side, in spite of everything I told you about him. You take everything he says at face value, but you won't consider anything that anyone else says about him."

"I wanted to take your side, Leda. I really did. But the only thing you and your friends ever had to show me was theories and suppositions. You can't persecute a man just because you think he might be guilty of something."

"If you love me, you'll just go back home. None of this has anything to do with you any more. Charlie isn't your father, and he's not going to want to see you again after tonight. Just go home and forget you ever knew me."

"Don't deliver that letter, Leda. It'll just get you in trouble, and it won't stop Charlie from marrying your mother."

"I'm not expecting this letter to stop him. I have a two-part plan. First Charlie reads this little blackmail letter fingering him for starting the tack room fire and stealing Running Fool's sperm; then, after he's good and rattled, my mother's going to grill him about a couple of things I clued her in to this morning."

"She won't ask Charlie any questions, Leda."

"Oh yeah, she will. She was really pissed off when I left her this morning."

"I saw your mother this afternoon. She drove up to Jupiter and tracked me down. I told her the whole story, and she knows that Charlie's not guilty of any of your accusations."

I braced myself for another angry explosion, but it never came. Leda just stared at me like I had just kicked her puppy. I could see the muscles in her face begin to tighten up as she tried to fight back the emotions welling up inside, and then the dam burst, and Leda was crying uncontrollably. I scooted over and swept her up. She lay limply in my arms, heaving in concert with the sobs that racked her body. She felt incredibly light and damp. I started stroking her hair and talking softly to her.

"I'm so sorry, Leda. I know things look bad now, but I'm sure it's all going to turn out all right. Charlie really isn't as bad as you think. Sssh, sssh, come on, Leda, even if everything you suspected about him were true, it's not like he could get away with anything. Your mom's as sharp as a tack. She'll probably make Charlie sign a prenup – besides, if she ever caught him with his hands in her purse, he'd end up having to learn how to tie his shoes with his teeth."

"Shut up, shut up, shut up! Will you please just shut up?" Leda straightened up and pushed me away. Then without another word, she got out of the Lincoln and ran to her Mini Cooper. As she drove away, I briefly considered following her, but then thought better of it.

I sat on the passenger side of my car for another ten minutes; contemplating the blackmail letter she had left lying on the floor. I felt like someone who had stayed behind in a movie theatre after the picture had ended. The show was over, the rest of the audience had gone home to resume their lives, but I was still sitting in the empty theatre wishing the film had ended differently. Leda was right. None of this had anything to do with me anymore. I just didn't know what to do now that the show was over.

Chapter Thirty-One

Recently, I had fallen into the habit of arriving late to work and leaving early. I decided it was high time that I reform my work ethic, so on Tuesday morning I made a special effort to arrive at Ace before anyone else.

When Jason walked into the office, he found me working at my computer. "Hey! Are we working in our shirtsleeves today?"

Ace reps are supposed to wear dark, solid colored sport jackets. I had two of these. One was at the cleaners, and the other was currently on the seat of my car. I had tried my best to clean it up, but the rum and coke had left little circles of light brown residue, and my wrestling match with Leda had torn my pocket and added an assortment of brown and green stains.

"No, I spilled something on my jacket yesterday. I was waiting for you to come in so I could go get my other one from the cleaners."

"Oh, well, hold on a second. I have something to show you."

He leaned over my shoulder, commandeered my mouse, brought up the web browser, and with a dexterous display of one-handed typing, entered a domain in the URL window. The website that came up had a sterile, prosaic design full of small print and enigmatic charts. Jason entered a name and password in a login window that brought up a screen full of more small type and charts. The title at the top of the page read: Acorn Labs DNA Paternity Test Exclusion Report (Motherless).

"This is the results from your and Charlie's DNA test. The lab emailed me after you left yesterday. As you can see, this report eliminates Charlie as your father just as we expected it would, but there's an interesting detail in the test results. This table shows eleven discrete locations on several different chromosomes. The first column of numbers identifies the chromosome and a specific location on that chromosome. The next two columns of numbers identify which alleles or genes were found at those locations for you and Charlie. You'll notice that you don't have any genes in common with Charlie on the first nine locations tested. That was enough to eliminate Charlie as your father with a 100% degree of accuracy, but you do share markers with him at the last two chromosome locations in this profile. I called the lab up to find out if there was any significance to these matches. Do you know what they told me?"

"I can't guess, but I bet you're going to tell me."

"Each gene has an established probability of occurrence in the general population. The probability of another individual sharing both those markers with you is only one in a hundred and thirty thousand."

"Well, in that case, why was Charlie eliminated as my father with a 100% degree of accuracy?"

"Because he can't be your father without any matches in the first nine chromosome locations."

"Okay, so he's definitely not my biological father."

"Not based on the evidence of this particular test, but the fact that Charlie just happens to be the one person out of a hundred and thirty thousand who matches you on those last two markers is a little suspicious, don't you think?"

"Here we go with the chimeras again."

"Well, what this indicates to me is some degree of relation. I think if we had run an avuncular DNA test, Charlie might have shown up as your uncle, and if we could get a sample of his sperm, we might still be able to prove he's your biological father."

I stared at him in disbelief. "His sperm?"

"Yeah, remember they couldn't get a DNA match for that one lady's children until they tested cell samples extracted from her cervix. If Charlie is a chimera, we'll need his sperm sample to get a positive result."

"Okay, Jason, that's it," I said standing up. "I'm through. I really, really appreciate you helping me on this, you've been amazing, but there's no way in hell I'm going to ask Charlie for a sperm sample. I have to walk over to the dry cleaners now."

"Hey!" he called as I headed towards the front, "you promised to tell me what happened at the bowling alley yesterday!"

"I know," I said, pausing at the door, "it's a real long story, though. Can we save it for after work? I have a lot to do today."

As I walked out to my car to collect my soiled jacket, I noticed Jason watching me through one of the office's big plate glass windows. After I got my coat out of the Lincoln and started walking toward the fence that separated Ace from the dry-cleaning store, I looked back at the office again. Jason was still visible through the glass, but he was engaged in conversation with Jody. She was talking and gesturing toward the rear lot. I smiled to myself. I probably would be called on to settle another dispute between my porters when I got back.

When I walked into the drycleaners, I found several other customers waiting impatiently for their turn at the register. The little Korean lady behind the counter was involved in an animated discussion with a fat balding man about missing buttons on his shirts. The next lady in line spent five minutes giving careful instructions on precisely how she wanted each one of her blouses, suits, and dresses laundered, dry-cleaned, pressed, folded and hung. The man standing in line right before me was picking up his cleaning, but he didn't have his claim ticket. When the Korean lady finally found his laundry, he insisted that a sports jacket was missing, and made her search her motorized conveyor for a light, brownish-grey jacket. After several minutes of "this it? No? How bout this one? No?' it suddenly occurred to me that this man was wearing a kind of light, brownish-grey jacket, and I asked him if the missing jacket looked anything like the one he had on. The man looked down at his own sleeve, looked sheepish, then paid for his dry cleaning, and rushed out of the store.

"Hi, Mr. Callisto!" the clerk said, expertly spinning her conveyor around until my clean jacket hove into view.

"Hi. Can you clean these stains out and get my pocket sewn back on?" I asked, presenting a sleeve of my soiled jacket that sported a fairly representative sample of Cuba Libre and battle stains.

She took the soiled jacket from me and examined it for a moment with her expert eyes.

"Oh no, very sorry, Mr. Callisto. Booze and dirt no problem, but green stains stay like tiger stripes. What happen? You fall in grass?"

"No, I fall in bush."

"Well, at least you still have this jacket," she said, handing me the one from the conveyor, "cow crap come right out."

"Horse crap," I corrected. I paid her, took the clean jacket out of its plastic bag, and put it on. Then I handed the plastic bag and my ruined jacket to the clerk. "Could you toss these in your trash for me?"

"Sure thing, Mr. Callisto. Come back soon!"

I had almost made it to the wooden fence separating the dry cleaner's from Ace Car Rental when I heard the little Korean lady calling me.

"Mr. Callisto, you forget something!"

I walked back to the door where she was waiting for me, and she handed me a small, brown paper envelope.

"We find something in pocket again. You almost throw it away with plastic bag!"

I thanked her, and she ducked back into her store. I walked back to Ace, ripping open the flap of the envelope as I went. The envelope was very light, and I thought it probably contained another restaurant receipt. As I turned the corner of the fence into Ace's parking lot, I reached a finger into the envelope to pull out the receipt, but I couldn't feel anything. I stopped walking, held the mouth of the envelope open by squeezing the opposing edges with thumb and forefinger, and inverted it over the palm of my free hand. A thin, white plastic straw fell into my hand. I recognized it as the 'souvenir straw' Leda had found and slipped into my pocket after Frisco Gal's artificial insemination. It brought back the heady memory of Leda giggling, prancing, and pirouetting at the end of my arm, and kissing me on the breeding room floor next to the standing stall. That's where she had found the expended sperm straw, hiding under the edge of the standing stall's floor.

I held the straw up so I could read the tiny black lettering on it. I saw the words 'Running Fool' and "Pender Lab," followed by a date and some other names and numbers. At first, I couldn't believe I was reading it right. The inscription on the straw should have started with the name of Charlie's horse, 'Thunder Tom,' but after rereading the straw's label several times, I was convinced I was holding an expended straw from the Triple Crown winner whose sperm had been destroyed in the tack room fire at Elara Downs.

The straw shook in my hand as its significance dawned on me. It could have been lying there under that stall for the last three years, or it might mean a cryogenic tank full of a Triple Crown Winner's sperm was sitting in Charlie's garage.

I was one of those people who feel the need for speed when faced with a crisis, and I had obtained a fairly high MPH by the time I burst through the front door of Ace's office. When I skidded to a stop in front of the counter, I saw Jody goggling at me from behind it.

"Where's Jason?" I asked.

For several maddening seconds, Jody stared at me with no sign of comprehension and then, just as I was about to reach over the counter and shake my teenage porter by her shoulders, she discovered that she was in possession of all the necessary facts to answer my question.

"Oh, he's gone."

"Where, Jody? Where has Jason gone?"

She gave another moment of careful consideration to this new twist on the question, and then after all the cogs of her cognitive processes meshed up with the proper gears, the facts of the situation lined up in her head, and a jackpot of information came pouring out of her mouth.

"Pitch got soap or something squirted in his eyes when he tried to unclog a doohickey in the carwash. We washed his eyes, but Mr. Singletary took him to the doctor to make sure he's okay. He asked me to watch the front until you got back."

Having successfully delivered her message, Jody began to walk toward the back door.

"Jody, wait up a moment. I might need you," I said.

She stopped and leaned up against a wall, while I came around the counter and picked up a phone receiver. Jason answered his cell phone on the first ring.

"Hey, Walt. Pitch is fine. They bathed his eyes, and the doc says no damage was done. I'll be back as soon as I finish the insurance papers."

"Good. Listen, Jason, I just found something amazing. I think your theory about Charlie switching the sperm might have been correct after all."

"Yeah? Wow! What did you find?"

"If I told you, you would only try to talk me out of doing what I need to do."

"Uh oh. Walt, listen, whatever it is you think you need to do can wait. Let me finish this paperwork, and I'll be back there in five minutes."

"Sorry, Jason, I won't be here. Every moment counts now. You don't know what I did to Leda yesterday, and I don't have time to tell you about it now, but I broke her heart. I betrayed her. I've been on the wrong side all along, and now I'm going to make it right."

"Walt! Put down your keys! You're not thinking clearly. Friends don't let friends drive when –"

I hung up the phone. I was afraid Leda might deliver another blackmail letter or do something else that would cause Charlie to move his tank of frozen horse sperm to another location, and that would ruin any chances of proving his guilt. I turned to face my teenaged porter. Her eyes had grown to the size of Ping-Pong balls.

"Jody, nod if you understand me."

Jody nodded.

"Can you watch the front until Jason gets back?"

Jody nodded.

"Good. Tell any customers that come in to just have a seat. Okay?"

Jody nodded.

Chapter Thirty-Two

On a hunch, I parked next to the vacant lot on the street behind Charlie's house. I got out of the car, walked over to the fence at the back of the lot, and pulled myself up until I could see over it. The yard on the other side was Charlie's back yard, as I had thought it might be. This would have been Leda's escape route, if Charlie had come home unexpectedly.

I went back to the Lincoln, popped the trunk, and removed the tire wrench. Young business professionals who want to work in the city but live in the country comprise the principal population of bedroom communities like Cobb's Station, so their neighborhoods are pretty much abandoned during daylight hours. Consequently, they employ a lot of security measures like the alarm that Charlie had on his front gate. I intended to avoid that alarm by creating a new gate. I approached the fence and quickly loosened the bottoms of three boards with the sharp end of the tire wrench. To make sure that I wasn't caught like Peter Rabbit had been when the young bunny had tried to make his escape from the farmer's garden, I carefully folded over all the nails protruding from the ends of the boards, before swinging them up and scrambling under them.

The next security sensor to worry about was the one on the side door into the garage. I intended to trip it. With modern electronics and cellular communication, successful break-ins have become more about speed than finesse. No matter how many phone lines are cut and sensors put out of commission, there is always the possibility of missing a hidden microphone or camera that's reporting a burglar's every move to the monitoring service over a battery-operated wireless transmitter.

I figured I had ten minutes to get in, locate Charlie's cryogenic tank, identify its contents, and scoot back under the fence before the community's security guard arrived. If I found the tank contained Running Fool's sperm, I intended to steal it and bring it directly to Elara Downs. When I showed the tank to Emily Taurus, the former owner and current manager of Elara Downs, and told her what was inside and where I had found it, she would instantly understand what Charlie had done to her. I would let Emily explain Charlie's villainy to Himalia, who would promptly stop the planned wedding and send a very grateful Leda running back into my arms.

Charlie could report the break-in, but not the loss of horse sperm that had never been his in the first place. More than likely, he would simply vanish, because Daniel Brookshire, the true owner of Running Fool's sperm, would be the next person Emily Taurus talked to. Daniel and other interested parties would have a lot of embarrassing questions for Charlie, once it was known that the frozen sperm had been recovered from his garage,

I smashed the door's little diamond-shaped window and reached through the opening to turn the latch on the inside. I braced myself for the loud noise of a siren and pushed the door open. Nothing happened, but now that I had the door open, I could see the little magnetic contact at the top of the door jam.

I walked into the garage and looked around. Nothing that resembled a cryogenic tank was immediately visible, but there was door at the back that obviously led to a small storage area. This door turned out to be equipped with a deadbolt, which I didn't have the time or equipment to deal with. After a short search, I found a hammer under the workbench, used it to knock a hole through the storage room's sheetrock wall and was immediately rewarded by the gleam of a steel cryogenic tank. Using the hammer and my hands, I widened the hole until I was able to pull the tank out of the closet. I noticed that "Pender Lab" and a 10-digit number were stenciled on both sides of the tank near the top – just like the straw Leda found.

Just as Charlie had a few days before, I lugged the large metal tank over to the workbench, deposited it on the wooden chair, pulled the cord hanging from the fluorescent light fixture and as it hummed into life, donned the safety goggles and cotton gloves that were lying on the bench. I took a big breath and carefully twisted the tank's lid in a counter clockwise direction. It was harder to turn than I thought it would be. I applied some extra pressure, and it suddenly popped open with a disconcerting whooshing sound as the pressure inside the tank equalized with the pressure in the room. The tank's thick metal brim instantly turned white with frost, and a cloud of white vapor poured over the sides.

I stepped away from the tank in alarm. I told myself that I needed to calm down and take my time. I didn't want to cause any more damage than I had to in order to identify the frozen sperm stored in the tank. My goal was to extract one straw and read the information printed on it. Doing so would probably take more than three seconds, and irreversibly damage the sperm in that one straw, but then I would know whether Charlie was storing the frozen sperm of the Triple Crown Winner, Running Fool in his garage.

I stepped back to the chair and looked into the neck of tank. I saw the tops of a number of metal canisters jutting up out of a gently moving cloud of white vapor. I had begun to pull on a metal cane inside of one of these canisters, when I realized that I needed a pair of tweezers. I opened drawers on the workbench until I found a long pair of plastic tweezers with rubber tips that was obviously made for the job. Remembering Dr. Norton's admonition to Charlie, I carefully raised one of the metal canes until the top of a translucent glass goblet was just visible but still below the frost line inside the tank. This took a while to achieve because my movements kept disturbing the vapor cloud inside the tank and the wisps of vapor that wafted up interfered with my vision.

Once I was able to see the tops of the straws, I reached into the goblet with my tweezers, drew out a straw, lowered the cane back into its canister, and turned to the workbench to examine my prize.

I held the straw up to the light, let out a moan of frustration, and dropped the straw onto the workbench. The horse named on the straw was Charlie's horse, Thunder Tom.

I decided to try pulling a straw from a different canister. I looked carefully at the group of canisters and noticed that the handle of each cane had a range of dates written on it. After holding up the first straw to the light, I was able to match the date on that straw to the handle of a cane I had just pulled. The dates written on the canes seemed to be sequential and cover a period of about six months. This discovery did not cheer me. It was looking increasingly likely that the sperm in this tank was drawn from a single stallion, but I decided to pull one more straw just in case the dates on these canes were not truly indicative of their contents.

I repeated the careful extraction procedure on another cane chosen at random and was holding the straw up to the light when I heard an electronic chime. Someone had just opened the gate. I dropped the straw and started to run for the door, but halfway there I remembered that I had left the cryogenic tank open, so I ran back, spun the lid on and raced to the door again.

When I got outside, I saw two fat security guards walking towards the garage. They saw me at about the same time, and the race was on. I sprinted for the fence and threw myself at the spot I had crawled under earlier. Unfortunately, the boards I ended up slamming into were not the ones I had previously loosened.

Chapter Thirty-Three

I came to lying face down on the floor of Charlie's garage. I tried to get up, but immediately felt the pressure of someone's boot on my back.

"Just settle down, sonny. The police are on their way."

I sank back to the floor with a soft moan of despair. The mention of police had brought home the serious nature of my predicament.

After I had spent about five minutes agonizing over the repercussions of my reckless actions, I heard the gate chime, and Charlie's voice talking to the other guard just outside the garage door. This was shortly followed by the sounds of someone bursting into the room, and rushing past me towards the rear of the garage. After that, I heard keys rattling, the storage room door being hurriedly unlocked, heavy objects being shifted around and a series of metallic clanks.

"Okay."

Charlie uttered this simple word like a man who had expected a bomb to blow up in his face, and then found it was a dud. I heard Charlie stride over to the vicinity of the workbench and, after a short pause, to my side.

"Okay, who are you, and who sent you?"

Charlie knelt down by me, and I struggled to turn my head up towards him. This movement drew an instant rebuke from the guard, but before my face had returned to the floor, I had seen Charlie staring down at me.

"Excuse me, sir," the security guard said, "but the cops wouldn't want you questioning the suspect."

"The police are coming?" Charlie asked.s "I don't think that's really necessary. I happen to know this young man, and I believe this is just a little misunderstanding."

"I don't know. I think your neighbors wouldn't want this kid running around loose."

"No, it's okay, really. He's not a burglar. He works at a rental car company in Jupiter. I'll take personal responsibility for him."

"Well, if you're sure, I'll call the cops and cancel, but give me a heads up in case you decide to press charges later."

"I'll be sure to do that. Thanks."

The guard walked outside, and Charlie stood in the doorway talking to him. I rolled over and sat up. I could hear one of the guards talking on his two-way radio, and the other guard asking Charlie to sign some paperwork.

I felt immensely grateful to Charlie. I knew any other man would have insisted on pressing charges against me. I stood up, removed the goggles, pulled off the gloves, and was dusting myself off when I heard the gate chime announcing the exit of the security guards. When I heard Charlie step back into the garage, I turned with the intention of thanking him for canceling the police and froze in my tracks. Charlie had a terrifying expression on his face and a black, automatic pistol in his hand.

"Okay, Walt, let's have a little talk."

I was scared spit less. I had never had a gun pointed at me before, and I would never have imagined someone like Charlie even owning one. I tried to talk, to explain, to plead, but my mouth felt like it was stuffed with cotton. All I could manage to do was nod, and I nodded for all I was worth.

"Good. I'm happy you agree. Now, I want you to walk over to the workbench."

I backed toward the workbench until I bumped into it.

"Watch what you're doing! You don't have to keep facing me like that! Turn around, and carefully put my tank on the floor."

I transferred the cryogenic tank from the chair to the floor, and then turned back to Charlie for further instructions.

"Well, go on," Charlie said in an exasperated voice, "sit down. Why do you think I had you put the tank on the floor?"

I wanted to explain that I was only trying to follow directions, but I decided it might be wiser not to interject at that particular moment and plopped onto the chair. Charlie walked up to the workbench, picked up the straws I had left lying there, and held them up with his free hand.

"You're not looking for your biological papa any more, are you, Walt?"

"No." I looked down, too frightened and embarrassed to elaborate.

"Well, what did you think you were looking for? You broke into my garage, and messed with my most valuable possession. Why did you do that? Who sent you?"

"Look, no one sent me. I'll tell you everything, and pay for any damage I've caused if you'll just stop pointing that gun at me."

Charlie stopped pointing his gun and started waving it instead. Then his face turned purple, and he began shouting at the top of his voice.

"You couldn't possibly pay for the damage, you moron!" He roared. "The sperm in that tank is worth more than you'll make in ten years!"

I was amazed and terrified. This was the first time I had ever seen Charlie lose it, and I was deathly afraid the pistol would go off in mid-wave.

"No, no, no. I was very careful. I only took the straws you're holding, and I didn't raise the glass vials above the frost line while I was removing them."

Rage drained out of Charlie's face leaving suspicion in its wake. He leaned across the workbench and looked narrowly at me.

"Who taught you all that?"

"No one did, Charlie. I watched Doc Norton do it last Wednesday, remember?"

"Okay, that explains how you knew the procedure for retrieving straws from a cryogenic tank, but it doesn't explain why you suddenly decided to start practicing what you learned in my garage."

"If you'll just put your gun down, I'll tell you everything"

Charlie pointed the gun to one side and pulled the trigger. It made the chunky sound of highly compressed air being released and a metal pellet ricocheted off the garage door.

"I keep this around to scare cats off with. I hate cats." Charlie slipped the air-pistol into his pocket and leaned against the workbench. "There's a lot of criminal activity in thoroughbred racing, Walt. I wanted to put up a tough front just in case you were connected to it. I don't really think that's the case now, but I'm still going to hold you to your promise to explain exactly what you were doing here. Then we'll discuss how you're going to pay me for my damages."

Now that the gun had been dispensed with, I felt a lot better, but this new tough version of Charlie made me sad. I knew Charlie had every reason to be angry with me, and I was grateful for being spared the humiliating experience of going to jail, but the remark about shooting cats with a BB pistol disgusted me.

"Fine, and I'll pay every dime. I made a terrible mistake, I destroyed some of your property, and it looks like I've made you really worried and upset. I'm sorry, and I appreciate your letting me make it up to you." I took a deep breath and let it all out with my next sentence. "I came here because I thought you stole Running Fool's sperm."

Charlie's mouth didn't exactly drop open, but there was an aspect of stunned surprise in his manner. "That's – bizarre. Why in the world would you think that? Where did you hear about Running Fool anyway? Have you been talking to Dean? I always had a feeling he didn't like me."

"I heard about it from several different sources, Charlie. Something about you just makes people suspicious. It's not fair, but that's the way it is."

"Well, did these sources of yours happen to explain how I was able to steal sperm that burned up in a fire?"

"Most of these people thought you set the tack room fire so Daniel Brookshire could collect the insurance money. My friend Jason was the one who thought you might have switched the sperm before you set the fire."

"That's absurd! I'm surprised you would believe such a crazy thing."

"I didn't until this morning. I thought everyone was just jealous of you. Then I found something that changed my mind. It wasn't absolute proof, but because Leda is so important to me and you were marrying her mother, I had to find out if you were guilty or not."

"So you broke into my garage and opened my cryogenic tank? Do you realize how insane that sounds? Why didn't you just ask me about it?"

"I know, it sounds crazy now, but –"

"Sounds crazy? Look at you! Your clothes are covered in sheetrock dust, you have a bump on your head the size of a walnut, and you're not making any sense. What could you have possibly found that led you to drive down here and knock a hole in my garage wall?"

I reached into my pocket, pulled out the little brown envelope, and handed it to Charlie.

"What's this?" Charlie asked.

"It's a used straw that Leda found on the breeding room floor after Frisco Gal's insemination. She stuck it in my pocket as a souvenir. I happened across it this morning."

Charlie pulled the straw out and held it up to the light.

"Running Fool – that's amazing! Where did she find it?"

"Under the edge of the standing stall."

"Oh. Well, that explains it. It could've been there for years."

"Yeah, or it could've rolled there after you dropped all those straws on the floor the other night."

"I see. You thought I purposely knocked those straws on the floor so I could switch them before Dr. Norton recorded the information off them. Walt, you have an incredibly convoluted mind. If I had stolen Running Fool's sperm, why would I carry the evidence of the theft back to the place I stole it from and risk getting caught? "

"I don't know, but you looked worried when Dr. Norton told you he was going to examine the sperm, and then after the procedure was over and everyone had gone to dinner, you came back to the breeding room."

"Yeah, Himalia sent me to fetch you and Leda."

"I know, but when I found that straw this morning, it occurred to me that you might not have found all the straws you knocked on the floor, and had come looking for the one Leda found – but we happened to be in the room you wanted to search."

"But that's all pure hogwash."

"I know that now. I only pulled two straws out of your tank before the security guards showed up, but it was enough to convince me that all the straws in your tank are Thunder Tom's. It wouldn't make sense for you to keep both horses' sperm in the same tank without some kind of obvious labeling system, and the fact that you have any of Thunder Tom's sperm at all proves that you didn't steal Running Fool's sperm. Jason said you would've had to repackage Thunder Tom's sperm in counterfeit straws to exchange with Running Fool's."

"Well, your whole theory was crazy to begin with." Charlie shoved the straw back in its little brown envelope and handed it to me. "Here. Take your souvenir back. I think you should keep it to remind you how much damage can come from listening to vicious rumors. Speaking of damages, I'm now going to dictate to you what mine are. If you don't want to accept my price, I'll just press charges against you for forced entry and malicious vandalism, and you can take your chances in court. Do you understand?"

"Yes."

"Good. I think I can get my door and wall repaired for around $500, but I'm going to charge you a grand to cover my time in attending to it. Any objection?"

"No."

"As far as Thunder Tom's sperm goes, I only have your word you were careful, and that's not good enough for me. I'm going to bring my tank in to the lab, and have them pull a straw from ten different goblets and test the sperm for viability. That's ten more straws that'll have to be destroyed in addition to the two you already ruined. That'll cost you fifteen hundred in lab fees and two grand for the sperm. Of course, if they discover any damage then you'll be liable for that as well. Let's hope all those little sperm are wigglers, because this tank has over a thousand straws in it, and I don't think you could ever pay me what they're really worth."

"So," I said weakly, "you think about five thousand dollars?"

"Yeah, you're getting off cheap, but I see no reason to hold you up just because you're mentally unbalanced."

"Okay, I – I have that much in my savings account. I'll write you a check, but you have to give me twenty-four hours to transfer the funds."

"I trust you, Walt. But we're not through here, the money's only part of the deal. You have to promise to never bother me again."

"You don't have to worry about that. You won't see me again after today."

"I'm marrying Himalia this weekend, which means you can't come to Elara Downs anymore either, and I'll expect you to turn down any invitations Himalia might extend to you."

"Okay."

"And finally, I don't want you seeing Leda anymore. I think you might be dangerous, and she gets into enough trouble by herself."

"I don't think you should make me promise that."

"Why not? It's not like you're seeing her anyway. Himalia told me Leda broke it off with you."

"It doesn't matter. You don't know what you're asking; hoping Leda will eventually come back to me is all I have to live for. I'm not going to promise you or anybody else that I won't see her again."

"Okay. If she looks you up, that's her business. But if you call, mail, or hang around outside Elara Downs, I'll contact my security service and have them forward their report to the police. Understand?"

"Yeah."

"Good. Then write me a check and get the hell out of here."

I pulled my checkbook out and wrote Charlie a check for five thousand dollars, which just about wiped out my savings. I handed Charlie the check, got up to go, and then turned to face him.

"I got the results on the DNA test. The results were negative."

"Of course they were negative. I told you I wasn't your papa the day you showed up on my doorstep, but you wouldn't listen."

I shrugged my shoulders, walked as far as the door, then turned for one last look at the man I once thought of as my father. Charlie was propped against his workbench with his arms crossed, smiling in much the same way he had when we first met. The smile that had seemed confident and friendly then, looked smug and conceited now.

"You know Charlie, there was one curious thing about those test results – we both happen to share genes on two different chromosomes, which wasn't especially significant by itself but for some reason Jason mentioned something about chimerism. Have you ever heard that term before?"

"What term? What the hell are you talking about?"

"Chimeras."

Charlie's smile vanished, and he waved a hand at me as if he was shooing away a fly.

"Go on, get out of here, Walt. Go find your real papa."

Chapter Thirty-Four

I made it back an hour before closing time. I would have arrived at Ace earlier still, but I had to stop by my apartment to change clothes and do my best to clean the plaster dust, dirt and grass stains off my Jacket. The grass stains wouldn't budge, and I was afraid the little Korean lady at the drycleaners would declare them to be 'tiger stripes.' On the way to work, I stopped by my bank and transferred most of the money in my savings to my checking account to cover Charlie's check. Afterwards, much to my surprise and shame, I spent five minutes weeping in my car.

When I arrived at the office, I found Jason beleaguered by return customers, and feeling more than a little guilty for leaving my partner in the lurch, I pitched in and helped him catch up. When we finally got a moment free, Jason said he had some banking to do and asked if I could cover for him. I had never known Jason to do any banking on a Tuesday, but I insisted he take the rest of the day off. I would have gone on to thank him for covering for me yet again, followed by an apology for running out on him in the first place, but a customer came in and cut my conciliatory speech short. I knew Jason was sore. I wanted to explain to my friend why I had felt compelled to leave Jody watching the front instead of waiting for him to get back from the doctor's with Pitch. And I wished I had some kind of reasonable excuse for all the times I had left Jason holding the bag during the last ten days. The problem was, I didn't have any explanations, and I was out of excuses. I was at a complete loss to account for my own behavior, and though I had found Charlie's snide remarks about my sanity insulting, I was beginning to wonder if there wasn't some truth to them after all.

I closed the rental agency by myself and drove the Lincoln back to Ganymede Apartments, where my calico cat was waiting to greet me. I crouched down by Io and spent several minutes communing with the one female in my life, besides my mother, that I knew still loved me.

I fed Io, boiled some water in the microwave, and poured it into a Styrofoam cup of ramen noodles. While my noodle soup was steeping, I walked into my living room and stared morosely at the fluorescent blue zero on my answering machine display. I didn't think Leda was ever going to call me, and if I had to follow Charlie's rules, I didn't think I would ever see her again. I wondered if Charlie really could have me thrown in jail after the security guards had already canceled their call to the police. I didn't know, but I suspected Jason would, or how to find out if he didn't.

I picked up the phone and dialed Jason's cell phone. My call immediately went to voice mail. I knew that meant Jason had turned his phone off. I was aware my friend was angry with me, but I thought turning the cell phone off was a juvenile maneuver that shouldn't be encouraged. So I called Jason's mother and asked if I could come over.

Jason's mom lived in the oldest, flattest part of Jupiter. The houses were all built of the same dark red bricks, manufactured by the town's now defunct brick company, and they all had full-sized basements. When I called Mrs. Singletary, she was getting ready for bed, but she told me she would leave the front door unlocked.

When I arrived, the only lights on in the house were coming from the basement and the front hallway. I let myself in, walked down the hallway, and rapped softly on the basement door. I heard the stairs creaking, and then Jason appeared in the doorway dressed in a t-shirt, shorts and house slippers.

"Hey, Walt. Mom told me you were coming over. I wasn't really expecting visitors, but come on down."

I felt a lump form in my throat. This remark wouldn't have sounded particularly rude to the unschooled, but this was about as nasty as Jason got. I knew my friend must be really peeved.

Jason led the way down the stairs and past the furnace to a cinderblock partition that served as the front wall of his apartment. There wasn't a door, and the walls didn't go all the way up to the floor joists, but as long as you didn't look up at the pipes and ignored the furnace, his apartment looked like any other tastefully decorated and furnished efficiency. It had its own kitchenette, a bathroom with a special toilet that flushed up instead of down and about five thousand plastic DVD jewel cases, arranged in floor-to-floor bookcases lining every available inch of wall space. Jason liked downloading music. The DVDs only represented a small portion of his collection; most of his music resided in a small city of hard drives stacked like miniature skyscrapers around his computer setup.

Jason directed me towards the daybed and then sat, with his arms folded and his legs crossed, on his computer station's pneumatic swivel chair. I settled uneasily onto the edge of the daybed and tried to compose my thoughts. There was a long moment of awkward silence and then both of us spoke at once.

"Jason–*Walt*–I–*what*–want–*the*–to–*hell*–apologize–*happened*–to you?"

My earnest statement of apology was covered up and mixed with Jason's demand to know where I had run off to. There was another slight pause, and then both of us tried to give the other the floor.

"*You go*–No you go–*ahead*–first." Jason ceded to me and visa versa.

After this bout of verbal head butting, we resorted to the use of hand signals to indicate to the other that he should speak first. Jason held out an open palm to me. I shook my head and pointed to Jason, who trumped my point by holding up both palms to politely refuse the honor. Finally, realizing I had the floor, I took a deep breath and bared my soul.

"Jason, I want to apologize for my bad behavior. The way I've been treating you lately is inexcusable. I let my personal life interfere with my duties at Ace. I came in late, left early, spent more time driving around than I did at the office, and when I did show up, I endangered both our jobs by leaving a teenager to watch the office while you were seeing to one of our employee's injuries."

"And you left me out of the loop!" Jason pointed out.

"And I left you out of the loop," I conceded. "I failed to tell you what happened when I saw Himalia and Leda yesterday. That was wrong, and I apologize. You have been involved in this whole affair from the beginning, and I had no right to cut you out."

"You saw Leda again?"

"Yeah, I'm sorry. I know I promised to share everything that happened at the bowling alley yesterday. I should've filled you in when you first asked me this morning, and I should've waited for you to get back from the doctor's office. If I had, you probably would've kept me from running down to Cobb's Station like a chicken with its head cut off, and saved me from making a total ass of myself at

Charlie's house. I've been acting stupid. I'm ashamed of myself, and I want to make it up to you."

"You just have!" he said, "Tell me about Leda. No, first tell me about your meeting with Himalia, then Leda. Then tell me what the hell happened to you today. Wait! Let me get a coke first. Do you want a coke?"

I didn't want a coke, but I waited patiently while Jason pulled one from his dormitory-sized refrigerator. I was grateful I hadn't permanently alienated my best friend, and smiled patiently as he settled back in his swivel chair with an air of keen anticipation.

"Okay, shoot."

I began by telling Jason about meeting Himalia at the Red Spot Lanes. I described my shock at learning how Maia had passed my confidences on to Leda and my dismay that my remarks had been misrepresented. Jason laughed when I told him about choking on Himalia's Cuba Libre, but congratulated me on realizing that Maia might have planned a two-pronged attack by sending a blackmail letter to Charlie.

I described the coat hanger and bubble gum device I had constructed to retrieve the letter, the exultation I had felt once I had the letter in my hands, and my shock and amazement at being caught red-handed by Leda. Jason started laughing during the blow-by-blow description of the first round of the fight with Leda and nearly fell out of his chair when I sheepishly displayed the bite mark Leda had left on my arm in the final round of the bout. He tried to reassure me about my rift with Leda by pointing out the tremendous passion I obviously inspired in her. Jason told me Leda wouldn't have been nearly as angry if she didn't really care for me.

I didn't find the intensity of Leda's anger especially consoling and didn't want to continue dwelling on the subject, so I segued to the discovery I had made that morning when I picked up my jacket at the dry cleaners. Jason jumped out of his chair the moment I mentioned finding the expended sperm straw. He capered around the room shouting that he *knew* Charlie had stolen Running Fool's sperm, and now we had the proof. I insisted that he listen to the rest of my story, and then described everything that had happened when I broke into Charlie's garage. Jason had few comments, but he made me repeat my description of the metallic clanking sounds I had heard when Charlie was inspecting his storage closet and the way Charlie had said the word 'okay' afterwards.

"He has more than one tank!" explained Jason, "Think about it, Walt. Charlie comes home to find his garage busted into and sees his tank of frozen sperm sitting out on the workbench, but instead of going to the workbench to check it out, he rushes to his storage closet to see what else you might have got into. I think the reason Charlie sounded so relieved was because Running Fool's tank was safe."

"Then why does he still have a tank full of Thunder Tom's sperm? I thought you said he used it all to manufacture the counterfeit straws he replaced Running Fool's sperm with before the tack room fire."

"I was wrong about that. I should have realized that he could've gotten ordinary horse sperm fairly cheaply from a number of sources. It didn't have to come from a thoroughbred; all the lab did after the fire was perform a test on a few straws to see if the sperm was still viable. Just because Thunder Tom isn't a Triple Crown winner doesn't mean his sperm isn't valuable. Thunder Tom is still a thoroughbred of respectable linage and standard horse breeders would probably pay Charlie a couple of hundred dollars per insemination."

"How many straws does it take for an insemination?"

"Around five or six."

"Then Charlie charged me for two inseminations of Running Fool's sperm."

"What! I thought you only pulled two straws."

"Yeah, but Charlie says the lab has to pull ten straws to make sure I didn't damage the ones in the tank."

"Well, since he expects you to pay for the damage you caused, he's obviously not pressing charges against you."

"Yeah, you didn't let me get to that part of the story. Charlie had the security guards cancel the police and sent them away. Then he had me explain why I was there. I told him about the stories connecting him to the tack room fire and your theory that he might have switched the sperm. Then I handed him the straw Leda found on the breeding room floor. He looked at it and admitted it belonged to Running Fool, but he pointed out that it could've been lying under the standing stall floor for years."

"He's lying. If the details of the story you told me about the tack room fire were correct, no insemination was ever attempted with Running Fool's sperm at Elara Downs. Remember, the vet who was performing the insemination that day had determined the mare wasn't ready, so the procedure was put off until after supper. They put Running Fool's cryogenic tank in the tack room for safekeeping, and it was irretrievably damaged when the tack room caught fire. No insemination took place that day, and none of Running Fool's empty straws should have been on that floor."

I stood up, and threw my hands in the air.

"You're right! Why didn't I remember that? I didn't need to prove Charlie had the sperm in his garage. All I have to do is show this straw to Dr. Norton and tell him where I found it. He'll contact Daniel Brookshire, and a ton of bricks will fall on Charlie's head. He won't be marrying Himalia, and he won't collect $5000 dollars from me because I'll damn well stop payment on the check!"

"You still have the straw? I thought you gave it to Charlie."

"Yeah, but he gave it back. Here it is, look!" I said, pulling the envelope containing the straw from my pocket.

Jason took the envelope and pulled the straw out. He frowned, rolled his chair up to his desk, took a magnifying glass out of a drawer, and examined the straw under the bright light of a reading lamp. Then he turned back to me and handed me the magnifying glass and straw.

"This straw still has sperm in it, and its not Running Fool's. Charlie gave you one of the straws that you pulled from Thunder Tom's tank."

I took the straw over to the light and looked at it under the magnifying glass. It was labeled with the names of 'Thunder Tom' and "Pender Lab," followed by a date and some other names and numbers. I dropped the straw and magnifying glass on the desk, stumbled back to the daybed, and lay down on it.

"Get up, you dunderhead!" Jason shouted, "This isn't a disaster! Don't you see that the fact he switched the straws proves he's guilty?"

"Only to us," I moaned. "We know he's guilty, but we can't prove it now that he has the straw."

"No, but you can still tell Dr. Norton about it. Once he knows what to look for, he can launch an investigation that'll tie Charlie in knots. Your sperm daddy is finished. He just doesn't know it yet."

I sat up.

"Yeah. That might work, but it would take too long. By the time anything came of an investigation, Charlie will already have married Himalia, and I'll have lost any chance of ever getting Leda back."

"Yeah, I guess you're right. But how hard should it be to stop a wedding? Now that you finally have absolute proof your sperm daddy is a slime ball, you don't have to hold back anymore!"

"Stop calling him my 'sperm daddy.' He's not my biological father!"

"Yeah, he is. I was right about Running Fool's sperm, and I'm right about this. He's a chimera, and your sperm daddy."

"Cut it out, Jason. Charlie's definitely not a chimera. I mentioned it to him, and it didn't even faze him. He just stared at me, and told me to get the hell out."

"He just stared at you?"

"Yeah."

"He didn't ask you what a chimera was, or where you heard the term or anything?"

"No."

"Hot damn! How much was that check you wrote Charlie?"

"Five grand. Nearly every cent I have."

"Stop payment on that check."

"I can't stop payment, Jason. He'll press charges if I do."

"Listen, Walt, I was right about him setting that tackroom fire and stealing the racehorse sperm, wasn't I?"

"Yeah."

"Yeah, well, I'm right about this, too. I don't know how I do it! I guess I must have some kind of sixth sense or something, but the moment I saw Charlie's face pop up in Bert's Facial Recognition scan, I knew he was your sperm dad – uh, biological father. When I first proposed the idea that Charlie might be a chimera, I didn't really think it was all that likely. But I *knew* he was a crook, and I didn't like the way he was pulling the wool over your eyes, so I started checking out seatechlimited.com. If you remember, that was the website you saw on the paperwork in Charlie's house for that rebuilt boat motor company he claimed to represent. It's a very slick, very professional, website. They have everything you would expect to see, but they never answer their email, their phone numbers go directly to voicemail and I couldn't find any references to the company on any other websites. Even the original manufacturer of the engines Sea Tech supposedly rebuilds doesn't mention them. The other day I tried to find out who owned the Sea Tech limited domain, but they had paid their registry to keep that information private. Anyone can have their registry information blocked to the general public for a small fee each year. Fortunately for me, I have a friend who knows how to get around privacy filters, and he emailed me the owner of seatechlimited.com this afternoon. The domain is registered to a Mr. Cecil Jones. Does that name strike a bell?"

I reflected for a moment, and then the image of a printed list of sperm donors surfaced in my memory. "Yeah, I think he was one of the aliases my sperm donor used. But that could be a coincidence. I've been running into an awful lot of coincidences lately."

"Walt, you're lucky I'm such a patient friend. Look, what if I could prove Charlie was lying about never donating sperm before? Would that be enough evidence for you?"

I started to answer impulsively, and then paused to seriously consider the question. Charlie had consistently maintained that he had never donated sperm before, but still agreed to take the DNA test. If Charlie was lying and had donated sperm before, then he couldn't have been certain the test would turn out negative unless he knew the DNA in his cheek cells didn't match the DNA in his sperm.

"Yeah, I guess so."

"So if I prove he has donated sperm under his own name, you'll agree your biological father is a chimera named Charlie."

"Jason, I'll even let you call him my sperm daddy. But how can you prove he's donated sperm before? I thought you said your friend stopped working at the fertility clinic."

"I'm not going to share my plan with you because I don't want you dwelling on it. I know you, Walt. You would worry all night and be completely worthless tomorrow. You'll just have to trust me. Okay?"

"Well, I have a feeling I'm going to regret going along with another one of your hair-brained schemes, but okay."

"Good. Now make sure you get up early tomorrow because you'll have to open Ace. Then call Marty and see if he can drive up and watch the store for a couple of hours tomorrow afternoon."

"Marty's not going to drive up here just to give us a long lunch break in the middle of the week."

"Yeah, he will. Just tell him I'm calling my favor in."

I agreed to open Ace and wait for further instructions, but I was starting to wonder what I was getting myself into.

Chapter Thirty-Five

A little after noon on the following day, Marty walked into the office carrying his pickle jar. I was glad to see him. I didn't know how Jason managed to juggle all the customers, phone calls, paperwork, and our teenage porters by himself, but now that I had tried it for half a day, I was resolved never to abandon my partner again.

"Hey, Marty. Thanks a lot for coming. I know it's a long drive for you to make just to watch the office for a couple of hours."

"I'm glad I could do Jason a favor. I owed him one."

"What did he do for you?"

"I messed up my daughter's laptop, and he helped me fix it. She left it at my house when she went to the Bahamas on spring break. I used it to download some, uh, well, you know, some games and stuff like that. Man, was her laptop fast! My desktop is slower than molasses on a cold day, but her little Toshiba made web surfing fun! Well, something I downloaded must have had a bug in it because the screen started going crazy. Boy, was I in trouble! That laptop had Sandy's dissertation in it, and it was due after the break. I called one of those technical support lines, but they said there was nothing they could do after the worm had already done its stuff. I was at my wit's end before I remembered good old Jason. Downloading stuff off the web is all he ever talks about. I figured if anybody knew about computer worms, he would. So I gave him a call, and he told me to bring it to his house. Man! Have you ever seen that Star Wars setup he has in his basement? Yeah? Well, I fell asleep on that little couch of his around three AM after spending hours watching him type messages to all the other geeks and nerds out there. When I woke up, he had Sandy's laptop working better than ever. He even removed all the stuff I had downloaded, so she wouldn't know I had been messing with it. Jason is tops in my book. Go take care of your business, Walt. I'll watch the store until you get back."

I spent a few minutes bringing Marty up to speed on our location's current business, and then drove to my rendezvous with Jason. He had called earlier in the day from a Fry's Electronic store on the outskirts of Buffalo, giving me an address in downtown Jupiter. I wasn't familiar with the place, and I didn't know what we were going to do there, but I had decided to give Jason my full and unquestioning cooperation. I didn't think the results of whatever plan he had in mind could be any worse than the disastrous consequences of my own efforts. Besides, it felt a lot better to be doing something instead of just sitting around with my face in my hands.

I had called my bank as soon as it had opened that morning, and stopped payment on Charlie's check. I didn't think Charlie would find out about it for a few days, and by then, Jason's mystery plan would either have pulled Charlie's fangs or gotten me in so much trouble that the prospect of going to jail wouldn't seem so bad anymore.

The address that Jason had given me turned out to be a multistory professional building close to Jupiter's largest hospital. I found a spot in the parking garage and rode the elevator down to the lobby to find Jason carrying a small briefcase and looking nervous.

"Hey, Jason."

"Okay, Walt, this is the next part of my plan. The fertility clinic my friend worked in is in this building. It's only been a week since she stopped working there, so they probably haven't got around to changing her logon or password. In this briefcase, I have a wireless router that should extend their network all the way to the parking garage once I hook it up to my friend's old workstation. All you have to do is distract the girl who took her place, while I install it."

"You mean, once you have the wireless router installed, we can come back here and get into the database without leaving our car? That's brilliant! How do I distract the girl?"

"Isn't it obvious? You go in to donate some sperm, and you have a little trouble doing it."

"Donate sperm! That's embarrassing. Why me?"

"Do you know how to install a wireless router in a UNIX environment?"

"No."

"Then I guess it has to be you."

"I don't think I can do it, Jason."

"Come on, Walt. You don't have to actually go through with it. You're just going to fill out the application, go back to one of the collection rooms with the attendant, and ask a whole lot of questions. They have all kinds of sexual aids to help donors get in the mood. Ask questions about them. Pretend you don't know how to operate a videotape machine. Just use your imagination. If it looks like you're not going to be able to keep her there long enough, faint, or throw a fit, or something."

"I don't know. The whole thing sounds really embarrassing to me. How long do you think you're going to need?"

"To be on the safe side, about five minutes."

"Five minutes! You want me to talk about sex toys and masturbation with some woman I've never met for five minutes?"

"Just do your best, Walt. Keep it up as long as you can, and when she starts to head back up front, tell her you've changed your mind and walk back with her, talking real loud all the way so I'll know you're coming."

"Now I see why you wouldn't tell me your plan ahead of time. All right, I don't like it, but I guess I'll do it,"

We discussed a few more details of his plan, and then Jason led the way to a third-floor suite with an 'Out to Lunch' sign on its door. On the way, he explained to me that the doctor never made appointments with patients on Wednesday afternoons; as a result, the office was practically deserted except for the occasional walk-in sperm donor. It was on a Wednesday that his friend had let him use her workstation last time.

We waited by the door until a middle-aged woman dressed in blue scrubs opened it from within. She smiled at us, removed the sign, and let us into the waiting room. She offered us both applications, but Jason told her he had only come along for moral support. She laughed as she went through the door that led to her office and the examining rooms beyond. Once her silhouette appeared behind the sliding frosted-glass reception window, Jason pulled another 'out to lunch sign' from his briefcase, quickly walked to the suite's entrance door, hung his sign on the outside, and threw the latch.

I finished my application and knocked on the reception window. The glass panel slid back, and the woman took the application. A couple of minutes later, she led the way back to a typical examining room that had, in addition to the usual equipment, a VCR and a small, well-thumbed collection of men's magazines.

"Okay, dear," she said, handing me a sheet of paper, "here are the instructions for collecting your sample. It's very important that you wash the areas indicated in the illustration with anti-bacterial soap from that dispenser before you begin the procedure. Here's your collection cup. If you need stimulation, you'll find magazines and tapes over there to help you. Do you have any questions?"

I couldn't think of anything to say, and we had been away from the reception area for less than thirty seconds. The nurse assumed my silence meant that I had no questions and started to leave the room.

"The soap!" I blurted. The nurse stopped at the door and looked inquiringly at me. "Uh, my skin is sort of sensitive. Do you think the anti-bacterial soap will cause a rash on my, my–uh..."

"Privates?" she asked, with a sympathetic smile. I nodded and the nurse picked up the dispenser and showed me the label. "We get this stuff in special. It's safe enough for a baby's skin."

She proceeded to read aloud the list of ingredients on the soap dispenser, but instead of listening to her assurances that the soap was hypoallergenic and safe for even the most delicate epidermis, I was frantically trying to think of more questions to ask. Consequently, I found myself nodding dumbly as she told me she had to return to her desk. The nurse had made it a couple of steps down the hall, when a question that Charlie should have delved into more thoroughly when he was donating sperm occurred to me.

"Oh, miss!" I called, and the nurse turned back to see what I wanted. "I need to ask a question about the privacy issue."

"Didn't you read the release you signed?" she asked, a touch impatiently. "All your privacy rights and responsibilities were explained in the release."

"Yeah, but I just want to make sure that any child produced with my sperm doesn't look me up twenty years from now."

"Look, young man, I've only been working here a week, and I'm not familiar with all the ins and outs of the legal issues. You're just going to have to decide for yourself if your privacy is protected or not. Now if you'll excuse me, I really have to get back to my desk."

As she started to walk down the hall again, I struggled to remember some of Jason's suggestions for delaying her. I looked franticly around the room for inspiration and spotted the VCR. This machine was hooked to a small color monitor with a short length of coax cable. I grabbed the cable, jerked one end off of the back of the monitor, hit the on buttons on both devices, and ran out into the hall.

"Oh, miss!" I shouted.

The nurse turned around at the end of the hall and stared balefully at me.

"What is it now, young man? I have work to do."

"Could you take a quick look at this video recorder? I think I must be doing something wrong."

The nurse glared at me and came stomping back down the hall.

"What kind of kid are you? I thought young people knew how to work video recorders."

I shrugged my shoulders and backed into the examination room. As the nurse started to enter, I realized that I hadn't put a tape in the machine. I reached out blindly and grabbed one off the shelf just as she was entering.

"Look" she said, savagely pushing the play button, "it's completely automatic. You just push the play button and it starts playing. Wait a minute; you don't even have a tape in here. Where's your tape?"

"Right here," I said, holding up the tape I had picked at random. "I ejected it when it wouldn't play."

"Well, let me see it," she said, taking the tape from him. "Lord love a duck! What kind of pervert are you?"

"I beg your pardon," I said, a little aggrieved by what I felt was a completely unwarranted slur. "I'm only playing one of the tapes you provided."

"This isn't a sexual stimulation tape. This is a educational tape for expectant mothers, depicting a live birth!"

"Oh! No, no, no. I just picked one up without looking at it. Here, I'll pick another one." I turned to the stack of pornographic tapes and picked the one with the largest number of naked bodies on the cover.

"Well," she said, somewhat mollified, "this is much more appropriate. I want you to know I have absolutely no bias against your sexual orientation."

Puzzled by this remark, I glanced at the label as she pulled the tape out, and turned bright crimson.

"No, I'm sorry. I made another mistake."

"Oh, then you don't want to watch 'A Gay Time in the Hot Steam Tonight'?"

"No, really, I'm not gay. I'm just a little nervous, and I'm not really paying attention to what I'm doing."

"Well," she said like someone who is not completely convinced, "tell you what, I'll just get this one rolling, and after I leave the room, you can eject it if you really want to. Okay?"

She slammed the tape into the machine and hit play. When a picture failed to appear, she spent a couple of minutes punching buttons on the tape machine and the television monitor it was hooked up to without results. Finally, she pulled the monitor away from the wall and looked behind it.

"Oh, here we go. The cable fell off again." She plugged the coax back in, and the screen filled up with naked men cavorting in a steam room.

"Well, enjoy. I have to run. I hear my phone ringing."

And before I could say another word, the nurse sprinted out of the room and down the hallway. I stepped out into the hall, half expecting to hear a scream and the sound of a struggle as Jason sought to escape the nurse's wrath. When I didn't hear anything, I let out a big sigh of relief, went back into the examination room, and turned off the video recorder. I thought that, for purposes of verisimilitude, I should wait in the room for a couple of minutes. Then I could approach the nurse and inform her that I had changed my mind about donating sperm.

It took all my discipline to spend two minutes alone in that room. It made me think of Charlie sitting in similar rooms, anonymously and dispassionately selling his own reproductive material hundreds of times over, without the slightest concern for the children that would be produced with it. I didn't doubt that there were high-minded sperm donors who refused payment for their donation and only wanted to help couples like my parents, but all anonymous sperm donations severed a child's roots to his or her biological heritage for the sake of convenience. During my search for my sperm donor, I had discovered several countries around the world that had already banned anonymous sperm donations, and I had recently read that the state of Virginia was considering a similar measure. I hoped the new law passed and was picked up by legislators in my state and other states throughout the country, because I thought children had a right to know their relatives, especially their fellow siblings.

When I walked into the reception area carrying my empty cup, I found Jason talking to the nurse through the sliding window.

"Oh, honey," the nurse chided, "you were supposed to call me when you were done. You can't go traipsing around with a cup full of live sperm. They're perishable!"

"I couldn't go through with it. Sorry," I said, handing the empty cup to her.

"That's perfectly okay, dear," She said with a sympathetic smile, "A lot of men can't perform under pressure. You can come back and try again if you like, but I won't be able to pay you this time."

"That's quite all right," I said. "Thanks for your patience."

"See you later, Angie," Jason said. "If you have any more problems converting jpegs of your grandchildren, just email me at the address I gave you."

On the way back to Jason's car, I asked how he had come to make friends with the nurse in such a short length of time. Jason laughed and told me that Angie had nearly caught him in her office. When the phone had started ringing, he knew his time was up and made a dash for the door. But he had only just opened it when Angie came running around the corner, so instead of continuing out into the reception area and alerting her suspicions, he pretended he was on his way into the inner office in search of me.

"I just reversed direction and made it look like I was closing the door behind me," Jason said. "I told her I thought I heard you calling for me, and she laughed and rolled her eyes. You know, Walt, I got the impression she thinks we're gay."

"That's because I picked up the wrong video tape."

"Oh, did you really?'

"Cut it out, Jason."

"Well, anyway, she seemed touched by my devotion to you, and we started chatting. I don't think she suspected anything, and she won't notice the router because I mounted it on the wall under the counter top. Someone might eventually find it, but they'll probably just assume it's an old installation. Even if they suspect the worse, they'll never be able to trace it back to me. I paid cash for it in a store over sixty miles from here."

"What about video surveillance?"

"I know what to look for, and I didn't see a camera. A camera in a doctor's office is a double-edged sword, Walt. The tapes can be used against the doctor as well as in his defense, and I can't see much purpose in recording transactions at a fertility clinic anyway. Besides, the kind of security cameras you find in office buildings are usually low-resolution pieces of crap that don't even have a decent archival system to store the fuzzy images they record."

They climbed into the rear of Jason's Escalade, and Jason fired up his laptop. He spent a couple of minutes negotiating with the fertility clinic's new wireless network, and then emitted a satisfied grunt.

"Okay," he said, "I'm in. Now, let's just search for anyone named Charles Bolero or Charlie Bolero, who sold his sperm between 1982 and 1986."

Jason typed in the search criteria, stared at the screen for a few moments, and then handed the laptop to me. The database record displayed on the laptop's screen listed a dozen sperm donations made at a clinic located in Canton,

Pennsylvania, over a three-week period in September of 1982. The donor was a Mr. Charles Bolero, occupation student, who gave a Southern Pennsylvania University post office box as his address.

"Okay, I guess Charlie's my sperm daddy," I said, handing the laptop back to Jason, "though he would probably say sperm papa."

"He would?"

"Yeah."

"Sperm papa doesn't sound as cool as sperm daddy."

"Well, Charlie likes the word papa. That's the last thing he said to me: 'Go find your real papa.'"

"And you did!"

"Yeah."

"You don't seem very pleased."

"I'm sorry. I guess I should be more excited about being related to a conman and a pathological liar who's destroyed my one chance at true love."

"Hey! Don't shoot the messenger. I'm here to help."

"Yeah, you're right, Jason. Congratulations. Your plan worked brilliantly. You're a genius."

"Oh, we haven't executed my plan yet. I just showed you this to prove I was right about Charlie – you don't think I'd go to all this trouble just for that, do you?"

"But what else can we do? We already know everything we came to find out, don't we?"

"There's a lot more to find out, believe me, and I'm going to stay here and find it. I hope you stopped payment on Charlie's check."

"Yeah."

"Good. You're going to need the money."

"What for?"

"For what we're going to do."

"What are we doing?"

"I'll tell you tomorrow. You'll need to open the store again in the morning, because I'm going to be up all night. When you go back to Ace, thank Marty for coming up. Tell him to call me anytime he has computer problems."

"You mean you're really not going to tell me what you're up to?"

"Nope. Not until I've done the research."

"Come on!"

"If I had told you what we were going to do here today, would you have gone along with it?"

"No."

"I didn't think so. This is the same sort of thing. If I told you about it now, you wouldn't want to do it. I want to put it all together and present it to you as a package, so you can see the true brilliance of my plan. In the meantime, I don't want you running off halfcocked. I know you're itching to jump in your car, drive down to Elara Downs, and tell Himalia you were all wrong about Charlie. Don't do it. You just gave Charlie a great recommendation two days ago. She's not going to believe anything you say against him now."

"Yeah, I know," I said miserably. "She'd just think Leda put me up to it. But how is your plan any better? She'll probably ignore any last minute stuff you pull out of that database too, no matter how convincing it looks."

"She won't be able to ignore what I have in mind."

"Yeah? Like what?"

"I'll tell you tomorrow. It'll be a surprise.

"Damn it, I hate surprises. Everybody's been springing surprises on me lately. I'm sick of surprises.

"Okay, one little hint – but I don't want to talk about it until tomorrow."

"Okay, fine. Give me your stupid hint."

"Papa's Day is coming early this year."

Chapter Thirty-Six

I was as nervous as a cat at a dog show. It was nearly noon, and Jason hadn't come to work yet. I thought I had a vague idea of what Jason was up to, but I couldn't see how it was going to help me with any of my problems. Despite Jason's admonition, I had tried to call Himalia at her ranch, but hung up when Charlie answered the phone. Now I wished I hadn't interfered with Leda's scheme to blackmail Charlie. I wanted to jump in my car, drive down to Elara Downs, and tell Himalia that every one of Leda's allegations about Charlie was true. She might not believe me at this late juncture, but I thought it might be better than getting sidetracked by another one of Jason's convoluted plans.

Jason was starting to worry me. I was pretty sure the law would frown on installing a wireless network on someone else's computer system and using it to break into their database. His little domestic espionage operation had been impressive, and I couldn't argue with the results, but it had seemed a little too much like the kind of sneaky, illegal stunt that Charlie might pull. I was musing over these disturbing similarities between Charlie and Jason, when the latter finally walked into the office and plopped down behind his desk.

"Okay, Walt, write me a check for $4,100."

"$4,100! That's almost all the money I have in the bank–"

"Don't whine," Jason interrupted. "If I hadn't made you stop payment on Charlie's check, you wouldn't have a dime. This way you stop the wedding, get Leda back, put Charlie out of action, and still have nine hundred bucks left in the bank."

"But what do you need all that money for?"

"A very small part of it is reimbursement for the wireless router, cables and mounting hardware I bought yesterday, some of it will cover charges I incurred last night on some people locator web sites, and the rest of it will go to pay FedEx."

"FedEx? Are you over-nighting a horse or something? What the hell are you up to?"

"I'm going to tell you, but I have to hurry. I have to get to the bank, cash your check, and drive to a FedEx office in Buffalo before they close."

"That doesn't make any sense. There's a FedEx office over by the airport. Why are you driving to Buffalo?"

"A couple of reasons. Buffalo is a major hub, so the envelopes will have a better chance of getting delivered on time. Plus the FedEx office I'm going to is used to seeing people walk in with large numbers of packages, so my little bit of business won't even raise an eyebrow."

"Why would anybody raise their eyebrows? Just how many envelopes are you over-nighting anyway?"

"A hundred and fifty-nine."

"A hundred and fifty-nine! Who are you sending them to? What's in them?"

"Your brothers and sisters, Walt, or at least some of them. I didn't include anyone under eighteen."

"All these people are Charlie's children? How did you find them?"

After you went back to work, I spent two hours in that parking garage tracing Charlie's sperm. He donated sperm an average of ten times at sixty-four clinics if you count the one where he used his real name. Charlie's fake applications must have been impressive because nearly all of the clinics he donated at found customers for his sperm, resulting in three hundred and seventy-six successful pregnancies in the years since then. I downloaded every child born before 1988 to my laptop and drove back to my house. When I got home, I called Vinny's and asked your cousin Tony about the Bolero wedding function. Did you know Himalia is having a Bacchanalian wedding?"

"No. What's that?"

"It's when you have the reception first and the marriage ceremony afterwards. They're going to start seating guests in the Explorers' Pavilion at two-thirty, but they're not going to have the actual ceremony until three-thirty. Then Charlie and Himalia are going to jump into a limousine and head straight to the airport. They're honeymooning in Tahiti."

"Well, that's all really interesting, but what's the point?"

"Hold your horses. I'm getting to it. I had a report that listed the names of Charlie's children and their mothers, but I didn't have any current addresses. It took me until five o'clock this morning to trace them down. Of course I couldn't find them all, and some of the ones I did find didn't live within driving distance of Vinny's restaurant."

"Why does it matter if they live within driving distance of my uncle's restaurant? What are you sending them?"

"Can't you guess?"

"No."

"Wedding invitations."

"Wedding invitations!"

"Wedding invitations."

"That's crazy, Jason. How is spending $4,100 on wedding invitations going to help me?"

"You see? This is why I wouldn't tell you about my plan last night. You're smart, Walt, but you don't have any vision, which is rather surprising considering who your genetic father is. Your sperm daddy might be a crook, but you got to admit he has vision. The letter I'm sending your half brothers and sisters is not just a wedding invitation. It's a confession, an act of contrition, and a monetary offer. Here," he pulled a folded sheet of paper from his pocket and handed it to me. "I underlined the variable fields on this sample, so you can see the information that changes on each letter. Check out the signature. I copied it off his rental agreement."

Michael T. Everet
20064 Chapel Blv.
Peyton, NJ 06043

Dear <u>Michael</u>,

    My name is Charles Bolero. <u>Nineteen</u> years ago, I donated sperm to a fertility clinic that your mother later used to help create you, my biological <u>son.</u> If you have attempted to locate me, you probably discovered that I used the name

Christopher J. Parks and listed Box 893, Number 12 Oak Rail Road, Burn's Creek, Pennsylvania, as my address. That name was an alias, and the mailbox was rented to Chris Fulton, a friend of mine. I was trying to disguise myself in case you ever attempted to find me. I regret doing that now, and I apologize if my deception has caused you any distress. I know you might be skeptical of my claim, so I am including documentation from your fertility clinic.

Life has been very good to me. I have been blessed with both good health and good fortune. Eight years ago, I was fortunate enough to found a very successful business. That enterprise has made me a millionaire many times over. I have everything life has to offer except family. I was an only child and never had any children of my own.

I realize you are only my biological child, and I don't expect your love; only the parents that loved you enough to use donated sperm to bring you into this world deserve your love. I only seek to make the lives of my biological children a little easier by giving each of them a onetime gift of $100,000.

It's my hope that this gift will be of some assistance in obtaining an education, starting a business or perhaps buying your first home if you're getting married like me. My impending marriage is what gave me this idea for a onetime gift to my biological children.

Since I'm an only child with no children of my own, I have no brothers, sisters, or children to invite to my wedding. So, I'm inviting you to come to my wedding this Saturday, 2:30 PM, at Galilei's Famous Italian restaurant in Juno, New Jersey. I have included the address and a map with this invitation along with the restaurant's fax and telephone numbers.

You don't have to attend to receive your gift, but my lawyer tells me that I might not be free to make these gifts after I'm married, so if you want to insure your gift goes through without any delays or problems, please try to make it.

I had to rush this project through to completion because I only thought of doing it three weeks ago. My lawyers were only able to obtain a few names from the fertility clinics in that short time, and I was only able to locate your address and a few others from those names. I just located your address today; that's why I am sending your invitation by Federal Express.

I know that it's very short notice, but I will be extremely grateful if you can make it. If you are able to come, please bring this letter and a means of identification.

Respectfully yours,

Charles Bolero

Charles Bolero

I read the letter a couple of times, then stared at Jason as though I had never seen him before. "You can't send this out. This is fraud!"

"Nope. You're wrong. Fraud is when someone collects money from someone else under false pretenses. Charlie committed fraud hundreds of times when he accepted payment for his sperm donations under a false name. This letter would probably be classified as a practical joke or at the worst, a hoax, but consider this: while no one is going away with any money, all of these people will have an opportunity to meet their sperm donor, and you of all people should know how important it is for sperm donor children to find and meet their biological father. After all, you just spent the last year of your life tracking yours down. These people might think they're coming for the money, but what they'll take away with them is far more important. We're giving them a precious gift, Walt, a connection to their biological heritage."

This argument touched a chord in me. The letter had shocked me, and I had been about to tell Jason I wouldn't go through with it. But now I wasn't sure how I felt about it. "Well, maybe it's not fraud, but this plan seems pretty iffy. I mean, how's it going to do all the things you said it would do? How will it stop the wedding, or help me get Leda back? Besides, how do you know any of these people will bother to come anyway? I don't think I would."

"Yes, you would, Walt. You were desperate for any kind of lead on your biological father. Even without the offer of money, you would've driven a thousand miles to attend that wedding. The only difference between you and your brothers and sisters is that you were lucky enough to find Charlie. Of course, not all of these people will be able to drive to New Jersey at a moment's notice. And a few might dismiss it out of hand. But out of a field of a hundred and fifty-nine starters, I wouldn't be surprised if a dozen or so actually showed up. That would be less than ten percent of our total mail out, and with this kind of offer, I think that's a reasonable expectation."

"I still don't see how this would stop the wedding. It would probably disrupt it, but Charlie would just tell Himalia and anyone who showed up waving your letter that it was all just someone's idea of a practical joke."

"She won't believe him, Walt. Tomorrow morning I'm going to send three identical overnight packages addressed to her at the restaurant by UPS, FedEx, and Express Mail just to make sure she gets at least one of them. I don't want her to receive them until just before the wedding, so Charlie won't have an opportunity to interfere with our plans. She'll be worrying about the contents of that package right about the time your siblings start showing up, and when they do, she won't be satisfied by a simple flat denial from Charlie."

Jason told me that there were two envelopes in Himalia's package. The first one contained documentation and a letter explaining how Charlie had begun selling his sperm under his own name at a clinic near his college, before he began making donations under assumed names at clinics that were further and further away. Jason had included a chart displaying Charlie's sperm donations in chronological order and copies of records from the clinic he used his own name at, and the next ten clinics after that. The other envelope had a letter describing Jason's latest theory on what happened to Running Fool's sperm. Jason had included Charlie's Cobb's Station address and a diagram made from my description showing the location of the sperm tanks. He had appended a sticky note on the letter asking Himalia to forward the letter to Dr. Norton.

I could imagine the scene that would ensue when Charlie's offspring began approaching the bride's and groom's table to introduce themselves. Charlie's denials would sound persuasive at first, but as more and more of his grown children arrived, cracks would begin to appear in Charlie's façade and

Himalia, armed with the information in Jason's package, would begin to ask tough questions.

I felt responsible for making it possible for my crooked biological father to marry Leda's mother, and I desperately wanted to stop the wedding. I thought Jason's plan was devious, unethical, and probably illegal, but I also thought it just might work, so I swallowed my reservations and wrote the check that Jason had requested.

After Jason left, a customer returned an Escalade that had been in a fender bender and sustained a crushed door. Doing the paperwork on the damaged vehicle and tending to some other customers kept me busy for the next couple of hours. When I finally had a chance to kick back, I began daydreaming about Charlie running out of the restaurant pursued by a mob of my half brothers and sisters. In my imagination, I could see Leda jumping up and down and cheering them on. As the imaginary young men and women ran past my mind's eye, I wondered how many of them had been trying to find Charlie before they got their invitation, and how many of them didn't even know they were the product of artificial insemination. I cringed as this last thought floated into my consciousness. What had I been thinking? I felt terrible. A lot of young people were going to find out, in the worst possible way, that they weren't related to their fathers.

Because I was in a panic, it took me three tries to dial Jason's cell phone. The whole time I was praying he had been delayed, preferably by a non-lethal event, like traffic or car trouble.

"Hello?"

"Jason! Tell me you haven't sent those envelopes off yet!"

"Why? What's wrong? Did something happen to Charlie?"

"No, no–"

"Good, because if something happened to Charlie, we just wasted your money."

"Oh, no! You already sent them!"

"Sure, thirty minutes ago. I'm on my way back. Why, what's the matter?"

"The children, Jason, some of them might not know they're sperm donor babies."

"Oh. That just occurred to you, huh?"

"You mean it occurred to you, and you sent them off anyway? How could you do such a heartless thing?"

"Calm down, Walt. It's not as bad as all that."

"It's worse, Jason. We don't have the right to interfere in other people's families."

"Look, Walt, all of these people are over the age of eighteen. That means they are legal adults who have the right to die on the battlefield defending their country. Are you saying that they don't have the right to know who their blood relatives are? Some of these people are getting married, Walt. They're having kids of their own now. What if a couple of them accidentally marry each other? Do you want that on your conscience?"

"No, you're muddying the issue. It's the parent's sole responsibility and right to decide when, where or if they'll tell their children about their biological fathers."

"If they haven't told them by the time they're eighteen, they're obviating their responsibility, Walt. All we're doing is correcting that oversight."

"My mother wasn't obviating her responsibility! She just didn't think I was mature enough to handle the facts until I was twenty-one."

"Look, Walt, I'm sorry you're upset, but there's nothing we can do now. I really thought you had already considered the possibility that some of these people wouldn't know their mothers had used donor sperm. I'm sorry I didn't ask about it. When I get back, I'll talk about it as much as you want. In the meantime, stop worrying. We live in very unsentimental times. Bee and Elmo are unusual; most of today's modern families pride themselves on their matter-of-fact approach to life. I wouldn't be surprised if everyone of these kids have known about their status since they were five years old."

I knew Jason's last remark was merely a sop thrown to my guilty conscience, but it made me feel a little better anyway. I decided it was wrong to blame Jason for my own poor judgment, and I believed my friend had acted in good faith. I told Jason I was sorry for yelling at him, and, despite recent evidence to the contrary, I really appreciated everything he was doing for me.

I made Jason promise to come in late on Friday. This made me feel better, too. It was like doing penance for my sins.

Chapter Thirty-Seven

I couldn't remember Friday. I knew there must have been a Friday. In my experience, Fridays usually followed Thursdays and preceded Saturdays, but somehow or other I had wound up at Ace Car Rental on a Saturday with absolutely no memory of having lived through a Friday to get there. This was the first day I had ever lost, and I wasn't sure how to behave. Pitch had given me a thumbs-up when I drove my Lincoln into the lot that morning, and Jody, though her hand still snatched my keys from the air with its usual alacrity, stood goggling at me. I was accustomed to Jody goggling at me, but I usually knew the reason for her protruding eyes. On this particular morning, that reason, like the day before, had escaped me completely. Nor did I have the least notion as to why Pitch would be hoisting an encouraging thumb.

Shrugging my shoulders at the inexplicable behavior of teenagers, I made my way to Ace's back door and down the hall to find Jason engrossed in an Internet game of GO.

I had seen Jason hunched over his simulated game board on many other occasions, but today the scene looked like a poorly pasted paper collage with some of the pieces curling up. For that matter, everything in the office seemed a little too sharply defined; objects appeared closer than they actually were, colors seemed oversaturated, and the fluorescent lights had iridescent halos around them.

"Morning," I mumbled.

"Hey, there you are," Jason said, swiveling around to peer up at me. "What happened to you yesterday?"

"I'm not sure. Was I here yesterday?"

"Of course you were here yesterday, dimwit. Where did you go after work?"

"After work?"

"Yeah, you stepped outside to give Pitch and Jody their paychecks, and you never came back."

"I'm sorry. I can't remember."

"What do you mean, you can't remember?"

"Jason, I don't remember coming to work yesterday."

"Really? Wow. Did you go on a bender or something?"

"You know, I do feel kind of hung over, but I haven't been on a binge since my twenty-first birthday. And why would I go drinking without you?"

"That's right, you wouldn't. You know it would hurt my feelings. Okay, it must be something else. What's the last thing you remember before waking up this morning?"

"Trying to get to sleep Thursday night. I was still worried about those overnight packages. I had to take a couple pills before I could get to sleep."

"Sleeping pills! Those things can cause amnesia, and all this stress you've been under might have made you more vulnerable to the side effects. Well, they're probably all out of your system now. But if I were you, I wouldn't take sleeping pills anymore. Try drinking a hot rum toddy next time you can't sleep."

"Does that help you sleep?"

"No, but it makes you feel better about being awake."

"Coffee makes me feel better about being awake," I grinned ruefully. "Let me get a cup while you fill me in on what happened yesterday."

"Like what?"

"Huh?" I asked, fumbling with the Styrofoam cups. I broke a couple before managing to pull an undamaged cup off the stack.

"What do you want me to tell you about yesterday?"

I put the cup down and tried to focus.

"You know, were there any problems yesterday? Did I do or say something that I need to know about? I don't know, Jason. I'm not thinking real clearly right now. Help me out."

"It's a good thing you don't remember yesterday, then. It was the Friday from hell. All the rentals came in at the same time, everyone was screaming about missing their flights, an airport shuttle broke down in the middle of our parking lot …we didn't get out of here until seven-thirty. It was a real horror-show. Jody and Pitch did a good job though. Both of them stuck with us to the bitter end –let's see, what else? Oh! Did you pick up your suit?"

"What suit?"

"Man, your memory was fried! You brought a brown wool suit from home and left it next door. Oh, and some girl called for you."

"Leda!"

"No, it was someone else. She asked for you, and I handed you the phone."

"Do you remember her name?"

"She didn't give it and you didn't say."

"I didn't tell you? That doesn't sound right. I tell you everything."

"I know, but this happened right in the middle of yesterday's nightmare. I just assumed it was a customer or something. If I had known you were going to lose your memory, I would've asked."

"Crap. Now I'm going to spend the day wondering who the hell called me."

"Nah, you'll forget all about it at Charlie's wedding. Damn, I wish I could go! Hey! Do you think you could take my digital camera with you?"

"The wedding! I forgot! I have to get ready for the wedding. I must have decided to wear my old brown suit. I better walk over to the drycleaners and get it."

I poured myself some coffee and made for the front door.

"Hey, where're you going, Walt? It's not even ten yet. You don't have to be there until two-thirty."

"I know, Jason, but I want to get there early and try to talk to Leda."

"No, don't you remember? We talked about this yesterday. We don't want Charlie to know you're coming until the last moment–"

I didn't hear the rest of Jason's comment because I had walked out the door. Shielding my eyes with one hand, I navigated across an unusually bright and colorful front lot, around the fence, and into the comparative calm of the drycleaner's. The little Korean lady laughed when she saw me come in.

"Hey you! I saw you with all the big shot movie stars yesterday."

I didn't know what to make of this comment, so I simply nodded and smiled. The Korean lady grinned, pushed the button on her carousel, and brought my brown suit and a couple of my shirts spinning into view.

"I take my smoke break out there," she said, pointing towards the corner of the fence. "Yesterday, I see big, big, white car, very long, and I see you get in with six movie stars! Very pretty girls, very, very pretty girls."

I nodded and smiled. I thought she probably saw a customer get into one of the airport limos that frequented Ace on Fridays. Any other time I would have tried to explain about the limousines that ferried customers to the airport, but at that moment I didn't feel up to the challenge of anything beyond basic communication, so I just thanked her, paid for my dry cleaning and headed back to the office.

Three cups of coffee, four aspirins, and an hour later, I was finally rolling down the interstate toward Juno. When I arrived at the restaurant, the front parking lot was about half full. Initially, I thought that my uncle was enjoying an unusually large Saturday lunch crowd, but then I noticed two white limousines idling in the parking lot and recognized Himalia's cherry red Mercedes-Benz and Leda's red Mini Cooper parked near the front door.

A glance at my dashboard clock told me it was only twelve-thirty. I wondered why preparations for the wedding were getting underway so early; it wasn't scheduled to begin for another hour and a half. I decided to drive around to the back of the building and go in the service entrance, just in case Charlie was hanging around in the lobby. I parked my car next to the dumpster, walked in the service entrance, and ducked into the kitchen. My aunt, her assistants, and most of the waiters were busy preparing the wedding dinner and didn't seem to notice me. I found my cousin on the other side of the kitchen loading glasses of ice water on a tray.

"Hey, Walt!"

"Tony, what's going on? The wedding dinner isn't supposed to start until two-thirty."

"Didn't Leda tell you? "

"Tell me what?"

"They moved it up. It's starting at one now."

"They moved it up! Why?"

"I don't know. Charlie said something about having to change their travel plans."

I sagged against the stainless steel counter. I had just spent my life savings inviting one hundred and fifty-nine half brothers and sisters to a wedding that would be over before they arrived.

"But that's not fair!" I moaned. "They can't just change when a wedding starts at the last minute!"

"Tell me about it. They sprang it on Pop yesterday. He was really ticked off about it, too. I mean, it's easy for them to change things around because most of their guests work at Mrs. Lobrelei's ranch or live close by, but we have to shift our whole lunch crowd around and–"

"Never mind about your lunch crowd, Tony. When will the wedding vows be exchanged?

"Not until two. Mrs. Lobrelei calls it a Bacchanalian wedding. The wine and food is served first and–"

I thought I could see a ray of hope. A few of our surprise wedding guests were bound to show up early, and if I could somehow delay the wedding ceremony until they did, Jason's plan might still work. I straightened up and grabbed my cousin by his arm.

"Look," I said urgently, "I need you to find Leda and send her back here, and whatever you do, don't tell the groom I'm here."

"Why don't you want him to know you're here?"

"It's a surprise, Tony. Just don't tell him."

"Oh!" Tony said, briefly assuming the appearance of someone with brains, "I get it! You and Leda are planning some kind of practical joke on the groom, huh?"

"Yeah, that's right, so make sure you don't say anything."

I smiled to myself as my cousin, glad for any excuse to leave the kitchen, shouldered his tray of ice water and went in search of Leda. Tony didn't know how close he had come to the truth, I thought. If Leda and I could delay Charlie and Himalia's wedding vows long enough, Tony would get to see one of the biggest jokes ever played on a groom.

To prevent tragic collisions, the kitchen at Galilei's Famous Italian restaurant had two separate swinging doors, one that swung into the kitchen and one that swung out. I had entered the kitchen through the Hall of Scientists corridor. The door that Tony and the rest of the staff used when they wanted to leave the kitchen opened on a hallway that passed by the Forum dining room. I knew that Leda would be coming in through the Hall of Scientists route, so I headed back across the kitchen to wait for her. I got there just as the door swung open to reveal an angry looking man dressed in a gold-flecked tux and a pink cummerbund. Charlie and I stood staring at each other for several seconds before he motioned me into the hallway.

I knew Charlie was trying to get me alone in order to threaten me, but I decided to play along anyway. Now that I had been discovered, I couldn't really see how it made Charlie any less vulnerable to the surprise he had in store, and if Charlie wasted enough time trying to scare me into leaving, it might even work to my advantage.

Once in the hallway, Charlie said he wanted to have a private conversation. I readily agreed and suggested the men's room, but Charlie insisted the parking lot was the only place where we could talk freely without danger of being overheard. This seemed okay, so I followed Charlie out the service entrance.

"Where's your car?" asked Charlie, once we were outside.

"By the dumpster. Why?"

"I thought it might be more comfortable talking in your car than standing out here by the entrance. Some of those musicians might come out here for a smoke break, and we don't want to air our differences in front of them."

"I don't want to sit in the car, Charlie. If you brought me out here to threaten me with the police, you can just save your breath because I'm not leaving. This is my uncle's restaurant, and I've just as much right to come here as you do. And another thing–"

I was about to tell him that I had stopped payment on his check in anticipation of escalating the argument and thus prolonging it, when Charlie suddenly stepped forward and put my neck in a chokehold. In the first moments of panic, I thought that Charlie intended to throttle me right there in the parking lot. But Charlie deftly flipped me around and frog marched me toward my Lincoln. I tried to struggle, but it's hard to resist when someone is squeezing your neck between a hairy forearm and an overdeveloped bicep. I felt one of Charlie's big hands invade my trouser pocket, and heard the click of a latch release as my captor appropriated my keys and pressed one of the remote-entry buttons. I was determined to break free when Charlie attempted to open the car door. But Charlie had not unlatched the door – he had opened the trunk, and I found myself being pushed face down into its depths. Charlie held my head against the floor of the trunk, removed my silk tie, then used it to bind my hands behind my back. The lid of the trunk began to come down, then paused in its descent as Charlie leaned over to speak into my ear.

"I found those overnight envelopes, Walt." Puffing a little from exertion, Charlie was speaking in an affable, offhand manner that seemed bizarrely out of place, as though he had won a game of tennis and was congratulating me on my hustle. "Someone signed for them, and left them on a table with the other cards and gifts. I wouldn't move around if I were you. It uses up oxygen!"

With that, the inside of the trunk was instantly plunged into darkness as Charlie slammed the lid shut, and everything became curiously quiet. I wasn't worried about oxygen. I knew the Lincoln's trunk wasn't airtight, and since Charlie had tied my hands, I was certain Charlie knew it too. If I were able to get my hands free, I would be able to unlatch the back seat, crawl into the passenger compartment, and let myself out a door.

Other than struggling onto my side, which took quite a bit of effort in the constrained interior of the Lincoln's trunk, I initially made little effort to escape my silken bonds. I couldn't see much point in effecting an escape, because, in my mind, I felt Charlie had already won. Even if a couple of the people that Jason had sent the letter to happened to show up early, Charlie would probably just pass off their claims as an elaborate practical joke. To make matters worse, now that I had given my stupid cousin the idea that Leda and I were planning a joke on the groom, Tony would almost certainly validate Charlie's claim by laughing hysterically, and boasting that he was in on the gag. Then the minister would perform the wedding ceremony, and Charlie would depart on his honeymoon just about the time his biological children were beginning to arrive.

It's difficult to keep track of time tied up inside the trunk of a Lincoln town car. I made a few halfhearted attempts to attract attention by shouting and kicking at the wheel well but the thick insulation lining the interior of the luxury car's trunk prevented the sounds from carrying very far. I couldn't begin to guess how much time had passed when a sudden realization jerked me out of my lethargic state and gave me new hope. It had occurred to me that if I could manage to contact Jason, he could print out a fresh copy of the paperwork Charlie had stolen, and fax it to the restaurant. All I had to do was escape from the trunk, call Jason, and try to delay the wedding vows.

My problem now was how best to achieve the first step of my bold plan. There were no sharp edges to cut my bonds, and pulling on the tie had only tightened the knot. Up to this point, I hadn't considered gymnastics because of the cramped nature of my confinement, now I decided to give it a try. Lying sideways, I drew my legs up to my chest and attempted to work my hands around my feet. This feat wasn't easy to accomplish inside the trunk of a car and my efforts were accompanied by a good deal of cursing and painful thumps against the walls of my prison. I had finally managed to get my bound hands past the obstruction of one of my feet and was straining to pull the other one free when I heard the sound of a steel blade scrabbling at the trunk latch. A moment later, the lid of the trunk flew open, and I was staring into the gold-toothed grin of Chic the stoop.

I was too astonished to say anything and just lay goggling as Chic's knife swooped down at me. For an instant I thought Chic meant to stab me, but instead of cutting into my flesh, the blade sliced cleanly through the silk tie binding my hands together. Chic helped me to untangle myself and climb out of the trunk. I couldn't begin to fathom why the little ticket-stooper was breaking into car trunks in my uncle's parking lot, but I was grateful nonetheless. Chic looked critically at me for a moment, and then pointed his knife at my head.

"Where's your cheaters?"

"Huh?" I quickly patted my head to ascertain if any ears or eyebrows were missing.

Chic rolled his eyes, poked around in the Lincoln's trunk, located my missing eyeglasses, and handed them to me.

"Chic, what're you doing here?" I put on my glasses and studied my unlikely liberator. "How did you know I was in that trunk?"

"I saw your car bouncing up and down. You don't usually find a Lincoln doing the parking lot rumba, so I got a little closer and heard you cussing and banging around."

"That's incredible, but why are you here?"

"I'm a wedding guest, just like you," Chic said a little stiffly. "Leda sent me out looking for you. Everybody's just about through eating, and the minister's fixing to do his stuff."

Chic folded his switchblade and tucked it in his vest pocket. He was wearing a handsome dark blue suit, and if he hadn't been wearing that same narrow brimmed checkered hat that he had on at the racetrack, I would have said the little weasel looked almost debonair. Even with the checkered hat and gold teeth, Chic still looked like a hero to me, and under any other circumstances I would have said so, but Chic's words had set a fire under me, and I took off like a rocket towards the back entrance of the restaurant.

When I rushed into the building, I could hear the string quartet playing over the noise of a hundred wedding guests happily eating and talking. I dashed into the kitchen, spotted my Aunt Lois plating cannolis onto saucers, and held a hand to my ear with the little finger and thumb sticking out. She pointed to some steel shelves that, along with industrial sized cans of olive oil and tomato products, held a all-in-one fax, phone and printer, and I made a beeline for it.

Jason was amazed that Charlie had intercepted the overnight envelopes, and assured me the fax was on its way. He also said the document amounted to over fifty pages and would take at least ten minutes to fax to the restaurant's machine. I didn't know how long I had before the minister administered the wedding vows, but I didn't think I could afford to wait for the fax to print. So, with the vague idea of sending someone back to the kitchen to fetch the fax, I headed out of the kitchen and shot down the hallway leading to the Explorers' Pavilion. Halfway there, I collided with a girl dressed in a white gown. The girl made an oomph sound and fell to the floor with me sprawled on top of her.

I felt something cold and metallic jabbing painfully into my right ear, and when I pushed myself away, I saw the offending object was a gold clasp with a group of classic feminine profiles sculpted onto its surface. Leda! This was the first thought that flashed through my brain, but when I looked at my victim's face, I recognized the beautiful, and in my mind, nefarious, features of Leda's surrogate mother.

"Maia, I don't have time to explain, but you have to help me–"

"Get off me!" Maia squeaked. I scrambled up and helped Maia to her feet.

For just the blink of an eyelash, she looked like a diner who had found a snail in her salad, then her features snapped back into the expression of motherly concern she had worn during my interview with her at the Marriott.

"Okay, come with me." She grabbed me by the hand and began towing me toward the rear entrance.

"No, Maia, listen." I pleaded, "I'm on your side now. I have a plan to stop the wedding, but first we need to delay..."

Maia suspended her towing operation and turned to face me.

"I know, Walt. We know about your plan, and we know what's gone wrong with it, too."

"You do?" I asked. "How could you possibly know about my plan?"

"You told us."

Chapter Thirty-Eight

Now that Maia had mentioned it, I discovered I did have a hazy recollection of telling someone about Jason's plan. I just couldn't remember when, where, or who I told it to. My mind sorted through the blurry remnants of my lost day until it focused on an image of my Korean drycleaner grinning at me.

"You and your friends picked me up in a limousine yesterday, didn't you?" This was more of a statement than a question – Maia, and her friends arriving in a white limousine would have looked a lot like movie stars to my Korean drycleaner. Our porters must have noticed my departure as well. My jumping into a limo filled to the brim with feminine pulchritude would explain Pitch's thumbs up and Jody's goggling.

"Look, Walt, we don't have time to talk about it. For now, you just need to follow me. We're going around the back way, so we won't have to walk by Charlie's table."

I had a lot more questions to pose, but avoiding Charlie made sense to me, so I let Maia lead me out the service entrance and around the building to the front of the restaurant. On the way, I tried to question her about what I had told her and her friends the previous evening. Her answers were terse and hurried, but I learned that Maia knew most of the details of Jason's plan, including the content of the redundant overnight packages Jason sent to Himalia.

When we reached the front entrance, I recognized another of Leda's friends, hovering by the door in her white gown. I stopped walking and tugged on Maia's arm. I assumed Leda's friends had a plan of their own for dealing with the complications that had arisen, but I didn't see how standing guard at the front of the restaurant was doing a lot of good. I thought we needed to talk strategy before we entered the building.

Maia listened impatiently while I reported my confrontation with Charlie in the parking lot and the unfortunate interception of the overnight envelopes. I told her about the fax Jason was sending, then pointed out that without the presence of Charlie's progeny, Himalia would probably just think the fax had been concocted by her jealous daughter and proceed with the wedding.

"So," I concluded, "even if Jason can fax us everything in time, it won't do us any good if we can't do something to delay the wedding."

Maia regarded me with an expression of weary forbearance, and turned to the girl waiting by the door.

"Helen, has that Express Mail package arrived?"

"No," she answered, "but Tony said the post office usually doesn't deliver overnights until after two on Saturdays."

"Okay, wait ten more minutes, and then come inside," Maia said, and turned back to me. "One or the other of us has been out here since 10 AM. Charlie only got what we wanted him to get– a few overnight letters and faxes from some of his children."

"Oh crap! Why didn't we predict that? Of course they'd try contacting Charlie if they couldn't come! Charlie probably got one of those faxes yesterday and tricked Himalia into moving the wedding up!"

"Yes, that's what all of us concluded last night," Maia said. "Fortunately, your blunder doesn't seem to have hurt anything, but you shouldn't have come here in the first place. You agreed it would be better if you were not involved in the plan's execution."

"I didn't know that. I can't remember anything that happened yesterday." I saw an odd expression flit across Maia's features, but it was gone before I could analyze its meaning.

"Well, since Leda asked me to take care of you, and you seem to have lost your memory, I'm making allowances for your behavior," Maia said stonily, "but from this point forward, I expect you to follow my instructions to the letter."

I was torn between congratulating Maia and challenging her. Although Friday was still a total blank to me, I had apparently participated in forming some kind of plan to deal with the problem of the wedding being moved up. I didn't trust Maia, and still couldn't believe I would have agreed not to attend the wedding, but I decided it was best to cooperate until I saw a reason not to.

As we entered the lobby, I saw two more of Maia's extended family dressed in their long white gowns, sitting with a young couple on one of the long padded benches lining the room. One of the two girls stood up and walked over to us. As she approached, I recognized her as Leda's friend Alice. When I looked back at the bench, I realized the other girl sitting with the young couple was Sara, the redhead who was attending Brown University.

"I'm going to slip you into the dining room and sit you at a table in the back where Charlie won't see you," Maia said. "Alice, please seat Walt at the table with our other special guests."

I looked back at the young couple sitting with Sara on the bench. The man looked older, maybe 22 or 23, and the girl looked to be a little younger. I had a vague feeling I had met them before, but couldn't remember where.

There were two sets of doors leading to the main dining room, located on either side of the lobby. Alice peeked through a small window inset into the top of the right hand door before opening it and quickly escorting me to a table in the nearest corner of the room. The overhead lights in the main dining room had been turned down even more than usual and I doubted if anyone at the far end of the room would be able to discern my identity until I came within range of one of the small candles on the tables.

"Alice," I whispered as she led me to my table, "who were those people with Sara?"

Alice leaned in close and whispered in my ear, "Your half brother and sister."

Her words echoed in my ear as though she had shouted them. Since I had first learned I was a sperm donor baby, I realized I probably had brothers and sisters, but now that I had actually seen two of them, I discovered there was a vast difference between simply knowing about something and actually experiencing it.

I desperately wanted to ask Alice more questions about the young couple, but we had arrived at our destination. One of the 'special guests' turned out to be Ralph Chicarillo, who greeted me with a gold-toothed grin and a broad wink. The other two men at the table were strangers to me. The table was a round six-top tucked between a corner of the Explorers' Pavilion and the entrance to the Gallery of Arts. This smaller dining room had a French door, one half of which was propped open in front of my table. My chair was positioned behind that door. Through its glass panes, I could see the string quartet playing on a small stage, complete with stage lights, set up at the far end of the dining room around a fountain with Christoforo Columbo standing astride two rocky crags. Several four-tops had been pushed together on a low dais in front of the stage to create a table long enough to accommodate the happy couple and the principal guests. The same three massive brass candelabras I had seen at Himalia's antebellum mansion were ablaze on the table and the same guests that had attended Frisco Gal's insemination party were occupying the seats of honor.

I could see Leda wearing the white gown I had seen her in at the Marriott, sitting next to Dr. Norton at one end of the table. Himalia was decked out in an incandescent tangerine wedding gown and Charlie wore his elegant tux, but most of the people at the main table and the guests from neighboring ranches at the surrounding tables wore the boots and hard-wearing clothing of their profession.

The two guests sitting next to Chic were an exception to this casual atmosphere. They were both immaculately attired in expensive suits and came across more like businessmen waiting for a appointment than guests at a wedding dinner. The man sitting directly opposite me looked like a banker or a Wall Street broker. His companion was an unusually large man who would probably be more at home in a boxing ring than an office.

The two men had not introduced themselves, and that was fine with me. I was too preoccupied with my own concerns to pay much attention to my fellow guests. If Maia had a plan to delay the wedding, I had yet to see any evidence of it. The guests were eating the last bites of their cannoli, and three of Leda's friends were circulating among the guests refilling wine glasses for the wedding toasts. I was wondering why Maia hadn't brought the young couple waiting in the lobby into the dining room to confront Charlie. She might be waiting for more of Charlie's children to arrive, but it was getting late, and I was worried.

One of Leda's friends filled the wine glasses at my table. She smiled and gave me a little wink as she left. As I was wondering what her wink meant, I saw my Uncle Vinny climbing onto the stage. The music came to a stop. The cello player put down his stringed instrument and pulled an electronic keyboard in front of him as my uncle began calling for attention.

"Attention! Attenzione tutto! Signore e signori di buon pomeriggio! I hope that you're enjoying yourselves. In a few minutes, Mrs. Lobrelei, one of my most charming and beautiful customers, will be getting married! Mrs. Lobrelei, please let everyone see how beautiful you are!"

Himalia stood up and climbed onto the stage, accompanied by a lively rendition of the famous Italian wedding dance, Napoletana Tarantella. My uncle took Himalia's hand, and they both danced a few steps of the Tarantella. With Himalia's red hair and tangerine wedding gown glowing in the stage lights, it looked to me like Vinny was dancing with a giant candle flame. The guests at the wedding party broke out in enthusiastic applause and began clapping in time to the music as Vinny danced Himalia around the stage.

"And now it's time to toast the bride and groom," Vinny announced after he and Himalia had whirled to a stop. "Charlie, you lucky devil, come on up here!"

Charlie bounced onto the stage and took Himalia's hand. She was smiling nervously, but I didn't think she looked extraordinarily anxious – and this worried me. I would have expected Himalia to look a lot more apprehensive and uncertain if she had read the material Jason had sent her in the FedEx. I was starting to think our plan wasn't going to work. Even if Maia were to parade the young couple in at that moment, Charlie might still manage to pass it off as a joke.

As these gloomy thoughts skittered through my consciousness, I noticed with alarm that a fat, jolly minister was standing next to the stage with a glass of wine in his hand.

One of Leda's friends handed Vinny a glass of wine. He raised it in the air, and everyone else in the restaurant raised his or her glass in response. "Cento anni di salute e felicità! May you have health and happiness for a hundred years!"

This kind of toast was usually made after a wedding, but the guests in the restaurant enthusiastically echoed the sentiment anyway and raised their glasses to the couple. As this toast started to die down, I heard my cousin Tony shout out another toast.

"Bacio per il bride!"

I winced and made a note to myself to strangle my cousin the next time I saw him. Tony's cry was enthusiastically picked up by every Italian man in the room, and after a hurried translation from Vinny, Charlie obliged by giving Himalia a big kiss.

My uncle stepped down from the stage, and the string quartet began playing the wedding march. I looked expectantly at the lobby doors, but my half-siblings failed to come through them. I looked back at the stage and saw the fat minister swaying slightly as he stood in front of the bride and groom. He looked ready, as Chic had put it, to do his stuff. I couldn't imagine what Maia could possibly be waiting for. When the minister opened his bible, I panicked. I jumped up with the intention of dashing to the lobby to retrieve my two siblings, but found myself being hauled back into my seat by Ralph Chicarillo. I rounded on Chic to demand an explanation only to find the little ticket stooper grinning widely and pointing toward the stage.

Instead of administering the wedding vows, the minister was suddenly gamboling about the front of the room like a puppy on its first outing. A puzzled and increasingly frustrated Charlie kept retrieving the wandering cleric and leading him back to the stage, where he would stand blinking for a few seconds, and then caper off again giggling like a schoolboy.

The trainers, breeders, and farm hands in the room loved it. They cheered each time Charlie managed to round up the straying clergyman and laughed hysterically when the besotted minister wandered off again. Charlie finally threw up his hands and, after a hurried conference with Himalia and Vinny, relinquished custody of the happy minister to my Aunt Lois, who led her charge back towards the kitchen.

Vinny got up on the stage and announced that there would be a short delay while my aunt got a couple of double espressos into the tipsy minister. The guests cheered and applauded, the string quartet started playing Italian wedding music again, and the room filled with the raucous conversation, ribald laughter, and general merriment of horse breeders having a really good time.

"Ah, Mr. Callisto, I see you're Johnny-on-the-spot as usual!"

I looked up to see Dr. Norton standing by my table. The old veterinarian smiled, patted me on the shoulder, sat down, and addressed the man I thought of as a banker.

"Here's a little reading material for you, Daniel," Dr. Norton said, offering Daniel a manila envelope addressed to himself in a script quite familiar to me.

I realized that this was Jason's letter describing how Charlie switched the sperm in Running Fool's tank. That meant the man sitting across from me must be Daniel Brookshire, the head of the Running Fool syndicate. This was Maia's special guest. I still couldn't remember my discussion with Maia and her friends the night before, but I believed Daniel Brookshire's presence was probably a result of that meeting. I hoped it had been my idea to invite him.

While Daniel was scanning Jason's letter, Dr. Norton turned to me and told me that Leda had asked him to make certain I stayed put until after the proceedings were over. Then, to my amazement, the crusty old vet actually winked at me. Everyone was winking at me. It was obvious to me that the people doing the winking thought I knew what they were winking about, but I didn't have a clue. I wondered what else had happened on Friday.

Daniel Brookshire slipped the letter into his coat pocket, and asked Dr. Norton how far Cobb's Station was from Juno. Then saying he had errand to run, he excused himself from the table and left the dining room with his large business associate following close behind. Looking pleased with himself, Dr. Norton got up, gave Chic and me a little half wave, and walked back toward the main table.

Twenty minutes later, the music stopped, and Vinny got back up on the stage to announce that the minister was ready to perform the wedding ceremony. The string quartet began playing the wedding march, Himalia and Charlie climbed back on the stage, and a flustered but sober-appearing minister shuffled forward and stood in front of the bride and groom. He opened a large bible, found the place in the text he wanted and took a deep breath.

But the minister never got to speak, because at that moment, all the overhead lights in the Explorers' Pavilion were suddenly turned up to their brightest setting, and Maia entered the room accompanied by four young adults. As they marched up to the stage, Leda's other three friends joined the procession, so by the time they had reached the stage, there were four beautiful women in flowing white gowns, escorting two young men and two young ladies to meet their biological father.

It was more than fifteen minutes until the original starting time of the wedding, but I was still disappointed by the turnout. I had hoped more than four of Charlie's children would have shown up by now.

One of the two girls that Maia had escorted to the stage was speaking to Charlie, but I was having trouble understanding her. There was a lot of noise interfering with my hearing, but it wasn't coming from the other guests. Except for a little whispering, the dining room was reasonably quiet. The disturbance seemed to be coming from the lobby. My table was close to the lobby, and it sounded like people were engaged in a loud disagreement right behind the door nearest to me.

I tried to ignore the noise and concentrate on what was happening on the stage. It appeared that Charlie was talking quietly to Maia and one of the two girls. From this distance, Charlie didn't even seem all that upset. I cupped a hand to one of my ears to see if I could catch what he was saying. This maneuver worked a little, and I was able to gather that Charlie was telling the girl she was the victim of a cruel joke. The girl said something in reply, but her words were drowned out by an increase in the noise coming from the lobby. Now, someone involved in the discussion in the next room began shouting. I decided to abandon my hiding place and move closer to the stage so I could hear.

Leda and Dr. Norton spotted me when I was halfway down the aisle and gestured frantically for me to go back. I ignored their signals and kept walking. I was one of Charlie's biological children too, and I thought I had a right to participate. As I approached the stage, Charlie spotted me and pointed me out to the four young people in front of him.

"There he is!" Charlie said. "That's the man who's perpetrated this cruel hoax!"

"No, Charlie," I said calmly. "It's not a hoax. These people are all your biological children, just like me."

I was proud of my rock-steady voice. I thought I sounded confident even though I had to speak over the noise coming from the lobby.

"You know that's simply not possible, Walt," Charlie said. "I told you I never donated sperm before. If I had, my name would be on the clinic's paperwork. Miss, would you please tell this deluded young man the name of the sperm donor listed on your document?"

Charlie was addressing one of the more recent arrivals. She looked at the clinic paperwork that Jason had included with each letter and nervously read the name of the sperm donor listed on it.

"Colby Farnsworth," she said in a meek voice.

"Not a bad-sounding name. You should be proud. And what was the name of your sperm donor?" Charlie asked the boy standing next to her. He looked blank for a couple of minutes, and then pulled his letter out of his back pocket and shuffled through the pages until he got to the clinic's paperwork.

"Charles Everwood," he read, his voice faltering a little.

"Well, at least the first name is right. And yours, young lady?"

"Chad Butterwick," she snapped, "but that was only an alias. You used a different name each time you donated sperm."

This was the girl I had seen sitting in the lobby with Alice and Sara. Maia had obviously been talking to her. I could tell that she was incensed, and I didn't think her anger had anything to do with not getting the money she had been promised in Jason's invitation.

"Now, now, that's a unfounded accusation. We can only go by the fertility clinic's paperwork. That is, if the documentation you have is really genuine. Walt's a devious young man. He might have faked the clinic's paperwork in addition to lying about my involvement. But that's beside the point. It doesn't matter if it's real or not, because my name is Charlie Bolero, and I've no connection to Chad Butterwick. Now young man, what's the name of your donor?"

The man that Charlie had just addressed was the other person I had seen in the lobby. He was taller and broader than me, and didn't seem at all intimidated by Charlie. He stepped up onto the stage, turned towards the wedding guests, and spoke in a loud, clear voice that everyone in the dining room could hear, even over the sounds of shouting and stomping feet issuing from the lobby.

"My name is Joe Turner, and the name of my sperm donor was Charles Bolero. His address was Box 19456 at Southwestern Pennsylvania University in Canton. The dates of his donations were September 9 through September 25 of 1982, and I'm not going to tell you how I did it, but I got all of this information myself, directly from the fertility clinic in Canton." Joe turned to Charlie and looked him in the eye. "I've been looking for you for two years. This wedding invitation just helped me find your sorry ass, Papa!"

Joe hurled the last word like a piece of rotten fruit, and Charlie, turning pale beneath his bronzed skin, took a step back.

I was astounded. At first, I couldn't imagine how this could have happened. Then I remembered that Jason had sent invitations to all of Charlie's adult children, including the ones conceived from sperm donated under Charlie's real name.

Charlie turned toward Himalia only to discover a roaring inferno of orange taffeta, fiery hair, and flaming eyes. One glance at his angry bride evidently convinced Charlie that Falstaff had had it right when he said the better part of valor was discretion. He suddenly turned on his heel and strode briskly toward the kitchen, only to find the way blocked by Daniel Brookshire. His oversized business associate was standing next to him holding a cryogenic tank in one brawny hand. It looked like the tank I had seen at Charlie's, but someone had sprayed black paint over the numbers stenciled on its side.

"Hello, Charlie. We've just been to your house," Daniel said. "I believe that we need to have a little talk."

Charlie, who apparently didn't share Daniel's need for conversation at that particular moment, abruptly turned and ran up the aisle. He had made it about halfway to the front of the dining hall when the left side lobby door burst open, and a herd of my half-brothers and -sisters, dressed in their Sunday best, thundered into the room. Their entrance drew a huge cheer from the horse breeders and trainers in the wedding crowd. Charlie screeched to a stop and stared in disbelief at the horde of offspring stampeding towards him. The wedding guests had been provided with little sachets of purple grapes with which to shower the bride and groom after the ceremony, and several ranch hands in the crowd began pelting him with these. Pivoting like a quarterback, Charlie ran between the tables on his right, weaving his way through the laughing and jeering wedding guests towards the other lobby door. Before he could reach it, however, a dozen more of Charlie's biological children erupted through that door as well. Now I was extremely gratified by the attendance.

"Get him! That's Charlie Bolero!" This rallying cry came from Joe Turner, the large young man who had just confronted Charlie on the stage. Apparently feeling that he had some unfinished business to conduct with his biological father, Joe jumped off the stage and ran towards the front to help his brothers and sisters run their papa down.

Thinking quickly, Charlie dashed into the Pantheon dining room, followed by a large group of his progeny. The rest of Charlie's adult children seemed uncertain about what was transpiring and what they should do next. Some of them simply stood in the aisle looking confused, while others wandered toward the front of the hall and gathered around the stage. I could hear tables crashing to the floor of the Pantheon, and the outraged protests of luncheon diners increased as Charlie and his pursuers made their way through Vinny's tribute to the seven deities of ancient Rome, the papal majesty of modern Italy and a mixed assortment of papal memorabilia, paintings of the Vatican, and photographs of recent popes. Then there was a gigantic crash, which led me to conclude that Charlie had just gone through the connecting door into the Forum dining room and knocked over Vinny's full sized plaster statue of Julius Caesar.

All of this frenetic chaos was accompanied by lively background music. For some reason or other, the string quartet, perhaps because their leader had seen one too many Hollywood depictions of saloon fights where the piano player kept playing right through the melee, or maybe just because he had a twisted sense of humor, had begun playing the Tarantella again. As my half-siblings gathered near the stage area, I could hear Charlie, and the crowd of sperm donor children chasing him, dancing over the rubble of Caesar, knocking down various mementos of Napoleonic history, smashing photographs, and upsetting tables in the Forum dining room.

The sounds of mayhem briefly subsided, and I could hear Charlie, frantically trying to reason with his pursuers, probably from the safety of a temporary blockade consisting of overturned tables and chairs. Negotiations apparently reached an impasse, however, and this short period of relative calm was suddenly shattered by the angry shouts of a mob that thinks its quarry is getting away. A moment later, a shocking explosion of glass, porcelain and silverware could be heard from the hallway, immediately followed by the appearance of a panic-stricken Charlie Bolero in full flight, his elegant tuxedo covered from top to bottom in a colorful array of pasta, sauces, and plaster dust.

The harried sperm donor executed a magnificent leap onto the bride and groom's table and ran along its top, sending candelabras, glasses of Chianti, plates of cannoli, and the friends and employees of Elara Downs flying in all directions. A crowd of my newly discovered brothers and sisters and four of Leda's friends were standing at the other end of that table with me, and I was the only one who failed to get out of the way.

There was a sickening sound of two bodies colliding, and I found myself lying flat on my back with Charlie sprawled across me. When I looked up, I saw a sea of my siblings' faces staring down at us. I heard a loud groan and felt Charlie's weight shift as he tried to push himself up from the floor. Then his angry face, festooned with plaster dust and pasta sauce, loomed into view only inches above my own. Biological father and biological son were face to face.

I sensed this was an important moment in both our lives. I realized that I had gained a new confidence and purpose in my own life, and I felt, deep in my heart, that this moment marked a new beginning for Charlie as well. I searched for words that would convey this truth, and mark this important occasion in a positive and memorable way. Finally, just as Charlie's face seemed about to explode, the perfect words popped into my brain. I smiled genially and said, "Happy Papa's Day, Charlie!"

Chapter Thirty-Nine

One of the things I had forgotten about was agreeing to go to Tahiti with Leda.

The night before the wedding, Leda had used her mother's credit card to cancel Himalia's and Charlie's honeymoon tickets, and to purchase new ones for us. That's why Leda's friends at the wedding had been winking at me. I was supposed to have arranged for a week's vacation from my job at Ace and be packed and ready to fly to Tahiti by the following afternoon. Instead, I had forgotten everything that had happened on Friday, surprised Maia and Leda by showing up at the wedding, and very nearly derailed the new plans that I had helped devise with Maia and the girls.

Leda thought my amnesia was probably a side effect from the drug Maia had surreptitiously put in my champagne during my limousine ride to the Marriott. Alice had taken Leda aside after the wedding and confessed to supplying Maia with an experimental drug that she had used to make me more cooperative. Later in the evening, after I had recovered my faculties, they had seen no ill effects from the drug, although I had no memory of the interrogation and thought I had voluntarily shared Jason's plan to stop the wedding with Maia and her friends. Other than complaining about a slight headache that I had attributed to the champagne, I had seemed fine. Alice hadn't learned about my amnesia until right before the wedding ceremony, when Maia had asked her to lower the dose they had planned on slipping into the minister's wine.

I knew I should feel outraged at being drugged by Maia, but Leda and I were riding in a limousine on our way to Jupiter, where I was going to throw some clothes into a suitcase, give a key to a neighbor who fed Io for me when I was out of town, and then proceed to the airport, where we would board a flight to a tropical paradise. What was a lost day here or there, I reasoned, when it meant flying to Tahiti with this amazingly beautiful girl?

With Leda in my arms, I relaxed in the cushioned luxury of the limousine and smiled. I thought that everything had turned out great for everyone, with the possible exception of Charlie. The last time I had seen Charlie, he was being ushered into another limousine by Daniel Brookshire's beefy companion.

Dr. Norton and Emily Taurus had been standing next to me at the time, and the old vet told me Mr. Brookshire was driving back to Cobb's Station to discuss the future disposition of Charlie's assets, both the frozen assets and the ones racing in Lysithea. Brookshire had promised to make up Emily's losses and to help her buy back Elara Downs if Himalia was willing to sell.

Some of the people who had driven to Juno to meet their biological father were angry they hadn't received the money they had been promised, but most of them seemed to feel the journey had been worth it. Everyone had begun talking excitedly to each other after Charlie had been driven away. They were exchanging names and telephone numbers, and several of the men and women who had come to meet Charlie actually knew each other and were astonished to discover that they were related. I hoped they didn't know each other in the Biblical sense. Joe Turner, the man who had confronted Charlie on the stage, was giving out a website he had established for sperm donor children. Joe knew about the legislation pending in Virginia that would make it the first state in the country to forbid anonymous sperm and egg donations, and he was urging his half siblings to join him in an effort to bring the bill to every state in the union. I got one of Joe's cards, and would have stayed to talk with him and the rest of my brothers and sisters if Leda hadn't pulled up in her limousine and whisked me away.

Now we were cruising up the interstate toward Jupiter, looking at the travel documents, and chatting about what we were going to do in Tahiti. Himalia had booked a deluxe tour that included three days in Bora Bora and every kind of activity from reef diving to 4X4 safaris. It looked like every moment of our seven-day stay was booked up for activities of one sort or another. I told Leda I would much rather spend the time alone in our cozy beachside bungalow and on the beach. Leda grinned and promised me that we would have plenty of time to ourselves, but said that on our second night in Tahiti we absolutely had to go to an open-air concert that featured several award-winning Polynesian bands.

"I love outdoor concerts," Leda said. "My mother used to take me to rock festivals and outdoor music concerts all over the world. I was conceived at a rock festival."

"Really?" I asked, nuzzling her ear. "Your mom and dad spent their honeymoon at a rock concert?"

"Oh, she wasn't married at the time. I was a love child. Does that shock you, Walt?"

"No, of course not," I said, kissing her on her nose. "I know you think I'm a prude, but I'm really not. I don't care how you got here. I'm just happy you're here."

"I'm glad you feel that way, Walt, because I've always thought the story of my conception was very romantic. Do you remember me telling you my mom was a New Age hippie?"

I mumbled and kissed my way down her neck.

"Well, I was conceived at a Black Sabbath Concert."

"What?" I was having a little trouble hearing because I had my face buried in her chest, but a loud alarm bell was going off in my subconscious mind. Slowly lifting my face out of her cleavage, I stared up at her with dawning apprehension. "Did you say you were conceived at a Black Sabbath concert?"

"Yeah! Can you believe it? Mom met a musician with one of the bands that opened for Black Sabbath."

I continued to stare at Leda, without speaking.

"What's wrong, Walt? Why are you staring at me like that?"

I suddenly pushed myself away from Leda. She goggled at me, her eyes expanding to the size of twenty dollar gold pieces.

"Walt, say something! You're scaring me!"

"You're my–you're my-you're my–"

"What? I'm your what?"

"You're my sister!"

"What?"

"YOU – ARE – MY – SISTER!" I shouted, clamping my hands over my head and squirming farther away from her. "Charlie told me he made love to a girl at a Black Sabbath concert! He told the girl he was a drummer for the backup band!

"No! Walt, that's crazy…"

But I didn't hear the rest of what she had to say. Jumping out of my seat, I ripped open the moon roof, and started climbing out of the speeding limousine.

Leda grabbed my legs and tried to drag me back into the car, but I continued to struggle until I was lying spread-eagled across the roof. The violent wind tore my glasses off and sent them sailing out of sight as I began cursing Charlie at the top of my voice. I couldn't hear myself over the roaring of the wind, but I continued screaming my lungs out anyway. After what seemed like an eternity, I felt the wind begin to abate as the limousine slowed down and pulled over on the shoulder of the interstate. As it rolled to a halt, Leda let go of my legs and stuck her head out of the moon roof. By this time my screams had subsided to a low sobbing moan. Leda reached out to comfort me, but I jerked away as though her touch burned my skin.

"Walt."

"Go away."

"Listen, Walt, we're not going to have a much fun in Tahiti, if you keep insisting I'm your sister.

"Go away."

"Why do you think I'm your sister?"

"I told you," I said wearily. "Charlie made love to Himalia at a Black Sabbath concert. He told her he was Charlie Vonante, the drummer for Glass Bird."

"That's not true, Walt.

"Yes it is, Leda." I rolled over, sat up, and gazed at her with a mixture of sadness and pity. I could tell she was in a state of denial. I knew none of this was her fault, but I felt I had to reveal the cold, harsh facts of her conception for her own good. "Look, did your mother happen to mention where she and this drummer of hers made love?"

"Yes."

"It was in a kosher hot dog stand, wasn't it?"

She stared at me and burst out laughing. I felt sorry for her. I knew people had different ways of coping with stress; my way, for instance was screaming my head off, while her way seemed to be laughing hysterically. I reached out and patted her on the arm. "Look, it's okay. I've always wanted a sister. We can still go to Tahiti if you want to…"

"Walt."

"Of course, we'll have to get separate rooms, but it should still be fun…"

"Walt, will you shut up and listen a minute?"

I stopped talking and waited for her to say whatever she was going to say. I was prepared for anything now. If she wanted to go to Tahiti, that was fine, and if she never wanted to see me again, I would do my best to live with her decision. I had been through the fire now, and had emerged a calmer, better, if somewhat sadder, man.

"Walt, do you believe for a moment that my mother would make love in a hot dog stand?"

"Well, didn't she?"

"No, she didn't. They made love in his tour bus."

I let out a long sigh and shook my head. "She probably just made that story up to make you feel better about your illegitimate birth. Your father was my father, the biggest jack-off of all time – Charlie Bolero."

"I wasn't illegitimate by the time I was born, you blockhead. After the concert, they drove to Reno and got married. They got a divorce two months later, but he kept in touch. He's a retired rocker now, living in England. I still fly to

London every Christmas to see him. And by the way, my father's name is Dave Pendergrass. He was lead guitar. My mom would never settle for a drummer."

I stared into Leda's amazing golden eyes and realized she was telling the truth. Visions of hot, sandy beaches and tanned bodies began to flash through my mind. "So, you're not my sister?"

Leda grabbed my shirt and began drawing me towards her. "And you're not my brother. So where do we go from here?"

"Well, for a start, Tahiti," I said, and kissed her. It was my first carefree kiss in a long time, and it felt great. Holding Leda tight, I climbed back into the limo and instructed the chauffeur in urgent tones to drive on.

I had suddenly realized that I had been living in fear for the last year. From the day I had discovered my mother's note hidden in my underwear until I had met Leda, I had avoided situations that might have led to sexual intimacy, due to the statistically small, but horrifying possibility that my next lover might turn out to be my sister – and a few minutes ago I had thought that nightmare had come true. At this moment, all I wanted to do was fly to Tahiti, soak up every intoxicating ounce of tropical romance the islands had to offer, and then, when the time was right, get down on my knees and pop the big question. Now that I had finally managed to find the one girl on the eastern seaboard who was definitely *not* my sister, I wasn't about to let her go!

The End

www.ingramcontent.com/pod-product-compliance
Lightning Source LLC
Chambersburg PA
CBHW070850120626
46556CB00002B/946